A Place
at the Table

Other Titles by Nathan Everett

City Limits

WHO AM I, really? It's a common question. It's part of being self-aware. But is it important? Are we really nothing more than our accumulated lifetime of memories? Or is there something inside that makes us inherently who we are? Stripped of his memories and identity, Gee Evars must come to grips with who he is as he attempts to make a home among strangers by simply doing the right thing. *City Limits* is the story of Gee's loss of memory and the life and love he gains.

Wild Woods

WHEN GEE EVARS wandered into town, he lost his memory in a daring rescue of a toddler in the raging Rose River. Now the man without a memory has become a force that even the Families need to reckon with. When the city votes to annex South Rosebud, Gee accompanies a small army of high school students to tear down the fence that has separated the cultivated hickory Forest from the Wild Woods. This is where the sequel to the popular novel *City Limits* begins. Gee and his crew must find a way to tame the Wild Woods, uncover its secrets, and live to tell the story. Gee's real work in Rosebud Falls has just begun.

The Gutenberg Rubric

TWO RARE-BOOK LIBRARIANS race across three continents to find and preserve a legendary book printed by Johannes Gutenberg. Behind them, a trail of bombed libraries draws Homeland Security to launch a worldwide search for biblio-terrorists. Keith and Maddie find love along the way, but will they survive to enjoy it?

For Money or Mayhem

COMPUTER FORENSICS DETECTIVE Dag Hamar has been hired to help a credit card company beef up network security, but are his new co-workers helping him or attacking him? Security video doesn't lie, does it? Dag is about to get dragged from behind his computer screen—away from the comparative safety of cyberspace—into the dirty streets of Seattle where an online predator has become a real-life serial kidnapper. But will he be in time to save his new romance and the daughter who is a victim.

For Mayhem or Madness

COMPUTER FORENSICS DETECTIVE Dag Hamar is on the case again! In this sequel to *For Money or Mayhem*, Dag is commissioned by the Financial Crimes Enforcement Network (FinCEN) to find and stop a dangerous hacker who appears to be a credible threat to national security. Follow Dag as he erases his own digital identity and goes on the trail around the world to track down and neurtralize Hacker X before he does something really dangerous like erase all the nuclear launch codes in the world. Or maybe, Dag should help him.

For Blood or Money

DAG HAMAR IS a hard-boiled computer forensics detective with all the trimmings: the Seattle Waterfront office, the sexy young assistant who adores him, and an attitude to match the constant gray drizzle outside his window. And a new missing person case. The only problem is he's a middle-aged computer geek who doesn't do missing persons. And the only clue he has is the missing man's laptop. Dag Hamar and Deb Riley discover hidden files and computer code can be as dangerous as dark alleys and flying bullets as they enter the high-stakes game of of tracing a missing friend and the billion-dollar fortune that disappeared with him.

Municipal Blondes

COMPUTER FORENSICS DETECTIVE Deb Riley has been cut loose to continue the work of her partner, Dag Hamar. He sent her to get the code from a dead man's tattoo. He told her she needed to crack the encryption on Simon's thumb drive. He told her he loved her. And then he died. Now Deb finds she is in possession of something everyone wants and will do anything to get. Including kill her. Enter the world of Deb Riley, code breaker, detective, and master of disguise, as she races into the heart of the mystery and risks discovery or worse in Seattle, Belize, and Croatia. She has Dag's reputation to live up to.

Stocks & Blondes

COMPUTER FORENSICS DETECTIVE Deb Riley is on the case again, this time with a dead woman named Georgia and a house full of computers. Georgia's father doesn't believe the police finding that she committed suicide. He's sure there was foul play involved. He had no idea how foul it was. Hacking into the computers starts a deadly game as neighbors, friends, and even Georgia, prove not to be what they appear to be. Infiltrating the cabal throws Deb into her deepest disguise ever while trying to balance her real life with a new boyfriend, who might also be different than he appears. Worse, it puts her in danger of ending up just like Georgia.

Steven George & The Dragon

STEVEN HAS ALWAYS known he was a dragonslayer, but on the day his village sends him to slay the fearsome beast he realizes he doesn't know what a dragon looks like, where it lives, or how to kill it. His quest is facilitated by the exchange of "once-upon-a-times" with the people he meets on the endless road. Think Grimm. For young adults, not children.

The Volunteer

JOURNEY INSIDE THE head of a chronically homeless man--a man that in a less politically correct age we might have called a hobo. Gerald Good, known now only as G2, volunteered to take the place of a homeless man, believing he would work his way back quickly. Ten years later, twenty... thirty years, find G2 alone in his head, his memories, and his boxcar.

A Place at the Table

Nathan Everett

ELDER ROAD BOOKS
LYNNWOOD WA

A special thank you to my editors and advisers
who stuck with me through this entire project.
Your help was immeasurable.
Michele Palmer
Lyndsy Fernandes
Margie Cantlon
Michelle Duncan
Denny Wheeler

Contents

1

Facing My Adulthood

Liam Cyning

I GOT BACK FROM LONDON with Mother and Father Friday night and was looking forward to a quiet weekend before my eighteenth birthday on Monday. We flew in a jet airplane! Father says it's the way of the future and the seven-and-a-half-hour flight meant he could go to London for a business meeting and return the next day. Sitting in an airplane in my suit wasn't comfortable. I seem to have had a growth spurt and as soon as I sat down my trousers were up around my ankles.

I can see the attraction for crossing the ocean by jet. There isn't much to see when you spend three days on an ocean liner. But it seems you would miss a lot flying over America from New York to Los Angeles. The train seems much better.

Of course, Grandmother wanted to have dinner with me and I would never slight her. Having an extra-long day with the time change won't hurt me; I'll sleep in tomorrow. In my life, Grandmother has always been my defender and friend. My parents have plans for me that I'm not quite resigned to. Father wants me to enter the business directly after my schooling at Elenchus Scholé is complete. Grandmother insists that I should go on to college so I'll have a better grasp of the world. I prefer that plan.

So, I showered and shaved and put on the clothes Erich had laid out for me. He always had the right wardrobe for me. I'd missed him in London but he'd packed my bag carefully so that I'd be able to tell what was appropriate when. I'm sure if he'd left it up to me, I'd have dressed each day in Levi's and a T-shirt. No. Not really. I just didn't always know what difference which tie I wore made.

Nonetheless, I presented myself at Grandmother's door at precisely seven o'clock.

"Liam! I'm so glad you could join me for dinner. I've been lonesome without you."

"Grandmother, I am always at your service. I wouldn't miss an opportunity to have dinner with you," I said as I kissed her on the cheek. I'm not that tall, but somehow leaning down to kiss my grandmother made me aware of her age. "How have you been while I was traveling with Mother and Father?"

"Well now, have a seat and I'll tell you all about it." We sat and Ricardo placed salads with slices of apple and crumbled gorgonzola cheese over spring greens in front of us. I noted I had a glass of wine that matched my grandmother's and was pleased that she was acknowledging my majority. "I've been very busy, as usual," she said. "Most tasks were simple. Thorne Larson wanted to buy old Mr. Jacobson's farm and the two could not agree on anything. When it came down to it, both wanted the deal to go through, but Mr. Larson wanted to think he'd gotten a good deal and Mr. Jacobson wanted to believe he'd made a profit on his years of toil. In the end, both were satisfied." She finished the salad and then continued. "I discussed an interesting piece of legislation coming before the state house this fall with the sponsoring representatives. They were quite concerned that it actually accomplished what they'd set out to do. Unfortunately, they hadn't really agreed on what they wanted to accomplish and decided they were not as far along in drafting the legislation as they thought. Oh, yes," she said as an afterthought. "And I hired a personal assistant."

"Is Isobel retiring?" I asked. My grandmother's personal assistant had been with her as long as I could remember.

"Oh, no. I hired a personal assistant for you."

"For me? Whatever for? What do I have to assist with?" *And shouldn't I have some say in hiring my own staff when the time comes?*

"Don't worry. Part of the reason is to get you used to working with an assistant. Another part is because life will be changing for you soon enough and you'll need advice on what course of action to take. And lest you think you have been permanently saddled with baggage, I have hired her for a six-month probationary period. If you want to ditch her at that point, you can make your own hiring decision. But I assure you, I have carefully considered what you will need in the next six months from a position of knowing things to which you are not yet privy."

I continued to eat in silence as Ricardo set a lovely chicken cordon bleu before us, complete with mushroom risotto and roasted asparagus and lemon butter sauce on the side. I learned my lesson about this dish some years ago. If you simply stick a fork and knife in it to cut, you are likely to spray ham, cheese, and chicken juices all over yourself—and possibly your companion as well. It requires you to gently stroke your knife across the meat rather than pressing down. The result, however, is heavenly. Cook's rendition of the dish is superb.

Well, things could be worse. I would have a lovely young assistant to run errands and keep me company. Grandmother had said 'she.' *Please let her be young and lovely!*

"When will I be able to meet my new assistant?" I asked.

"She will attend your birthday celebration dinner Monday evening. It is always best, I think, to meet in a social setting rather than try to jump right into business without knowing each other."

"Oh. Of course. Mother and Father...?"

"Have approved my choice. They would rather it had been a lawyer, I'm sure, but the interview process has been going on while you were still at school and they agreed I had found the best alternative for you. She is of the Advisor class."

"Those I have met in that class have always impressed me as very level-headed and even-tempered. I'm sure I will learn a great deal from her," I said. I wondered what subjects she could give me advice on. It seemed my first date of my life this spring had gone poorly. I'm pretty easy going and happy to interact with people except when I'm facing a single female one-on-one. Lonnie laughed at me and said I just needed to pick myself up and get out there again, as if I'd fallen off a bicycle.

"And what class have you evolved into?" Grandmother asked. Classes are very important in our society. In fact, much of our elementary and secondary edu-cation is focused on discovering our class and preparing for participation in it.

"It seems the boundaries between the classes shift back and forth a lot," I sighed. "I think I could be a Leader, but sometimes I behave like a Commander. I find myself attracted to Inquirers, but not so much so that I can't think of anything else. What do you think, Grandmother? Have my instructors made a suggestion?"

"Let's start with the Dexters." She reached for my hand and turned it palm up, showing it to be clean and soft. "I don't believe you are physically bent toward working with your hands. Or really with any other part of your body, even though you do play sports. We'll eliminate that. A Cognoscente? Yes, there is potential. I don't think you would be satisfied with a mental task performed repeatedly, even if there were problems to be solved. You'd want more variety than that."

"I know I'm not an Aspirant. I'm sometimes drawn to one vocation or another, but mostly to find out what it is all about. I don't feel called to any form of service or any profession. And the same is true of Creators. I like to dabble with my drawings and paintings or play a bit on the piano, but I have no passion for it or any other field of interest."

"We can leave discussion of vocation for another time. I'm sure you will find work that appeals to you. I don't think you have as compulsive a drive toward order and regulation as a Defender would have," Grandmother continued. "And much to your parents' disappointment, you show only scant traces of being a Promoter. I'm sure your father has already been at you about joining the business and learning it from the ground up. Which wouldn't be a bad thing, but is probably not where your heart is. I'm sure you have some of the necessary entrepreneurial skills, but not the mindset to become a Promoter."

"That brings me back to Leader or Commander," I sighed.

"Or Advisor."

Grandmother's suggestion was disturbing. Advisors were always in the background, nudging people toward where they should go. Whether leading or directing people, I tended to like the spotlight. I found that aspect of my ego mildly disturbing.

"No," Grandmother continued. "I didn't think so. Leader or Commander. What do you think?"

"I probably have enough ego to be a Commander. But when it comes down to actually telling people what to do, I'm not that great. I can rally people to an idea, get everyone behind us, but it's always Lonnie who starts assigning jobs and telling people what to do," I said. Lonnie was my best friend, my roommate for the past eight years, but if I compared myself to him as a Commander, I was unlikely to come out favorably.

"So, a Leader. I believe your teachers agree. Now, it remains to find out what kind of a Leader you will be."

"That is a problem. I'm not even sure what a Leader does. It seems I need to have a vision before I can get people to follow it." I found our class structure to be confusing at times. Some of my schoolmates, who had truly settled into their class already, were incredibly proud of it, no matter what class they had discovered. It made sense. I'd heard in my schooling that there were various kinds of personality tests that would show your 'true class.' They were often used in the public schools.

Elenchus Scholé spent much more time on discovering our class with educators trained in spotting identifying traits and encouraging their growth. But discovering one's class when it was an integral part of one's personality and character was often a long and sometimes painful process. Still there was something satisfying about knowing where you fit in society as a whole. It gave you tools for facing life.

"So, that will be your task for the next six months, and hence your need for an assistant," Grandmother continued. "She will want things to run smoothly and to keep obstacles out of your way so that you can lead on a clear path. In order to do that, however, she will need to see what your path is. She will advise you when you have choices to make. She will discuss with you your philosophy of life. She will probe for your inner character and help you bring it out."

"She must be very wise and mature."

"In some things. In others, you will find her as naïve as yourself and you will use each other as a sounding board to find your way."

"I will learn all I can from her and do my best to become a Leader you can be proud of, Grandmother."

"I am already proud of you, Liam. Become a man *you* can be proud of."

ON SATURDAY MORNING, I rose at my usual time of five-thirty, despite the long day previous, to find Erich had already been into my dressing room to lay out my running things. I couldn't believe how well my valet understood me. Better than any of the other adults in our household, including my parents. He'd been a constant for me since my tenth birthday. He didn't follow me around, but seemed to always be where I needed him.

For example, the year I began attending Elenchus Scholé, a boarding school in Covington—I think it was a relief to my parents to have me out of the house, even though the school was scarcely twenty-five miles from home—Erich could not lodge and be near me at school, but my clothes were always laundered, my bed made up, and my room tidied when I came back from classes. At first, I thought Lonnie had been industrious, though it didn't seem to be in his character. And his side of our room was just as tidy as mine. If there was a snack waiting for me, there was one waiting for him as well. It took both of us putting our heads together to realize Erich was coming in each day while we were in class.

Which was both a comfort and a pain. It was nice to have everything picked up and tidied and laundered, but it also meant that someone saw exactly how we lived.

Lonnie didn't seem to care. He felt he deserved to be waited on. Grandmother had cautioned me when I was living at home to never misuse my staff and to always try to make their jobs as easy as possible. By the end of my first year at Elenchus, I was making my own bed before I left the room for class in the morning. I made sure my laundry was picked up and in the bag provided for it. Lonnie discovered that after I started making my own bed, his remained unmade. We got a few demerits for leaving the room a mess before he got the message that he needed to take care of himself.

This morning, I needed to run. I needed to clear my head to think about what it meant to be a Leader. And how on earth was I going to relate to having a personal assistant? One thing I knew was that I didn't dare misuse or abuse her any more than I would Erich.

As I pounded down the path with Leonard at my heels, I tried to figure out what having a personal assistant would mean to my relationship with Erich.

Oh. Leonard. What a perfectly stupid name for a dog. Especially a dog that was assigned as my bodyguard. He was a lean Afghan/Setter mix, reddish gold in color. Not what you'd expect as a guard dog. But Leonard had been at my side for as long as Erich. I'd received a horse and appropriate riding gear as a gift from my parents on my tenth birthday. When I went to the stables for my first riding lesson on Sim—Persimmon, but never called by his full name—Leonard had been in the same stall. We've been together ever since. When I was twelve, I decided I hated my family—my parents, really—and decided to run away. I ran to the farthest edge of the estate and started to climb the high fence. Leonard prevented it. Guard dog or babysitter? Well, he was still a good running companion.

Yes. Back to Erich and my assistant. I should have asked Grandmother for her name, but I was sure I wouldn't know it anyway. That was one thing that would be different. Since she was a woman, she certainly would not be laying out my clothes or coming into my room to straighten things. I chuckled a bit as I passed the two-mile post on my running trail. Perhaps if she was extremely pretty, I might get her to... That wasn't a good line of thinking. One did not become involved with a member of the staff. Better if she was much older and not so pretty.

What are the things I must do to discover what my role as a Leader is? There were obvious things like organizing a volunteer effort or, as Grandmother did, negotiating a real estate sale or a studying and guiding legislation. I knew Grandmother was a Leader. People simply came to her for help. She settled disputes and often spoke at motivational rallies. More than anything, a Leader brought people together with one mind.

That made me wonder what the difference was between an Advisor and a Leader. Perhaps they were not so far apart. An Advisor might suggest to a Leader where he should go and then fall in line behind him to follow. An Advisor more or less led from behind the Leader, then. In a strange way, that made sense. It still did not leave me any nearer to understanding what my personal assistant would do for me. I ended up in the shower, still unsatisfied with my progress.

"AH. ERICH?" IT was Sunday afternoon and we were sitting with the newspaper on the patio having coffee.

"Yes, sir?" Erich was always respectful, even though we had been on a first name basis all my life, it seemed. I was certain he was at least seventy years old—almost a surrogate grandfather. We could sit comfortably with a soft drink on the patio to talk, or he could act as my chauffeur, even driving me on my dates. Date. I'd only successfully asked one young woman out and she politely told me afterward not to ask again. I think Lonnie had convinced her to accept a date with me in the first place. I never had difficulty going out with a mixed group, but facing a single girl gave me butterflies I couldn't control.

"Do you know a great deal about classes and how they interact? I'm having difficulty understanding the role of my new personal assistant. All I know is that she is Advisor class and I've no idea how to interact with one,' I said. Erich laughed.

"What makes you think you don't know how to interact? Are our encounters so stressful?" he asked.

"Our encounters?" I paused looking at the laughter in his eyes. I suddenly realized that I had no perception of class difference with Erich. I had always assumed that the staff were all Dexters—cooking, cleaning, chauffeuring. But there were also staff who kept the family accounts. There were staff who managed other staff members, planned parties or events, and even consulted with my parents and grandmother. "Erich! Are you an Advisor?"

"Well, now that you mention it, it's the class I've belonged to for over fifty years."

"But you do so many menial tasks. You collect my laundry and drive me to school. Why are you not advising me and, since I have you, why do I need another personal assistant?" I was completely confused. I knew in my head that occupation and class were two very different things. I'd even studied Leaders who were soldiers, presidents, and outback outfitters and guides. Why did it suddenly surprise me that my valet would be an Advisor?

"Who advises you regarding what you should wear?" Erich asked. "Who taught you table manners, provided dancing lessons, and suggested the venue for your first date?" The failure of that date had nothing to do with the perfectly sensible suggestion of taking her to a well-chaperoned school dance. Or my dancing ability.

"I must be the densest brat alive! I never thought of you in those terms. In truth, I most often think of you as my friend and don't consider your job at all."

"Then I have been successful and will be able to retire with pride."

"Retire? Erich, are you leaving me?" Well, that sounded like a dramatic break-up of a marriage. I felt foolish. "I mean, I don't want to lose you and I'm concerned that you are provided for in retirement. You're not that old, after all."

Erich laughed. He was a spry fellow, trim, a bit bald, always dapper.

"Liam, my young friend, I am seventy years old. I have had a life of helping young people become ladies and gentlemen. I have had, literally, generations of being an Advisor." He sipped his coffee and tossed the newspaper aside. "Employment in the Cyning household is an honor. And I assure you, my retirement is well-provided for. I won't abandon you. I'll phase slowly out of my job as your personal assistant phases into hers. And I will always be your friend. You can always call upon me."

I DIDN'T FEEL any different on the morning I woke up as an eighteen-year-old. In fact, it was a fairly normal day. I ran. I rode my horse for a while. I had a swim. I had luncheon with my parents. That wasn't unusual, but we didn't take all of our meals together. Sometimes I joined Grandmother and sometimes I simply ate at the kitchen nook where I wasn't much bother to people. But this was my birthday, so my parents wanted me with them.

My parents, Lydia and Thomas Cyning, were not neglectful, though much of my life had been spent at boarding school or in the care of Erich—or before him, with a nanny. I'm much closer to Grandmother. But I've traveled the world with my parents.

"Your clothes no longer fit you." Father observed, pointing at my trouser legs. He held a bit of pungent cheese to his lips and paused for another sip of wine. I drank coffee. My parents' coffee was untouched as they settled in with their second bottle of Grand Cru Saint Émelion from Chateau Cantenac.

"Even the trousers you are wearing no longer have cuffs. Erich had them let out to lengthen the inseam." Mother plucked a grape from the cluster and popped it into her mouth. "We've a card for you. Present this at Monsieur LeFevre's shop in Covington and he will help you pick a new wardrobe. You're old enough to shop for your own clothes now. I know your casual wear at Elenchus is Levi's, but do not go overboard on buying them. You only need a couple of pairs for weekends. The card will let you charge common items at Browning's as well."

"Thank you, Mother. With luck the growth is over. I don't think I'll get much taller than my current height of five-eight." They simply nodded.

"Nonetheless, be conservative in your initial choices and save some of the budget for next season, even if you don't grow more. You never can tell how your needs might change." Father was no taller than I. Even Grandmother was nearly five-seven when she was younger. I wondered if it was a family trait. There was a 'big book of ancestors' that sat in the library at Buxton House. I resolved to have a look at it.

"I will do as you say, Father. And thank you, Mother. I am becoming a bit self-conscious about my clothing. This will help immensely." I learned long ago to appreciate any gift my parents gave me. Monsieur LeFevre might have been instructed to give me cruise wear for all I knew.

I DRESSED FOR dinner and looked critically at my pants legs. They barely touched the top of my shoes when I stood, and were around my ankles when I sat down. I would keep my feet under the table and absolutely never cross my legs. Erich was in the outer room and I presented myself for inspection.

"I know you are uncomfortable with your trousers," he said. "You put on height rapidly, even while you were in England. We'll get you shopping as soon as possible. Perhaps it is something you can get your personal assistant to help with."

"That would be interesting. I'll just have to stand straight and ignore it," I laughed. "I think my feet grew, too. My shoes feel tight."

"It is nearly time for guests to arrive," Erich said. "Endure this night and as an independent eighteen-year-old, you can shop for new shoes later this week. What an opportunity."

I left my room and turned right along the hall. There are a lot of halls and rooms, some divided into suites and others just rooms for guests. Buxton House is a monstrosity that was repeatedly built onto as generations of the family married and stayed. I was the only resident on the third floor now so I was surprised when I saw a tall, slender redheaded woman leaving the room just a few doors down from mine.

"Who are you and what are you doing up here?" I asked.

"This is my room," she said, turning toward me. "I am the new..." We both froze in place.

"Oh, my God. Look who has come to make my life miserable," I whispered.

2

First Impressions

Meredith Sauvage

I KNEW when I accepted the position that Liam would be a little put off. I hadn't known his grandmother would not tell him who his new personal assistant was. I suppose she wanted to keep him from whining at her until I arrived. We had not always gotten on well.

"Mr. Cyning. My apologies for startling you. I had not expected to meet you until after five. I hope my appearance is not disconcerting to you," I said. I would need to handle him carefully and try not to set him off just by being here.

"As long as you keep your fists to yourself, I'm sure I'll learn to tolerate you," he said. I wasn't sure if he was joking or not. On his tenth birthday, he'd been insufferable about wanting the boys to stay away from the girls. When he'd taunted me by calling me Meri the Savage, I'd punched him in the nose. Got it good and bloody, too.

"I've learned much sharper jabs since our last encounter. They don't leave visible marks, though." I was certainly not going to be cowed by him. I was an impulsive twelve-year-old when I'd struck him and Mrs. Cyning the elder had given me implicit permission to 'set him straight.' I think it was my first test on the path to becoming his assistant. I'd been trained for eight years for this day.

"Must I then be on my guard at all times?"

"No. Being on your guard means you expect me to be on the offense. I have no reason to attack unless you are being an insufferable prat. Even then, I've learned to ignore most malfeasance of that sort. I trust that even if rocky in spots, we will be able to develop a positive working relationship." I held his eyes, even though I had to look up at him now, unlike when we were children and I stood nearly a head taller. Still, I guessed our heights were only two or three inches apart even now.

"We shall need to apply ourselves to the challenge." He smiled a little. "Miss Sauvage, I am intrigued by the prospect of working with you. I have no doubt that you were chosen by Grandmother as a test of my maturity. I expect you will not be the last such test. May I escort you to the patio where guests will gather for drinks before dinner?"

"I would be delighted to take your arm, Mr. Cyning." He offered and I accepted his elbow as we walked toward the stairs and the party that was already beginning. I would not often be on his arm. We would have to see if we could even stand being in the same room.

WE WALKED DOWN the stairs companionably, but when I saw that people had already begun to gather, I extracted my hand. Liam turned a questioning look on me.

"I'm sorry, Mr. Cyning. I'm your assistant, not your date. It would not look right for me to appear on your arm," I said. It was also my first day on this job and I didn't want any of the Cynings looking at me and wondering what I was up to. I stayed near Liam, but not in an intimate proximity.

"Oh. I suppose so. The party is mostly old people. I see Lonnie and his girl-friend, though. Let's go." I laid a restraining hand on his elbow again.

"You are the host and even these old people are your guests," I whispered. "Don't ignore them." He sighed, but nonetheless began working his way around the room, greeting each of the guests politely and introducing me as his new assis-tant. Eventually, we reached his friend and roommate, Lonnie.

"Quite the drag having to talk to everyone," Lonnie said. "We haven't met anyone since your parents greeted us at the door. Who is this with you?" Lonnie leaned around Liam to see me more clearly and I stepped out to greet him.

"Is that a way to greet an old school chum?" I asked as I extended my hand to him.

"My God! Meredith Sauvage? You certainly turned out to be a beauty. How did Liam manage to pick you up? Did he finally apologize?" Lonnie asked. His date looked petulant and pulled on his arm. "Oh, this is my friend, Susan Ritter. Susan, Meredith went to school with Liam and me back before we were all sent to board-ing schools eight years ago."

"I don't believe I've met you before either, Miss Ritter," Liam said. "Welcome to Buxton House and the party."

"Thank you," she said. She still looked a little angry at Lonnie. I thought she must be a bit younger than the rest of us. I was more than two years older than Liam and Lonnie was between us.

"Miss Sauvage is my new assistant," Liam said. "I'm told that I'll have increasing responsibilities this fall and her help will be much appreciated."

"We need to get together then," Lonnie said. "We could all go out and catch up on our lives."

"By the way, Lonnie, did you meet Jack Lenova? I see him at the bar. Ladies, can we bring you drinks?" Liam asked. Susan and I gave our preferences and I suggested we sit at a nearby table.

"How do you happen to know Mr. Porras and Mr. Cyning?" I asked. I was going to try to get her to behave a little more formally. The four of us were certainly the youngest at the party and I guessed she was the youngest of us.

"Lonnie is my *boy*friend," she seethed. "I never met Liam before. Lonnie just said it was a birthday party and would be fun. There's only old people here."

"Mr. Cyning's parents, I'm told, were responsible for the guest list. I doubt they know many young people."

"Why do you call Liam Mr. Cyning? He's younger than you are," Susan said.

"It's polite. And besides that, he is my employer. Age alone does not indicate one's station in life. We should always try to be polite, especially until we actually know a person and are invited to familiarity," I explained. I had a feeling my words were falling on deaf ears.

I looked for Lonnie and Liam and saw them just parting with an older gentleman I assumed was the Jack Lenova Liam had mentioned. He seemed vaguely familiar, but any memories I had of Buxton House were eight years old.

"Sorry it took us so long," Liam said as the boys handed us our drinks. "I wanted to be sure Lonnie met Mr. Lenova, my father's corporate attorney."

"He could be important to my career," Lonnie nodded.

"You don't have a career. You're just a student," Susan chided.

"Well, let's pretend that one day I shall have a career. Okay?"

"What are you studying these days, Mr. Porras?" I asked.

"Well, Father said that the best step into politics is law. I'm not completely convinced, but it can't hurt and Elenchus has a pre-law specialty with just an extra year. It should at least give me a head start when I move on to law school."

"Oh, sorry to interrupt," Liam said. "Grandmother just arrived with Mrs. Grosvenor. Please, let me introduce you to her." We stood, leaving our drinks on the table and followed Liam to his grandmother's side. Of course, I'd been interviewed by her half a dozen times in the past few months and I was sure Lonnie was often a guest of Liam's, but it was a nice gesture.

"Grandmother, I would like to introduce you to my friends, if I may."

"Of course, Liam. I would love to meet them." I always found myself at ease around the elder Mrs. Cyning, even though I was a bit in awe of her. I held back and let Liam introduce his friends.

"This is Lonnie Porras and his date, Miss Susan Ritter. Lonnie and Susan, my grandmother, Mrs. Cyning. And this is our friend, Mrs. Grosvenor." His grandmother seemed to know a lot about Susan as well as the rest of us.

"I'm pleased to meet you again, Mrs. Cyning," Lonnie said. "Mrs. Grosvenor, a pleasure."

"Hi," Susan added. Not the most elegant greeting or the politest response, but she was only fifteen, I'd discovered. And Lonnie was nineteen. I could make allowances for her.

"Miss Ritter, is your mother not Angela Ritter, the newspaper columnist and author?" Mrs. Cyning asked.

"Oh. Yes, ma'am. Do you know her?" Susan was suddenly standing straight and on her best behavior.

"I read her column every day. She is insightful. Perhaps one day you could arrange for us to meet."

"Certainly, Mrs. Cyning. I'm sure she'd be happy to meet you."

"Grandmother, may I present my... friend and new assistant, Miss Meredith Sauvage. I believe you have met before. Meredith, my grandmother, Mrs. Cyning, and our friend Mrs. Grosvenor." It did not escape my attention that Liam was making a genuine effort to bring me into his circle of friends.

"It was so kind of you to allow me to return for this special occasion. I promise to be on my best behavior," I said, grinning at the woman as she smiled back at me. I took her offered hand and dipped in a small curtsey.

"Welcome back, Meredith."

"WHAT'S THAT ABOUT being on your best behavior?" Susan asked as we began moving toward the dining room.

"Oh, please, Meredith. Let me tell the story," Lonnie laughed. "After all, I'm the only impartial observer here to be sure the truth is told." I laughed and nodded my approval as Liam hid his face in his hands.

"It was a bright and sunny day, exactly eight years ago, that half a dozen school friends and the usual array of adults gathered right where we just were on the patio to celebrate Liam's tenth birthday. Liam had been given a horse as his birthday gift and was in the process of convincing the boys that we should ditch the girls and go to the stable. Meredith overheard the plot and stepped up to ask what we were planning to do."

Liam looked at me and I could see the red blush on his face as he mouthed the words "I'm sorry," to me. Lonnie was on a tear and laughing at being able to tease his roommate.

"Our Liam was a bit of a brat when he was that age and told Meredith it was only of concern to the men and not to stupid girls. He might have escaped at that point if he hadn't punctuated by calling Miss Sauvage 'Meri the Savage.' At which point she delivered the best right hook I've ever seen and bloodied Liam's nose. I did have a moment of heroism as I helped him to his feet and into the house to get cleaned up. When we returned to the party, the other five of our classmates, including Meredith, had left with their parents."

"I never did discover where they went, but that was when Lonnie and I found out we were going to Elenchus Scholé and would not be returning to the public school with our classmates," Liam said. We found our places at the table and waited for Mrs. Cyning to be seated before Lonnie and Liam pulled our chairs out and we were seated.

"As I have learned," I said, "all six of us, Lonnie included, received full scholarship to private schools where we have been studying ever since."

NEXT TO LIAM, a Mr. Ferguson engaged in a conversation involving Lonnie and Mr. Lenova across the table. It was a lively engagement and we were all included.

"I say we should keep them out of the country entirely," Ferguson said. "We've enough of our own poor. We should not need to take care of poor immigrants as well. We can't feed our own." He stuffed another healthy bite of prime rib into his mouth. I saw Liam's grandmother raise an eyebrow at Liam, nodding almost imperceptibly toward Mr. Ferguson. Liam put his silverware down quietly on his plate. I could see Lonnie's eyes pop open and a look of expectation come across his face.

"Excuse me, Mr. Ferguson. May I ask a question of you?" Liam looked as innocent as he could when Ferguson turned toward him.

"Of course, young man. How are youth to learn if they don't ask questions?"

"I'm intrigued by your statements. You say we can't feed our own poor. Does our country not have enough wealth to feed its poor?"

"You need to understand the economics of it," Ferguson plowed on. "When you give sustenance away to people, then they feel entitled to it without contributing. People who *do* work for their income become demotivated and eventually feel they should not need to work for their living either. Soon, no one is working and the entire economy collapses because there is no money to keep supporting them without work."

"So, then the problem becomes one of employing the people who are poor so they can earn a living wage, does it not?"

"There are plenty of jobs."

"Do those jobs pay enough to feed the poor?"

"If they are not living above their means."

"Shouldn't anyone who works be able to afford decent housing, food, and education?"

"People need to adjust their expectations based on what they are capable of earning."

"What work do you do, Mr. Ferguson?"

"I own businesses and invest my money."

"Isn't that the same as being entitled to something that is paid for by other people? Is it not the Dexters who actually earn your income through their hard work? That in itself must be demotivating to poor people who see you enjoying a good life based on their efforts." Liam maintained his innocent expression, gazing intently at Mr. Ferguson.

"I believe I have contracted a bit of indigestion. If you will excuse me, Mrs. Cyning, I think it would be seemlier if I retire from our current conversation until such time that we can continue it in private and not interrupt this august social gathering." Mr. Ferguson stood to leave and tugged at his reluctant wife's chair. With a sigh, she, too, stood.

"Of course, Mr. Ferguson. Please forgive us for not accompanying you to the door." Mrs. Cyning smiled graciously at her guests. "My responsibility, as you know, is with the guests at the table. Ricardo will see you out."

"Certainly. Good evening." The Fergusons begged the pardon of the other guests and Mr. Ferguson paused to assure Liam that he would like to continue the conversation at a later date. When Ricardo returned to the room and nodded to Mrs. Cyning, she stood and began applauding. The other guests joined her applause, though some seemed hesitant.

"Happy birthday, Liam. It is nice to see that you are learning something at Elenchus Scholé." She seated herself. "Mr. Porras, you were right in the middle of things and heard best the nature and context of the conversation. I understand you consider yourself an impartial third party when it comes to telling tales. As a classmate at Elenchus, please give us your analysis of this discussion." Lonnie cleared his throat and glanced at Liam. Liam smiled and gestured for him to stand and take the floor.

"If I may say, ma'am, Mr. Ferguson was an easy target, caught up in his own fantasy of wealth and not expecting an ambush. Had he been prepared for this encounter, as I assure you, he will be the next time they meet, Mr. Cyning would not have gotten the edge with the questions he was asking."

"Would you have had different questions?"

"It is easy to construct better questions after the fact than in the heat of debate. In retrospect, however, yes. Mr. Cyning's questions took too long to get to the central question of the trickle-down theory and, in fact, did not quite get there before Mr. Ferguson excused himself. I believe he would have reached that point more expediently by directly asking Mr. Ferguson why he did not employ more of the poor and pay them a living wage. That is my opinion, ma'am, and I am certain our teachers would be equally proud of the way Mr. Cyning handled the conversation." Lonnie sat back down and Regina Cyning looked around the table as if looking for consensus before she began applauding again.

"This is the brilliance of the Elenchus Scholé." She silenced the applause. "These two young men have not been taught a series of facts to recite. They have been taught to question and discover. I am sure they will apply themselves in different directions as time goes by, but both have very sharp minds and will go far." She raised her glass for a toast and everyone responded. "Again, happy birthday, Liam."

AFTER CAKE AND champagne, dinner ended and the party began to break up. I had really only placed my travel bag in my room in order to dress for the party. The next day, I would need to go home and pack for a longer stay. I was unsure yet of all the protocol in the huge old mansion. I didn't even know how to get a meal if someone didn't invite me. I turned to say goodnight to Liam.

"Mr. Cyning, perhaps we should set a time to meet in the morning so we can begin a plan as to what our roles will be. I do not expect to be staying here full time, but I have been granted a room so we can spend time working together," I said. I hope he didn't assume we'd be working together in my room.

"An excellent idea, Miss Sauvage. Why don't we meet for breakfast and then we can get on with our tasks for the rest of the day. Would six o'clock be suitable?" Liam asked. I looked at him in disbelief.

"Six? In the morning? Will rising at such an ungodly hour be a requirement of this job?" I couldn't believe the suggestion. We had all day as far as I knew. Why would we need to start before I was even awake?

"I'm sorry. That was inconsiderate. I'm used to getting up at five o'clock each morning. But I have other things to do in the morning that don't need to wait for breakfast. In fact, they seldom do. I was letting enthusiasm govern my suggestion rather than good sense." He really did look apologetic.

"Are you so enthusiastic?" I asked.

"I find that I am. This day has awakened in me a sense of excitement for the future. And a bit of fear of the unknown. I'm hoping you can tell me what I'm supposed to do."

"Perhaps we can discover that together."

"What time would be comfortable for you to join me for breakfast?" he asked. I considered telling him noon, but I didn't want to be that snide.

"Could we make it nine o'clock?"

"Brilliant! I'll be able to get a full run in, shower, and shave before we meet. I'll see you then."

"Uh... Mr. Cyning... Where?"

"Oh! I usually eat in the kitchen. I have a table there for casual meals. I could... meet you in the hall at nine o'clock and show you how to get there."

"That would be excellent."

"Shall we walk up to our rooms? I'm ready to call it a night." I wasn't sure how to take that suggestion. Yes, my room was just a few doors down from Liam's but I wasn't sure I wanted to be saying goodnight at my door. The decision was taken from me.

"Liam, please come to the library. Your mother and I wish to speak to you," his father demanded. Liam looked sadly at me and shook his head.

"Some other time," he sighed. "Goodnight, Miss Sauvage." He followed his parents into the library.

3

Frustrating Children

Liam

"LIAM, PLEASE COME to the library. Your mother and I wish to speak to you."
I looked apologetically at Meredith but she just shrugged her shoulders and said
goodnight. I followed my parents into the library.

"Whatever came over you, Liam? It was unconscionably rude to challenge Mr.
Ferguson at a dinner party filled with friends who came to celebrate the achievement
of your majority." Mother accepted a glass of scotch from Father as she scowled at me.

"Were those my friends, Mother?" At my birthday dinner, most of the guests
had been my parents' friends or people they hoped to impress with a dinner at
Buxton House. I was merely an excuse for the event.

"This is not a debate," Father snapped. "Keep your Socratic questions for
your conversations with your grandmother. She is the only one amused by them. I
happen to be in negotiations with Fergie that could be worth millions."

"I'm sorry, Father. Do we need money?" Father scowled at me and I conceded
defeat. They had long since learned how to handle my attempts to turn the conversation to my own ends. The Socratic method really only works well when you
can control the flow of the conversation. It was time to make a straight-forward
justification and explanation. "I'm truly sorry, Father. Mr. Ferguson was throwing
around unsupported opinions and theories that were disproved decades ago. He
was, in fact, directly insulting one of my close friends. Remy Fortier came to this

country to get an education and seek the opportunities our nation is reputed to offer all. I could no more sit by and let my friend be insulted than you could help being offended by my treatment of *your* friend."

"Remy Fortier does not fit the profile Fergie was describing," Lydia interrupted. "He's a good and talented boy and scarcely even has an accent. And he is a virtuoso on the violin."

"In other words, because he is white?"

"We are not racists! I employ people of all races in my companies and treat them all equally. Their advancement is based on merit and merit alone."

"Father, it is all too obvious that even assignment to a class has become culturally discriminatory. How can one develop into a Leader if there are no opportunities to lead? How can he become a Commander if all he has ever known is being bossed around and told what to do? We espouse the idea that classes are based on inner character, yet people like Mr. Ferguson continue to promote discriminatory practices under the guise of saying 'It's their own fault.' That simply isn't acceptable."

"What is unacceptable is for you to challenge and insult people who came to honor you on your birthday. That is not the sign of a Leader," Mother said. That stung a bit and I suspected she was probably right.

"I am eighteen years old today. Perhaps the next time there is a party to honor me, it might be with *my* friends and associates."

"Go to bed." Mother tossed down the rest of her drink before continuing. "We'll discuss this with your grandmother. She egged you on. She can decide the appropriate punishment. If *we* punish you, you will automatically believe we are being unfair."

I was relieved. I didn't like these conversations with my parents. I'd grown to see, over the years, that regardless of class, they honored wealth. And I was a beneficiary of that. I lived in a mansion and never had to worry about anything. I had a feeling that wealth was an obstacle I would need to overcome in order to be a Leader.

Angela Ritter

I'M SURE THERE ARE DAYS in every mother's life when she wonders what she did to deserve such a troublesome daughter. I've spoken to enough mothers to know in my head that it doesn't last forever, but perhaps we could just skip the teen years. And having a precocious teen is even more problematic. She shouldn't have grown up so fast!

I looked at the notes I'd made for next week's articles. Being a daily columnist had its good parts, but I was itching to get started on my next book. A stack of research on "Leaders of Our Age" looked abandoned on the edge of my desk as I fought with the outlines for my series on "Influencing Class." It was an ageless argument between the influence of heredity and environment on class determination. Our society had long abandoned the notion of a hereditary class system, and just as quickly abandoned classes based on wealth or position. "Inherent Character" was supposed to be the determination and most of our educational system was supposed to identify and enhance a student's class characteristics.

I wondered, sometimes, how effective it was. Was there a reason that certain schools turned out large numbers of Dexters—people who were 'happiest' working with their hands and bodies—while other schools had more Creators or Commanders or Defenders? I had a stack of research on the teachers in those schools and still had little in the way of conclusive results.

I needed to know why. I guess that's what makes me an Inquirer. I couldn't identify anything in my own childhood environment that influenced my class. I had simply always wanted to know the Why and the How of things.

Currently, I wanted to know *why* my fifteen-year-old daughter was only now getting in at a quarter past midnight.

"THEY WERE SO pretentious," Susan answered my question about how the party was. I disciplined myself not to mention the rumpled state of her party clothes and smeared lipstick. "We weren't allowed to take pictures and I had to leave my camera at the door. I only wanted a couple of snaps to show my friends I was really there. No one will believe me otherwise."

"It's an honor to be invited to Buxton House at all. I'm sure if you call, they would arrange a photo tour for you. It's not polite to just point a camera and take photos of other people's homes without an invitation to do so," I said. I'd seen a notice that tours of the old mansion were available for groups, though I'm sure they were closely monitored and did not get to see private areas of the old house. It was one of the original estates that went back nearly two hundred years. It was architecturally grotesque as every generation seemed to add its own touch to the house and grounds. At one time, it was said, over a hundred people had lived there, including the staff. There were only four family members now. I wondered how many staff they needed to maintain the old monstrosity.

"Everyone was so formal," Susan continued. "Mr. This and Mrs. That. There were only four teens there. Some celebration for an eighteenth birthday. We called each other by our first names, except Liam and Meredith. I mean Lonnie and I used their first names and they used ours, but between the two of them, they were Mr. Cyning and Miss Sauvage."

"Meredith Sauvage?" I said. "So, she's the one who won."

"Won what?"

"It's long been assumed that Liam Cyning would settle into a class as a Leader, Commander, Promoter, or Inquirer. In any of those positions, he would require an assistant. It could even have been your Lonnie who got that job." I had been reasonably certain the selection would be made soon but was unaware of a choice having been made. One didn't probe deeply into the affairs of the Cynings, but rumors had surfaced nearly ten years ago that teachers were looking for class-mates of Liam to train as assistants.

"Lonnie, an assistant? Hardly," Susan scoffed. "He'd be Liam's boss. But I don't think Liam would make a very good assistant, either. He's too full of himself. Do you know he started an argument with one of the guests? Rather than pursue the argument at the table, the guest got up and left."

"Was the guest offended?"

"I don't think anyone dares to be offended there. How do they rate? I mean, they're rich, but so are Lonnie's parents. And Lonnie's house isn't as big but it's much prettier. Buxton House was designed by a dyslexic monkey," she twittered.

"Oh? When did you see Lonnie's house?"

"Um… We stopped by so he could introduce me to his parents. Once. They were quite nice." My daughter was lying. Of course, unpleasant people can adopt an air of politeness when social niceties called for it. I was pretty sure they wouldn't consider Susan as anything more than a convenient toy for their son and not worth the time of an introduction. Mr. Porras was a Senator and Mrs. Porras managed his career, his campaigns, and his money. "Oh, Lonnie said to be sure to tell you that Mrs. Cyning would like to meet you."

"Liam's mother?"

"No. His grandmother. I don't know why you'd want to meet that old lady." *My clueless daughter.*

"Well, perhaps your relationship with Lonnie Porras wil have some benefits after all." I was afraid the relationship between the two was to be short-lived. A boy four years older than my daughter and screwing her on their second date. I did have sources of information. But what was I to do? Forbidding her to see him would simply mean she would sneak out to be with him. Still, I wondered how traumatic the breakup would be.

"So why do you want to meet her?"

"Regina Cyning may be the most important woman you will ever meet," I said. "The thickest of my folders of research over there contains everything I've discovered about her. I've sent half a dozen requests to interview her. Regina Cyning has her fingers on the pulse of America. Not the pulse in the wrist, but the pulse in the neck."

"What's the difference? Don't they both show how fast the heart is beating?"

"To that extent, yes. But if I placed my fingers on the pulse in your wrist and squeezed tight, it would hurt. Perhaps your hand would go numb. Cutting off the flow of blood might be serious enough to lose your hand. Compare that with the pulse in your neck. If I squeezed there hard enough to cut off the flow of blood, you would soon lose consciousness. You might even die."

"Is she really that powerful? What does she do?"

"She leads. These days, she contents herself with working at a low level, negotiating agreements, reviewing legislation, even arbitrating disputes."

"Like a judge?"

"Not so formal. People seek her out to resolve their conflicts and problems. In times past, she and her husband frequently met with presidents and dignitaries. Buxton House was the site where treaties were signed, trade agreements made, and even marriage partners introduced. It is a trait of true Leaders that people are willing to follow them."

"So, do you think Liam will be having that kind of party in the future? I mean with presidents and dignitaries?"

"One doesn't begin there. Even in leadership, there is a path from the simple to the great. Who knows how far along that path he might go?"

"Lonnie is far more commanding. He's more likely to go places than Liam is. Even he seemed a little cowed by Mrs. Cyning, though."

"And much though I wish it was different, you fit with Lonnie much better than with any Cyning. And not because I think you will go through life blindly following his orders, sweetheart. You think alike."

"What do you mean?"

"Why did you choose Lonnie?"

"He's a good catch. He's rich and he's going places. And I wasn't about to let Josie Lebrun get her hooks in him."

"So, you caught him. With sex."

"Mother!" She stopped and looked me in the eye. There was no way she could deny it. "Yes, I made love to him. And I do it as often as possible. We like it. It's not like I'm selling myself. I'm not a whore."

"I didn't say you were, dear. You are a woman. There was once a time in ancient days, when women had very little choice in the matter. Their value was as breeders. So, they used their sex to attract and capture the man who could protect and provide. We women opened our sex to capture the man and produced children to hold him. Sex has always been a transaction. But the times have changed. Our class system is now generations established. Within the classes, women are neither inferior nor superior."

"Are the classes discriminatory? I mean… do men and women have an equal chance at being chosen for any class?" Susan was getting to the real problem. It is what I was studying so fervently.

"There are few compiled statistics that would answer that question," I said. "On the surface, the criteria for evaluation are non-discriminatory. But are there inherent traits in women that indicate a tendency toward one class or another? Perhaps. Let's take Defenders for example. At first glance, we might see the traditional military force as being a natural home for defenders and it is more likely to be male than female. But the determination to maintain order, discipline, and protect others can be seen as easily in housewives who spend all their time focused on the home and the children as it can be in a soldier. In that instance, women are far more likely to be classed as Defenders. The tasks are different but the class is the same."

"I don't want to be held down in what I can achieve. And I don't want to be lumped into a particular class because I like having sex with my boyfriend."

"That is less likely than you think. We women are strong enough and independent enough to not need a man to protect and provide. I earn three times what your father does. I bought this house. Why do I need him?"

"Are you talking about love?"

"That comes into play, but in our day and age, love is often an aftereffect of sex rather than a reason. Even after marriage in many instances. Your father has access to much of the Commander class, even though he, himself, is an Advisor.

He opens doors for me. And over the years, I *have* come to love him. Even though my reputation has grown to the point that I might open most of those doors myself, if I ever mistreated him, I would find them slammed in my face." I hugged my daughter to me and she sighed. *How I wish she had not grown up so fast.*

"You need to pay attention to Lonnie in more ways than spreading your legs or you will lose him. Much of the benefit of being with him is yet to come. He will open many doors and will go far. If you can show him you can open doors for him as much as he opens them for you, you will keep him."

"I'm going to lose him. I could see it at the party tonight. He held my hand but he never took his eyes off that girl, Meredith Sauvage, even though she paid no attention to him or to anyone but Liam Cyning. It was obvious she was only there to set her hook in him. Why would Lonnie want her instead of me? I'm much prettier."

Angela laughed. She couldn't help herself. She threw back her head and let the laughter roll. Susan stood and stomped her foot.

"It's not funny. I'll fight her for him."

"Oh, you won't have to, daughter. Meredith Sauvage was bred and born to be with Liam Cyning. It would take someone far more persuasive than Lonnie to interfere with that."

"You mean she has a marriage contract with him? Is that even legal?"

"I doubt very much they will ever marry. Possibly. She might help him pick his wife eventually. But no matter of that, she has a bond with him that will last a lifetime. They'll have problems, no doubt. My research has shown significant areas that are a doorway to conflict. But essentially, they are complementary in much the same way you and Lonnie are. You could be his one true love, or you could lose him by being in contention with him instead of cooperation. t will be mostly up to you."

"How do you know so much about these people?" Susan seemed to seriously be pondering whether she would ever be cooperative enough to stay with Lonnie. It was one of the reasons I regretted her having moved into this relationship so quickly.

"It's my job and my passion. I am an Inquirer. I research and write about society, politics, and economics. I can see who the influencers and the manipulators are. I study them. I speak about them. I write books and columns about them. I have to know about them. And now, thanks to you, my dear. I will have an opportunity to know Regina Cyning."

"You'll write about the Cynings?"

"If she permits it. There are certain things I can never expose to the public. It would be a kiss of death. Hopefully, only to my career. But if she permits me to put my hand on hers, I, too, might feel the pulse of America."

4

Seeking a Direction

Liam

I STOOD QUIETLY outside Meredith's door at five minutes until nine in the morning. Whatever else she might think, I didn't want her believing she had to wait for me.

"Oh!" she said, startled to see me standing there when she opened her door. "Mr. Cyning. You are prompt."

"I find it best not to keep others waiting for me," I laughed. "Are you ready for breakfast?"

"Yes. Coffee at least. A little something to eat would be good," she said.

"Are your quarters satisfactory? I could inquire about something more suitable if you find this... possibly... I mean... I hope you are not upset that our rooms are so close on the same hall. I've been living alone up here for so long that it startled me to see you in the hall yesterday and I could see you were startled by my presence this morning," I said. For the past eight years, I'd attended an all-boys school. Seeing a woman on a residence floor was somehow scandalous.

"The room is lovely. I've not even explored it all yet. I agree that it was disconcerting to find a man in the hall. I've been at Green Hill Women's College for eight years. The only men we see are those coming to pick up their dates."

"Do you...?"

"Please don't make any other arrangements for me, Mr. Cyning. It is simply something we must get used to. The proximity will serve us well if we are to work

together." She was being particularly charming this morning and I was having difficulty maintaining an employer/employee detachment. Even though I'd had no
use for girls at the time, our clutch of friends seemed always to be together. We
would probably have become friends if we'd stayed at the same school. I wasn't
even certain what else I would say to her this morning. If there were five girls there,
it wouldn't be a problem. I wouldn't need to relate to any one of them. But with just
one, I was having trouble getting my thoughts together.

We reached the kitchen and I pulled a chair out for her. I'd called down to
Cook to let him know there would be two for breakfast. My parents took nearly all
their meals in their private dining room and Grandmother even had a small kitchen
in her suite. Only occasionally had I eaten a meal she cooked, though. Usually
when I dined with her, Cook sent Ricardo with our meals.

I grabbed two cups from the counter and filled them with strong black coffee.

"Do you take anything in your coffee?" I asked as I set Meredith's coffee in
front of her.

"I believe everything is on the table," she said pointing to a creamer and a
sugar bowl. I didn't take anything in my coffee and couldn't remember seeing those
on the table before.

"Here we are, Mr. Liam. Miss Meredith. Enjoy your breakfast and let me know
if you need anything. I'm just getting ready to prepare the evening meal. Will you
both be here or with either of the elder families?" Cook asked.

"I believe we'll take the meal here," I said. "No one has invited us anywhere else."

"Very well. As usual, there will be luncheon items in the refrigerator for your
convenience."

"Thank you, Cook." The meal looked incredible. Bacon, ham, sausage, a
mound of hash browns, pancakes, and eggs. I dug in and really had no time for a
pleasant conversation while we were eating. Perhaps, in fact, I was focusing on my
food in order to avoid talking. I was sure Meredith noticed.

By the end of breakfast, my plate was clean while Meredith's still had half the
food left on it. "Did the breakfast not suit your taste?" I asked.

"I shall—just this once—cross into a subject that would not normally be discussed in polite conversation. Liam, how much do you weigh?"

"Me? Weigh? I suppose around one-forty or one-forty-five. And you?"

"I repeat, that is normally not considered a polite question. However, I started
this to give you precisely that information. I weigh about one-oh-five. Now, considering a forty-pound difference in our weights, the fact that you have burned

over twelve hundred calories in a morning run, and your athletic metabolism, how could I possibly eat as much as you?"

"Oh. Oh! I see. I'll discuss the matter with Cook."

"No, please don't. This is for me to discuss with Cook. We are both on staff. Getting you involved would make him nervous." I could see Meredith's point. I'd never be able to address the issue without stumbling all over myself anyway. "Now that breakfast is out of the way, why don't we have another cup of coffee and chat for a bit?"

I couldn't avoid it any longer. Meredith and I needed to talk and I had no idea what to say. Erich had talked me through a list of conversation starters before my first date. I figured that was as good a place to start as any. As far as I knew, we had no work to do, so we might as well get to know each other better.

"Meredith, where do you go to school?"

"I attend the Green Hill Women's College where I have studied for eight years," she said. "The women's college starts as a middle school and goes through a baccalaureate degree if one stays there long enough. I fancy it's not much different than Elenchus for boys. And by the way, that was a great question. Would you like to know what I study?" When I'd asked that question of my date last spring, she'd looked at me blankly and said, "High school stuff, of course. This is my school."

"Yes, please. I have no experience with schools other than Elenchus and the public school where we first met."

"My major focus is now Social Studies."

I was puzzled. "Is that like Sociology?"

Meredith laughed at my comparison. "Not quite. Sociology is a science, sometimes considered a part of Social Studies, that deals with the development, structure, and functioning of human society. Social Studies is a broader and less scientific study of social interaction and the various roles people play in society. It includes history, government, economics, civics, sociology, geography, class structure, and anthropology. Green Hill is the only school in the state that has a program defined as Social Studies. Years ago, it was called women's studies but it was expanded to the broader topic since everything at Green Hill is a woman's study of some sort."

"I like your laugh." *That was totally inappropriate.* I needed to find more questions. What was next on the list?

"Thank you. I find many things amusing that others don't. I was afraid I might laugh and offend you and you'd ask me to leave."

"Why ever would you think that, Miss Sauvage? Am I such an ass?"

"Oh, no. I just didn't want you to think I was laughing *at* you. We're very different people. And I'm sorry to say that before we were split up and sent to different schools, we never really had a chance to become friends, though it seemed we were always in the same group of friends," she said.

"I have to take the blame for that. I was decidedly antisocial when it came to girls. I can't believe how stupid I was. It took me about six months at Elenchus to realize that I really missed having girls around. And now that I've been there eight years, I find that I have no idea how to interact." That was probably more than I'd said to her at one time since we met the day before. It seemed so strange to have been apart so many years and now be next-door neighbors.

"It is typical of that age group. You were right on the cusp of learning to appreciate girls and I'd already started wanting to be closer to boys. It was probably for the best that we were sent to boarding schools. In many ways, we've lived in different worlds."

"How so?" I was learning a lot about Meredith in this conversation.

"You're an only child raised by Promoters in a Leader's household. I am the youngest of five—all brothers—raised by Creators."

"Was that difficult?" I tried to imagine what it would have been like to have siblings. I rather thought it would be fun.

"I wouldn't call it difficult, exactly. It was certainly interesting. I think having brothers helped shape my determination to stand up for myself. And contributed to the power of my right hook." We both laughed at that. It was still embarrassing but I held no ill will toward her for disciplining me. "Much to my parents' disappointment, none of us turned out Creators. I like things more dependable and smooth running. Not to the extent a Defender would require. But I never knew when 'the mood' would strike my parents. They called it inspiration. I thought of it as mood swings."

"They became depressed?"

"No. Not usually. For example, I might be all dressed and ready to go to an event with them, or even out shopping, and suddenly they'd disappear. It might be two hours later that we left or we might not leave at all."

"Where did they go?" I didn't even know what her parents did. Creators were often artists, musicians, or performers. Vocation was not the same as class, though.

"Oh, to the studio, the garden, the kitchen, the bedroom. Their passion leaks all over everything." She laughed again. I found I wanted to hear that sound often.

"Miss Sauvage, I have no idea what I am supposed to be doing in life. I have an interest in many things but nothing grabs and holds me with the passion you describe." I took a deep breath and plunged on. "Do you suppose it will be possible to recapture that lost moment from our childhood when we could have become friends?" Her green eyes bored into my own and for a moment, I was afraid I'd offended her. Then her expression softened some.

"I should like that, Mr. Cyning. I should like that very much."

WE RELAXED AS we chatted over coffee. It wasn't the first time I'd talked to a woman one-on-one but it was the first time I could remember not being completely tongue-tied. Except Grandmother. I never had difficulty talking to her.

"So, since we don't have a packed agenda this week and are still working on figuring out what we're doing, I won't be spending every night and every day here, if that is all right. I made a commitment to help with the Children's Hospital Auxiliary this weekend. They are having a fund-raising and awareness festival at Patriot Park," Meredith said. That sparked something in me. I was on my vacation and seriously doing nothing. I'd just been thinking this weekend about volunteer activities.

"Could you use help? I'm not skilled at anything, but I could run errands or help with games. Whatever." I looked at her rather anxiously. "I'm not trying to push my way into something you're involved with. It just seemed like a good opportunity to do something useful."

"Really? You'd really volunteer? That's wonderful! I'm sure we could use another person when it comes to rounding up a few hundred children and getting them involved in games. I'll gladly arrange for you to help!" Her enthusiasm sounded genuine and I breathed a sigh of relief.

"I've been trying to figure out what I should do this summer to discover my... whatever I'm *supposed* to do. This past weekend, I was thinking that I could volunteer for something but I had no idea what. This would at least get me started," I said. My relief was not only at her acceptance, but at the thought of having found something useful to do.

"Mr. Liam," Erich said as he approached the table. We'd been sitting there most of the day. "Your grandmother has extended an invitation to dine with her this evening if you do not have other plans. Both you and Miss Meredith."

"Oh. We need to tell Cook we'll be with Grandmother instead of still occupying this table tonight. Miss Sauvage, are you available to dine with my grandmother and me?" I asked.

"That would be lovely," she said.

"I'll let Cook know," Erich said as he left.

"I'll need to freshen up before dinner," Meredith said. "Do we have more you'd like to cover this afternoon?"

"I think this has just been a getting to know you day," I laughed. "And I am delighted to get to know you. Would you like a quick tour of the house before dinner?"

"Oh, that would be nice. I had no idea where to get breakfast this morning until you invited me."

We walked through the lounge.

"Tell me, do you find our house too ostentatious? I've been looking rather critically at my lifestyle lately." I led Meredith through the main rooms of the house—lounge, formal living room, library, dining room, a small ballroom I didn't remember ever having been used. I pointed down the first-floor hall toward my parents' suite and paused on the second floor to point out Grandmother's suite and the opposite direction to the resident staff rooms.

"Are you uncomfortable here?" she asked.

"I wouldn't say that so much as that recently, I've begun to question how our society is organized. Your specialty, I believe. I feel a bit embarrassed by my family's wealth, which I have had nothing to do with acquiring but certainly benefit from. It is a shift in worldview I am struggling with."

"If you are asking if I live like this, no, not at all. My parents do not have a suite separate from the rest of the house. I grew up with four older brothers. That might be why, when younger, I thought an appropriate response to an insult was to slug a boy in the face." We laughed over that and I felt we had truly gotten past it. "If you are asking if I would like to live like this, my answer would be a bit more ambivalent. It's hard to imagine myself in a setting like this, but the thought is somehow pleasant. I guess I will discover during my tenure here, how much I do or don't like it." We walked on up to the third-floor hallway that, until yesterday, had been my sole domain. We paused for a moment to finish our conversation. "Now, if you are asking if most people live like this, you must understand that it is not only your wealth that sets you apart, but your class. You would be of the same class even if you were penniless, but being a Leader is a natural magnet for wealth. It is in your character."

"It seems so unequal. Or should I say inequitable?" I puzzled over the idea of wealth in the hands of only a few people. *I accused Ferguson of being unemployed and living off the work of others. I am just as bad.*

"Helping a class to prosper does not require another class to suffer. Prosperity is not a limited resource."

"WELCOME, WELCOME," GRANDMOTHER said when we presented ourselves at her door. We joined her immediately at the table where salads had already been set. We politely waited for Grandmother to begin with the first bite before we started. "I'm not going to make a habit of prying but I simply wanted to check in on how your first day has been. Are you going to manage to get along or should I have a boxing ring put in the ballroom?" We all laughed.

"I believe Miss Sauvage and I will avoid coming to blows, Grandmother. I hope that was a lesson that needed to be taught only once," I said.

"We have both learned better use of our words," Meredith agreed. "We've had a good day getting to know one another. Mr. Cyning has volunteered to help with the hospital benefit Saturday."

"Excellent. Well done, Liam. Have you made arrangements to go shopping yet?"

"I didn't even think of that. I rather dread facing Monsieur LeFevre and trying to describe what I need for school. I'll probably end up with much the same things as always."

"Perhaps I could *assist* your endeavor," Meredith said. She looked at me. I was certain she had chosen that word intentionally.

"Is helping me shop for clothes a part of your portfolio?" I asked. "I would love your assistance if it is available."

"Shall we plan tomorrow afternoon? I'll make arrangements with Erich to drive us so we don't need to worry about where to put your packages." She was in control. I was amazed.

"Liam, what do you think a personal assistant is for?" Grandmother asked. I admitted I had no idea. "It is good that Meredith is thinking in terms of what she can do to help smooth out the path you travel."

"I somehow thought I would need to identify tasks and ask her assistance," I said. "Frankly, the thought terrified me. I would never have thought to ask for help shopping."

"You will undoubtedly need to direct me at times," Meredith said. "I'm not a mind reader. I will try to keep ahead when tasks have been identified."

"Thank you."

"I will identify one or two tasks to have you work together on," Grandmother said. "The volunteer idea is a good one. You should continue to look for other ways you can be of service in the community. You have led a rather sheltered life, Liam. I believe you respond well and deal with other gentlemen without difficulty. I threw the two of you together so you would begin to relate to a woman. You should consider what other ways you can engage with individuals and groups. Two that come to mind are dating and parties. Put your heads together to figure out what social events could be arranged. We have the pool, the stables, the tennis courts, the patio, and acres and acres of trails. They've been terribly underused since you started at Elenchus. Have a party!"

"Grandmother... That is a great... I don't even know who to invite, let alone how to plan a party!" Meredith raised her hand to about shoulder level and waggled her fingers at me. "Miss Sauvage, would you assist me in organizing some simple party?"

"I would be delighted, Mr. Cyning."

"And how long are you going to keep that up?" Grandmother asked. I turned a blank look to her.

"What?"

"You two are, hopefully, entering into a partnership that will last a long time. I know the probationary period is six months. I hope we will be able to measure your association in years. The time will be excruciatingly long if you continue to address each other as Mr. and Miss. Now, I don't mean in public, of course. There is a time and place for everything. You should be able to plan a party and not be using last names." She looked at us and I know I blushed. "Not now. This is something else for you to deal with in private. Is your office adequate, Meredith?"

"I've not even seen it yet, I'm afraid. I have an office?"

"Lupe will escort you to your room this evening and introduce you to your entire suite. I know you've scarcely brought anything with you so far but please understand that your rooms are yours for so long as you remain attached to Buxton House."

"Yes, ma'am. Thank you."

I'M AFRAID I was pretty quiet through the remainder of the meal and through coffee and dessert in Grandmother's sitting room. There was much more to this whole personal assistant thing than I imagined. I thought of my father and his assistant. I only ever associated him with the office. I suppose that might be more of a professional assistant than a personal assistant? An association that would last for years?

I needed to examine this carefully. If 'years' was the expectation, I needed to be very sure I could tolerate an association with Meredith for a long time. And the 'personal' part of personal assistant obviously meant something more... intimate than I had imagined. Not that she and I would ever be intimate in one sense. But she was going shopping with me for my fall wardrobe! She would know my measurements, my taste in clothes, the style of my underwear! Could I allow her to get that close? Only Erich knew me so well.

And what of these other plans? Did Grandmother actually tell me that Meredith should help me plan dates and events at which I might meet other women? That would be... I could almost imagine Meredith waiting up for me in a rocking chair, knitting when I got home from a date. What a motherly thing to do. Would she ask if I had a good time? What we did? If I like the girl?

How could I possibly ever talk to her about things like that?

"Liam, you look a bit feverish," Grandmother said. "Are you well?"

"Yes, Grandmother. I just feel a bit flushed. If you will forgive me, I think I will retire early this evening. I'm sorry to drag you away..."

"I am going to ask Meredith to stay for a bit longer so we can chat some more," Grandmother said. "I'll have Lupe show her back to her room and give her a tour." I rose and kissed my Grandmother on the cheek.

"Until tomorrow, then," I said to Meredith. "Why don't we plan to leave about eleven and have a bite of lunch before we shop?"

"That would be lovely. Until then." I left and rushed to my room.

5

Dressing for Success

Meredith

"YOU HAVE CONCERNS?" Mrs. Cyning asked as soon Liam left the room.

"Of course," I answered. "I am concerned about our ability to work together and worried that the honeymoon, so to speak, will be over before we really resolve our relationship. So far, I believe I have seen Liam on his best behavior and it is difficult to not imagine he will turn around one day and still be a brat. It's worrisome."

"Well, we all have our ups and downs. Do you believe you'll be able to weather the storm when it breaks?"

"Yes. Oddly, I am more concerned as to whether Liam will be able to weather it. I don't want to destroy what is being built. But I don't dare let him walk on me. I appreciate your concern and the opportunity to vent about mine."

"We shan't have these talks often, I'm afraid. I don't want Liam to think that you are running to me with stories about him. You report to him. I just wanted to confirm in my own mind that we made the right choice with you." Mrs. Cyning paused for a moment and looked me hard in the eye. "I am confident we did. You've been carefully prepared for this responsibility which I do not place on you lightly. Do what you must to expose Liam's leadership qualities. Help him to see them in himself. Goodnight, Meredith."

"Goodnight, Mrs. Cyning."

I STEPPED INTO the hall to find a woman waiting for me in a household uniform.

"Good evening, Miss Meredith. I'm Lupe. I was asked to give you a more extensive tour of your suite and let you know where and how to get meals, laundry, and help if you need it."

"Thank you, Lupe. Today has been exhausting and I've not really taken time to learn anything about Buxton House." She led me first to the kitchen and explained the protocol there. She also told me I could ask for a meal to be sent to my suite if I wanted. When we got to my room, she pointed out the huge walk-in closet and that she had already pressed and hung my clothes. In the dresser, my lingerie had been neatly folded. Fresh toiletries had been laid out on the bathroom sink. Unlike Mrs. Cyning's suite, mine did not have a separate sitting and dining area. But there was a small table and chairs where I could eat if I wanted, and a lovely easy chair with a reading lamp. It was obvious the room was not set up for entertaining.

"This is your office," she said, opening a door opposite the bathroom. "It is not completely set up yet, as we wanted your input on preferred décor and furnishing." The room was large and had only a desk and chair in it, making it seem even larger. "The door here is to the hall so you need not take guests through your bedroom to reach the office."

"And what is that door?" I asked. The third door was in the wall opposite my bedroom.

"That is a connecting door to Mr. Liam's study. It is a security door and must be opened from both sides. You needn't fear being interrupted or interrupting Mr. Liam."

"Not much need for that, I think. If Mr. Cyning wishes to come to my office, he can use the hall door, like everyone else."

"Yes, of course, Miss."

I ROSE FROM bed, showered, applied makeup, dressed, and still made it to the breakfast table by eight o'clock. There was no sign of Liam. I went to talk to Cook.

"What would you like for breakfast, Miss Meredith?" he asked. "I can whip up nearly anything, but if you have a regular sequence of meals, it makes it go more smoothly."

"Thank you, Cook. I'll try not to be a pain. I feel awkward calling you 'Cook.' Do you prefer to be called by name?"

"I'm James Harrison, but I actually prefer being called Cook. It's what I was called in the Army."

"Then Cook it is. I eat lightly in the morning, preferring fruit, coffee, and some type of cereal, hot or cold. I'm not very picky."

"That is not a problem at all. This morning, we have an assortment of fresh berries and oatmeal. Most of the staff just finished eating."

"I'll try to be earlier tomorrow. When does Mr. Cyning usually eat?" I followed Cook's pointed finger to get a coffee mug and pour my own.

"He's usually in and out by six-thirty when he's here at Buxton House. Always has been an early riser." I groaned. It would be hard enough to get to the kitchen while the other staff were eating but I was not going to suggest breakfast meetings with Liam.

As soon as I had finished my meal, I returned to my room. There was no telephone in my office but one sat by the bed. I looked up the number I wanted and called Elenchus.

"Good morning. This is Meredith Sauvage. I am assisting Mr. Liam Cyning in selecting clothing for the coming season and would like to ask about the uniform requirements and other clothing he will need at Elenchus Scholé this fall."

"Of course, Miss Sauvage. I'm Ray Wellborn, the dorm parent for Mr. Cyning. On matters of fashion and dress, however, it would be better for you to speak to my wife. Will you hold, please?"

"Yes, thank you." It took only a few seconds for Mrs. Wellborn to come to the phone.

"Miss Sauvage, so nice to meet you. I am Lucille Wellborn, dorm mother. I understand you wish to pick out clothing for Mr. Cyning. May I ask your role in this?"

"Of course, Mrs. Wellborn. I have been hired as Mr. Cyning's personal assistant as he explores his class potential."

"Oh, you're the one. Wonderful! I am so glad he is moving smartly into his class. I'm sure you will have your hands full, but a finer young man you will never find. Here is what we have as our standard list." Mrs. Wellborn read through the list of clothing. It included uniforms, what she referred to as 'play clothes,' and athletic wear. "I hate to see you spend a lot for a full closet of uniforms. We have noted that Mr. Cyning is expected to matriculate to the university after Christmas. I would suggest dropping at least one of the uniforms and preparing to purchase a few items for the less rigid university lifestyle."

"Thank you, Mrs. Wellborn. I will take your advice. I do hope you have a pleasant afternoon. It has been a pleasure to discuss this with you."

"Good day, dear."

I looked at the list and reduced the uniform blazers from two to one. The standard uniform slacks were suitable for casual wear as well as with the uniform but would be boring if he had no other choices. Even though white shirts and ties could always be worn, Liam would need a selection of ties now instead of just the school tie. He would need at least one new suit for dressier occasions. He would look handsome in a Norfolk jacket and wool slacks, and the Norfolk could also be worn with jeans.

Yes, this would be fun.

OUR FIRST STOP was at the Serenity Garden, a tea shop where we enjoyed a light lunch while I told Liam about the art of shopping.

"You need to drive the conversation when we reach Monsieur LeFevre's. If he detects you are not in control of your own wardrobe, it will be the same as if you were shopping with your mother. I'll support you and supply comments about things that would be nice on you or things that you should avoid. Shall we go?" We entered the shop.

"Ah, Mr. Cyning. I see you are shopping for your own clothes. And with a lovely companion. I have laid out all the usual attire if you would come this way." We followed the tailor into a fitting room where an array of school blazers and slacks were hung. Monsieur LeFevre began by getting a new set of measurements as I browsed through the selection.

"You shan't need as many school uniforms this year, Mr. Cyning." I separated out just one jacket and two pair of slacks. "I'm told you will be starting at the University mid-term."

"Really? I mean, of course. In that case, I'll need fewer school uniforms and more casual attire for the University, Monsieur LeFevre. I'd prefer the bulk of my winter wardrobe to be more in keeping with the college atmosphere. I'm thinking I will need only one school blazer and would like two appropriate sport coats with an assortment of slacks to go with them. One of the jackets could be another blazer, but I'd like one to be a Norfolk style in an estate tweed. Will that be possible, sir?"

"Of course, Mr. Cyning. Let's look at a couple of fabrics and see what you like. With your coloring, I would recommend you stick with the blue or gray as your primary colors. Don't you agree, Miss?"

"For the more formal pieces, I agree, sir. I think though, Mr. Cyning could launch into browns for his tweed." I fingered a wool fabric and tugged the corner out a bit to show Liam. It was amazingly soft. He smiled.

"I think I like this one, Monsieur. Do you think it would make up nicely in a Norfolk?"

"That is a very good fabric, Mr. Cyning. You have a good eye. This is Suri Alpaca wool from the Argentine Andes. The fabric is woven of natural colors and has not been dyed. It's more durable than other alpaca wools and considerably warmer so it makes a very good jacket for cool days. Your choice of a traditional Norfolk will go excellently. And for your blazer?"

"I'll go with your recommended gray," Liam said. The shopping continued until Liam had selected the bulk of his fall wardrobe.

"Shall we deliver these to you at school?"

"I'll be at Buxton House for another few weeks before I return to school. Can you have them sent up to me there?"

"You can expect them in seven days."

I walked ahead of Liam to the door where I paused and let him open it. Erich met us with the car and we proceeded into the larger retail area of town.

"**WHEN WAS I** supposed to find out I was going to the University this winter?" he demanded. "That was a bit of a shock."

"I apologize. I assumed that since it was information so freely given to me, it was common knowledge. I had no idea you didn't know!" I was surprised and worried that I'd let out news that was not supposed to be public.

"I suppose this is Grandmother's doing. Why do you suppose she's having me wait until mid-term to transfer?" Liam mused, somewhat mollified.

"I would think they have a transitional course planned for you this fall. Aside from that, how are you surviving the day so far?"

"I feel a bit like a mannequin," Liam laughed. "But I do like the combinations we selected. The charcoal pinstripe suit is sure to become one of my favorites."

"Let's see if we can't add a little color to your choices with the casual wear. You needn't always dress in black and white and shades of gray. You handled Monsieur LeFevre very well. It's your confidence that changes things."

"I did not *feel* confident and thank you for giving me subtle hints where he could not see them. Oh! I will need new shoes, as well. I believe my feet have quit growing, so at least new dress shoes, a pair of loafers, and a pair of tennis shoes would be good. And I suppose athletic shoes, too."

"Your confidence is strong even when I am the only audience. Very well done. Let's head for Browning's."

"I'M HEADING HOME now," I said when Erich dropped us off in front of Buxton House and indicated he would take the boxes to Liam's room. "It would be good for both of us to list out some of the things we want to accomplish in your few months before enrolling at the University. Also include any topics you would like to discuss. Subject areas you want to investigate. That sort of thing. I'll plan on spending more time here next week as we establish more routines. This was all sprung on you rather suddenly."

"Are you supposed to be my teacher now? Giving me assignments?" Yes, he could still be a brat.

"As a matter of fact, that is part of my job. I can scarcely prepare to either assist or mentor you if you don't share with me your interests. It will be best to increase our exposure to one another gradually so we don't come to blows at once." I did laugh to lighten that little sting. He smiled.

"There are things I would like to discuss, but I'm not quite comfortable doing so yet. I will make sure they are on my list."

"For my part, if we are having a serious discussion, I promise not to be judgmental or patronizing. I'm sure we'll work it out."

"Thank you, Miss Sauvage. I will see you at the park on Saturday for the festival."

"I've given Erich the necessary information on timing and meeting places. I'll see you then."

I SANK INTO the driver's seat of my car and breathed a sigh of relief. I'd acquired the automobile as soon as I was hired. I was thankful for the guidance of Erich while Liam was still in England. I would not have been able to afford the used Studebaker Commander, but it was deemed as necessary for my job and I was thankful to have it.

I needed to return to my dormitory and make an appointment with Dr. Parolini. One half of a week and I felt incredibly tense. I knew I needed to guide

Liam with a firm hand but I didn't dare attempt to manage him. He would definitely respond negatively to that. Yet I knew it was not only Liam but Mrs. Cyning who was observing how well I handled this.

I needed to figure out what I was assisting him with as well. I was going to be very careful how I approached what an eighteen-year-old boy might want help with.

I had left a list with Lupe this morning, indicating what I needed in my office. I would spend more time this week gathering together references about state and local history, interesting sights, a business profile. It would need to be quite general until I learned more about his interests. I just needed to be where I could focus without being in the next room over from him.

"RIGHTS OR PRIVILEGES? What are your expectations?" Dr. Parolini addressed her three students at an informal roundtable. For the past year, it was how most of my classes were held. Some few were one-on-one with an instructor. My classmates had been with me for eight years. Peggy Anne and Karen—the same girls who had been invited to Liam's tenth birthday party. All three of us had received a full scholarship and allowance to attend Green Hill. We all knew we were being groomed as a mentor and assistant to Liam. We had all three been interviewed by Mrs. Cyning before I was selected. I was a bit concerned about their reaction to me now. Dr. Parolini continued.

"We all have basic rights: Life, Liberty, and the Pursuit of Happiness. Our constitution guarantees certain other rights that fall in the category of civil liberties. But society gives privilege to some and not to others. We all have equal rights but not necessarily equal privileges. Privilege is afforded to people with rank, wealth, or class, and it often comes with attendant responsibility. A study of any civilization would show that people with wealth, rank, office, or authority seem set aside as special. And some societies even perpetuate classes like Royalty, Bourgeoisie, and Serf that are nearly impossible to break free of."

"Our class system is not hereditary, though," Peggy Anne said. "Any person might be chosen for any class."

"That's true. Nearly a hundred years ago, when the nation was in turmoil over perceived divisions of society and privilege as a result of the Civil War, a select commission was chosen to study and define a class structure for America. They examined, as you have, the class and caste structures of many societies to determine a set of characteristics that would lead a person to be considered a member of a class. They were careful to define the classes in such a way that they would not be based on wealth, heredity, or occupation. In that way, anyone might be chosen for any class. Does it work?"

"The idea of choice enters the picture," Karen said. "I can't just choose to be a Cognoscente. I had to work very hard to shape myself into the characteristics of the class I wanted to be part of."

"It is actually your own volition that helped reveal the characteristics of that class in you. The desire to be something and putting forth the effort to become it is an indicator of proper class assignment," Dr. Parolini continued. "Still, the three of you were all trained for the same occupation—to be a personal assistant and mentor—even though you are all three of different classes. Cognoscente, Creator, and Advisor."

"Doctor Parolini, now that Meredith has been chosen, what is the likelihood that Peggy Anne and I will ever find a mentor or assistant role? We've known from the outset that the Cynings would choose one of us or one of the boys, but we have never considered what will become of the others." Karen was the most outspoken of us, focused on a career as a lawyer. She was advancing quite nicely through her studies and I wondered how she would have responded to Liam now that we were older and supposedly more mature. When we were twelve, we'd all been somewhat intimidated.

"That is a difficult question. You have the opportunity to have a career that has been afforded by your education. You might apply your education to any number of things. Perhaps you would one day want to teach law. Or to become an advisor and mentor to a Commander or Promoter or even an Inquirer. It is not only Leaders who can use such guidance. Peggy Anne might become a mentor to any number of people who are soothed by music, including another Creator. And either of you might yet be called upon to mentor a Leader. Liam Cyning is not the only one in the world."

Dr. Parolini had worked with us for eight years. She was not much older than we were now when she began teaching. "I was also trained as a mentor, though my class is Inquirer. Sadly, the young woman I was brought to was a frail girl. She succumbed to a fever when she was just growing into womanhood. Let me tell you that losing your disciple is an emotional tragedy I would wish on no one." I was shocked. I considered Katherine to be more than a professor; she had become my best friend.

"Dr. Parolini, how did you cope with it?" I had no emotional ties with Liam aside from the intensity that we had all trained to become his assistant. Occasionally, I still wanted to teach him a lesson. He could be charming one moment and aggravating the next. But I'd worked hard for this position and was not about to consider losing it.

"I was invited to stay in the household and await the blossoming of a second child but I chose to leave. I was brokenhearted. Everywhere I looked there were reminders of my precious Leah. I wandered for a year, simply traveling. I got my advanced degree in Social Studies and was contacted by this college to mentor three bright young women. You three have made me very happy. I am so proud of all of you."

"Dr. Parolini, I understand your grief but what does this have to do with rights, privileges, and expectations?" Peggy Anne seldom challenged her teachers but she did want to get to the point.

"Meredith, how do your rights compare to your disciple's rights?"

"I believe our rights are the same. Isn't that what you're getting at? Rights are guaranteed to all of us. Everyone has the same rights. But he still confuses his privileges as rights. His wealth and his family ensure he has more or different privileges than other people who have the same rights."

"Wanting great privileges for all is a fine trait in a Leader. In a Dexter, that expectation might cause great frustration and anger. In essence, even though we are an egalitarian society and no class is considered better than the others, the occupations and inheritance of wealth or social status often make a great difference in the way we are treated."

"MEREDITH, PLEASE STAY a moment." I returned to my seat at the table with Dr. Parolini. "We are going to graduate you. I believe it will be best if you begin at once at the university."

"Isn't it too late for me to get enrolled? Classes begin in less than a month!"

"Arrangements have been made. Your tuition and expenses will continue to be covered. Your major task this term will be to find suitable housing for yourself and for your disciple. You need to think carefully about what is suitable. Your quarters should be near but not the same. Liam will need private quarters, to enhance his maturing as well as to entertain his… ah… dates. Do you understand?"

"Yes, Katherine. I can't say I'm comfortable moving to the university, but it is clear why it's necessary."

"When you locate suitable housing, the Cynings will rent it or buy it."

"I will make it a topic for us to discuss as we are both floundering a bit regarding what my job is supposed to be," I said. Moving to the University. I suppose I should have expected it, but I'd been very happy here at Green Hill Women's College. It would be a big adjustment.

"I am very proud of you, Meredith. You have one of the most difficult and at the same time rewarding tasks possible. You may not become wealthy, but by association, you will be afforded many of the privileges accorded to Liam."

"It has many rewards. I have discovered a few. I will serve the family by advising the son. And that, frankly, is reward enough."

"You should prepare for your move. Temporary housing will be available in a University dormitory. I don't, however, believe that is the right place for either you or Liam to stay. Blessings on you, Meredith."

"WHAT ARE YOU doing back? Isn't this your first week working for Mr. Wonderful?" Hana demanded of me when I walked in.

"Puh-lease! It's just a job. He's not quite the indolent little kid I remember from eight years ago, but he still has his moments," I said, hugging my roommate. "And I'm not going to live with him. All the time."

"You're going to live with him part of the time?" Hana laughed.

"Well, as a member of the staff, I have a room and an office at Buxton House for convenience when I'm working on a project. They've all been very nice to me so far."

"Mmm. That would make it convenient!"

"Hana! Don't embarrass me."

"Sweet Meredith. We've roomed together for five years and across the hall from Peggy Anne and Karen. In that time, I could have made a fortune if I had a dollar for every time any of you mentioned his name or started a sentence, 'When I'm working for Liam.' You may be able to tell the rest of the world it's just a job, but you can't tell me that." Hana led me over to sit down. Our apartment had two bedrooms, a bath, and a sitting room study.

"It's different than I thought it would be. I pictured us... doing things—solving world problems. The truth is that neither of us know why he needs an assistant at the moment. We talked ourselves out on Tuesday, went shopping on Wednesday, and I came home to have a session with Dr. Parolini. The only thing we have planned is that he will volunteer on Saturday for the Children's Hospital festival in the park.

I don't even know what he'll do." I was more concerned about that than not know-ing what I should do as his assistant.

Hana was right, though. For eight years, six of us—three boys and three girls—had been thinking of working for Liam Cyning. He wasn't really always a brat, when we were all in school together. There was something about his presence. Kids always looked for him to organize a student art show or suggest a game or to explain a concept. He didn't like girls at the time, but we knew that would change. I was two years older and expected a different level of maturity from him.

"Well, at least if he's volunteering Saturday, I'll finally get to meet the man. Maybe I'll just take him for a test drive for you." Hana always had a solution to my problems that involved her getting lucky. Unfortunately for her, none of the solu-tions were long term.

"Careful. I might just suggest he ask you out."

6

Physician, Heal Thyself

Hana Ito

I HAD FUN teasing Meredith. She took her education seriously and her desire to work for—or under—Liam Cyning overflowed so much I was surprised she was classed as an Advisor instead of an Aspirant. But I suppose merely loving your chosen line of work is not the same as being called to it. If she'd not been chosen as Liam's Personal Assistant, she would have been disappointed, but she would have found something else to do. For me, nothing could possibly replace my calling to become a healer—a doctor.

The cost to my personal life was high, but it didn't make a difference to me. I'd had a few relationships. I was, after all, two years older than Meredith. But relationships ultimately got in the way of my studies or work at the hospital. As soon as that happened, I was single again.

We were up early on Saturday. The event wouldn't start until eleven, but the core volunteers needed to be at the park by eight to get things set up. We had portable grills for the hot dogs we'd be serving. Games with courses to lay out. And areas for the different age groups of children who would be present. If a child in the hospital was mobile and deemed fit enough, he or she would be brought to the picnic with a nurse watching over them. But there would be dozens—we hoped over a hundred—of children who were not sick but just came for the festival and hopefully would make friends with the patients.

People started arriving at ten-thirty and there were a few moments of panic as we tried to get things started. I was to light one of the grills and get started. Unfortunately, it was quite uneven and I struggled trying to get it level so I could start the charcoal.

"May I help? We could put a small stone under the short leg," a young man said, moving at once to his knees to lift the short leg and scrape some small stones under the leg. "How does that look?"

"Much better, thank you. I'm afraid I didn't have the strength to lift it up. I don't think the hot dogs will roll off the grill now." I looked up into the young man's gorgeous blue eyes and smiled. He wasn't too tall, but I'm only five-one. I get nervous around giants of six foot or more. I expected him to say something to me.

"Well… um… I guess I'll try to be useful somewhere," he stammered. He looked away from my eyes and I was afraid he would flee.

"Why don't you help with the grill here. Can you light the charcoal?" I asked.

"Oh. Yes, certainly. I'll have it started in a few minutes," he said.

"I'll go get our plate of grillables. I'm Hana, by the way."

"It's very nice to meet you, Miss Hana. I'm Liam."

"We'll be sweating over the grill together shortly. Please just call me Hana." I turned to get the food out of the coolers while Liam showed some skill in getting the charcoal to light. Liam. It could only be Meredith's Liam. I had a flash of jealousy. It was silly, but he was cute and terribly shy. I wondered how he had ever managed to be classed as a Leader. Well, I was ready to follow him.

In half an hour, the smell of grilling hot dogs and hamburgers rose from our grill as he worked, placing cold meat on the grill while I removed cooked meat to the picnic table. A small child ambled up to where he was grilling with her head turned up trying to smell the savory aroma. She couldn't quite see over the edge of the grill. I gasped as I saw her reach to pull herself up on the grill.

Liam didn't hesitate. He reached down and scooped the little girl up and safely back from the grill.

"Did you want to see what was grilling?" he asked. "I'll show you. But it's very hot. That's why I hold a long-handled pair of tongs to turn the hot dogs over." The little girl pointed at a hot dog. "Is that the one you want to eat?" he asked. "It's almost ready. Hana, could you put this hot dog on a plate just for my little friend? What's your name, precious?"

"Wendy."

"Wendy, Hana is getting a paper plate. She'll put your hot dog on it and carry it to the table so you can sit up and fix it the way you want. Just remember, the hot dog will be hot at first. Okay?"

"Okay." He pointed at the hot dog she'd indicated to make sure he got the right one. She nodded and he put the food on the plate I was holding. She squirmed a little and Liam put her down, placing himself between the little girl and the grill. She immediately reached for my hand and I led her to the table where children were busily digging into their food.

LIAM STOOD GUARD over the station as he doused the coals in a bucket of water and scrubbed the grill. He stayed there until he was sure the grill was no longer hot enough for a child to get burned. I saw him step away and the same little girl come over to meet him. It looked like he had a fan.

I saw Meredith across the park as she started toward him. We were both too far away to listen to the intense conversation they were having. Then Liam stood up and took hold of the little girl's waist as she led him off yelling, "Choo choo!"

"Come get on board the train," Liam called to nearby children. They began to flock toward him and he guided little Wendy around as more and more children attached themselves to the train. Meredith and a few other volunteers fell into line, encouraging the children to make train noises. Before long, nearly all the children were in line, nurses helping their charges move with the train while Liam and Wendy led them on a long follow-the-leader game. It was near the end of the party and I stepped up beside Liam and asked him to lead the train to the station so the parents could take their children from it. He pointed to the bandstand and I hurried to tell parents where to pick up their children.

The nurses broke off with their charges to return to the hospital. Parents took mini trains to the parking lot where they said goodbye to their friends. I maneuvered Liam out of the way a bit.

"Thank you so much for your help today, Liam. You really stepped in to save the day. That was probably the easiest conclusion to a festival imaginable."

"It was really fun," Liam said. "I'm glad I got to help." We'd had several minutes to chat while grilling and transporting food and it seemed like he was more comfortable as the party ended.

"Excuse me for being forward, but this would be a good time to ask me out next weekend," I said. I knew it was brazen. He stammered a bit.

"Really? I mean. Of course. I mean. Um… Hana, would you like to go out next weekend? Maybe Saturday night?" he asked.

"How nice of you to ask. I'd love to go out and get to know you better. Let me give you my phone number and you can call to make arrangements." I'd already written my name and number on a paper napkin and pressed it into his hand.

"I'll look forward to it and call tomorrow."

"Not before ten. I have a night shift tonight and will sleep late."

He smiled and I saw Meredith headed for us again. I winked at her and left. I saw them in a conversation as animated as the one Liam had had with little Wendy.

MY PHONE RANG after ten on Tuesday morning and Liam sounded like he'd rehearsed what he wanted to say.

"Miss Ito… uh… Hana, I have tickets for the symphony Saturday evening. Would you be my guest for the concert and dessert after?" he asked. Very charming.

"I hope this is Liam Cyning calling," I said innocently.

"Oh my gosh! I'm so sorry. I forgot to introduce myself. Yes. This is Liam Cyning. I hope you remember our conversation Saturday afternoon."

"Yes, I remember," I giggled. "I'd be delighted to go to the symphony Saturday. I love classical music and I understand they are doing Berlioz *Symphonie Fantastique*. It's one of my favorites."

"I'm so glad I found tickets then. Shall I pick you up at seven?"

"Do you know where I live?"

"Um… not yet. My driver could pick you up though if you let me know."

"Oh, a driver."

"Yes. I've never had a reason to have a license before. I should think about that."

I'D BEEN PREPARED to tell him I couldn't go out after all. He was cute, but in a teenager sort of way and Meredith had fumed a bit after his call on Sunday. Not that she would say anything, but I could just tell she wasn't happy. He said he would work out arrangements for something based on a few suggestions I gave him. Then when he called on Tuesday and suggested the symphony, what could I do.

I had a huge amount of studying to do and continued night shifts through Thursday, but I had the weekend off. Until Sunday night. I got straight to work.

IT WAS FRIDAY before I saw Meredith again. I got back from the library and she had just returned from her alternate residence at Buxton House. I opened a bottle of wine and poured us each a glass.

"How was your week with the new job?" I asked cheerily. She growled at me.

"As if you haven't talked to him as much as I have."

"Meredith, that's not true. We've only spoken a couple of times. I was going to turn him down for the date, but then he suggested the symphony and I crumpled. You know how I love the symphony."

"Oh, yes. Who do you think suggested it and got the tickets and made reservations at Chez Panisse for you?" she groused.

"Meredith! I'm so sorry. He had you make all the arrangements?"

"I'm his personal assistant. And, no. He didn't ask me to make the arrangements. He wanted to sit down first thing Monday morning and talk. Well, first thing when I got there. I didn't attempt to get there for breakfast like when I'm staying there."

"What happened?"

"He was a nervous wreck. Hana, he's only ever been out on one date. He's eighteen and has had only one date! And from what he told me, it was unremarkable and she declined his invitation to go out a second time. It's really quite amazing that he got up the nerve to talk to you Saturday."

"He was so helpful! And the way he rescued little Wendy when she was about to put her hand on the grill and just took over cooking. And then when he led the children all around as a train. Everyone just jumped aboard. It was quite amazing. I guess I was a little infatuated from the start," I admitted.

"He quite surprised me, as well. I hadn't even spotted him arrive and all of a sudden, he was with you manning a grill. I had children at the tether ball and never got away to even ask how he was getting on," Meredith said.

"So, what did you talk about Monday?"

"He had a regular confessional. Told me about his lack of confidence in speaking with women and his disastrous first date. Which apparently was a well-chaperoned dance, but he couldn't find anything to talk about. You may need to carry the conversation tomorrow night. Then he was in a panic about what to do on a date. I finally suggested the symphony and dessert. You wouldn't believe how relieved he was. He was going to call you at once, but I suggested he make sure tickets were available. Of course, I was the one who made the call, reserved the table, worked out the timetable with him."

"Well, I can only say thank you. I'm sure nothing will come of this, either. You know my luck with men. As soon as they find out I work eighty hours a week at the hospital or in classes or studying, they realize I don't really have time for them."

"Perhaps one day you'll find another Aspirant who considers his calling to be taking care of you."

"Oh, my! Wouldn't that be something?"

"Then guess what happened Wednesday morning?" Meredith giggled, in full gossip mode.

"What?"

"He asked me to take him to get a driving permit and teach him how to drive. He said he'd only just realized what an imposition it was for him to not be able to fend for himself on a date. For a minute, I thought he was going to ask me to chauffeur him tomorrow evening. But Erich will be the driver." Meredith sighed and took a drink of her wine.

"Why didn't he ask Erich to teach him to drive?"

"It's one of those quirky little things. He explained that part of Erich's job was to drive him and he didn't want to make him feel that Liam was dissatisfied or was trying to push him out. He also explained that while I might need to drive him somewhere at some time, chauffeuring him was not part of my job and he would feel it was a huge imposition on me. It was really quite touching."

"Meredith, do you want me to not go out with him?"

"I'm not his girlfriend, Hana. Have fun."

I ANSWERED THE knock at my door to find Liam ready to pick me up. He looked quite handsome in a charcoal pinstripe suit.

"Good evening, Miss Ito."

"Please. Let's not get started with Mr. and Miss. Call me Hana like you did at the park."

"Yes, Hana. May I escort you to the car?"

"I can't think how else I would get there." I laughed and locked the door, then took Liam's offered arm. His driver held the door open, I got in and fastened the seatbelt. Liam ran to the other door. I wasn't sure if I should have slid over next to him but that seemed a bit forward. The position wasn't conducive to talking much, though.

"Um… Miss… Hana, I mean. I'm afraid I'm not very used to this. I completely forgot to give you this small gift of truffles. I was… um… overcome with how stunning you look. I'm sorry I did not comment on that immediately."

"Oh! Chocolate. You know the way to a woman's heart." I ignored his comment about my looks but I was pleased. I did get dressed up. I wore a sleeveless black dress with a strand of pearls—simple and elegant.

At the theater, he quickly jumped out of the car to run to the passenger side and give me his hand as I stepped out. A perfect gentleman. I took his offered arm and we went into the theater.

An usher guided us to the center section, six rows from the stage. *Wow!*

"Oh, these are very nice seats, Liam. I love the pieces they're performing tonight. Berlioz is one of my favorite composers and *Symphonie Fantastique* is my favorite of his works." I was going to continue by telling him Berlioz was seriously on drugs when he wrote the piece, but the conductor arrived on stage and the audience applauded. We'd talk at intermission.

Unfortunately, the lines for the restrooms were long and we barely made it back to our seats before the orchestra launched into Paganini's *Violin Concerto No. 1 in E-flat major.*

"**WHAT A FANTASTIC** concert!" I said, taking Liam's arm as we walked across the street to Chez Panisse. "Berlioz was wonderful and the pianist for the Mendelssohn was beautiful. But do you know how rare it is to hear the Paganini played in the original E-flat? Nearly all modern performances are in the later D-major version."

"What is the difference? Why would they step down a half step?"

"E-flat is an extremely difficult key to play on strings. So, what Paganini did was brilliant. He didn't want his soloist overwhelmed by the strings in the orchestra so he wrote the soloist part in D-major with *scordatura* tuning. That meant the soloist's violin was tuned half a step sharp so she could play the dominant note on the open D-string. The rest of the orchestra, playing in E-flat, was more muted because the strings could not play on an open string. Brilliant!"

"Do you play?"

"Liam, have you ever met an Asian who didn't play either violin or piano? It is part of our upbringing. No matter what class or what occupation, we take years of piano or violin lessons. Playing the piano, as I do, is simply part of my daily routine."

"I had no idea. I've a friend who plays violin. He's French."

"Well, Asians don't have a corner on the instrument. Most of the music we learn is from Western Europe."

Liam gave his name to the host at Chez Panisse and we were led immediately to a table where he held my chair for me. The waiter took our order for coffee and soon a French press was steeping on the table between us. Bittersweet chocolate and caramel profiteroles were delivered just as the waiter pushed the plunger down on the press and poured our coffee. It was well-orchestrated.

"Not that I would have chosen differently, but did we order this?" I was puzzled by the puff pastry.

"I'm so sorry. When we ordered coffee and dessert, they automatically brought this. I didn't know what was on the menu tonight. This restaurant only fixes one dessert each night," he explained.

"You are giving me a wonderful new experience tonight. Thank you."

"I've delighted in your company. I'm afraid I am not very experienced in the world of dating. I'm constantly unsure of what I am doing."

"I'm afraid my schedule is such that it doesn't allow for much dating, either."

"Tell me about your calling," he asked. Well, he knew I was an aspirant. It was nice that he was interested. And he was easy to talk to.

"It's not like I'm mystical or spiritual. I dabbled in all the things children do. Séance, Ouija Board, Sunday School, Yoga. They didn't really do anything for me. I wanted to live life to the fullest—experience everything," I said.

"I can appreciate that."

"It was all great until the day Deborah almost died," I continued. "She tried to copy a back flip I did and fell short of the full revolution. I was horrified to see her lying there on the pavement. I yelled for someone to get an ambulance and then knelt beside her. She was still breathing and had a pulse. I just wanted to straighten her broken body. Deborah opened her eyes.

"'Owww! It hurts?' she cried.

"I knew better than to move her but I asked her to take a deep breath, which hurt, of course. I guessed it was probably a broken rib. I set about removing her skates and checking to see if her toes moved.

"'My neck hurts,' she complained.

"This is where the story gets strange. I closed my eyes and laid my hands on Deborah. I focused all my energy and poured it into her. *Heal. I send you all the healing energy you need. Heal and get up and walk,* I prayed. Of course, nothing happened. People don't get healed that way. People get healed because they go to doctors and doctors set the bones, operate on bad parts, and prescribe medicine. I knew right then, I needed to become a doctor.

"It was like turning on a light in my life. It was crystal clear. I need to become a doctor. I need to heal people."

"I'm in awe, Hana. I truly find Aspirants to be an inspiration. I don't feel that kind of intense calling to any one thing," he said.

"Yes, but you are a natural Leader. The way you captured the children Saturday just showed how quickly people will follow you. I have my own bit of envy," I laughed.

WHEN WE LEFT the restaurant, I let my hand slide down his arm to his hand. His driver opened the door for me and I slid in, but didn't let go of his hand, pulling him into the car after me so we sat closer together.

"Coming down from a beautiful evening like this always makes me feel cozy. Thank you again for a wonderful evening."

"Shall we plan something for next weekend?" he asked. He was so sweet.

"I can't. I'll be at the hospital on weekend shifts for the next two weeks. I'm sorry, Liam. I'm a very difficult person to date. I'd love to carve out some time for another date, but I'm afraid it won't be soon. The hospital is very important to me. If I can finish my med school by the end of winter, I will be able to start full time at the hospital. Won't that be wonderful?" I suppose my enthusiasm was lost on him. Perhaps we would manage another date sometime.

"Truly wonderful."

The car pulled up in front of the dormitory and Liam walked me to my door. I saw him come toward me to kiss my cheek and couldn't help myself. I pulled his lips to mine and lost myself in a real kiss. He was startled, but he certainly responded quickly. We were both breathless. I needed to move inside quickly before I lost control completely.

"Goodnight, Liam." I opened the door and went inside, seeing Meredith, sitting at her desk in her pajamas. I quickly shut the door. And I forgot the box of truffles! *Darn it!*

"I THOUGHT YOU were going out this evening," I exclaimed.

"Yes. I did. Rich called and we went to a movie but the guy is an octopus. I finally left the movie and told him to take me home and not to call me again. I hope Liam was more gentlemanly."

"He was... I kissed him. I didn't mean to, but I did it. I'm sorry." I felt so guilty. I might not have felt so bad if I'd had time to settle down before I saw Meredith. She was quiet and looking at a paper she'd written. "Meredith. Please. You know I'm not going to see him anytime soon again. It was a spur of the moment thing and I sort of lost control."

"It's okay, Hana. It's silly of me to be jealous. It was only yesterday that we agreed to use each other's first name. I just wish he hadn't seen me sitting here in my pajamas. I'll die of embarrassment Monday."

"You know, just from the look on his face, I think he may be more embarrassed than you."

7

To Earn a Living

Liam

I LEFT A HURRIED NOTE on Meredith's office door and ran to catch Father as he got in the car. Dennis, my father's driver, pulled away from Buxton House. I was going to work. Father had sprung this on me Sunday over brunch. I'd worked at the clothing factory some last summer and apparently Father thought it would build character if I put in a month this summer as well. Of course, only half days, but I definitely wasn't used to hard manual labor.

"Liam, we're going to Lincoln Arms this morning, not to the clothing factory. We've been managing the company for three years now and I want you to use your skills when you enter the company. Your grandmother is often bragging about your accomplishments at school. I'd like to see them in action."

"What do you mean, Father?"

"I'm not assigning you a specific job on an assembly line or in an office. Your mother and I have had a feeling that something just isn't right in the company since your grandfather passed away. I can't put my finger on it. Even when I practice the same skills you learned in your time at Elenchus, I'm afraid my position inhibits real interactions. Lincoln Arms came into our possession three years ago at the passing of your grandfather. Neither your mother nor I are fully comfortable with it. I'd like you to not use more than your first name so the Cyning name doesn't influence your conversations," he said.

I was puzzled. This was a much different approach to learning the business than what he'd taken last summer. I was being cut loose to find out... something. And in the arms company, not the clothing factory.

I knew my father had reservations regarding the Lincoln Arms and Munitions factory. He had other businesses as well—two years ago I'd worked in a food processing plant. But the arms factory had come into the family as part of my mother's inheritance. It had taken father off his other pursuits. And still, he and Mother split the operation of the factory. He rose early and was at the office by eight o'clock. No hardship for me. But at one o'clock, Mother arrived at the office and Father went to check up on his other businesses. Usually, both got home around six.

"Have you any idea what is making you uncomfortable?" I asked.

"It could be nothing," he responded. "I just get a feeling people are not being forthright about some things. I don't know if it is in materials, craftsmanship, design, or even shipping. It could be something happening in the office. Your mother has also mentioned it and agreed to have you investigate. You can have free access to all parts of the office and factory."

"Hmm. Perhaps I should have a cover. Why not make it what it really is? I'm William Thomas, a student working on a thesis project on the various aspects of how a business is run. That should allow me anywhere and people will know to answer questions."

"Excellently done, son. We'll take you to the HR office and get you a badge as a student intern."

I HAD CARTE blanche access to every part of the company. I spent my first morning doing a survey of where each department was located and what it was responsible for. A very high overview was all I had time for. The operation was large and involved everything from sales and marketing to design to fabricating to testing to shipping. There were so many steps I could scarcely draft out a general organization structure. It was going to take the first week just to figure out what the chain of command was in the company. HR's simplified org chart was only vaguely helpful, especially since it still had my grandfather's name as the CEO. I wasn't even certain how Mother and Father split their duties.

I had barely jumped in the car before Dennis pulled away from the factory and headed for Buxton House. Erich and I would have had a pleasant conversation in that time, but Dennis was quiet. At Buxton House, I stepped out of the car, gave Mother a kiss on the cheek as I handed her into the car, and watched them drive away. I sincerely hoped Meredith could help me organize some of this data.

I skipped up the stairs and paused at what I was told was her office door. I knocked. In a moment, she opened the door.

"Liam. I'm glad you're back. Your note was not forthcoming," she said. I sensed a slight rebuke and realized I should have been more detailed when I wrote it but I wasn't yet sure what I was going to be doing.

"Yes, ah... Meredith..." It still seemed just a bit casual to refer to her by her first name, but we'd been school mates before employer/employee. I hoped one day we would be friends. "I have a job."

"A what?"

"A job. As in, I need to go to work each morning. It's only for half a day, but it will be Monday through Friday. In fact, I've just returned and before we get busy, I'd really like to shower and change. Can you join me for lunch in thirty minutes?"

"Of course, Liam." She wrinkled her nose. "You *are* carrying an interesting odor with you. Like machine oil." I blushed and excused myself.

IN THE KITCHEN, I pulled sandwich makings out of the refrigerator. Cook was always careful to mark anything I was explicitly not to touch but otherwise left my noon meal to my own devising unless I requested something specific. I seldom did, but a hamburger sandwich was occasionally provided. Meredith poured iced tea and we sat at the table to make our own sandwiches.

"This is pretty casual," I said. "I trust you've made your meal requests known."

"I had a lovely chat with Cook. I'm not a picky eater and we had some common ground to discuss food on. In general, I eat whatever the staff is eating."

"I just don't want you to feel neglected. I'm beginning to see what an important part you will play in my life."

"Like arranging your dates?"

"Meredith, please. I had no idea you were roommates with Hana. I never intended you to feel uncomfortable." I blushed. I didn't want to specifically state the reason she might be uncomfortable. I'd seen her in her nightclothes.

"I had no intention of being home when you brought Hana to the door. I had a rather unsuccessful date, myself," she said. I was gobsmacked.

"You had a date?"

"Don't sound so completely surprised, Liam. I have a life outside my employment."

"Yes, of course. I didn't mean to imply... I'm sorry. First, I find out that my date is your roommate and then that you were also on a date. And I'm sorry you had an unsuccessful date. Truly."

"You are so sweet at times, Liam. How about your date? Did you have a good time?" she asked.

"Yes, yes. I did. Quite a good time. A little surprising. Quite fun. Quite."

"Liam? What?"

"You know, it's not that I want a steady girlfriend, but I would like to know a girl is interested enough in me to see me a second time."

"I know." She reached across the table and laid a hand on mine. Then quickly withdrew it. "Believe it or not, it has not been that long since my first date. I was certain no boy would want to date the redhead with the flaring temper."

"You've not impressed me with a flaring temper since that time eight years ago," I chuckled. She had flattened my nose with that right hook. I deserved it.

"I hope I've learned a bit about self-control since then. That doesn't mean I wouldn't like to punch you sometimes," she laughed. I adored the sound of her laughter. I began to relax.

"Well, perhaps you can give me some dating tips. I still feel like such a rube whenever I speak to a single woman. I stutter all over myself. I was so surprised... Did you know that at the festival, Hana actually suggested that I should ask her out? I would never have... I just said okay."

"We're doing a pretty good job having conversations. And from what I could tell, once the ice was broken, you did fine with Hana. She seems to have enjoyed herself." We ate our sandwiches quietly for a few minutes.

"It wasn't... I didn't... I am so embarrassed."

"Why, Liam. It was me sitting in my pajamas that you saw."

"I'm terribly sorry about that. I didn't mean to. Honestly."

"I know that. Don't think about it again. What has you embarrassed?"

"I never expected my first kiss to be quite like that," I said. My face felt hot and I squeezed my eyes shut. "It took me by surprise." Meredith sat there looking at me with her mouth slightly open, as if she were about to take a bite of her sandwich.

"I had no idea. Liam... There are many kinds of kisses. It surprises me that was your first, but even so, it should be something you remember fondly. Don't be embarrassed about it. My first kiss was certainly something less exciting than Hana Ito!"

"Meredith!" I laughed. Still, she'd broken my momentary embarrassment and we were able to go to the library and discuss my project at Lincoln Arms and brainstorm some ideas on how to approach the process. Working with Meredith and a chalkboard, we were able to map out a series of questions, a path through the company, and a basic outline of how I could approach the whole project. I was amazed at how much clarity Meredith added to my own thinking. I was very glad to have her as an assistant.

"MEREDITH, DO YOU ride?" I asked over dinner. We'd simply gone to the kitchen when Erich told us Cook was ready for us. I hadn't even thought to ask whether we could eat in the kitchen. Cook had a casual meal set out for us.

"Horses? I've had lessons and have proper attire."

"I was wondering if we might take a ride tomorrow afternoon. We could recap my day's investigation as we enjoy the out-of-doors. I feel like I've been neglecting my horse this summer and it's such glorious weather," I said. I barely had time for a three-mile run in the morning now that Father and I were leaving for work at seven-thirty.

"That sounds lovely. I'll run home in the morning to pick up my things. Oh. I don't have my own horse."

"We have several in the stables. I'll call out to Ray after dinner and ask him to prepare a suitable ride. Yes! I definitely need a ride to clear my head after a morning at the shop."

"I'll be delighted, Liam."

"MAY I ASSIST you?" I offered my cupped hands for Meredith's knee and gave her a boost into the saddle. Then I began adjusting her irons. She looked like an accomplished horsewoman in her riding clothes. "Ray says this mare is gentle but lively enough to keep up with Sim. Her name is Skydancer. We just call her Sky."

"Is that the same horse you got on your birthday so long ago?"

"Yes, Persimmon," I said. "I considered changing his name to Nosebleed, but thought better of it."

"Well, he is rather red, isn't he?" We laughed and headed for the woodland trail, my faithful dog Leonard padding along with us. "I love Dancer's white socks. She's so elegant." I noticed Meredith had already changed the mare's name to suit herself. I hoped we'd ride often.

"Sometimes I just need to drift in the wilderness for a while," I sighed. "Not that this is really wilderness. I like to run and get a few miles in each morning early, but running is not really peaceful. Not that I don't think a lot while I'm running, but there is so much to do to keep pace, watch the path, and keep arms and legs moving. When I'm on Sim, I don't even need to guide him if I'm really absorbed. He knows the trails and will carry me while I'm lost in thought."

"I think that's lovely. I hope you are getting time in to ride often enough."

"I admit it has been a little touch and go. You know, having a personal assistant is a great deal of work," I laughed.

"Oh? And how am I so difficult?"

"It's not really anything about you. It's that I'm a teen and I was saddled with an assistant I had no idea what to do with. I felt like I needed to think up things for you to do or spend my time discussing them all the time. Otherwise you would become bored and it would be my fault."

"I'm able to stay busy, even when you are 'at work.' Did you know that Erich brought me all your school papers yesterday for me to sort and organize into files?"

"Oh, God! He didn't! There's no need for you to read my school papers. How utterly boring!"

"I'm not reading all of them. All I need to do is get them cross-referenced and organized in folders so you can find them. Occasionally, though, one will pop out and I need to take time to read it," she said.

"Like?"

"Your essay on Sun Tzu's *The Art of War*, for example, was unusual. What inspired you?"

"Ah. Peoples... He's one of my instructors and my academic counselor. You know none of my classes have names. Our schooling at Elenchus is quite freeform. I can't tell you what he is an instructor of. He makes me think—sometimes one-on-one and sometimes with a group of guys interested in the same thing. Peoples said if I am to be a man of peace, I must know the art of war. Meredith, there is nothing I desire more than to be a man of peace. Do you see?"

"That explains much of your theme in the paper. The question regarding whether wars are to be fought for stability or for victory." We rode on, pointing out a bed of violets in the shade of a tree. "Oh, that reminds, me," she said. "Not the violets, but your mention of Mr. Peoples. I assumed we would discuss that when we were back in the library. He called this morning, saying it was not necessary to return the call unless you have specific questions. However, he would like you to put together a paper and presentation on what you discover at Lincoln Arms. He referred to it as an audit of their corporate health."

"I'll bet my father had something to do with that. When I took on the task, I adopted the identity of William Thomas, a student doing a thesis on the running of a business. I'm sure Father called Peoples and suggested the project would be a good one for me. I think he still hopes I'll turn out a Promoter or a Commander. He's not comfortable with the Leader class, despite his parents. He says they make decisions without having authority to carry them out."

"Yet, he called you in to use your skills to discover what is wrong." I waved Meredith over to a fallen log and dismounted. I helped her down from her saddle and very much appreciated the softness of the woman in my arms. I tried not to linger and took a pack from my horse. We sat on the log to share a few cookies and the canteens of water I'd brought along.

"What do you do when you want to clear your head, Meredith?" I asked.

"Me? I like riding, but since I do not have a horse, that is scarcely a regular option."

"Anytime you wish to ride here, just call Ray and give him the word. He'll happily bring Sky... or Dancer, if you will... out of the barn and saddle her for you. I hope we'll be able to have more rides together. What else do you like to do?"

"Well, I walk. There is a lovely walk along the river not far from Green Hill. When I am considering weighty matters or need to refresh myself after studying, I often walk there. Or... I'm embarrassed to say..."

"Please tell me."

"I like to bake cookies."

"Ah. Please feel free to clear your mind anytime you are at Buxton House." She laughed at me and we walked a while, leading the horses.

"How was work today?" she asked.

"Puzzling. I'm still too new there to draw any conclusions. I've just been wandering around and observing. Haven't really even started asking questions yet," I said. "I feel it, though. What Father feels. An unsettling undercurrent. I think I need to start listing places where something *could* go wrong. Where could someone benefit by sowing discontent? Or how could someone subvert something to harm the business? And why?"

"A threat analysis?" she asked. I nodded enthusiastically.

"That's it, exactly. There are obvious places, like embezzlement. I somehow feel the disquiet more in the manufacturing facility than the office, though. How about when we get back to the house, we park ourselves in the library and work on listing possible threats. It would help me focus. Would that be okay?"

"I am your assistant. It is what we should do."

I was so enthused that I leaned over and kissed her. Not a huge kiss. Just a peck on the cheek. She was startled and turned toward me so quickly that our lips brushed against each other.

"I'm so sorry! I was just excited and you said something so perfect that I wanted to kiss you. I shouldn't have done that!"

"Please do not apologize. It wasn't unpleasant—just surprising. I... Liam, you should not attempt to develop a relationship of that sort with me. There are ramifications." We'd stopped short after my faux pas and looked at each other.

"Of course. You wouldn't be interested in such a thing. I'm not... Well, you probably have a line of suitors."

"No. But my role is as an assistant—a mentor and advisor. As an advisor, it is my responsibility to tell you what you 'should' do—not what you 'can' do. Think about it carefully."

I boosted her to her saddle and we continued our ride, returning to the stables and brushing down the horses in silence. In addition to riding, I had long ago discovered that the simple act of grooming my horse also served to clear my mind. As I considered her words, I found it difficult to lose myself in the simple act of currying my horse.

CHARTING OUT THE potential threats to the business, Meredith and I resumed a pleasant and uncomplicated working relationship. I found her comments and questions helped me clarify my own observations and we continued through the week. I gleaned information during my mornings at the plant and, together in the afternoon, we listed my findings on the chalkboard, which Meredith transcribed the following morning. I could see this was not going to be a job to go to for a week and be able to resolve the uneasy feelings my parents had.

On Friday, we met briefly and Meredith took the remainder of the weekend to attend to her personal business. She said she had some studies of her own to complete and that she needed to register for fall classes at the University. She was putting in many more hours than I thought I would ever need from a personal assistant. When we met in the afternoons, we often talked through dinner. And she was working in the mornings organizing our notes and typing them up.

The ironic part was that I wanted to spend more time with her. I had considered asking her to a movie Saturday afternoon, but I hadn't yet reconciled the meaning of her statement in the woodland. I 'shouldn't' attempt to develop a more personal relationship with her. But underlying her refusal to say otherwise, was an indication that I 'could.' I had no time to worry the subject. Mother and Father had asked for my attendance at their dinner table Friday night.

"**WHAT HAVE YOU** discovered in your first week prowling around the factory?" Mother asked. I had very little overlap with her during the day as I left the factory in time for her to return with Dennis. I chatted briefly with Father on the way to work in the mornings.

"I have discovered that you two seem to be respected, but mostly because of Grandfather. No one knows quite what to make of you, just that you 'aren't the old man,' as I've heard your father kindly spoken of. It's way too early for me to have uncovered any discontent or nefarious behavior. But I feel the same things you seem to," I said. I'd prepared my notes to bring with me to dinner. We would not do more than touch the surface of the subject while eating, but I assumed my parents would want an outline of my strategy after the meal.

"My father was a Defender," Mother said. "He never looked at the company as an end in itself. He owned a company to enable him to focus on providing a secure future."

"Was he a military man?" I asked. I couldn't remember there being any mention of service while the old man was alive. He'd died before my fifteenth birthday and my parents had already started taking over the operations of the company by then.

"No. Nor should you consider the class of Defender to necessarily be military or police. Defenders are very much about order and security. In my father, those characteristics showed up in maintaining a clear production path and orderly sales path, and in creating security for his family and employees with a successful business. He would probably have been as comfortable with any kind of sustainable business. Manufacturing arms and munitions was opportune, but secondary to having a clear set of objectives that could be reached with a specific plan. Some of those plans, we are still executing today," Mother said.

Cook had prepared three courses for the evening meal, including a cold soup, veal saltimbocca with *piselli alla romana*, and a fruit and cheese tray. As always, the meal was exquisitely prepared and paired with a nice pinot noir. Since my eighteenth birthday, I'd been allowed a glass of wine when I took meals with my parents or Grandmother. We moved to my father's study for the cheese and coffee.

"Let me see your notes, please," Father said. "I talked to Peoples at Elenchus and he expects you to have a solid survey of the business written and prepared when you return to school. I thought you might take the task more seriously if it was to fulfill a class requirement." He started looking through the notes and nodding his head.

"I do take the task seriously Father. I would not give you less than my best."

"Yes, I know, but this gets you credit for it as well as your modest wage. This is good. Has Meredith been typing up your notes?" he asked.

"When I return in the afternoon, Meredith and I go over what I've found, what my questions are, and how I should structure my next day's investigation. While I'm at the factory, she organizes and types the notes," I said.

"I had my doubts about choosing Meredith for the role of personal assistant. I was afraid you would get... distracted," Mother said. "In my opinion, it was too early to start you with a personal assistant. I'm glad to see she is functioning in such a useful way."

"In fact, I think we need to consider you full time rather than part time. You are putting in much more work than I anticipated and I had high expectations," Father said looking up from my notes. "It looks to me like she is putting in a lot of time on this as well."

"Thank you, Father."

"Try not to let this take up all your time this summer, though," Mother said. She poured herself and Father another glass of wine, their coffee untouched. "We did not intend to make it so you don't have any fun on your vacation days."

"Thank you, Mother. Meredith and I did Tuesday's work on horseback so we could get out in the fresh air for a while. I'll make sure to take some time off," I laughed.

"Speaking of which, are you seeing that young woman again... Hana Ito? I looked into her a bit and she seems very nice, if a bit old for you."

"Mother! You had my date investigated? I'll never be able to face her again. Which is likely anyway. Hana is an Aspirant. She is devoted to becoming, not just a doctor, but a healer. She doesn't really have time for a regular relationship. I'm afraid I'm seeing no one this weekend."

"Take Meredith out," Father said.

"Um… Meredith suggested that I should not try to form a close personal relationship with her."

"I'm your father. I told you what you *can* do, not what you *should* do."

"I see."

"Why don't you have a party so you can meet more people. A little summer barbecue," Mother suggested.

"Grandmother suggested that, but who would I invite? My schoolmates are all male."

"Put Meredith to work on it. Have a little mixer. Meet some new people. She went to a girls' school. Certainly, she must know some girls."

"I suppose. I'll talk to her."

I also decided I'd talk to Grandmother. Somehow, I trusted her guidance more than my parents'.

8

Building a Good Relationship

Meredith

"SO? WHAT'S HE LIKE? You've been over there for three weeks now. Is it dreamy or is he still a brat?" Karen asked. She and Peggy Anne had seen me come in Friday afternoon. They were sitting in my room as I folded and packed my life into boxes. I was really leaving Green Hill Women's College. I had thought I would stay through my baccalaureate, but I needed to get established at the University before my charge arrived in January. But that meant moving out of the room I'd lived in the past five of my eight years at Green Hill. Peggy Anne and Karen roomed across the hall.

"He's different than he was. I mean, I should hope so. He's eight years older, just like we are. I don't know. Those extra two years between his age and mine are a huge gap in experience." I folded another blouse and sat on the edge of the bed. "There are times when he's still just a little kid—in a good way. He has a sense of wonder about him that shows in everything new he sees or touches."

"Is he a good kisser?" Peggy Anne asked. She had a devilish look in her eyes.

"Peggy Anne! What a horrid thing to ask. How am I supposed to know if he's a good kisser? I'm his personal assistant, not his girlfriend." Everything had been quite proper since our horseback ride.

"You can't tell me you haven't thought about it. Personal assistant? What eighteen-year-old boy needs a personal assistant?" Karen mocked.

"You'd be surprised. He's not just lying by the pool all day. He actually goes to work in his parents' company each day. His father gave him a special investigation to conduct and when he returns at noon, we discuss his findings, brainstorm ideas, consolidate his notes... I even type them and collate them in the mornings while he's at the factory. And then there are his social engagements."

"What kind of social calendar does he have?" Peggy Anne asked.

"Well, it hasn't been much so far. He volunteered at the hospital festival and was a big hit. Especially with my roommate," I laughed. It *had* been one of his more lovable days.

"Hana met him?"

"Oh, met him, wooed him, and got him to take her out on an elaborate date for the orchestra and dessert. If you want to know what he kisses like, ask Hana."

"She didn't!"

"Didn't what?" Hana asked as she entered the room. I suppose we'd been a bit loud, but it was almost time for her to go to her shift at the hospital.

"You made out with Liam Cyning?" Peggy Anne asked. We generally considered her the shyest of the three of us girls, but she certainly had a fixation on kissing Liam.

"Maybe not making out. I had just enough presence of mind to break the kiss and dash inside. If I hadn't assumed Meredith was sitting in the room, I might have dragged him in with me," Hana said, shocking us all. "I'm afraid, though, that he's just too young to be serious about. I'm twenty-two and he's only eighteen. He's quite intelligent but I'm sure we'd run out of things to talk about quickly."

"And if you can't talk, you may as well kiss."

"You, girl, have a fixation. I need to leave for work. This is a twelve-on, twelve-off weekend. No kisses for me."

IT TOOK ME until nearly ten to finish packing and load my car. It would take a second trip as well but looking around my room, I decided I couldn't really spend the night with all my bedding packed.

I drove 'home.' To my parents' house. I suppose I could have simply moved my room to Buxton House, but that was a move I was not yet ready to make. Although, I discovered I was taking more with me on each trip. Still, I'd need a dormitory room at the University. Once classes started, I was sure Liam and I would both be spending more time in town than at Buxton House. He would still have another term at Elenchus.

I could hear the tones of my mother's piano as I walked in the door and my nose was welcomed with the sweet smell of fresh cookies.

"Hello, Mama, Papa!" I called. I set a box down and turned to get another from the car.

"You've boxes? Are you moving home, sweetie?" Mama said.

"I'm kind of in transition. What I'm definitely doing is moving out of Green Hill," I said.

"Let me help carry. You must have accumulated a great deal in your years at the college," Papa said. I loaded his arms and Mama's before scooping up the next box and locking the car.

"The rest can wait until morning. I've just torn apart my room at the college and needed a place to crash. It feels funny to think of going out to Buxton House on the weekend."

"I'm glad you've come home," Mama said. "We've hardly had a chance to talk since you started there."

"Wait. I have fresh snickerdoodles and cold milk," Papa said, rushing back to the kitchen.

"Oh, that makes coming home worth it," I laughed. I hugged Mama and she led me to the sofa.

"Now tell us about your job. You've been spending some nights at Buxton House," Mama said as Papa brought the cookies and milk. "Are they always demanding, like so many wealthy are?"

"Oh, no, Mama. Everyone, including Liam, has been very polite and proper. I have a lovely suite of rooms of my own with an attached office where Liam and I can meet when we need to. We spend most of our professional time in their library, though." I didn't mention going horseback riding or walking through the woods.

"We worry, you know," Papa said. "The Cynings have always been people of fine character—at least Regina Cyning. But sometimes people with money think that exempts them from proper behavior. You should never feel that you are required to do something unprofessional."

"I know, Papa. In fact, Dr. Parolini and I had a talk about that. But they have also done so much for me that I **am** grateful."

"You needn't be too grateful. Before we accepted your scholarship to Green Hill, it was explained carefully that they were giving six scholarships and that no one should feel obligated in any way by them. We always knew they would choose one of the six as an assistant to Liam if at all possible. But even then, you had the option to turn the opportunity down," Mama said.

"I wanted this opportunity, Mama. I've wanted it since I've known about the chance. And even now that I am officially part of their staff, the Cynings are continuing to pay for all six of our tuition and board. Even though I'm moving to the University this fall." I let that little bomb drop and waited for my parents' response. It wasn't long in coming.

"The University? Why aren't you continuing at Green Hill for your baccalaureate?"

"I will be enrolled at the University so I can be prepared to help Liam when he enrolls mid-term. It will be good for us to be at the same school so I can help with his enrollment, lodging, and incidentals."

"I worry most about his incidentals. Are you being paid well?" Papa asked.

"I don't know," I said. "I never asked. It would not take much to consider myself paid well since my meals and lodging, tuition and books, car, and even clothing allowance are covered in my usual scholarship. I suppose I shall need to inquire about that. I'll do it when it's convenient."

"Tell us about your day when you are working."

"I arrive at Buxton House mid-morning on Monday and check notes and messages. Sometimes there is something from the weekend that needs tending to, but I have a number of menial tasks like filing that have been neglected for a long time. Liam gets home from work shortly after noon and we have lunch together."

"Work? What kind of work does Liam do?" Papa asked. He seemed impressed that Liam had a job.

"His parents have asked him to investigate their arms company and get a general feel for the process and the employees. Something is bothering them about the company."

"Probably guilt," Mama scoffed. "Why would anyone choose to be in arms and munitions as a business?"

"Let's not be judgmental, dear," Papa said. "We don't have a mission to judge others."

"You may be right, though, Mama. They inherited the business, you know. Most of the family industry is in clothing. But Liam is developing a threat matrix and I've been able to do a great deal as an assistant. We spend most afternoons discussing what he has discovered in the morning, jotting down notes, and brainstorming next steps. We do have some leisure time. Earlier this week we went for a lovely ride around the estate. I didn't realize it was so large!"

"So, you are helping him with a job he is employed at. It seems like Thomas and Lydia are getting two people for the price of one."

"I suppose so, but it has been rather fun and exciting to work on the project. We often have dinner together, served casually in the kitchen. The staff is very nice. It's almost like being next to your kitchen." I knew one of my parents' concerns about the job was that I would be shunned by the rest of the household staff. We'd heard stories of how difficult it sometimes was to be a newcomer in an established staff.

"Speaking of which, you must bring him by for dinner."

"Really, Papa? You wouldn't mind?"

"Of course not. If you keep eating what that fancy French chef of his cooks, you'll both weigh 300 pounds before you are out of college." Papa knew the Cynings' cook and felt a touch of rivalry with him. It would be good to show Liam what Papa could cook.

"Yes. We should get an opportunity to meet your boyfriend away from his palace."

"Boyfriend?! Mama! Liam is not my boyfriend. No no no. Not my boyfriend. We have a professional relationship. We aren't dating. In fact, he took my roommate out on a date last week. I know I've talked a lot about Liam over the past years, but it isn't as if I'm in love with him. He is too young for me for one thing. Whatever would we have in common? I'm to be an advisor on how to behave in social situations. I even arranged the orchestra tickets for his date last week. And I had a date as well. With Rich. No, Liam is not my boyfriend!"

"Have you run out of protestations now?" Mama asked after a pause. I blushed. My heart was racing and I'd responded like the twelve-year-old I'd been at Liam's party eight years ago. I'd popped him in the nose and then Mama and Papa had taken me home. The other schoolmates left as well, except Lonnie. Mama had teased me about liking Liam and not knowing how to act with a boy. That was a little girl crush, and I had denied liking him in the least. But over the past eight years, his name was a common element of our conversation.

"Yes, Mama," I whispered.

"It is okay to like him and enjoy his company. Probably much easier to do your job if you do. I just don't like the idea of you being subservient." Mama hugged me.

"When have you ever known me to be subservient?" I snorted. "I was raised with four older brothers. I've learned to hold my own. In fact, I believe that was a key element in my being selected for this role. I don't know about the boys, but

Peggy Anne and Karen would be too easily manipulated. I daresay the boys would have dominated him."

"And you can withstand his charm?"

"He is charming... most of the time. So far, I've been able to subtly guide him. He is a bit... naïve."

"And you are still seeing Rich Biggers? I thought you put an end to that relationship," Mama said.

"No. I'm not seeing Rich. I thought we could go out casually and see a movie. I was wrong. I ended my date early and asked him not to call me again."

"Well, you know your heart and mind, dear. You know you can always talk to us if you need."

"OH GOOD, MEREDITH. I was just thinking of you," Mrs. Cyning said. I'd just arrived Monday morning and picked up a cup of coffee from the kitchen to take to my office when Liam's grandmother stopped me. "I was going to get a cuppa myself. Won't you join me in the lounge?"

"Certainly, Mrs. Cyning. May I get your coffee for you?"

"You aren't a servant, Meredith. I don't even ask Ricardo to run silly errands for me. Just keep me company for a few minutes if you would."

"While I'm pouring my own, how would you like yours?" I asked. She laughed and I handed her a cup of coffee.

"How are you getting on with Liam?"

"I think we're learning how to work together and beginning to understand the scope of things we can work on. The project at the arms factory has been enlightening for both of us," I said. We sat in the lounge to sip our coffee.

"One of the things I've been concerned with is Liam's social life," Regina said. "I don't actually want to meddle, but it is easy to see that the time he's spent at Elenchus has left him comfortable around men and backward around women."

"We have had some awkward moments but I understand from both Liam and Hana that their date a couple of weeks ago was enjoyed by both."

"That's good. I'm not implying he's incapable of enjoying company, but only that there are few opportunities for him to socialize with other young people. I thought perhaps you might suggest he have a casual party this weekend. Perhaps a barbecue on the patio and some friends to swim. You could work together on who to invite, but try to make sure there is a good mix of male and female," she said.

I swallowed. I knew planning events would be a part of my responsibilities but was not anticipating needing to suggest events. Nonetheless, if I could talk Liam into it this afternoon, it would be a pleasant diversion this weekend.

"I'll suggest it to Liam this afternoon," I said. "I should find out what notes he's left for me to work on this morning. He's very intent on the project."

"Lincoln Arms and Munitions has weighed heavily on Thomas's mind for some time. I wish he would put it on the market and divest, but it was Lydia's inheritance. It is simply very different than their various clothing and textile interests. I'm not sure either of them has the stomach for it." The old woman paused and shook her head. "I should let you get to your work and I should get to mine. Don't hesitate to ask for advice, dear. We all want a successful relationship."

"Thank you, ma'am. I appreciate your guidance." I took her cup with my own to the kitchen and rinsed them before heading to my third-floor office.

"YOU DID A lot of work this weekend," I said when I joined Liam for lunch. It was now a commonplace ritual to busy ourselves in the kitchen when he returned from the factory. Cook always had a cold lunch prepared for us. We only needed to assemble the component parts. Today, we were enjoying a tuna salad niçoise.

"I didn't really have much else to do and made notes on a book on gun-making. I've seen the process in action, but there are so many steps where something could go wrong, I'm still not following them all. I wiggled around in the storeroom this morning, though, and discovered a stock of some 5,000 rifles that are not even listed in our catalogue and I can't find in inventory. It might be nothing, but I can't fathom why we would have a stock of so many rifles with no orders and no catalog. It could be nothing more than an oversight, but I think I'll need to bring it to Father's attention."

"We can work on the questions to investigate after lunch." We chatted for a bit as we ate and I worked around to the subject of a party. "It has been such glorious weather lately, it seems a shame to waste it."

"Wanting to go for another ride? I'd be interested in that."

"Oh, yes. That would be lovely. I was thinking though, that perhaps you'd like to invite a few people for a cookout and swim this weekend. I'm sure I could get Cook to prepare things for a party that aren't too elaborate. Somewhat like we did in the park for the festival." I thought reminding him of his prowess on the grill at the hospital festival might go a long way toward encouraging him.

"Hmm. It would be good to see some of the guys over the summer before school starts. Don't know who's available, though."

"If you give me a list of people you'd especially like to invite, I'll supplement it with a few women. It's much more fun to have a swimming party if there are both men and women."

"I'm sure I would only embarrass myself," he sighed. "It's difficult to talk to a woman as it is, let alone a woman wearing a swimming costume." He blushed.

"But it would encourage the men to come if they thought either their dates would be welcome or there would be other women around. You know Lonnie would be far more interested in a gathering if Susan were also invited."

"I suppose you're right. I just don't know any women to invite."

"Trust me?"

"What? Of course I trust you."

"Then I will balance out the numbers of men and women. Just give me a list of people you don't want me to miss."

"Do you suppose Hana would come?"

I swallowed my catty retort and smiled. "I will be sure to invite her unless you would prefer to invite her yourself as a date."

"Oh. Um... That seems a bit... no, just as a party invitation. If I'm to be a host, I should be equally attentive to all who are there. It would be much too embarrassing to spend my time... to see... Ah! Meredith, could you please make the arrangements? I'm sure it will be great fun, but I'm simply tongue-tied when it comes to calling people."

"I believe this could be considered within the realm of an assistant's duties," I laughed. "I will, however, want your input on some details. It is *your* party."

"Yes, yes. Of course. I don't think I can concentrate on work at the moment. Why don't we take the horses out?"

"That would be fun."

"I'll call out to Ray and let him know we'll be out in half an hour."

THE RIDE WAS lovely and Liam definitely relaxed the moment he was in the saddle. He'd said riding was what he did to purge his mind. It also seemed to loosen his tongue a bit and I used the opportunity to find out more about his lack of confidence around women.

"I've had a superior education," he said as we rode along. "It seems to have been complete in all areas except relationships. On the list I'll give you, there will only be three boys. I don't hang out with many of the fellows. Lonnie, of course, is my roommate. Wonder what he'll do when I move to the University. Remy Fournier and I became fast friends when he immigrated here three years ago. Fantastic violinist. Roald Adams. Sharp mind. We often debate each other. I always learn something from him. The only others I spend significant time with are on a team or such and inviting one would mean inviting a whole team, which would make for a raucous and boring party, I'm afraid. Or professors. Seems most of my meals are taken up in conversation with one or more professors."

"While they are no doubt valuable conversationalists, for most persons our age, they would tend to put a damper on things. When was the last time you saw Donnie and Richard?"

"Who? Oh! Defoe and Lingam. We ran into each other a couple of years ago when they were in town for a break. Decided to put in a few rounds at the shooting range. Military school put them way ahead of me in marksmanship. If they are in town, that would be excellent. Aren't they at the academy now?"

"Well, they may have some time off. I'll check to see." We rode in silence for a while, pausing to watch a squirrel chattering at us from a tree limb. Liam's dog Leonard was alert as if the squirrel posed a clear and present danger to us.

"MEREDITH." WE'D STOPPED next to one of the small ponds on the north side of the estate to let the horses have a drink and I could tell Liam was in a contempla-tive state. "Why is it that I'm so nervous around other women but I feel completely comfortable talking to you? I mean, it's not like I'm ready to reveal my darkest secrets, but I don't have a difficulty being with you. I'm not even afraid you'll sock me anymore." He laughed but it was a little nervous—like he might still be a little afraid I'd slug him.

"I don't know, Liam. But I'm glad you feel comfortable with me. I confess, I was a bit nervous being thrown together with you for so much of the day when we started. I'm feeling more comfortable now as well. So far, we've managed to build a good working relationship and—I hope—at least the beginnings of a friendship. I guess you can just assume you will be more comfortable with other women as you get to know them better." The idea of Liam becoming more comfortable with other women was unsettling to me but I determined not to let that become an obstacle between us. Part of my job was to get him better socialized. I would do nothing to sabotage any relationship he developed. I promised myself that.

"I suppose you're right. But there is something else as well. I feel like we have a common bond that is more than our working relationship. I would like at times—frequently—for us to be able to ignore the idea that I'm an employer. I suppose that's asking a lot but something about being out here riding horses—even when we aren't talking or working—feels right. I feel like I can depend on you."

"I hope that is always the case, Liam. I will always try to be dependable." I wasn't going to rush into anything with Liam but, if the situation allowed for it, I was open to being his friend. Or more. I shook that feeling off. Regina Cyning certainly didn't hire me to seduce her grandson and I would not tread that path.

"Shall we go out for dinner this evening? I'm sure Cook will be okay with us missing whatever he has planned for dinner. The family is always rather casual about when and where they take meals. I'll give him some warning as soon as we get back to the house. Besides, I still need my driving lesson today." He laughed and looked at me as though he had just solved a major riddle. Hmm. This might just be a good opportunity.

"I've an idea of where we could go for dinner. Before then, I'll work on our guest list for Saturday. Unless you have other work you'd like to do."

"No. I'm a bit tired just now. I think I'll take a nap before dinner. I never thought how tiring getting up to go to a job could be. I need to get used to this!"

"MEREDITH! WELCOME, DEAR. I didn't know you were coming in this evening. I can have your usual table ready in just a moment." The hostess in the restaurant kissed me on both cheeks before hurrying away. In just a minute we were led to a table near the back of the restaurant and on one side.

"You're known well here?" Liam asked.

"It's a favorite retreat when I'm at school. I come here frequently." We were seated at our family table and Jasmine raised an eyebrow. I just shook my head and she left us. It would be a surprise for Liam.

"Since you are so well known here, what would you recommend? The menu looks very good."

"Oh, it is, I assure you. Everything on the menu is delicious, but in the interest of helping you on your first time here, I would recommend the chicken pot pie."

"A pot pie? In a restaurant?"

"Trust me. It is my father's signature dish." Liam placed his order and then seemed to realize what I'd said.

"Your father? Does he create recipes?"

"Yes. And cooks them. He wanted to serve you a meal sometime but this will be our little surprise to him and he won't have time to fret about it. He's the chef here at Rangers."

"Will you ever run out of surprises for me?"

"I hope we will be able to surprise each other often, Liam."

We chatted over soft drinks until Papa himself rushed out of the kitchen with our dinners.

"You didn't tell me you were coming this evening! It's not nice to give your old papa apoplexy," he teased. "Mr. Cyning, need I apologize for my daughter suggesting such a humble meal? If there is something else on the menu you would prefer, just say the word."

"Not at all, Mr. Sauvage. Meredith tells me this is your signature dish and I am looking forward to it."

"Well, enjoy your meal. If there is anything you need, let us know." He paused long enough to kiss me on the head and then rushed back to the kitchen.

LIAM SEEMED TO enjoy the meal immensely.

"This has been lovely, Meredith. That pot pie was incredible. So many distinct flavors to have all been in a single dish. What is proper for me to tip and how do I settle the bill?"

"Shh. My father would never let a friend of his daughter pay for a meal here. I don't abuse the privilege, but I eat here often and anytime a friend is with me he or she eats as part of the family. Papa has always asked me to come here whenever I can. Leave a nice tip for our server and let's depart." When Liam hesitated with his wallet open, I selected a bill and he left it discreetly on the table. Papa hurried out of the kitchen as we stood to leave.

"Come again any time!" he said. "This table is always open for you."

We returned to Buxton House and I said goodnight, rather proud of having been able to surprise Liam.

9

Follow the Leader

Donnie Defoe

MEREDITH SAUVAGE. My, my. I've lusted after that redhead for eight years. Ever since that fateful birthday party when she'd bloodied Liam Cyning's nose. I didn't bear any ill-will toward Liam. He went off crying with Lonnie. I would have stood toe to toe with Meredith and given it right back. She was fiery and defiant. Wonderful. Then we were all sent home. Richard and I were sent to military school in Virginia. Lonnie went to Elenchus with Liam. The three girls went to Green Hill Women's College. My first erotic dream had been of stancing toe to toe with Meredith exchanging blows.

It was fine to have sent Richard along to the academy even though he wasn't very military. At least we'd had a friend in each other. He just wasn't cut out for the military. Except when you put a gun in his hands. He wasn't the sharpest shooter in our class, but he knew more about weapons than anyone else in the school. He could disassemble and assemble any weapon given to him with his eyes closed. He could identify any firearm by weight and feel. He could tell how far and how accurately it would shoot. He could examine a jammed firearm and release the jam safely. If there was a faulty part in a firearm, Richard could fix it. Lately, he'd been working in the machine shop learning to mill his own parts so he could build a rifle. I was surprised he'd chosen to go on to military academy and even more so that he was accepted. I bet the Army would be using him in a development lab someplace, surely not as a commanding officer. Richard was a real Cognoscente. A pure craftsman.

"Donnie, it's Meredith Sauvage calling."

"Well, hello. What can I do for your prettiness today?"

"Oh, please, Donnie. Has that line ever gotten you anywhere?"

"I would never tell," I laughed. *Yeah. However I felt about Meredith, it wasn't returned.*

"I'm calling to invite you to an informal party. Are you still on break?" she asked.

"We have all of August off. How much of my time would you like?"

"Just an afternoon. Liam's arranging to have a few friends over for a cookout and swim. We thought that if you were in town, it would be nice to get all of us together."

"Oh, yeah. You're his assistant now, aren't you?" We all knew, of course. In May, Mrs. Cyning had called in each of the six of us for an interview. We'd all trained to be number two to Liam Cyning, but all in different ways. It would have been a good job, but I wasn't disappointed to have been passed over. I had good prospects for an Army career and being an assistant to a guy who might never have a job no longer appealed to me. I was a Defender and the lack of order in Liam's life left me cool toward the job. I supposed someday he might need a bodyguard. "So, he's got you handing out his invitations?"

"It comes with the territory. Besides, I'm inviting Peggy Anne and Karen, too. And Lonnie, of course."

"Of course. It would be nice to see everyone again. Can you promise to bloody Liam's nose again?"

"Will you listen to you? You'd think you didn't like Liam."

"I do like him. Always did. This Saturday? I think I can make it."

I did like Liam. That was the hell of it. I could laugh about his awkwardness or lack of skill at something, but I was still ready to follow him if he had an idea. At the moment, the idea of a party was one I was ready to follow.

HONESTLY, THE IDEA of seeing Meredith, Karen, and Peggy Anne in swimming costumes for the afternoon was quite appealing. I hoped Meredith was inviting some other women as well. With Liam's money, he should have far more women than he could handle.

I had a feeling one of the reasons we'd been shipped off to Virginia for military school was to keep us away from the girls. At the time of Liam's last party, we'd already been exploring with each other a little. Well, not with Meredith, but Karen and I had kissed. In Virginia at an all-boys military school, we didn't meet any girls for the first three years. And then I had mixed results. None of them particularly satisfying.

Before I left on my summer break, my girlfriend promised that this fall she'd go all the way with me. Of course, last year it had been 'at Christmas' and then 'in the spring.' It wouldn't surprise me too much if she'd latched onto an upper classman during the summer and failed to tell me. I was getting tired of carting my virginity around with me.

Unlike Richard. For a guy whose mind is so chaotic, he sure scored with the girls. He'd met a girl from a women's college near the school in Virginia and spent almost as much time in her apartment as he did in our barracks. Then they kissed goodbye and two weeks after we arrived at the Academy, he was dating a local girl who was happiest when she was under him. I was probably the only one who knew he was still sweet on Peggy Anne. If he met up with her at Liam's party, he might not even return to school.

Karen Reese

"HAVING A WILL is important for everyone, not only those who own a lot of property. Without a will, anything the deceased owned will be managed by the State and after taxes and fees will revert to the next of kin. If no next of kin can be found, it will revert to the State. But avoiding probate is an inadequate reason to have a will. Think of your family. In times of great stress, like the death of a loved one, family members tend to focus on small things they think they can control. Mother's diamond brooch may become a matter of great contention. An insignificant pile of letters might become more important to everyone in the family than a bank account with fifty thousand dollars in it. Your will should deal with the small things."

I sat in the class, taking copious notes. Estate Planning was not only the name of the course, but one of the things I hoped to do as a career. My academic advisor suggested that I focus on family law, but conflict gives me the snakes. Maybe that's why I wasn't chosen as Liam Cyning's assistant. As soon as I received news that I could attend Green Hill Women's College with all expenses and maintenance paid, my parents' marriage fell apart. The squabbles became fights. The fights became insurmountable obstacles to their marriage. Divorce—long, drawn-out, nasty divorce—ensued. I didn't want to ever deal with divorce or child custody cases in my career. They were just too hurtful.

I'd carefully chosen law as my focus, thinking Liam, whom I would be sent to mentor and assist, would need to navigate the waters of legal agreements and situations. I planned to be well-prepared to help him. He could do the negotiating and I would put the formal words on paper to make it airtight.

I didn't understand why Mrs. Cyning didn't agree with me. It hit me hard that I wasn't going to be the successful candidate. It was explained to the three of us on our first day of school at Green Hill that we should follow our hearts as far as what we studied, but that we would also be given special courses in how to support, assist, and even mentor another person. We all knew the person we'd be helping would be Liam Cyning. Even back then, we knew Liam was a Leader. Or would become one. Yes, he was a bit of a brat at times, like when he tried to lead the boys off to the stables and give the girls the slip, but we were two years older. We knew boys just didn't get it as early as girls did. We hadn't known at the birthday party that we were being tested.

Of course, Meredith plunged in and decided to teach him a lesson right then and there. I couldn't believe she socked him. And then we were all asked to leave but told that we'd all been such good friends to Liam that Mrs. Cyning was funding a grant for our education. Meredith, Peggy Anne, and I would go to Green Hill Women's College. The term 'college' being applied to grades down to intermediate school. Richard and Donnie were sent to a military academy in Virginia with the same instructions. And Lonnie went with Liam to Elenchus Scholé. Peggy Anne said it was because Lonnie came to Liam's aid and helped him into the house to get patched up. I laughed at the thought of having one of the girls help him into the house. Would we have become his roommate? Of course not. Lonnie was nearest to Liam's age. It was natural that they'd go to the same school.

But somehow, it never occurred to me that it wouldn't be me chosen to be his assistant. I was happy for Meredith. We three had been inseparable since we'd started school and were the three girls closest to Liam and the three boys. I'd kissed Donnie behind our school just before it let out for the summer. It was just an experiment, but I liked it. Maybe I'd find out how life was going for him at West Point and see if we could renew our friendship after having been separated for eight years. Ah, well. It was a consolation prize.

I'd decided to pursue estate law. Maybe someone else would need a personal assistant with a good background in law. Lonnie? I figured he'd be going into politics. Following his father's footsteps. A Commander could always use a Cognoscente to advise him. But planning an estate was a matter between the lawyer and one client. The assets belonged to that one person and that one person could determine how they should be divided and among whom.

I'd finished most of my pre-law requirements at Green Hill. Dr. Parolini suggested I move to the University Law School at midterm. I was tempted to register right away, but I knew there were still a few courses I needed here, no matter how accelerated our education had been. Dr. Parolini said my expenses would continue to be paid and law school would be tuition free. As soon as I had that in writing, I'd plan my move.

"OH, GUESS WHAT," Peggy Anne said when I got to our apartment. "We've been invited to a party this weekend at Buxton House."

"Really? When?"

"Meredith called to invite us. Saturday afternoon at two. Pool party and cook-out," Peggy Anne said.

"I knew Meredith was living there, but I didn't know she could throw a party." I was a little shocked at that. According to Meredith, when we'd talked last, she'd only been living there part-time and working on some sort of project with Liam. Having a party made it sound like she was more a member of the family.

"Oh, it's Liam's party. Meredith is making all the arrangements and inviting the guests."

"Boys and girls?"

"Even Donnie, Richard, and Lonnie. Plus others, I gathered. Apparently, Liam doesn't get out to meet many people he's not in school with."

"Hmm. You know what that means? We need to go shopping! A pool party? With boys? We need new swimwear!"

"Oh, my God! They'll be looking at our... legs!"

"Honey, they'll be looking at more than your legs. You'd better get a suit with extra support." Peggy Anne was busty. In fact, I was a little jealous. I didn't need a suit with extra support. Or any support. But a party with boys meant looking our best with what we had. We really didn't get that many opportunities to socialize with guys. Peggy Anne blushed, but agreed to meet me after my class the next day to go shopping.

Peggy Anne Ransburg

I WASN'T SURPRISED not to be chosen as Liam's personal assistant. When Dr. Parolini had told us to follow our hearts in what we studied, there was no question but that it would be music for me. I loved playing the piano and it was possible that I might even be able to play concerts eventually. There were times when the required courses seemed like an interruption to what I really wanted to do.

But I owed it to the Cynings to give it my best. They were paying for my music education.

Nonetheless, we were going to a party at Buxton House Saturday. And yes, I was going to get a new swimsuit. Afterall, there would be other boys there besides Liam. Like Richard.

THERE WERE ABOUT a dozen at the party, pretty evenly divided between boys and girls. I sound like a baby. Between men and women. But that meant when I took my wrap off to swim, everyone could see me. I quickly tucked my hair under my cap and dove into the pool. I was first in the water, so I could turn and see the others as they prepared to dive in. All the girls had gone for very sexy swimsuits, forgoing the ones with little skirts. Meredith's was backless, which I thought was very daring. But the two young girls—I was introduced to one as Lonnie's girlfriend and the other as a friend of hers—were in scandalous two-piece outfits that left their stomachs bare. I had to shrug it off. They were the youngest at the party, everyone else being over eighteen.

"Hey, it's good to see you," the man's voice said next to my shoulder. I turned in the water and was face-to-face with Richard Lingam. I'd noticed his swimwear, too. All the men had racing suits on with their tank tops. He looked good.

"Nice to see you, too, Ricky. How do you like West Point?" I asked.

"It will be better this year, now that I'm no longer a plebe. You know, you're the only person I let call me Ricky, Peg. Please don't do it around the younger girls." Richard blushed a little.

"Sorry. I didn't think of that. Talking to you once a month, I guess I've slipped into bad habits."

"It's okay from you. I just don't want it to get back to the cadets. And Donnie would *not* understand." We treaded water silently for a bit. "What are you going to do now that the selection has been made? Did the conservatory respond?"

"I'm still waiting to hear. It's bad timing to get in anyplace by fall term. They have invited me for an audition, though." I was friends with Meredith and Karen—roommates with Karen—but Richard and I started writing to each other when we were just sent to school. Later, when we had that privilege, we began talking by phone but could only really afford once a month. We shared a lot of our life goals with each other and how we felt about what we were doing. I knew Richard hadn't been certain he should go to West Point, but the opportunity was too good to pass up. Just as the opportunity for Karen to go to law school, Meredith to go to the University, Lonnie to go wherever he wanted.

In a way, the five of us who had not been selected were all treading water. We'd all been waiting for this day, not knowing what we would do after it. Richard was my friend and I knew we'd see each other through the next few years as we had the past.

Richard Lingam

GETTING A CALL from Meredith Sauvage shocked the hell out of me. I knew, of course, she'd been chosen to become Liam Cyning's personal assistant. I wasn't too disappointed. I supposed I had something I could contribute if I'd been offered the position, but I wasn't pining away about it. Liam was a good guy, but it wasn't like I really counted on being his assistant.

I was a Cognoscente—a craftsman in my own terms. And the thing military school had awakened in me was my affinity for firearms. That's what finally convinced me to accept the appointment to West Point. They'd laid out a plan for me to work in the design and fabrication of weaponry. I couldn't imagine what good that skill would have done Liam. And I certainly wasn't going to make his bed for him. I only made mine under threat of inspection.

But it would be nice to see the old gang back together again. We were a pretty strange crew back in primary school. Liam was never fond of having the girls around, but usually he treated them fairly. He really had a stick up his butt the day Meredith hit him in the face. The thing was, we were all ready to go along with him. He said "Let's go see the horses. The girls won't miss us." Lonnie was already plotting out the route we'd take when Meredith showed up. We'd all called her Meri the Savage at one time or another—though never to her face. Liam really lost it when he brought the name out in front of her. *Pow!*

It was sure *I'd* never call her that!

IT WAS ALWAYS like that, though. Not the name-calling or hitting. I mean, Liam coming up with an idea that always sounded so good. "Let's go get ice cream after school. That test was brutal and we need a treat." Well, yeah. We'd all agreed with that. Then Lonnie got in on it. We'd need to give the slip to our teachers and miss the bus. If we met at the north entrance of the school at the bell, we could slip from there into the woods and around to the main road. Donnie would come up with routing and timing. At exactly 3:15, when the bell rang, we were out that door and off into the woods. Meredith stopped us at the edge of the woods.

"It's all good so far," she said. "But we all need to ask ourselves if this is the right thing to do. We could still make it to the front of the school in time to catch our buses."

"Are you saying you won't do it?" Liam asked.

"No. I'm with everyone else if we do this."

"As long as you all promise not to leave me alone to take the blame for any-thing and come to my defense if I get in trouble, I'm in," Karen said.

Peggy Anne and I just looked at each other and shrugged. The ice cream was great. The restrictions put on us by angry parents weren't. But we lived and learned.

WE GREW INTO our roles—into our classes. Liam was a Leader. Lonnie was a Commander. Donnie was a Defender. Meredith was an Advisor. Karen and I were Cognoscenti but of very different types. And Peggy Anne was a Creator. Sweet and gentle and always coming up with a beautiful bit of art or music.

"HEY, RICHARD," LIAM said as we filled our plates with burgers and potato salad. "I have a question to ask you." We sat at an end of the table and everyone was too busy eating to bother with our conversation. Though I noticed Peggy Anne sat beside me and Meredith next to Liam. "Lincoln Arms has a stockpile of rifles that have a hold on them for some reason. I can't get anyone to tell me why they aren't being shipped. I can shoot but I don't have any particular skill with firearms. Donnie tells me you are specializing in that."

"Yes. I'm not the best shot in the world, but I can break down and reassemble any weapon you give me," I said proudly.

"Meredith said you're still in town for a couple of weeks. Would you be interested in coming in for a tour of the plant and to take a look at these rifles?"

I grinned. Tour Lincoln Arms? I hadn't realized Liam had an in with the firearms and munitions factory. *Yes!* "I could do that. Do you have permission to take someone in there?"

"My parents are the majority stockholders in the company. It was my mother's inheritance. They've given me carte blanche to learn everything I can about the company this summer. I'm sure I can include you as an expert guide."

I suddenly had a sinking feeling. I'd considered myself to have nothing to offer as Liam's assistant. Now I find out that his parents own an arms factory. I could have kicked myself all the way to the pool and then drowned myself. If Liam one day inherited that factory, he'd need an arms expert. What was I thinking?

I agreed to go with him Monday morning and take a look at his rifles.

Lonnie Porras

"MEREDITH, DID LIAM tell you about the time we put an entire putting green in the lobby of our dorm?"

"You're kidding."

"No," I said. We were all sitting around the firepit on the patio relaxing after the afternoon of swimming and then eating. We'd all had a beer or two as well, though none of us were inebriated. I'd made sure Susan and Rosemary didn't have more than one. Meredith had asked me to bring an extra girl and I delegated the task to Susan. But they were both only fifteen. "Nappy didn't even ask anyone else in the dorm. He came straight to Liam and me."

"Boys, I believe you have a cleaning job that will keep you occupied for the rest of the weekend. If you finish before Monday morning, you can continue cleaning the dining room and hallways," Liam mimicked our dorm parent.

"He sent us to our room and told us he expected us to start cleaning by eight o'clock Sunday morning. We had to clean it up and scrub the entire lobby before the cleaners came on Monday evening." Everyone was laughing and Liam was shaking his head. The whole thing had been his idea and everyone in the dorm thought it was a good one. None of them helped Liam and me clean.

"Why such a big deal about a green carpet on the floor?" Susan jumped in on the conversation She looked confused. Meredith was looking at Liam with an eyebrow raised. She must remember some of his ideas in primary school.

"We didn't use green carpet," Liam said. "I'd have been happy with that, but once Lonnie started planning how to do it, it got a little out of control."

"It was perfect," I said. "We sodded the entire lobby and had a five-hole putting green. Mr. and Mrs. Wellborn had gone out for the evening and we had everything ready to move in as soon as they were out of sight. The guys stacked all the furniture in the dining room. We didn't figure Nappy would mind since he's an avid golfer. Came straight to us and told us we'd need to clean it up in the morning. Then he spent two hours with his own putter practicing on our green!"

Everyone started laughing at that.

"Let's see. Seven of us knew each other in elementary school. Two more guys go to school with us at Elenchus. And I've brought two gorgeous coeds from St. Agnes. How did you meet Liam, Hana?"

"I met Liam at a charity festival for the Children's Hospital," Hana said. What a dish. If I hadn't been attached to Susan, I'd have been all over her. She'd been blind to anyone all afternoon but Donnie. I thought Karen was over-compensating with the attention she was paying to Roald Adams. Sure, the guy was sharp and an Inquirer but Karen could do so much better. By default, that left Remy Fournier and Rosemary Dean quietly facing each other. Remy was a little shy. If he'd been a little more forward, he'd probably have gotten on well with Peggy Anne. They're both Creators. I wasn't sure yet where Rosemary was going to settle. Susan had only recently been told she was on track to be a Commander, which suited me fine. Rosemary? I thought she might be a Promoter.

"Liam does charity events?" Karen asked.

"He did this one. Handled the grill like an expert. Then he got down on the level of a little girl who was feeling lost. He told her he was sure they could find her mother if they got on the Mommy Express. They started choo-chooing around the park with all the kids attaching to the train as they yelled, 'All aboard.' And sure enough, when they pulled into the station, the little girl's mommy was there to take her home. It was so sweet."

"Geez, Liam. I know you don't have a girlfriend, but isn't five a little young for you?"

Roald missed the point. I knew Liam had taken Hana out the next weekend. But what they didn't want to tell people, I wouldn't volunteer. Even if I wasn't going to be his assistant, I was pretty sure I'd still be managing his ideas eventually.

10

Quality

Liam

FATHER WAS CONVINCED there was simply an incorrect entry in the inventory and it would be straightened out as soon as he got accounting to do an audit. I couldn't argue with that as it may well have been a typo. But Father didn't see anything wrong with me checking out a case of the rifles and taking them to the test range. He wrote the order and assigned a delivery driver to me. We picked up Richard on the way to the office Monday morning.

"So, what are we looking for?" Richard asked as we headed to the warehouse.

"I don't know," I answered truthfully enough. "I've listed it as being a test so we can write copy for the catalog and develop a brochure on the rifle. So, we'll check performance, sighting, clustering. I'm certain the test range has calibration equipment and we can check the ballistics, muzzle velocity, gauge, and whatever else we want. I just want to know what these guns are."

"WHAT ARE YOU doing here in here?" the warehouse manager demanded as our driver fired up a forklift.

"We have permission to extract a random crate to take to the test range," I answered, shoving Father's official memo at him.

"These weapons have been tested and sealed."

"It will only be one crate. The test is to compile information for a marketing catalog," I responded, smiling at him. "There's no data on file that we can use to create the marketing pieces. You know how the bosses are about marketing. He decided my internship should include building the brochure from the ground up."

"Take the end case. I had it prepared for just this kind of contingency. Knew someone from marketing would be meddling with them," the manager said. He turned on his heel and went back to the office.

"We'll take this one, Joe," I said, pointing to a case in the center of the third row. He'd have to shift three other crates in order to pull that one out.

"Mr. Wilcox said..."

"The boss said take a random crate, not one that had been prepared for marketing," I said. "He wouldn't like it if he thought someone had prepped a case for us to use." I left Richard to watch the unloading to make sure we got the crate we wanted and took the information from the end of the box to a phone on the wall near the door. "Mr. Daniels? This is William Thomas, the intern working for Mr. Cyning. We're bringing a crate of rifles out to run some tests on. He called you? Good. We'll need a case of 270 over 30 ammunition according to the crate spec. 130 grain. Yes. There are eighteen in a crate according to the spec. And they load six shells. We'll run at least a full chamber on each rifle. Thank you. We should be there in half an hour." I walked back to Richard and Joe was moving the forklift back to head to his truck.

"I told you to take that crate! What do you think you're doing?"

"Sorry, Mr. Wilcox. The boss specifically stated that we were to take a random crate."

"What's the difference between that one and the one I pointed to?"

"I don't know, sir. Should we take both and compare them?" I thought he blanched.

"You're only authorized one crate. Get out of my warehouse!" He turned on his heel and headed for the office again. I looked back as we left the warehouse and saw him on the phone.

"WHAT ELSE CAN I do for you?" Joe asked. There was no forklift on the range, so we'd manhandled the crate to the loading table where the range master met us. It weighed around 200 pounds. He issued goggles and ear covers.

"It's going to take us a while here, Joe, but you're welcome to stick around if you aren't scheduled for anything else."

"Mr. Cyning said I was assigned to you for the day. I'm even to take you home if necessary," Joe said. He was a nice guy and I didn't mind him sticking around. Mr. Daniels, the range master, clipped the bands on the crate and lifted the lid.

"Oh. Nice," Richard said as he lifted the first rifle from the crate.

"Please take the rifle to the loading table and strip it," Daniels said. "No rifle goes to the shooting range without having been stripped and cleaned."

"Yes, sir!" Richard snapped. I decided to watch the process since I really didn't know the first thing about stripping a rifle. Watching it in Richard's hands was like magic. It just fell apart into neat order on the cloth. He swiftly ran a cleaning cloth through the barrel and wiped each piece, all while talking. "Nice rifle. Good solid stock adds weight at the shoulder but isn't uncomfortable or too heavy to lift. Twenty-two-inch barrel. This weapon has been modified from a bolt action to semi-automatic. It will take six shells and auto-eject the casing each time the rifle is fired. As the casing is ejected, the next shell is chambered. Estimated overall weight is between nine and ten pounds. Recoil will be moderate. Field scope has also been modified for sighting up to one thousand yards. Sir, weapon has been cleaned and reassembled. Ready for loading." It had taken him a total of five minutes.

"Well done, soldier," Daniels said. "Are you active duty?"

"West Point, sir."

"Glad to have you on the range. Six shells are on the firing table. First target is 200 yards. Second target is 500 yards. Third target is 800 yards. See how it handles while I give instruction to your friend." Richard took the rifle to the firing table and a horn blasted as a warning to clear the range. Daniels turned to me and showed me how to strip down the rifle and clean it. It took me much longer than five minutes. By the time I was finished, Richard was standing next to me stripping and cleaning the rifle he'd fired six shots from. I turned to him and asked how it went.

"Nice. Marksman quality at 200 and 500 yards. I'm not an expert at 800 yards, but hit the target. There's an interesting click as the shell advances," Richard said.

"Do you mind if I run a set through it?" Daniels asked.

"Please be our guest," I said. "Expert opinions are what we need here." He directed me to a firing table where he laid out the six shells and watched as I inserted them and closed the chamber.

"Take your first six and see if you can get a cluster on the 200-yard target," he said. "I'm going to see how it performs on the 800." Richard already had another rifle out of the crate and was showing Joe how to strip it and clean it. I had a feeling we were going to use more than the 108 shells I initially projected. While I'm not great at stripping and cleaning, I am a fairly good shot. I'd been hunting with our groundsman on a number of occasions and he taught me carefully about gun safety and targeting. I lined up and squeezed the trigger, near enough to the target center to have made a kill if hunting. My next three shots clustered near the first. I was feeling good about my performance when I squeezed off the fifth shot and nothing happened. I looked at the rifle but couldn't see anything. I raised it and attempted to fire again. Nothing.

"Liam! Stop!" Richard shouted. Daniels had just finished his sixth shot and stepped back from the table at the shout. I immediately laid my rifle on the firing table. "You've got a jam. Did you hear the click as the last shell ejected?" I confessed that I hadn't been listening for it. Daniels confirmed that he'd heard it in the first rifle. We stepped back from the table and Richard quickly but carefully broke down the rifle and cleared the jam. He held up the jammed cartridge and inspected it. He held it up for Daniels. "I don't see severe damage but it's scratched."

Daniels pulled a pair of pliers from his pocket and removed the bullet from the shell. He tipped the powder out on the table.

"We don't reload a jammed shell," he said. "I'd like to run a set through that rifle if I may." We nodded and he loaded. We stepped back and watched as he put six shots into the 500-yard target. No jam.

"Must be Liam's... uh, William's loading," Richard snickered. He stepped up to the firing line and sighted in on the 500-yard target. After four shots the fifth cartridge jammed, just as mine had. "I don't like this," he muttered as he cleared the jam and handed the damaged cartridge to Daniels.

The rest of our morning proceeded much the same way. We ran at least two full sets through each weapon and averaged a jam every third set. One rifle jammed on the first cartridge. Daniels went into his office and emerged with a toolkit and magnifying glasses. He and Richard both sat to examine the rifles in minute detail.

"If we put a .30 caliber barrel on this and used .303s in it. I don't think we'd be having this problem," Richard said. Joe had run out to get us sandwiches and the four of us sat in Daniels' office to eat. "It's the stepdown shell that's creating problems. There's too much give room in the head. It wobbles going into the chamber. If these rifles were in the hands of the military, our guys would get killed. No one can afford to clear a jam every ten to twenty shots. It loses the whole advantage of the semi-automatic delivery."

"I'd have to agree," Daniels said. "It's hard to believe our company is putting out something like this. The Old Man would never have tolerated it."

"Well, the boss has been trying to discover what has things out of kilter. It's difficult to come into a business like this and take over from such a legendary founder. Three years is not that long."

Daniels eyed me speculatively. I think he'd caught onto the fact that I wasn't here just as an intern working on a school project. Before he could say anything else, though, Richard jumped up.

"I've got it!" he said. "We could resolve the issue with some machining and salvage the bulk of the current equipment."

"What do you think?" I asked.

"The problem is in chambering the stepdown cartridges and the fact that when they removed the bolt, they tried to squeeze two more cartridges in. It would be a comparably simple process to convert it to a magazine. We could even expand the capacity to maybe ten. I could build one if you'd like," he said. Daniels nodded.

"I think you might have something there. You'd need to re-machine the chamber to take the magazine feed instead of the rotating action of the current feed. It would speed reloading as well."

"What would you need to set it up, Richard?" I asked.

"A machine shop and tools. It wouldn't take much more."

"I have a shop here at the range," Daniels said. "I often rebuild old weapons out here for the museum."

"May I use your phone?" I had to dial Father at the clothing factory as he'd already left the office at Lincoln Arms. "Mr. Cyning, it's William Thomas. Yessir. Our day has been profitable. We—and I mean by that, Mr. Lingam and Mr. Daniels—discovered a design flaw in the D-270 that causes a jam every ten to twenty shots. Mr. Lingam believes he can machine a replacement part that would enable us to refit the rifles in a cost-effective manner so they could safely be put in the catalog."

"Liam, I'm distressed at your discovery and pleased with the solution. I believe I have found the missing inventory record but it was not listed with the same model number. If Richard can work there at the range with Daniels, he's hired. Have Daniels get him any material he needs. Other than the jam, what's the quality?"

"We've decided overall it's an excellent weapon and is probably within the specs for military usage. But as Richard says, the military wouldn't touch it if it jams all the time. People would die."

"Very well. Let me speak with Daniels and I'll authorize the work. Keep the crate of rifles you have out at the range and if possible, update all of them."

"Yes, sir." I handed the phone to Mr. Daniels and motioned Richard outside. "How long do you think it will take to make the conversion and generate patterns that the machinists can follow?" I asked.

"I should have the first part milled in a week," Richard said. I could see him nodding to himself. "A lot of custom millwork to get the first piece right. Then I can generate the pattern and we should be able to turn out enough pieces to refit this crate within three weeks."

"Three weeks? How does that stack up against when you need to be back at school?"

"Oh, damn! What day is this? No, it should work. I report September fourth. I can get this done before then."

"According to the Boss, you're hired. And Richard, thank you."

"Thanks? This is fun!"

"MEREDITH, CAN YOU work late tonight?" I asked. I'd barely made it home before dinner.

"Of course, Liam. I was staying here tonight. What's up? You must have had a productive day with Richard," she said as we sat at the table in the kitchen.

"We did. Richard is working at the range machine shop for a couple of weeks. Father says he thinks he's found the missing inventory entry and we discovered why it's stacked in the warehouse without a listing. I need to work on that report. I want to make sure Father has all the details before he makes a move at the plant." I was hungry and the sauerkraut and German sausages Cook prepared were perfect.

"Makes a move? You sound like there might be culpability involved."

"I'm afraid so. Two hundred seventy-five crates of rifles don't get shuffled into a corner and forgotten. I estimate the market value for these would be well over $300 each or a total of around one-and-a-half million. That's a huge hole in accounting."

"Who would try to hide a million and a half dollars of inventory? And why?"

"That's a big part of the question. Lingam thinks they were built for military use. If that's true, the question is, 'Whose military?'" That's what had been bothering me most of the afternoon as we continued to test the rifles. If they were loaded with only four shells instead of six, the jams occurred less frequently. Joe proved to be quite helpful in cleaning and preparing the rifles. Richard and Daniels did most of the test firing while I wrote notes.

We finished our dinner and headed to the library.

"Meredith, I wanted to thank you for preparing the party this weekend. It was good to see the gang again. I don't know why I've never thought of having a group over before. Mostly, the only guests are guys from school and then only one at a time. Remy was quite taken with Rosemary. I think they'll go out." I hesitated to mention the next but I knew Meredith would know. For some reason I felt there would be no secrets from her. Ever. "I uh... asked Hana out again this weekend. She said she is off the weekend schedule at the hospital for another week. I thought we might uh... Oh, God," I sighed.

"What is it Liam? Hana's a wonderful woman."

"Yes. It's not that. It's just that I opened my mouth and just sort of asked her if she'd like to go out this weekend and she said yes. And I have no idea what to do! What do people do on dates? She already said she doesn't expect anything as fancy as another concert. But I don't know what people do? Where do they go? I'm lost!"

I didn't expect Meredith to start laughing. When she did, I realized how ridiculous I sounded. A beautiful young woman had consented to go out with me without knowing what we would do and I was asking my assistant—who was every bit as beautiful and who would be a wonderful partner if I could muster the courage to ask her out—to help me plan a date with another women. It was ludicrous.

"I'm sorry, Meredith. I don't expect you to plan dates for me. It isn't fair. If you have advice, though, please let me have it."

"Oh, I will. And thank you for excusing me from planning your dates. It's not the kind of thing you should delegate. A woman you go out with should know you put some thought into it, not that you had your assistant plan it."

"It's not just that," I said. "When I talk to you about planning a date, I feel bad that it is not you I'm taking out. That seems unkind."

"Um... Liam, you shouldn't think that way about me. I will always do my best to assist you. You don't need to feel sorry for me."

"I see. You think I'd only take you out for sympathy? That wouldn't be likely. I don't feel sorry for you. If anything, I feel sorry for myself." *What an idiot! I'm making a mess of this.* "Just never mind. I'll call Lonnie and ask him."

Meredith started to respond and then backed off.

"Very well, then. Shall we start outlining your report?"

"Yes. I suppose we should do that."

"She does like Italian food," Meredith said just loud enough that I could hear her. She started drawing an outline on the chalkboard and I quickly joined her to fill in the blanks. We worked for about two hours. Meredith took the notes and promised to have them assembled and typed up by the time I got back from the factory tomorrow.

"Let's plan on an afternoon ride if the weather holds, can we?" I asked. She smiled at me.

"That would be nice, Liam. Goodnight." She headed for the stairs. I stepped out to the patio to look at the stars and think a bit.

FATHER HAD MY report and said he'd be meeting with Mother this afternoon to determine what they should do. It was clear there had been a massive coverup of weapons that were faulty. People were going to be fired. I wasn't satisfied that we knew the story yet. Wednesday morning, I wandered back to the warehouse to look at the inventory again. I expected to be accosted by Mr. Wilcox when I entered, even though I wore a proper hardhat and goggles as required in the warehouse. I glanced through his office window but he wasn't there. I could hear the forklift moving somewhere farther on so followed the sound, noting what arms and munitions were stored where.

As I turned down the last aisle, I saw Wilcox operating the forklift. For a minute I watched, unable to figure out what he was doing. He seemed to be shuffling crates around at random. As I started toward him, I saw more clearly what he was doing. Crates at the top of the stack leaned out toward the aisle. He'd been stair-stepping the crates with each layer stacked farther out over the one below it. And they didn't look stable at all.

"Mr. Wilcox! Stop! You'll get hurt!" I ran toward the forklift. He apparently heard or saw the motion of me running because his head snapped toward me. There was something wild in his look and the forklift pulled back then jammed forward into the bottom row of crates, lifting and tilting. I pulled up short as the top row of crates began to slide off the pile toward the forklift and a domino effect started everything within yards of the forklift began to tilt and slide. "Run! Run!" I screamed but he simply stared at me as the first crate came over the lift and slammed into him.

In a second twenty or more crates had tumbled out of the wall and onto the forklift and its operator. I ran to the wall and slammed my hand on the emergency alarm button next to the door. The klaxon sounded and I ran back to see if I could uncover Mr. Wilcox. I started shifting crates. These were slightly smaller than the D-270 crates we'd moved on Monday. A lighter weight weapon or number of units per crate. While I could barely lift one, they had bounced quite a lot, causing units to come loose from the other side of the aisle.

There was no question in my mind that Wilcox had set this up deliberately. The forklift—and Wilcox—were buried under a mound of crates. It would take me forever to shift them if someone didn't hurry up and get here.

"Stand aside," a man yelled at me. I looked and saw a red armband with the words 'Safety Officer' emblazoned on it. He was accompanied by six other men, all equipped with the required warehouse equipment. More were arriving.

"There's a man under there on the forklift!" I yelled.

"We need to assess whether moving things will cause others to fall," he responded. "We'll get him out." I was pushed back by the men with armbands and watched them start to work. "Here," the officer said coming up to me. The men were moving steadily forward to stabilize the mess. "Take this tape and run it across the head of the aisle and get on the other side of it. Make sure no one crosses into this aisle." I nodded and took the tape to block the aisle, stepping to the other side.

I wrapped a piece of the tape around my own arm and as people came into the warehouse, I waved them back unless they had a safety officer armband on. Three more of those arrived. A shop foreman joined me at the head of the aisle and started shouting for people to clear out of the warehouse and head back to their jobs. Before long the area was cleared of all but a few management types who were being given hardhats and goggles like anyone else.

My father came straight to me.

"What happened?"

"Mr. Wilcox was operating the forklift and a row of crates fell on him." He looked at me with an eyebrow raised. I glanced at the other managers in the aisle and he nodded his head.

"Avery! See that Wilcox's relatives are notified of the accident and kept informed of where he has been taken. Someone open the far door for the ambulance; I can hear the siren. Jack, stay with me. Everyone else clear out of the area."

It took half an hour to uncover the broken body of Wilcox. The ambulance crew had him loaded in the ambulance and was screaming toward the hospital. They hadn't covered his face, so perhaps there was a chance for him to survive.

Father pulled Jack Lenova and me to Wilcox's office. Jack started examining the desk and drawers while Father and I sat to talk.

"Now you can tell me what really happened."

"I didn't see everything, Father. I'd just gotten to the warehouse, intending to ask Wilcox who had given the order to warehouse the D-270s. It doesn't make sense that he would have been the person responsible for them. It has to go into the manufacturing area, design, and probably sales. He wasn't in his office but I could hear the forklift down that aisle. When I got into the aisle, I saw Wilcox on the forklift rearranging crates. He was stair-stepping them out at the top. When he saw me, he rammed the bottom layer with the fork and lifted and tilted until the crates started falling. The whole wall of crates came down on him and caused crates from the other side of the aisle to fall as well," I said.

"You think it was deliberate, then?" Jack asked.

"Yes, sir. There's no way he'd have been stacking crates like that if he didn't intend for them to fall," I said.

"A trap for someone else?" Jack asked. I just shrugged my shoulders. I didn't know.

"How is Richard getting on out at the range?" Father asked, changing the subject.

"I was going to give a call out there this morning before all the chaos started," I said.

"Go ahead. I'd like to know if it still looks like a good refit will be possible."

I picked up the phone on Wilcox's desk and looked at the card of numbers next to it. I dialed the range. Daniels picked up. He didn't want to talk at all and put Richard on the line immediately.

"Richard, how's the progress?"

"Liam, we may have a bigger problem than sloppy machining of the chamber."

"What? What else is wrong?"

"Something we didn't notice when we were test firing Monday but became aware of as we were drafting plans. Are you sure these weapons were manufactured at Lincoln Arms? There's no manufacturer's mark and no serial number on any of them."

11

Results and Celebrations

Meredith

POOR MR. WILCOX didn't survive the accident at Lincoln Arms. Liam told me about what he saw and that Mr. Wilcox had planned the accident deliberately, but that didn't stop either of us from having sympathy for him. Liam had spent the day with adrenalin pumping into his veins, first with the accident and then with the news from Richard that these guns might not even have been made by Lincoln Arms. The decision regarding what to do about them hasn't been made, but Richard is continuing to upgrade the crate of rifles he has at the range.

When he got home, the adrenalin was wearing off and he looked sad and somehow much older than he'd been when we were riding the previous afternoon. We sat in the kitchen at lunch and when he looked up from his food, his eyes were filled with tears.

"I've never seen someone die before," he said. "It wasn't as if I sat by his bed as he slowly died from cancer, nor like I saw blood from a gunshot wound. But I saw a man looking at me as his world came to an end. What was so terrible for him? Why would he choose to end his life rather than face the consequences?" He left his food and I followed him from the table to the library. When he turned to face me again, the tears had let go and ran from his eyes.

I don't know if what I did was right or wrong, but I folded him in my arms and sat with him as he wept, my own eyes overflowing. I held him against my breast and petted his head and whispered comforting words. When we had cried ourselves out, he pulled himself upright. He saw the wet spot on my cress and leaned in to place a soft kiss on my lips. I responded, welcoming the life-affirming sensation of his body against mine. We broke the kiss and moved apart, both of us embarrassed by our emotional display.

I didn't mention the kiss, nor did he apologize. I simply opened a notebook and began to organize his thoughts on the day as he spoke them. Did Wilcox have an accomplice? If the rifles were manufactured at Lincoln Arms, it is almost certain that he did. They would need designs and materials and manufacturing. The scale of a coverup that implied would have been like having a shadow company operating along-side the regular work. That seemed to indicate the arms weren't manufactured here. They could have been brought in and warehoused with no one but Wilcox the wiser.

From where? Small arms manufacturing was common. There were at least three dozen manufacturers in America. The Cynings considered Lincoln Arms to be a second-tier small arms manufacturer, far behind the major names in fire-arms—Barrett, Remington, Colt, Ruger, Henry, Mossberg, Springfield. They were major defense suppliers as well. Most of the second- and third-tier manufactur-ers would have as difficult a time manufacturing and then losing 5,000 rifles as Lincoln would. But why would a first-tier manufacturer need to hide weapons in a small company's warehouse?

"Foreign?" I suggested. "Could these have come from a foreign country?"

"Oh, God. It would mean they'd been smuggled illegally into the country. Stashing them at Lincoln Arms could make us an accessory. Who would imag-ine the CEO and COO of the company wouldn't know of such a deal? And with Wilcox out of the picture there is no one else to point to."

We finished the report and sealed it in an envelope to hand to Liam's parents.

"HE SAID TO wear casual sporting clothes," Hana said after we'd chatted for a minute. She called me at the office and was agitated about her upcoming date with Liam. "Do you know how big a range that includes? Of course you do. But I don't think Liam does. What kind of sporting? Indoor or outdoor? Will I sweat? He has to tell me more. How am I to guess what I should wear?"

"My, Hana. You certainly seem anxious about dating Liam. Why don't you just call him this afternoon? He's a nice guy," I said. I was still working on our report from the night before.

"You mean you don't know what we're doing or where we're going? I can't just call him and demand to know more. Wouldn't that be awfully forward? It's not like I think we'd ever have a real relationship. He won't wait around for an Aspirant to suddenly have time for him."

"Well, he did seem to favor you at the party last weekend."

"Ha! Donnie occupied all my time, and nice though Donnie is, I'm not going to try to manage a long-distance relationship and remote deployments. I like Liam. I know we're not really together. A second date doesn't imply anything, but he is fun. It could be two months before we have another opportunity to meet. I shouldn't be taking the time this weekend," Hana said, working herself up.

"Okay. I'll let Liam know he needs to call you and give you more details."

"You're a doll, Meredith. And don't worry. When you're ready to start a relationship with him, I'll be long gone."

A relationship? I couldn't help but think about how we'd wept together yesterday afternoon. And then that long gentle kiss. *Well, that's not enough to base a relationship on, is it?*

I TOLD LIAM he needed to call Hana and explained why simply saying sporting clothes was inadequate for a date to prepare properly. He finally got it.

"Meredith, I'm... I mean, about dating... It's just that... What I'd really like..."

"Liam, don't struggle with it. Enjoy it. Isn't this your first second date? Soon it will be more comfortable," I laughed.

"That wasn't what I was struggling with, but I suppose you're right. I should concentrate on what's before me and not worry about the future for now."

"Instead of the library, why don't we pick up soft drinks and go to my office for our work this afternoon. In fact, make your call and I'll fix a bit of afternoon snack for us and meet you there."

"Is that all right?" he asked.

"I can't see why not. I run up and down the stairs to my office two or three times every afternoon while we're working. I suppose it is good exercise but I don't think I need it. Do you?"

"Ah. No. Of course, I've been terribly inconsiderate of you," he said. "Certainly, we should use your office. That's what it's there for."

He went to his room to make the call to Hana and I headed for the kitchen.

"Miss Meredith, are you here for a little snack?" Cook asked.

"Liam and I will be working in my office this afternoon. I thought we could use a little more energy," I said, heading for the refrigerator.

"I have just the thing. Why don't you go ahead and I'll send Lupe with your snack in half an hour?"

"Really? That would be so kind of you."

"Truthfully?" he whispered. "Lupe is afraid you don't like her because you never ask her to do anything. This will make her feel important."

"I had no idea! I just don't want to abuse her service. I'm only an assistant."

"You are an assistant and Lupe is a maid. Her job is to clean and serve for you. Any little errand you can send her on, she would be thrilled."

That shocked me a little. I'm simply not used to having household staff. At home we did for ourselves. I knew Lupe came into my bedroom each morning while I was working. I'd tried to make her job easier by being sure my bed was made and my clothes were hung. Did she think that meant I didn't like the way she cleaned? I wondered about Ray in the stables. I went out to ride two or three times a week and always insisted on grooming Dancer and saddling her myself. I'm not so small nor she so big that I can't handle the task. But did Ray think I didn't like the way he worked with the horses? I would need to rethink my relationship with the household staff.

I WAS IN my office, facing the door between our rooms, when Liam knocked. I turned quickly and opened the hall door.

"Oh! You're here."

"You were expecting me, weren't you?" he asked.

"Yes, of course. I just... I thought you would simply use the door between our studies," I said. I was somehow embarrassed that he had come to the hall door. I wasn't sure why.

"What door between our studies?"

"Oh! Well, that one," I said pointing at it.

Liam crossed to the door and opened it, facing the blank door on the other side. "This goes into my study?"

"You were unaware of it? Lupe told me when she gave me the first tour."

"I don't have a door on that side. I need to talk to Erich about it. My entire wall on this side of my study is bookshelves."

"Oh, that's funny! You didn't even know a door was there? It makes no difference. We have this door and we are not engaged in clandestine activity."

"Clandestine? Uh... People might get the wrong idea if I was using a private door between our quarters. That's true. I'll discuss it with Erich. Now, shall we get to work?" Just then Lupe knocked at the door.

"Miss Meredith? Mr. Liam? Is it convenient to serve your snack?"

"Yes, Lupe. Thank you. Please place it on the table." I turned to Liam. "I'll get my steno pad and you can tell me how we are outlining the final report while we eat, Liam."

Lupe set the sandwiches and a teapot on the table with napkins and spoons. It was a far more elegant setting than I would have brought up. The egg sandwiches were trimmed of crust and cut in neat triangles. They were served in the center of the table so Liam and I could reach them from either side. Our teacups and the pot were on a serving tray and she poured for us, setting a cup and saucer on the table next to us with our napkins and spoons. She curtseyed to us and left the room, closing the door behind her.

"I don't think I've ever seen Lupe look so happy," Liam said. "I wonder if she has a boyfriend." I simply smiled.

Liam

I WAS VEXED to discover I there was a door between our studies I knew nothing about. It was like having a secret passage in an old castle. My imagination was quick to create adventures through the secret door. Yes, I am a fan of magical tales and secret adventures.

Meredith and I worked on the final report for my parents all afternoon and well into the evening after dinner. We included a chart of conclusions and possibilities, which I drew out on the chalkboard and then went to my own study where I had a drafting table and could draw the chart more carefully for inclusion in the report. I also had the diagram Richard had drafted of the new machining it would take to convert the D-270 rifles to D-270A, magazine fed semi-automatic.

Then I rejoined her in her study and we assembled the report. I was quite happy with it and thought this might be the end of my internship at Lincoln Arms. I thanked Meredith sincerely and took the report with me when I retired.

"AN EXCELLENT REPORT," Father said. "I have launched a full investigation into the origin of the rifles and have found no design or manufacturing records here in the plant. We can only conclude, as you did, that they were delivered here for some clandestine purpose and without our one link, Mr. Wilcox, there is no way we can track down the culprits."

"After considering the legal aspects of it, we're putting a team on stripping them all down to components and melting down the barrel and chamber pieces," Mother said. "As you have pointed out, the stocks are good quality maple and we see no reason not to build a different rifle on them. This was truly excellent work, Liam. Your grandfather would be proud of you."

"Thank you, Mother and Father. I'm glad you find it acceptable," I said.

"Now, tell us what you learned," Father said. *What?* I'd just given him the report. Did he want an oral presentation?

"I learned there were crates hiding in plain sight," I said hesitantly.

"No. No. Not the result of your investigation, but what you learned for yourself. What important discoveries did you make by being an intern at Lincoln Arms?"

"Oh. I see. I learned the importance of our family name. When I was simply William Thomas, an intern, people were friendly and open, willing to help. But when it came out this week that I was your son, I felt people grow cautious around me. I could call it respectful in some instances, like Mr. Daniels at the range. But the line workers—even the ones I'd shadowed to learn what their jobs were—looked at me suspiciously, as if I'd been spying on them."

"In a way, you were," Mother said. "But you became the spy revealed this week."

"What you discovered was a fundamental problem with management. Your mother and I had suspected something was wrong for several months, but whenever we walked the floor of the factory conversations hushed and people were focused on their jobs. We hold their jobs in our hands and there is an automatic division that results from having that kind of power."

"I'm not certain my father had that same division. He worked side-by-side with many of those people on the floor. They built the business together and had mutual respect for each other. Even after three years, in which we have made no major changes to the operation, we are still considered outsiders and a threat. I'm afraid we will never be on an equal footing with the workers."

"I think that is sad," I said. "I understand the division of labor and management, but it seems a closer alliance between the two might have prevented an incident like we just discovered."

"Very possibly. What else did you learn?"

"I learned that I learned more by listening than by talking. I know that's obvious and I've always believed it, but I'd never experienced it as I have over the past four weeks. Everyone I spoke with wanted to know why I was asking questions. I learned the shorter the response I gave, the more information the person was willing to share with me. It didn't require me asking questions or explaining what I wanted to know. It was while listening to a driver that I discovered there were crates of weapons in the warehouse that weren't even listed on inventory. That showed that some of the lowest people in the organization also had information to share," I answered. "I think the same is true of having asked Richard to just take a look at the weapons so I could describe them accurately that led to his enthusiastic response and discovery of both the jamming problem and the lack of serial numbers and manufacturing information. It was a case of bowing to someone else's expertise."

"I think you've done well," Father said. "I'm concerned, though, about the paper you will present to Mr. Peoples when you return to school. I don't believe he should be privy to proprietary information that is contained in your report to us. Do you have information to pass on that will not implicate the company in any wrong-doing?"

"I think Mr. Peoples is more interested in what I learned than in the actual information contained in your report. The questions you are asking now will help me formulate my thesis for him."

"Anything else?" Mother asked.

"Um... Yes. It's more personal."

"If you can share it with us, it will help us know how to support your continued growth as a Leader," Mother said.

"Well, I guess I learned how valuable a personal assistant can be. Meredith helped clarify my thoughts, suggested avenues of inquiry, proposed methods of evaluation, and did a bang-up job preparing the finished report," I said. "I've come to respect and value her in ways I hadn't imagined when she joined my staff. Working with her has been challenging—in a good way—as well as being very pleasurable. I find I look forward to seeing her each day and that I miss her on her days off. I'm looking forward to working with her for a long time."

My parents just smiled.

"WELCOME. I'M SO glad you could join me for dinner," Grandmother said when Meredith and I arrived at her door Friday evening. I'd asked Meredith if she was okay working into the evening on Friday instead of taking off for the weekend as she normally would. I found dining with Grandmother to always be an experience and I looked forward to sharing it with Meredith. She seemed pleased to be invited.

"Thank you, Grandmother. You know I always like dining with you and feel the past few weeks have been shorting me on family time. And thank you for inviting Meredith as well," I said.

"Welcome, Meredith."

"Thank you for inviting me, Mrs. Cyning."

"Let's sit for dinner. Erich arrived just a few minutes ago." I hadn't known Erich was invited to this dinner but he was smiling at us when we entered the dining room.

"Hi, Erich. Fancy meeting you here," I joked. I'd seen him just half an hour ago when he laid out my clothes for this evening. I wore my gray blazer with black slacks and the lavender shirt and narrow tie Meredith had chosen as my 'edgy' clothes. Meredith had chosen a turquoise cocktail dress. The top, with a classic round collar, was fitted exactly to her shape but at the waist the skirt fell in gentle waves to her knees.

"Cook has outdone himself for our little dinner," Grandmother said. "He has sent up hors d'oeuvres that we should partake of at once. Let us sit at the table."

The hors d'oeuvres were splendid. Each place was set with a lacquered tray. In the four compartments were garlic shrimp, seared scallops, codfish balls, and hollandaise sauce. Chopsticks were the utensils.

"I think Cook is showing off," I said as I snatched a codfish ball, dipped it in hollandaise, and popped it in my mouth. "He sent up a lovely afternoon snack yesterday while Meredith and I were working on the final report for my parents."

Erich chuckled. "I daresay, Cook has upped his game since Miss Meredith began here. Your father has quite a reputation and Cook wants to be sure his food measures up to your standards."

"Oh, dear. I must go to the kitchen after dinner and thank him personally for the effort. And to assure him he need not worry about my father. He never cooks continental or Asian cuisine like Cook does. He is an all-American sort of chef."

"The pot pie was certainly the best I've ever had." I smiled at Meredith, remembering how surprised I was to find the chef at Rangers was her father. He was a jovial man and you would think 'cook' immediately upon meeting him.

"Hmm. Perhaps we should arrange a cookoff. We could invite half a dozen of the top chefs in the county to participate." Grandmother nodded as if she were actually considering such a contest. Meredith looked both horrified and honored that her father would merit such attention. "Of course, then someone would need to judge the contest when all we really want is to sample their food. Perhaps a food fair would be more appropriate. I'll have my secretary investigate the possibilities. It sounds like a good event to have next summer when everyone can be out of doors."

"Grandmother, perhaps we could make it a charity event. We could have the proceeds donated to the children's hospital."

"Excellent suggestion, Liam. Oh! I do love these garlic shrimp."

The meal continued with good natured conversation. The main course was lamb boulangère garnished with fresh herbs and a side of roasted brussels sprouts. Flatware was set by Ricardo for this course. He also poured each of us a glass of pinot noir which accented the lamb perfectly.

"What courses have you registered for at the University, Meredith?" Grandmother seemed keen to discuss her schooling.

"There are a few required courses. I think the University has come to realize people come from a wide variety of educational backgrounds and they use these courses to level the playing field. For example, I am required to take an English composition class."

"Writing and composition are skills every student needs. If the student cannot express herself in writing, she will not succeed in composing essays for history, reports for science, or philosophical treatises. What else, dear?"

"I will continue my Social Studies with a view to achieving a master's degree. Supplemental to that, I will study sociology and psychology. I am intentionally carrying a light load this fall as I find I have other responsibilities."

"Am I such a difficult task for you?" I grinned at Meredith and she lightly tapped my shoulder.

"And how are the two of you getting on?" Grandmother asked. "I don't need to discuss your report to your parents. They gave a favorable review. But is your relationship beneficial to both of you?"

"I wasn't sure there would be anything for me to do when I got here," Meredith confessed. "It seemed I was making up things to do the first week or two. Then suddenly we were in over our heads in the work for the factory and it has been very stimulating."

"I had no idea what I needed an assistant for either," I said. "But this project has shown me how much I value you. You were much more a collaborator than an assistant. I honestly believe I would not have discovered what I did without your prodding, and I believe together we accomplished at least three times what I could have on my own."

"So, I take it you are pleased with the arrangement and wish to continue it?" Grandmother asked.

"Oh, I very much want to continue working with Merecith!" I said. Perhaps I was a bit too enthusiastic. She smiled at me.

"I am quite in agreement. Do you think we will have as much to do together when school starts as we have the past month?" she asked.

"I believe Liam will need advice on many matters—personal and social, perhaps even academic at times—and making sure his household when not in residence at Buxton House is well maintained and appropriate," Erich said. "As there is no residence at the University for him, one of your next responsibilities will be to locate suitable housing."

Grandmother took over from Erich. "We haven't really discussed your compensation, Meredith, except for the preliminary agreement we reached before you started. We should make that formal so Liam knows your status as well. All your expenses will be taken care of. You will have adequate funds for your personal use as well as an account to meet the expenses of maintaining the household. That will include your personal quarters, which should be convenient to my grandson's but for propriety's sake, should not be in the same house or apartment. Similar to what you have here at Buxton House. Do you think you can find accommodations?"

"Yes, I'm sure of it," Meredith said. I was too stunned to respond. I hadn't even thought of where I would live at the University. And I had no idea how to look for something. I'd been in a dormitory at Elenchus for the past eight years.

Ricardo entered the dining room from Grandmother's lounge. "Cook has prepared an exquisite cheese tray for your after-dinner enjoyment. I have placed it in the sitting room and Martin has paired several wines especially for the cheese and fruit."

"Thank you. Let's sample these after-dinner treats." Grandmother led the way from the table, attended closely by Erich. I took my cue from him as proper gentlemanly conduct and held Meredith's chair for her. She took my arm just as Grandmother took Erich's. They looked very comfortable together.

The cheese board was elegant and delightful. Seven different cheeses were on the board, interspersed with fruit and nuts. There was a tangy Italian *mostarda di pere*—not a mustard in the usual sense, but a blend of macerated pears with oil and seeds of mustard. A quince paste from Spain accented the Manchego. Three bottles of wine were open and at the side. I thought we might be drinking more wine in one evening than I had ever before. I hoped I was up to the challenge.

"Martin kindly provided instructions," Erich said, reading from a note. "We are to start with the lighter cheeses and a Riesling. Then, in the middle of the board are soft and spreadable cheeses. We are to drink the Beaujolais with them. Finally, the hard and strong cheeses are to be accompanied by tawny port."

"Meredith, my dear, I trust you are not planning to drive home tonight," Grandmother said. "We don't want you driving after we have indulged ourselves."

"Thank you, Madam. When you invited us for dinner, I phoned my parents to let them know I would be staying in my quarters here," Meredith said.

"Speaking of which, what kind of accommodations should we look for at the University? I've been excited about attending ever since I found out but hadn't given a single thought about where to live," I asked.

Erich took over the instructions and described several different possibilities as well as a budget for housing I thought was extravagant. Whatever Meredith was able to find would be far better than my accommodations at Elenchus.

WE WERE BOTH a bit tipsy when we left Grandmother's suite. I wouldn't say we were quite drunk, but we leaned on each other as we made our way up to our rooms on the third floor, laughing at an insane pun Erich had pulled just before we left. Meredith's hand slipped into mine as we climbed and she did not immediately retract it when we reached her door.

I don't know what came over me, but I bent to kiss her and soon found my arms around her and an enthusiastic response to my forwardness. I pulled myself away before I lost all sense of control and kissed her fingers as I looked into those green eyes.

"Thank you for a lovely evening, Meredith. You are a perfect companion."

She looked at me and smiled shyly. "Goodnight, Liam. Sleep well." She slipped her hand from mine and entered her room, closing the door gently behind her.

The next morning, I began emptying and removing the shelves that covered the door between our studies.

12

Dating

Hana

"ROLLER SKATING? This is wonderful! I haven't been on my skates in years. How did you know?" I couldn't believe it when Liam told me to wear clothes comfortable to skate in. I tried my skates on just to make sure they still fit. And we were holding hands as we made our way around the rink the first time, just getting used to wheels beneath our feet.

"I try to be attentive. I miss things and I don't understand others, but I pay attention," he said. What a sweet boy. "You told me the story of your calling and said you and your friend had been roller skating. It sounded like you really loved it."

"I did. I do. I just haven't had time for a while." The movement felt good and familiar. I'd be sore tomorrow. I turned and skated backward as he held me in a dance pose. Liam wasn't a great skater, but he was good enough to hold me while we skated. I did all the spins and fancy moves. He just kept the momentum going around the rink.

Roller rinks aren't the greatest places for conversation, but it was a great way to make contact, so to speak. We skated for almost two hours!

WHEN WE GOT to the restaurant, I was pretty used to touch ng him and held his hand until we were seated.

"Come on, fess up," I said. "I know I didn't say anything about Italian food being my favorite."

"I know. I overheard Meredith say something about it."

"Overheard her?"

"When I told her I wasn't going to have her plan my dates for me, she turned away and mumbled, 'She does like Italian food.' I took it as a hint. But I chose the restaurant." We were seated at a nice table and presented with a large Italian salad and bread before we'd had a chance to look at the menu. I ordered spicy chicken rigatoni and Liam showed some savvy about Italian food when he ordered linguine with clams in white wine sauce.

"It's a good thing we skated first," I said. "I won't be able to move after this meal. If you chase me, I'll have to let you catch me."

"Hana, I wouldn't do something like that. I'll be too full to put up much of a chase." He made light of it, but I got the feeling that if there was any chasing to be done, I'd be the one doing it. We'll see.

"Tell me about your job. Meredith said you went to work."

"Technically, it ended yesterday. It was a short-term project for my father. I studied what was running smoothly and what could use adjustment. This week, I have to put the report together in a non-proprietary format to hand in at school when classes resume," he said. "I don't think I could have done it without Meredith's help. She kept coming up with ideas and helping me brainstorm situations. She typed up the reports when I'd written a draft and was really supportive. I'm glad I have her as an assistant."

Somehow, I got the impression Liam was happy with Meredith. In fact, maybe more than happy. I doubted very much that I'd date Liam again. Although I doubted that after the first date, too. He might not be aware of it yet, but he was fixated on my former roommate. I sighed out loud.

"Hana, I'm sorry if that came off sounding like more than it is. Meredith and I have a professional relationship. We aren't dating."

"It's okay, Liam. We've always known it would be difficult to have and maintain a relationship with each other. I hardly ever have time to see anyone and you have a whole new path ahead of you. Let's just enjoy the food and company. Are you having dessert?"

I was still comfortable with him. I knew he wouldn't be overly aggressive with me but I was interested in more than holding his hand. I cuddled next to him in the back seat as his driver took me home.

"Walk me to my door?" I asked.

"Of course." We held hands and when we reached my apartment, I pulled him to me and brought my lips to his. It was like striking a match to tinder. I lost myself in the kiss and in his touch. I fumbled for my key and opened the door, pulling Liam toward me. He stopped without crossing the threshold. He bent and kissed me tenderly again.

"Thank you for a lovely evening, Hana. Maybe we'll be able to do this again sometime. Good night." My lips tried to follow him down the hall. I sighed. If things were different, I wouldn't have let him go.

Meredith

OUR LAST WEEK before school would start was filled with working on Liam's paper for Mr. Peoples and generally getting things organized. That included a trip into Covington to do last minute shopping and get Liam his driver's license. I didn't know what he'd be driving normally, but I let him drive my car for the test.

We met my parents at Rangers for dinner Wednesday evening at their invitation. Liam wanted to return to the restaurant and try another dish. My father was eager to show him some more of his cuisine. Erich drove and we waited for him to open the door. I took Liam's arm and went in.

"Meredith, how wonderful to have you and Mr. Cyning with us this evening. Your mother is already at your usual table. I've never seen your father so nervous. Here we are." The hostess showed Liam and me to the table where my mother stood at once.

"Please, Mrs. Sauvage, don't stand for me. It is so nice to see you again." Liam was a perfect gentleman, holding our chairs for us. Of course, I expected nothing less. Just in the few weeks we had been working together, I'd noticed a new maturity in his bearing. The incident with Mr. Wilcox had affected him profoundly.

"You are very kind, Mr. Cyning."

"Meredith and I are very close and I am sure we will see you frequently. Please call me Liam."

"Then you must refer to me as Kendall and Meredith's father as Rainer." Mother was Mother, of course—charming and relaxed with her quick smile. She's very physical and frequently reached over to touch one of our hands or arms.

"Meredith, did you know you have something of the same sparkle in your eyes that your mother has?" he asked.

"Liam! I... How kind of you to notice." He was flirting! No wonder Hana was infatuated. I was still puzzled that when I called, she said she had a wonderful time and really liked Liam but wouldn't be able to see him again—at least not soon. I wondered at her attitude but she just said the new term was starting and she couldn't afford an entanglement that might distract her from her studies.

"Even *my* heart jumped a beat with that," Mother said.

Father emerged from the kitchen bringing us each a bowl of hot soup and a plate of bread.

"Good evening, Mr. Cyning..."

"Just Liam, sir. Please."

"Wonderful. Liam, have you noticed the weather getting cooler? Lovely, of course, but I thought our meal needed to start with a hot soup. I hope you find this French onion soup to your liking. And don't worry about your breath. The characteristic odor of the onions is muted by the broth and cheese. I'll join you for the entrée but must ask that you excuse me from the soup." He nodded his head and ran back to the kitchen.

I watched Liam savor the soup.

"This is heavenly! Mmm. It warms one up, doesn't it?"

"Yes. It is one of our favorite winter soups. Rainer was torn between this and the minestrone, but chose this because it is warming but not so heavy as the minestrone. I'm so glad you like it," Kendall said.

"I do. Meredith, what kind of cheese is this that your father uses? It seems so unusual."

"The usual in this area is to melt Emmental on the top. Father found an old recipe that used gruyere. They are both Swiss cheeses but the gruyere is a little softer and sweeter than the Emmental," I said.

"It's delicious. I wonder if I've ever had that on a cheese tray. I'd like to sample it sometime. Could you assist me in selecting cheeses for a tray some evening? Perhaps we could serve my parents and grandmother. I do owe them something for their tolerance this summer."

"I'd be delighted." I smiled at him. He could have just told me to do it and as his employee I would. But it sounded much more fun this way.

"Here we have the entrée," Father said as he and a server returned to the table. "For our dining pleasure this evening, I have chosen a lamb fricassee with avgolemono sauce. You will discover, however, that I have included greens in the sauce, which lightens it and enhances the flavor of the lamb. Bon appétit!" Liam leaned forward and inhaled just to savor the enticing aroma. He started eating and moaned his pleasure.

"The avgolemono is exquisite! I've never had anything like it."

"It's why I serve this only with crusty bread. It is the best way to get every last sop of the sauce." Father was being very formal, explaining dishes as if Liam were a food critic from the newspaper. When I teased him, however, he started telling stories—some I found quite embarrassing.

"Meredith, I didn't realize you had four older brothers. Did you have a difficult childhood?" Liam turned to me, picking up Mother's mannerisms and touching my hand.

"Oh, not so terrible. I learned a great deal from my brothers. Including, I'm told, a vicious right hook." We all broke up laughing at that.

"We never quite forgave her for that. To think that she would bloody the nose of the host! I died of mortification."

"Kendall, please forgive her as I have. I was being insufferable and deserved the punishment and embarrassment. I assure you, both Meredith and I have learned more civilized behavior since that day." Desserts arrived.

"How colorful, Papa!"

"It's a parfait with layers of fruit and frozen cream."

"This is ice cream? It's so rich!" Liam scooped past the creamy layer into the fresh berries beneath.

"Not ice cream, precisely. It is frozen cream. I have a good relationship with a local dairyman. He skims the top of the cream for me. It is so thick a spoon will stand up in it without whipping it or freezing. When lightly whipped and frozen, it retains a pliability that is softer than the typical ice cream. I did not even sweeten it."

"It is a wonderful capstone for a delightful meal, Rainer. I can scarcely thank you enough for this invitation," Liam said.

"We hope you will not be a stranger to us here. As Meredith knows, I have this table ready for her or for you at any time. Please join us often.'

"Thank you for your generosity, Rainer." Father excused himself to check on the kitchen and encouraged us to take our time over coffee. Liam decided it was time for us to leave, too.

"I'll go into the kitchen now," Kendall said. "Sometimes there are little tasks Rainer has left for me so I can feel useful."

"I'm going to run in and give Papa a kiss before we go. I'll be right back, Liam." I moved quickly to say goodnight to Papa.

THURSDAY EVENING, WE sat at the kitchen table at Buxton House and shared a meal of steak au poivre. Cook served it with a layer of mashed roasted potatoes, crisscrossed with asparagus spears. The steak rode atop the stack with abundant sauce over all. I wondered if Cook felt threatened by our having dinner with my father the night before. This was a basic meal if you thought of it as simply steak and potatoes but it contrasted nicely with the lamb my father had cooked.

"We start classes Monday," Liam sighed. "The summer is over."

"Well, since you finished your paper this afternoon, you can have a long weekend to enjoy the last of summer before Monday."

"I am glad to have the paper finished. Of course, Peoples will want a complete discussion of it as soon as he's read it. That will be okay."

"I was surprised," I said cautiously, "that you gave so much emphasis to our working relationship. It was a little embarrassing."

"Oh, Meredith! I didn't do it to embarrass you. I really don't think I could have produced what we did on my own. Even this paper, you helped tone down some of my statements and direct me in positive ways. I've learned so much from you these weeks that I can't possibly keep your influence hidden," he said. I could feel the heat in my face.

"Thank you, Liam. I suppose we will have less interaction this fall. I can scarcely be in the next room when you are at Elenchus."

"Nor can I expect you to help me with my studies when you have your own at the University," he said. "But perhaps, at least on the weekends, we could study together. I would like that."

"I think that could be arranged."

"I tell you what. Why don't we spend tomorrow going for a ride and having a picnic? There are beautiful places in the woodland I've yet to show you. Would you join me?" His enthusiasm almost overrode my good sense.

"I suppose that during our work hours we can do nearly anything you need help with," I said. I wasn't sure, but it sounded more like he was asking me on a date.

"No. That won't do. I'm officially giving you tomorrow and the rest of the weekend off. It is your own personal free time. Would you consent to joining me during your free time to enjoy a ride and picnic?"

He *was* asking me for a date! I should have turned him down. He shouldn't have asked me.

"I would love to go riding and for a picnic tomorrow," I said.

WE MET IN the kitchen a bit before noon and instead of sitting to eat, we made sandwiches and packed fruit and water bottles. Liam had his saddlebags with him and carefully packed our lunch. Cook had thoughtfully provided a potato salad in a container for us. I stepped out to change clothes and when I returned, Liam was in his riding clothes and his saddlebags seemed much plumper than they had been in the kitchen.

"Ray, I so appreciate you having Dancer prepared and cared for when I ride," I said. I wasn't sure when I'd be out for a ride again. Liam's Sim was prancing around next to the mare waiting for us to get going. Liam gave me a gentle boost into the saddle and patted my leg before he led Sim to the mounting block.

"I'll need to make a fool of myself mounting from the ground after the picnic," he laughed. "I don't need to start the ride like that." I was glad I hadn't shown off by vaulting into the saddle. My riding instructor had made sure I was equipped to mount under any circumstances and taught me a few tricks.

"I went for a morning ride yesterday and found how peaceful and still things were at the duck pond. You might go that way," Ray said once we were mounted. He attached Liam's saddle bags and a rolled blanket. "There were a dozen mallards in the pond when I passed by."

"Thank you for that suggestion, Ray. We're taking a leisurely ride and having a picnic, so don't wait for us if you have a Friday night engagement. We'll groom and cool the horses," Liam said. My! It was only just after noon. He must expect us to ride for a very long time!

"Certainly, sir. Enjoy yourselves."

THE POND WAS well-maintained and quite far from the house. We rode for nearly an hour—sometimes on trails I'd ridden before—when we reached the picnic location. It had only one fully cleared shore of about fifty feet of gently sloping grass. On this there were two covered swings, large enough for two people in each. I wondered if they were ever both in use at once as Liam lifted me from Dancer and spent several long minutes holding my hand and listening to the birdsong and the light breeze rustling the leaves as we swung.

Suddenly becoming aware we were holding hands, I pulled away and suggested we busy ourselves with the picnic. We spread the blanket and Liam surprised me by pulling a tablecloth from his saddle bag to lay over the top of it.

"I confess, I did some preparation last night," he said. "We have a bit more than just the sandwiches and fruit we packed at noon. I hope you don't mind. I did it myself—with just a bit of help from Cook. We needn't try to eat everything. I'm afraid I packed enough food for a crew."

"Oh, we should have invited company," I laughed. He looked at me uncertainly but realized, I think, that I was joking. I reached over and lightly laid a hand on his. "Thank you, Liam. This is lovely. We can spend all afternoon eating if you like."

"Well, the horses carried it all out here, so I suppose they'll still be able to carry us after we've eaten. Try a Scottish sausage roll. Cook instructed me on preparing the filling and baking the rolls. There are deviled eggs, as well."

"Goodness, Liam. I had no idea you were so domestic."

"It is something Grandmother suggested I learn before I need to fend for myself in college. I'll never be the kind of chef Cook or your father is, but I did enjoy preparing food for you. May I pour you a glass of wine?"

"Oh, this is delicious. Yes, thank you. Wine would be lovely."

"Cook cautioned me not to overindulge. We do need to sit our horses later."

I looked at him, sitting opposite me on an edge of the cloth. He was pleasant to look at, but I wouldn't have considered him a model. He continued to chat on about various things in his bag, including a cheese tray and thermos of coffee, wine glasses, plates, cups, and flatware. No wonder his bags had been bulging!

Leonard, always accompanying us, lay down at one edge of the blanket and was happy to receive bits we fed him.

"Did you know," Liam said, "my father is still disappointed I didn't become a Commander or a Promoter? As if he believes it was my choice. And I'm not saying I would choose either of those anyway, but I thought our classes were supposed to be revealed, not chosen. Of course, he's suggesting that I could still learn to manage the business. That type of work just doesn't appeal to me."

"It's true that our class is revealed and not chosen. However, it is our choices that reveal class," I said.

"What do you mean?"

"Would a Commander choose to turn, say, your team captainship to someone else more able to plot and strategize the plays? Or would he simply assume he is the best for that role? Yet you chose to nominate Lonnie as your team captain."

"It's true, but I've always known Lonnie is better at actually making things happen. It goes back to when we were kids. Even if I came up with an idea, he'd organize it and get us all working together."

"He's always known it, too. But how did your teammates know that?"

"Well, I nominated Lonnie and said he was the best to be our captain because he understood the playbook and when to use each play best of any of us."

"And what did the team do?"

"They voted for him."

"That is the difference between a Commander and a Leader. The team voted in your direction. I've scanned your school papers while organizing them, you know, including the notes attached by instructors and coaches. They confirm the same behavior. When strategy and tactics are needed, Lonnie or another Commander are called upon. When consensus is needed, all eyes turn to you."

Liam paused in the midst of biting his ham sandwich. His eyes seemed focused on something far away. I just watched his profile and saw the strength and character in it. He finished his bite and turned back toward me.

"So, you are saying it is not my choice to be a Leader, but the choices I made revealed my Leadership. It feels like more of a burden now than it did. What do I choose? I will be thinking of every suggestion I make," he said.

"Oh, don't obsess over it. You have seldom led anyone astray. People need to know someone is incorruptible. If you are struggling over a direction, it is probably the wrong time to attempt to lead," I said. I found, however, that I was more willing now to follow him than ever before.

"I certainly was not leading well on my tenth birthday. I attempted to sneak the boys away."

"And they were ready to follow you. If you had some ready reason to give to the girls, we would have let you go. An insult, however, brought home the consequences. And as soon as I struck, Lonnie took charge. He waved us away and took you to the house. Donnie, of course, thought he was sucking up and was ready, instead, to hit me back. Peggy Anne and Karen thought I was a brute."

"And Richard?"

"I'm not sure because it all happened so quickly, but it seems that Richard was examining the mechanism of the lawn sprinkler and missed most of the action."

Liam laughed and shook his head. "And it took us eight years to all get back together." He turned on his elbow and looked across the food at me. Those piercing blue eyes made me think he was looking right into me. "Are you happy, Meredith?

Is being with me—around me—too much? I find I've come to depend on you in ways I never knew were possible."

What a difficult question to answer. Not because I was unhappy but because the kind of happiness I had when I was with him had nothing to do with my job or responsibilities. I was suddenly conscious of where we were and how we were behaving. Riding and picnicking with Liam were not part of my official duties. Our conversation could be considered mentoring, but it was not so different than any couple might have on a date.

A date. We were alone and undisturbed with food and wine and conversation. I'd kept the notion away from my conscious mind through all our preparations. But now I could not restrain it. We were on a date. And I was thrilled.

"I'm very happy, Liam. I hope we will continue to have opportunities to develop our understanding of each other and to work together. It pleases me to spend time with you."

He reached across the table spread and I let him take my hand. He brought it to his lips and kissed my fingers. Then he let them slide away from him. We continued our chat, packed the remains of our luncheon, and he lifted me to my saddle. It was a very good date.

LET ME HELP you with your boots," he said, kneeling before the bench where I sat in the entry.

"Really? You don't need to do that for me, Liam."

"It's my pleasure if you are not offended by it."

"Oh, certainly not! I just... thank you."

I was a bit self-conscious. Riding boots are not particularly breathable and feet tend to sweat in them. I'd been wearing mine for at least five hours and was afraid my feet would smell. Liam pretended not to notice as he gently removed them and massaged my feet before slipping house shoes on them. It was heavenly.

I stood and struggled to get him to sit while I returned the gesture and we began laughing so hard we simply fell together and then my lips were suddenly against his and I realized we were kissing and I wasn't fighting it. At all. I panted as I finally pushed away from his embrace. My! Did Hana teach him to kiss like that?

"Shall we tell Cook we'll be ready for dinner at six?" he asked. I took a deep breath.

"I should really be getting home this evening," I sighed. "We both need to be ready to move into our dormitories this weekend. I'm sure you have as much preparation to do as I have. I... I'll say goodnight and go change to my traveling clothes. Have a good evening, Liam."

I tried not to run as I fled from the possibility of another kiss.

13

School Dazed

Liam

I MOPED AROUND a bit Friday evening. Meredith fairly ran from me. I supposed I might be feeling how Hana felt when I left her abruptly last weekend after a lovely kiss. It simply left me wanting more. I needed to get control of my feelings and not become fixated on Meredith. She'd warned me, but then she'd also been a willing participant. Girls were very confusing.

I hadn't finished painting my room. The bookcases had been emptied and Erich helped me move them away from the wall where the door between my study and Meredith's had been hidden all these years. I needed some physical labor to take my mind off things, so I checked with Herman, our caretaker, and he helped me gather paint and gear from the work shed. He offered to help me with my task, but I felt I'd already kept him too long on a Friday and encouraged him to go on about his weekend. This was a project I could do. I could repaint my study.

The mindless repetition of painting helped to calm me and free my mind from dwelling on a possible relationship with Meredith. I needed to pack my school things and be ready to move to the dormitory Sunday afternoon. Grandmother had already announced a family dinner for before Erich drove me to Elenchus.

I cleaned my paintbrushes and rolled the tarp before showering and heading for a peaceful night of sleep.

THERE WAS NEVER enough time once a deadline was set. My project stretched on through Saturday as I decided the entire room needed a fresh coat of paint. Erich came in to help me paint the trim in the room and move the bookcases into their new locations. By then it took both of us to get suitable clothing, books, supplies, athletic gear, and my attitude packed for school. After a very pleasant meal with my parents and grandmother, he took me to Elenchus and helped move my things into the dormitory apartment I shared with Lonnie. There was already a party going on down the hall and the boisterous return to the hallowed halls of academia was more like a soccer match.

"So, are you doing Meredith yet?" Lonnie asked as soon as we were alone in the room.

"Geez, man! What kind of question is that? You know Meredith is my employee. I can't just start *doing* her. And that's a gross suggestion." Sometimes Lonnie was a little hard to deal with. Nonetheless, he was my best friend and we'd been roommates for eight years.

"I looked it up. There's nothing wrong with having a relationship with an employee as long as it is clear her employment is not dependent on it. You could transfer her and have her report to your grandmother to take care of you and then you'd be out of her chain of command. Everything would be fine."

"No. What makes you think we'd have that kind of relationship?" I asked.

"My friend, were you so oblivious during your party a few weeks ago? You might not have intended it, but by the time we were roasting marshmallows, it was a couples' party. You'd done quite an effective job of pairing everyone up. I wasn't a problem, of course, because I had both hands full of Susan. And believe me, those are nice handfuls. You introduced Hana and Donnie and neither of them saw anyone else all afternoon. Karen was so upset that you wouldn't pay attention to her that she practically seduced Roald right by the pool. I brought Rosemary to the party specifically because Meredith said she wanted you to meet more girls and she ended up all over Remy. Of course, Richard and Peggy Anne have had a little thing for each other since primary school. Wonder how that will go now that he's back at the academy. My point is that everyone was paired up and you spent the day with Meredith. She was the only woman there you were interested in."

"Not true!" I defended myself. "I took Hana out the very next weekend. And I can't help it if I'm uninterested in girls as young as you go for. The rest of us were just re-establishing old friendships. That's what the day was about."

"Okay. I rest my case. If you can't see the look in Meredith's eyes when she sees you, you'll be old and gray and still wondering what happened." We finished our unpacking while talking about the new soccer season and who would be ready to move up and take our places as we matriculated to the University.

"WHO WINS?" MR. Boyer strode around the class positing various scenarios in interpersonal relationships. "We have two people who each think they've been wronged. They have a confrontation. Who wins?"

"Doesn't that depend on the definition of winning?" Roald Adams was a good friend and I was glad we were sharing this class. I could see him preparing to debate and shuffled through some of my notes. "I mean, is it getting the other person to apologize? Is it correcting some behavior? Is it replacing a precious object? We can't really tell who wins until we know how each defines winning. Right now, you've set it up so that neither will win no matter what the outcome."

"That's just the point, though, isn't it? In a situation like this, the optimum solution is that both win, not that both lose. You can't win an argument, even if you defeat your opponent." I loved getting into it with Roald.

"You both have excellent points. Roald has indicated an important piece of the puzzle. What constitutes winning for each of them? No peace can be negotiated unless both walk away feeling like they've won, as Liam has suggested."

"Then how do we get to the point of discovering what winning means for each? Do people really go about finding what the other person wants or needs before they have a confrontation? I'd question whether either even know their *own* definition of winning." I was puzzled regarding how people ever succeed in relationships. I didn't even know what I wanted myself. Lonnie's insistence that Meredith and I were a couple was absurd. *Wasn't it?*

The discussion continued for more than an hour, the class periods being somewhat less defined at Elenchus than other schools, I was told. Students arriving for the next class simply sat in the back or stood against a wall to observe the debate. Even a couple of faculty members, including Mr. Peoples, with whom I had my next class, arrived and watched.

"Do we actually have two different scenarios here? If Roald and I have a falling out, we should both be aware enough of this dynamic to find out what the other really wants and then work together to resolve our difference. But if either or both of us do not have the tools or education to get to that point, we are automatically in a lose-lose situation. Is that what we're ultimately coming down to?" I saw Roald nodding. Somehow, the two of us never had difficulty reaching a consensus. Mr. Boyer stopped in mid-stride as he paced the room and turned to stare directly at me.

"That is where *you* come in. *You* have the education. *You* have the skills. You need to practice this over and over so attempting to find what a person's win is and how you can effectively give him that without another losing becomes an automatic response, even if that person does not have the education or tools to discover it himself. And you need to be available for those who cannot find a resolution to help them through to it, even if you are not personally involved in the conflict. I think we've carried on enough for today. Let's get everyone to his next class and we'll deal with another dilemma tomorrow." Mr. Boyer motioned to us to leave and the boys who had entered took their seats. I was lost in thought. Mr. Peoples interrupted me and suggested we walk to the cafeteria for a cup of coffee and a 'chat,' which was his code for the next lesson.

"**TELL ME MORE** about your employment experience," Peoples said when we had coffee and sat in a corner of the dining room.

"Um... I'm not sure how much I can divulge without slipping into proprietary company information," I said. "It was a good experience, though sometimes shocking and emotionally draining."

"I detected that key events were redacted from your report. Without describing events, tell me about the emotions that you experienced while fulfilling your responsibilities." I figured that was a pretty safe area, so I collected my thoughts and tried to put them in words.

"I guess the first day was a mix of excitement and frustration. I was unhappy that I wasn't working with my new assistant. I hardly knew what we were doing yet. So, I guess I was relieved at the same time. The excitement was because I was facing a new challenge. In fact, everything seemed to be a new challenge that month. Working with Meredith, analyzing operations at the factory, exploring what it means to be a Leader. And there was apprehension. I didn't want to fail my father and mother. With limited guidance around what I was to accomplish, I wasn't sure I knew what a standard of success was."

"Enthusiasm makes any number of other emotions seem less important. Your report certainly exposes your enthusiasm."

"I think that came partly from discovering Meredith and I actually had a project to work on together and it finally made sense to have an assistant. I remember feeling a sense of awe about the whole mechanics of the organization. Everyone had a part to play and missing any of those pieces would affect the performance of the whole. I think the impression of efficiency and performance is what made it so hard to discover the piece that was out of place. It wasn't obstructing the process, but it wasn't contributing to it, either."

"How did you feel when you finally discovered the problem?"

"Wow! What a mixture. Of course, there was the elation of having made the discovery but it came with a sense of betrayal. The company came into the family from my grandfather, who founded it. My parents were never that enthused about the arms foundry because their other businesses are clothing and food related. But it was a family business and they didn't want to just dissolve it and lose that legacy. Someone in the company had betrayed them all, including my grandfather and, by extension, me. That made me angry. I went for a long horseback ride with Meredith and talked it out so I could see the various possible permutations and pathways through the company the problem could have taken. She encouraged me to also look at what long-term damaging effects it could have."

"I see. You weren't concerned about the stock value?" Peoples asked.

"Hmm. That didn't really cross my mind until I was doing the analysis afterward. I suppose that if my father had started me off with a concern about profit instead of one of a vague unease, I would have seen that as a more prominent issue. As it was, I didn't experience a concern for profit or even legality until I'd discovered the nature of the problem. Then I felt despair and sadness. I was glad I didn't have to make the decisions regarding a path forward."

"This should show you a certain short-sightedness in your approach. You let the way the problem was described to you influence how you searched for a solution and perhaps even what you discovered. When you approach a problem like this, it may be helpful to describe alternate problems before you start looking for resolution. It's not unheard of, for example, for a small problem that can be easily discovered to hide the existence of a much larger problem. As you discovered in your debate with Roald this morning, in order to successfully negotiate resolutions to conflict, you need to discover what 'winning' really means. If you could give both parties everything they said they wanted, and one was still unhappy, what would you have missed?"

"That's a tough question and one I'll need to talk to Meredith about. I find that talking my way through things with her helps me clarify my direction."

"You get along well with your assistant?"

"Yes. Better than I thought we would. We haven't always had a cooperative relationship. But I value her insights and intelligence. She's really cool. We can work side-by-side on a serious project one moment and switch gears to planning a party the next. And she's fun to be around. Just lying on the grass for a picnic and talking is a high point of my life. And when... um... I mean... she..." I was suddenly at a loss for words. I'd nearly said 'when we kiss,' but those were isolated instances and not a basis of our relationship. Still, I wouldn't mind kissing her some more.

"A key element in having a successful relationship with your assistant is developing trust and not taking it for granted. In order to facilitate that, you should be aware of the same things you are aware of when investigating a problem at a company. Are there underlying problems that might be hiding a larger one? You may well develop a deeper relationship with your assistant than with your wife."

Wife?

Meredith

SCHOOL WAS HECTIC from the start. I was used to the relaxed environment of Green Hill Women's College. The University was far more intense. Of course, there were many more students, a wider area to cover in going to class, and classes with a hundred or more students in a lecture hall. I had orientation sessions to attend in addition to classes and was one of the older students in those sessions. It was more typical to begin college between eighteen and nineteen years old but I was a transfer student with two years completed and only a few credits needed for my baccalaureate. I could only imagine how confusing it would be for Liam when he began at mid-term. From our conversations, I detected Elenchus was not much different than Green Hill.

My dormitory room, once a quiet retreat where I could study and focus, was a horror. Hana and I had enjoyed separate bedrooms with a common area between us in our dormitory apartment. The room I was given at the University was scarcely bigger than my former bedroom and included two beds, two desks, two wardrobes, and shared a bath down the hall with a dozen other double rooms. I thought of my luxurious quarters at Buxton House and nearly wept.

Neither Liam nor I had time to spend the next weekend at Buxton House. It looked like we might not get back there for the month. We did meet for lunch on

Saturday, but mostly we both described what getting back to school was like and how overwhelmed we were with classes and how exhausted we were from studying. Of course, Liam also had soccer practice and any free time was spent working with his team. Liam and Lonnie were 'senior members' of the team and were not eligible to play this year, but they worked with the younger boys every day.

We finished our lunch and went back to our job or studies. My focus for the afternoon included running to various real estate and rental agencies to pick up brochures and fliers on properties for rent or sale. Just returning to my dorm room was motivation to begin studying where and how to get living quarters as soon as possible.

I SPENT SOME time daydreaming over the next week. I'd come to believe our rooms at Buxton House were perfect, but part of that was having meals served to us and someone coming to our rooms to clean and tidy things. We had a swimming pool, horses, tennis courts—all things we would not have in a new home. I even imagined myself cooking and cleaning for us as part of my duties and recoiled from the image in horror. As a personal assistant, I had a great many responsibilities but cooking and cleaning were not among them! I would not become Liam's maid and cook, even if we were to marry.

Where had that come from? I was certainly not hired to become his wife. Liam was a nice boy, sort of handsome, kind, wealthy, and... And absolutely too young to even consider as a possible mate. I needed to introduce him to some other girls as soon as I could arrange to do so.

Still...

AFTER TWO WEEKS of further study and being immersed in school, I still hadn't made much progress in my search for housing. I determined I had to make appointments to see something or I would never succeed. I made several calls on properties I had seen advertised when I began this search, only to find they were already let. Others said to simply give them my requirements and they would 'find something.' Eventually, I spent another Saturday going from place to place.

My first appointment was with an apartment rental agent who looked the requirements page over carefully. Liam and I had spent our Saturday luncheon the previous week drafting a list. I had typed it up and sent it to a few agencies, of which three had called me.

"You are requesting two apartments. One large and one small. That is unusual," the agent said.

"My needs are unusual. I assure you, both will be occupied."

"I see. Near the university."

"Preferably walking distance. Students, you know."

"We seldom rent to students. I thought we were talking about an older couple. Students generally have no discipline, make a mess of things, throw loud parties, and are unreliable about their payments."

"These would not be your usual college students." I remained calm but could tell already I would not be interested in anything this agent showed me. She was quite condescending.

"Miss Sauvage, let me be blunt. We are not in the habit of renting to a man and his mistress or a woman and her kept man. I am not claiming that you are on either end of that spectrum but, based on your information, I'm afraid there are too many red flags here to consider renting to you." The agent stood to conduct me to the door. I pulled a card from my purse. Mrs. Cyning's assistant, Isobel, had kindly provided professionally printed business cards for me, a task I felt I should have done myself.

"I can find my own way out, thank you. Should you suddenly find a change in your company policy, please call me. I daresay there are other properties I can find, though, so don't go to any special pains." I handed her the card and hurried out the door. I was in my car when I saw the office door fly open. I pretended not to notice and drove away.

That had not gone as I hoped. I hadn't wanted to use the Cyning name to open doors. This agent would be leaving me messages about over-priced rental properties by the time I got back to campus, I was sure. I had little hope of finding an apartment anyway. Regina told me to consider looking for property the family could purchase. I had to prove to myself the old woman was right.

I PARKED MY car back on campus and made my way to fraternity row. I steeled myself for the notorious way frats were reputed to treat women on campus. But joining a fraternity was definitely an option for Liam and my dormitory was only two blocks away. I didn't relish the idea of staying in a dorm room long term, but if the fraternity had a good reputation and space, I would do what was best for Liam.

"Miss? Excuse my surprise. We don't often get single ladies calling on our house—especially in the middle of the day."

"I'm sure most call in the evening or late at night. I am looking for a suitable fraternity for a friend transferring in at mid-term. He's eighteen and could use a reliable big brother environment—for which your fraternity is known."

"Oh. We have a few problems there. First, we don't automatically invite every pledge to join our fraternity. Second, first year brothers are advised to live in the dormitory and await available space in the frat house. Eighteen is the minimum age we allow students to pledge, but it is a rigorous pledge process. You are over eighteen, are you not? Would you like to come in for a personal tour of our house? I will gladly show you what we have to offer."

"I see no sense in that since my friend would be ineligible. Perhaps you would be kind enough to call my office if you think of a good place to refer him." I handed the surprised boy my card and moved immediately up the street. The scenario was repeated at three additional frat houses. I didn't stop at every one but felt four scattered through the district would get a buzz going. It might even reach the sororities. I giggled at the thought of what knowing the Cyning heir was coming to the University might inspire among the sororities. In one way or another, I had been propositioned at each frat house I visited.

I went to the library to see if other Leaders had attended the University and whether any of them had joined fraternities. While the classes were equal, institutions of higher education tended to take great pride in educating Leaders or Commanders on one hand and Inquirers or Creators on another. Schools were simply known for the kind of people they attracted and tended to use their alumni to attract more of the same.

The fraternity situation looked bleak, but at least I had options to share with Liam should he decide to accept a party invitation.

LIAM AND I decided it was too nice a day the next Saturday to spend in our dorm rooms studying. I picked him up about ten and we headed to Buxton House for the weekend. When she found we were planning the weekend, Mrs. Cyning immediately asked us to play tennis in the afternoon and have dinner in the evening with her. We quickly agreed.

When I appeared dressed for tennis, Liam stopped and stared at me.

"Is there something wrong with the way I'm dressed?" I'd played tennis in this outfit before. It was a sleeveless white blouse and a short white skirt over my tennis shorts. I wore white socks and freshly whitened tennis shoes. Liam was dressed in white with shorts and a knit shirt.

"You're just... so beautiful. I... Your... legs... You will make it difficult for me to focus on the game." My face heated.

"You're too kind, Liam. Haven't you looked enough?" Belying my comment, I suppose, I posed like a fashion model in the hallway. We laughed and I couldn't believe my brazen display. We quickly walked to the tennis court and I was amused to see Regina dressed almost exactly like I was.

"Hello, Grandmother. Erich. You remember Meredith, do you not?" Liam led me onto the court where the older players had been warming up.

"How could one ever forget? It's only been a month! How are you, Meredith? I'm so glad you could indulge this old woman's whim for a rousing game today."

"It is my pleasure, Mrs. Cyning. I hope you will forgive me for my lack of skill. I'm afraid I don't play often."

"Nonsense! Do you see the fifth window from the left on the second floor of the house?" Liam's grandmother pointed back at the house. I nodded. "That is the window in my sitting room. I have a perfectly clear view of the sports court and have watched you and Liam play twice this summer. I hope you weren't planning to let me win. Erich, prepare for a contest!"

We lined up on opposite sides of the net and began a warmup volley. Soon the game was underway and there was no time to consider 'letting them win.' We split two sets and decided that was enough. We walked toward the house together as we caught our breath.

"You would not have won that last point if Lonnie had been playing instead of me. He's twice the competitor I am." Liam was laughing at having muffed the last shot.

"Pfft. If Lonnie had been playing, he'd have missed the shot just to make sure I won. He works hard at ingratiating himself with people he thinks will further his ambition. There is no need for either of you to behave in such a way. But let's not bog ourselves down with replaying the match. Meredith, I trust you have come prepared to spend the night. I had Lupe refresh your room. Let's plan on dinner in my suite at seven. You two can occupy yourselves until then, no doubt."

"We have a lot of catching up to do, Grandmother. We've not had much time to get together since school started." I squeezed his arm and only then noticed I had taken it as we walked. I noted that Erich had offered his arm to Regina, so I didn't feel awkward.

We went to our rooms to clean up and promised to meet in the lounge before dinner.

WHEN I HAD showered and dressed, I went into my office and saw the flashing light on the answering machine. If there was anything important, I would need to figure out a way to collect messages during times away from Buxton House. I sat at my desk with a pad of paper and a pen to listen to the messages. After the first two, I started laughing. By the third, I was in hysterics. I opened the door between our studies and rapped lightly. A moment later, Liam opened the door. He'd also showered and shaved and smelled quite nice.

"Meredith! I was sitting in my office trying to decide if I dared knock and disturb you. Is everything all right?"

"Yes, Liam. But please come in and listen to the messages I've received this week after going out looking for an apartment last weekend. They are too precious not to be shared," I laughed. I realized how forward it had been of me to knock on Liam's door and began to stutter. "I'm sorry for disturbing you. I don't know what came over me. I didn't stop to think that I might be interrupting your studies."

"Meredith, please, knock any time. Do you know this is the first time we've opened that door since I cleared away my books and repainted the room? Look! Don't you think it is nice?" I dared to peek through the open door at his private quarters. He had books open on his desk, but the room was tidy and looked comfortable. I backed into my own study and Liam followed, leaving the door behind him open. "Really," he whispered. "I hope we will be working together for many years. You don't need to be afraid to knock on my door. It's not improper and I promise not to be ungentlemanly."

"Thank you. It is a very nice room. Uh... Please, listen to this first message from an apartment rental agent who was downright rude when I met her."

"Why ever would she leave a message?"

"I left her my card." I handed one of my cards to Liam. I didn't think he'd seen them. It was quite lovely with the Buxton House crest in one corner and raised type that boldly declared, 'Miss Meredith Sauvage, Personal Assistant to Mr. Liam Cyning of Buxton House.' It included the phone number.

"Oh, my! What did she have to say?" I pressed the button to begin the playback again.

"Miss Sauvage, it was so nice to meet you in our office this afternoon. I felt terrible that we had nothing in our inventory that was suitable

*for your purposes. I made several discreet inquiries, however, and have
found a property I believe would be perfect. It is a penthouse apartment in the Excelsior complex, which I'm sure you know is only minutes
from the University while still having the kind of upscale environment
your employer would be interested in. The penthouse has twelve rooms,
including a lovely staff wing that would be suitable for your needs. It
could accommodate not only a personal assistant but also a valet, cook
and maid. I would be delighted to show you this stylish new property.
Please call at your earliest convenience to arrange an appointment. As
I'm sure you are aware, an exclusive property like this will not be on the
market for long. Good day."*

"My word! A twelve-room apartment with room for *all* my staff? How could
we miss?" Liam laughed. "She must think I'm eighty years old!"

"She thinks you are rich. That makes a great deal of difference to her. She was
unwilling to rent to you and your 'mistress' as she said, or to me and my kept man,
but for a price she was able to find a prestigious address where you can live with all
your mistresses!"

"Oh, Meredith!" Liam looked truly shocked. "We've put you in a terrible position. To have your honor questioned! I'm so sorry. I'll take over the search for an
apartment myself!"

"Liam! It's not as bad as you make it out to be. I could have presented my card
as soon as I met the woman but I don't want to be presented with penthouse apartments simply because your name is recognizable. There are times to cast your
name about and times when it should stay concealed."

"Like when I went by William Thomas this summer at the factory," Liam
mused. "I see the sense, but it offends me deeply to have your character dispar-
aged when simply carrying out a work assignment. Perhaps we could get another
business card that is somewhat less forward in presenting who you work for."

"I think this will work well enough," I said. "Wait until you hear the next message." I advanced to the next message and pressed the 'play' button.

*"Miss Sauvage, this is Daniel Trimble, president of Tau Epsilon Alpha
Fraternity on the University campus where you recently visited. I believe
my fraternity brother, Samuel Davis, to whom you spoke, may have
overstated our society's position on not accepting applicants until they
have been at the school for a year and pledged our fraternity. In fact,*

there have been many exceptions to that guideline. We would like to invite you and Mr. Cyning to tour our house and let us show you the true hospitality that Taus are known for. If you would call me directly, at this number, perhaps we can arrange dinner. Please give my best and heartiest welcome to Mr. Cyning."

"Do you suppose the invitation to dinner was for both of us, or only for you?" Liam asked. "It would be embarrassing for both of us to show up if he was really only interested in you."

"Oh, I assure you, brother Samuel Davis was very interested in arranging a private showing for me. I wasn't sure of what," I laughed. "This next one, though, we, or you, might consider. It is a bit less direct."

"Play on." I pressed the button to begin the next message.

"Miss Sauvage, this is Miss Carolyn Dubois. We've not met, but it has recently come to my attention that you have joined our peers at the University and I would like to extend the welcome of Gamma Delta Epsilon Sorority. I understand you have inquired at several fraternities, looking for suitable housing for your employer, Mr. Cyning. What a horrid thing you must have endured to approach any one of those houses! I honor your courage. I met with some of my sisters here at Gamma Delta and we thought we might be able to help you in your quest. We are organizing a social mixer here at the sorority house on October tenth and would like to invite you and Mr. Cyning to attend. I assure you this is not a recruitment event and will have guests from several of the more reputable Greek houses on campus. We would all like to meet you and show you that the Greek societies are not just party houses, but are service-oriented organizations striving to make the best of our education. Please let me know if you and Mr. Cyning will be able to attend."

"That sounds very nice. Do you suppose it is genuine?" Liam asked.

"It's hard to say, but since they clearly invited both of us, it should be safe. And it would be good to meet some of our fellow students informally. If I recall, there's a football game at the stadium that day. We might make it your official college visit day," I said. "Why don't I make some inquiries and if it all looks good, accept the invitation?"

"Just don't leave my side," Liam sighed. "If I find myself suddenly surrounded by women, I might panic and run."

14

Home Sweet Home

Liam

BY THIS TIME, I shouldn't have been surprised to see Erich in Grandmother's apartment. He'd played tennis with us this afternoon and it was completely reasonable that he should be invited to dinner. It seemed, however, that I saw him more and more often in her company.

"Let's sit," Grandmother said. "I'm eager to hear how school is going this fall. Cook fixed game hens for us this evening." Cornish game hens are among my favorite treats but I was worried about how messy they could be. I wasn't very good at stripping the meat from the bones with a knife and fork. I didn't need to worry about that right away as we had a yummy Greek salad to start with. I do like feta cheese and Cook serves it with a large slice on top, not crumbes.

Grandmother got us right into telling about our school projects and guided Meredith and me in comparing the experience of Elenchus and Green Hill with the University. I could see right away that it would be a different experience.

"Seriously?" I asked Meredith. "You have a class with a hundred people in it?"

"It's not unusual for lectures to combine three or four groups that then have follow-up classes in smaller classrooms. I guess it saves the lecturer having to repeat the same lecture four times."

"It will be very strange for me to sit and listen to a lecture without being able to respond. How do people learn anything?"

"The smaller follow-up classes often have more discussion, but they are usually led by a senior student and not the lecturer. The professor is the authority on the subject and the discussions are to be sure we understand what he said."

"It will be a new experience for you, Liam," Grandmother said. "At Elenchus you are encouraged to question and even challenge your instructors. That is not the norm for mass education. Undergraduates are expected to listen and recite. It is assumed that the instructor knows what he or she is talking about. At the master's level, you are expected to demonstrate that you not only have learned what you have been taught, but that you have a mastery of the subject and understand it thoroughly. Only at the doctoral level are you expected to contribute to the body of knowledge or to disprove something from the canon."

I was at a loss for words and could only hope that I'd survive the lectures. I still wasn't sure how I was supposed to learn in that environment. I contemplated it through the remainder of my salad.

The main course of game hens with wild rice was served. Grandmother immediately attacked her bird with her fingers and tore off a wing, freeing the rest of us to use our fingers as well. Grandmother called it "delightfully messy."

"And how goes your other task, Meredith?" she asked.

"It's generated some interesting responses. I'm afraid people are somewhat reticent to discuss renting to people as young as we are but as soon as they see the Cyning name on my business card, they become inappropriately helpful."

"Would you believe, Grandmother, that one rental agent who had rudely dismissed Meredith at first suddenly discovered a twelve-room penthouse with quarters for my staff. The inquiry Meredith put out was very specific regarding our needs and that was way out of line."

"I believe you will need to purchase something," Erich said. "We ran into the same thing with your father and with your grandmother."

"You had this problem, Grandmother?"

"Oh, yes. Even though it might have been less a problem with Erich as my assistant than if I had a young woman, he met with much the same kind of prejudice. He was told a property was in a respectable building and they weren't going to lease it to him for his lover. Then when they heard the name Barone, they fell over themselves with several 'discreet' properties we could have."

"Your father ended up simply living here and having me drive him to the University until he felt it was too much bother and established his first business. He didn't continue his schooling after that," Erich said.

"I can't believe they thought Grandmother was your lover!" I said.

"Well, I was, dear. You can't blame them for that."

Fortunately, Meredith was there to shove a piece of chicken into my open mouth. I nearly choked.

"You would think he would know by now," Erich said. I offered Meredith a bite and found her mouth in a similar state of gaping. My body was suffering from far too much stimulus. I turned to look at her and she simply shrugged her shoulders.

"But you were married to my grandfather, weren't you?"

"Yes. My parents felt I was damaging their name, so they arranged a marriage to William Cyning. It was my negotiating skills that made the situation tolerable. And William was a good man whom I came to love. But I explained to him up front that where I went, Erich went. I would otherwise be a faithful wife, but he needed to understand that was part of the deal."

"And he agreed to that?"

"You need to understand that your grandfather was a so a product of his times and that the marriage was arranged against his will as well. There was some thought that classes could be inherited like British nobility if both parents were of the same class. It was a most stimulating negotiation and set us both on the path of accepting each other." Grandmother looked down at the bones in front of her. We'd all stripped our birds completely. But grandmother was not finished. "Part of our agreement was that we would have children only with each other. I'm happy to say your father was the product of that union, so don't imagne that Erich might actually be your grandfather. Your father also was proof positive that classes don't breed true."

"Yet, here I am," I sighed.

"Cook set our cheese and coffee in the sitting room," Erich said. "Regina, may I escort you?"

"As always, Erich. As always."

AT LEAST THIS time we did not overindulge in wine and cognac, though I was sorely tempted. We paused outside Meredith's door and I turned to her.

"Meredith," I began. She placed a finger to my lips.

"It is too soon to speculate on that, Liam. We've a lot of new information to digest. I don't believe your Grandmother hired me with the intent that I should become your lover. You... *We* both have a great deal to learn at the University, not the least of which is our studies." She reached up and placed a soft kiss on my lips and then withdrew immediately. "Goodnight."

"Goodnight," I responded.

I HAD A lot to think about. My grandmother had told me she was my valet's lover. But the subtext was that a relationship with my personal assistant and mentor was not unacceptable. I wondered how my parents would feel about that. But it was also clear that many people had a special tutor who had helped them along the road to maturity. Erich had been my father's valet and mentor until Father started into business. Jack Lenova had become my father's personal assistant when it became clear his class was Promoter. But the shift was not one that heralded a failure of any sort. It was simply to gain an assistant who was more capable of dealing with the demands of that class. I knew my father respected Erich.

Already, I couldn't imagine a time when I would want an assistant other than Meredith. But did that mean I wanted to be her lover? On a very base level my mind screamed, "Yes!" But I could recognize my own hormones driving me and could have screamed the same thing about Hana. Meredith was right: It was too early to contemplate that.

Still, the thought kept me awake and after a restless hour in bed, I rose and put on my robe. I removed my carefully concealed pack of cigarettes from my desk drawer and went down to the patio to have a smoke. I watched the stars and contemplated my life. Eventually, I fell asleep there.

"THIS IS EXACTLY the position I was in when I decided not to return to the University," my father said, startling me awake. I quickly tried to conceal my pack of cigarettes, but to no avail. "Can I hope that you have been considering joining me in the business? I believe you could rise rapidly in your grandfather's arms company. And frankly, I'd welcome you there." He reached for my cigarettes and helped himself to one. It was too early in the morning for me to indulge in that particular vice. Father was in his swimming trunks and despite the chill was obviously headed for the pool.

"I hope I'll always be of help to you in the business," I said. "But I confess, I have no love for it that would drive me to quit school and come to work."

"I thought not, but I had to check." He crushed out his cigarette after only a few puffs. "Join me for a swim?"

"I'm not dressed for swimming," I said.

"What difference does that make?" He tossed off his robe and stepped out of his trunks. "It's a great way to wake up in the morning." He dove into the pool and after a moment's hesitation, I stripped off my pajamas and dove in after him. I wasn't convinced of its being a *great* way to wake up, but I was certainly awake!

Meredith

IT WAS AN INTERESTING WEEKEND. Liam and I spent a good share of Sunday studying. I also took down the details from the calls on my answering machine and learned how to access it remotely. Not having a phone in my dorm room made the process awkward but at least I could find out if an agent had a unit I was interested in.

Regina Cyning took me aside for a few minutes and told me she had placed a substantial sum in a drawing account for Liam and me. She handed me a checkbook and encouraged me to shop for something we could buy instead of rent. Liam and I went through the classified ads Sunday and circled one or two that I would follow up on. Monday morning, we rose early and I dropped him at Elenchus as I continued on to the University.

It was a busy day. I returned the call from Carolyn Dubois and she was as pleasant to talk to as her phone message had sounded. I accepted her party invitation for Liam and me, stressing that we were trying to maintain a low profile and to please not make a big thing out of introducing Liam.

I called several real estate agencies and faxed our specifications. Two called back and I arranged appointments.

THE FIRST REAL estate agent I met with professed to know just what I needed and had the perfect property to show me. The agent met me at the gate—yes, gate— to the mansion she was selling. I groaned inwardly. The agent chose to show what she thought we could afford rather than what we specified we wanted.

"Now, I know you can't mention names, dear, but this is exactly the property a Leader needs." She'd obviously done a lot of research to discover who I was representing. I'd worked out the wording with Mrs. Cyning. This was precisely what we'd tried to avoid. "Not only is it convenient to the university—only two miles—it will make a fine addition to the family estate. It would not surprise me if the family came to stay here on occasion, even after college is left behind. The house has twelve bed-rooms, a library, a study, formal dining room, formal living room, and casual lounge. I looked up all the available information made public and I know this is perhaps smaller than your client is accustomed to but generally has the same amenities. Lacking the stables, of course. There is an ordinance forbidding livestock in the city limits. You will find there are quarters for the maid, attendant, cook, and other essential staff, while I'm certain you would find the lovely apartment above the carriage house suitable for your own dwelling. The utmost discretion is desired and this would be perfect with an office, small suite, and a large bedroom. I have a decorator standing by who could have the entire property up to your standards in two months."

"I'm afraid you have missed our criteria." *Maid, attendant, cook, personal assis-tant?* I mentally added a groundskeeper and at least two lackeys to do whatever was needed. "I appreciate you having so diligently researched my client, but our criteria are firm. A two-bedroom unit and a one-bedroom adjacent unit. Mr. Cyning is to be a student here. We want his life to be as normal as possible when compared to other students. Simply being in off-campus housing is a stretch. I'm afraid I must decline to make an offer."

"Cyning? The Cyning heir is coming to the university as well as the Kendrick daughter? I'm so sorry, Miss. I took you to be Elizabeth Kendrick's personal assis-tant. Are you certain Mr. Cyning won't be interested in this property? If so, I need to be proactive in contacting the Kendricks." I excused myself and the agent rushed to her car.

This was new information I should make Regina aware of. I needed to research the Kendricks and specifically the daughter Elizabeth. This could be an accident or it could be a setup. Whatever, I needed to be on top of it.

THE NEXT STOP was to see an apartment for sale. The fax I sent out specified that I was looking for a two-bedroom unit plus a nearby mother-in-law apartment. This company suggested they could help with adjacent apartments. I arrived and sat waiting for my appointment Wednesday evening as I glanced through *House Beautiful* and other decorating magazines.

"Miss Sauvage? I beg your pardon. I was expecting someone older and you certainly couldn't be the mother-in-law." The cheerful agent shook my hand and said she hoped I hadn't waited too long.

"I'm actually working for a client," I said. "I understand your confusion."

"I shan't pry but I understand your client then needs a two-bedroom apartment with an attached mother-in-law apartment within wa king distance of the university. It's always exciting when a professor comes to our community." I didn't rise to the bait. "We don't have a property that *exactly* matches your description, but I have two adjacent apartments which might be modified to suit your client's needs. Shall we take a look?"

The woman led me to the third floor of the building and down a long hall. Many of the apartments had decorated front doors. "We encourage our owners to personalize their dwelling in one way or another. The street view, as we call it, says so much about the resident. There is a door that might as well have a sign on it that reads, 'Ask to borrow a cup of sugar.' This next one just screams Inquirer. If you knock on his door, prepare for a long discussion on an important topic. And these two. Both Cognoscenti of different sorts. Lived next door to each other for as long as I can remember. He passed away after a serious illness with his family gathered round his bed. She never woke up the next morning. A sad story but mysteriously one of great hope as well. Don't you think?"

"It sounds like a very sad romance."

"Legendary. Shall we look at this one first?" She unlocked the apartment on the right and led me in. "The family has cleared out personal possessions but would like to sell the furnishings with the apartment. If your client doesn't want them—and I certainly understand that—we can assist in disposing of them. Take a look around, dear. You don't need me following you around to show you what a sink is and where the windows are. Just try to imagine your client in this space." I nodded and wandered around. Liam *could* live in this space. The problem was it had only one bedroom and he really needed the second for his study space. On the other hand, it had a large living room and a formal dining room with a small entryway room that seemed to have no purpose at all.

"Raymond kept his tools in here. And a piano. It was always in pieces. He was a piano tuner and a fine one at that. Of course, the family removed all his tools and the piano."

"Of course. I have a picture of him in my mind's eye, turing and testing. My mother is a pianist. I've always adored her art."

"How lovely."

"The apartment is beautiful, but it has only one bedroom," I said. I'm sure my disappointment came out.

"Let's look at the other unit and I will describe my idea."

We entered the apartment next door. It was a mirror image of the one we just left, but with no furniture in it.

"The rooms are much larger than I visualized with all the furniture in them. The gentleman certainly liked to fill every inch with something, didn't he?" I mused.

"Yes. Usually antiques that he took in trade for his tuning services. I know that's not to everyone's taste. Ms. Emerson's apartment was far neater. Every piece of furniture had a purpose. You could see that she could entertain precisely three people and that they would leave at the end of the evening. Her friend next door could have slept three people just on the sofas he had. Not that he would, of course." The agent stifled a giggle and I wondered about the relationship. There was no sign of a connecting door between the two units.

"Tell me your idea, please. This is far too much space for the mother-in-law unit." I continued to look around as the agent went on.

"If both properties are to be owned by the same person or couple, they could do some rather extensive remodeling. I was thinking this wall from the bath to the outside wall could be removed. Then partition the dining room space off the second apartment and make it into a second bedroom for the larger unit. That would remove the dining room from this side, but most older people don't really use a dining room."

Hmm. That's an interesting concept. If Liam's study were in the new room, I could use a portion of my sitting room as an adjoining study. Then there could be a connecting doorway. I was becoming obsessed with connecting doorways. But still...

"I should like to bring my client to view the site and an architect to draw the plans. Pending approval of both, I believe this is exactly what we are looking for. I'd like to put a hold on both units if I may. Will I need an earnest deposit?"

"Yes, of course. The board also has to approve the sale. While the building is not a retirement facility, we do have restrictions on small children. Are there small children involved now or in the foreseeable future?"

"No. None for so long as this is owned."

"Then what I will need next is your client's name and a deposit of one thousand dollars for each unit." I caught my breath at the thought the first check I wrote would be for $2,000. Mrs. Cyning, however, had started the management account with a generous $10,000. I pulled the checkbook from my bag and produced a card for the agent. *I should have made a lower offer but it's too late now.* "The deposit will need to be in the form of two checks since we are holding the deposits on behalf of two different sellers. Oh, my!" the agent gasped as she read my card. I filled out the first check. "The young man is to be the owner of the units and reside in the large one?"

"Yes. I do hope there is no silly rule about an eighteen-year-old owning property in the building, though it will be considered a family asset."

"And I assume you are the mother-in-law," the agent laughed.

"Yes. I need to be near enough that I can respond to his summons if he needs me. Our current working arrangement is inconvenient as I am at the University and he is at Elenchus. He will, however, be at the University come mid-term."

"It may be... We'll make it work. I'm sure the board will have no difficulty approving it. It would be very difficult to dicker about price, though, if this information were known."

"Use it at your discretion. I have offered the full asking price as it is stated in your brochure."

"Yes. Of course. Pardon me for being nosy, but from Buxton House? He is a Promoter? A Commander?"

"A Leader. Regina Cyning's heir. That is not widely knowr yet. As I said, please use it with discretion."

"I assure you I will. Word will leak out in the building though. Are you sure you want an apartment?"

"He's a teenager. A house, I fear, would be far too ostentatious and difficult to manage. This will be a nice step up from his dormitory," I said.

"They all start the same, don't they?" The agent took the checks and bade me goodbye at the door.

THE REST OF my week was filled with preparations. I informed Liam and Mrs. Cyning about the offer I had made. Liam was a bit ambivalent, happy that I had managed a deal and unconcerned about what I had chosen. Regina heartily approved.

I contacted an architect and arranged to tour the units with him on Saturday. I suggested Liam join me as I reviewed the plans. He was more than happy to and wandered through the apartment nodding and saying "Good. Good." The architect promised sketches in a week and building plans by the end of the month.

"Now, Liam, you need to dress appropriately for a college party," I said as I took him back to Elenchus.

"I believe I have everything I need," he said. "I am so glad you are accompanying me. I'd be a lamb led to slaughter without you. It's not that I dislike women. They're just so confusing to talk to. With other guys, we would just fall into a discussion of sports or politics. Or we'd be discussing girls, not talking to them. I'm so glad you will be my date."

"I'm pleased as well, but let's not get hampered by that, either. We both need to talk to others—men and women. I don't doubt that one or more women will want to monopolize your time. You're wealthy, you have a good name, and you're rather handsome, even if I do say so myself."

"You flatter me. But I'm certain I will be too busy guarding you from the fraternity brothers to take time with any of the women."

"Liam, remember what I said about it being too soon. We should both try to find someone at the party to go on a date with. It will be a good introduction to college life."

"I suppose," he sighed. "Perhaps I'm just seeing the easy way out. You're here. You're smart, beautiful, and personable. I like you. I can't imagine finding anyone who compares."

"Better you discover the truth of that now than in five or ten years," I said. I understood what he meant, though. There is a song I heard on the radio in the dormitory that went, "You'd be so easy to love." It would be the easy way out.

15

Class Struggles

Randy Peters

I LIKE MY JOB running a shoe lasting machine at Covington Shoe Factory. It's good steady work and with my wife working as well, we're managing to raise our kids in a healthy environment most of the time. I have to stay alert so the leather is properly aligned on the last before it's vacuum-formed. I pay attention to what I'm doing. But Sally and I still daydream about one day going to Hawaii and having a real vacation.

I'm a Dexter; that's what I was told. A person who is best suited to working with his hands. Somehow my wife, Sally, was classed as a Dexter, too, though the principal handwork she does is typing. In fact, it seems that about ninety percent of our classmates at Covington Central High School were classed as Dexters. I know some didn't finish school when they received their classification; they just quit and went to work. Sally and I both finished with hopes of going to college and really making something of our lives. But no college was interested in 'wasting scholarships' on a Dexter. And there was no money to pay our own way, so we went to work. That was twenty years ago.

At one time, cobblers would have been considered Cognoscenti. They worked with their minds as well as their hands. There are still a few around. I even spent time on weekends hanging out with one of the last cobblers who still handcrafted shoes. I learned a lot from him, but in a factory producing nearly a million pairs of shoes a month, it's one man, one job. I insert the form in the rough cut upper and use a machine that combines pressure and steam to mold the shoe to the last. Then the machine trims the excess leather away. The shoe, complete with the last, is sent down the line where the sole is stitched in place and trimmed. The joke that runs down the line is that we lasters create heathen shoes because they have no soles.

The work isn't stressful, though injury is certainly not unknown. A break in concentration and a hand could be caught in the last and formed into a shoe. I have the current record for fewest rejects of all the lasters. I've held most of the jobs on the assembly line at one time or another, but as soon as I found the last, I knew it was where I wanted to stay, especially since I work on the high-end products—formal men's shoes. Everyone on my line is proud of what we produce.

You need to take a break sometimes, you know. When the noon whistle blows and the machinery shuts down for fifty minutes, I hustle to one of the lunchrooms with my bag lunch and join several buddies to play cards. Of course, we can't gamble on the company grounds, but none of us have money to waste on that anyway. The guys mostly enjoy playing pinochle. You have to sit carefully on the rickety folding chairs and not lean on the table. The lunchroom's a place where any subject can be talked about—mostly sports and job gripes, but occasionally women, wives, children. The women workers in the plant usually use a different lunchroom or sit away from the card players, so I don't know much about what they discuss. The guys, though...

"What gets me is that we only got a nickel an hour increase *last* year. It was an insult. What good is an extra two bucks a week? And this year nothing?"

"It didn't even cover my baby's birth. Why are doctors so expensive, anyway? We didn't borrow money to go to school."

"That machine on line seven is a deathtrap. The guard on it's been broken for months. I told them flat, I won't work that one until it's fixed."

"Anybody else getting pushed to work overtime? They're not even offering a bonus for working weekends."

"Bet Mr. Moneybags got a bonus. On our backs."

"We should write a letter and send it to the big boss. Tell him we're not going to put up with this anymore."

"Hey, Randy. You got a typewriter at home. Why don't you type it up? I'd volunteer but we sold the typewriter to pay for the baby. We're selling everything else we can."

"Why me? They won't listen to a Dexter." I'd done a little griping, too, but writing a letter was serious business.

"You're smart. You read books. Type up a letter like it was n one of them books you read." It was true. Sally and I spent nearly every evening reading. And not just dime novels. She'd brought home a book on the socio-economics of class structure from the library a few weeks ago and it was really interesting.

"Well… I suppose I could. We'd better write down what it is we want, though. If we can agree on what we should ask for. Let's make a list." One of the guys grabbed an announcement off the bulletin board and turned it over so I could write on the backside. I had a stub of a pencil I sometimes used to mark uppers I reject at the last.

That turned our lunchtime meetings into brainstorms about what should be done. I brought more paper with me from home and took notes, the pinochle cards forgotten. I noticed the women no longer sat quietly on the other side of the lunchroom. They were right with us listing out the issues we should write about—sick pay and time off for childbirth. Sally and I went over the notes and started composing the letter in the evenings. That weekend, she typed multiple copies up for me to distribute at the plant and get comments on. She sure liked the idea of challenging the Promoters. She felt she should have been classed as Inquirer, but she'd been working a part-time job to help raise her younger brother and sisters when the classifications came out and school automatica ly gave her a Dexter certificate. She was stuck, just like me. It was like the school cidn't believe anyone there could be anything but a Dexter. I'm so glad we found each other. My head would go numb if I didn't have such a smart wife.

"SO HERE IT is. Everybody should read it and make sure I wrote what we really want. Pass copies around to the other departments and night shift. I don't want to suggest something that doesn't agree with what you said and everyone wants." I read the letter aloud and waited for responses. The free pair of shoes each year was something Sally had added but it sounded good. No one who worked in the factory could afford the shoes we made.

"We shouldn't put this around where any of the supervisors can see it," Barbara Workman suggested. "We don't want them thinking we're plotting something."

"Right," Jim Baggins said. "Even if we are."

A week later, the copies got back to me—smudged and tattered but still legible. There were a few notes from people suggesting ridiculous things like free meals in a company cafeteria but mostly it was approved as written.

"That's real good. Now you should sign it on behalf of the employees of Covington Shoe Company. And send it in the mail. If it comes from the post office, it always looks more official," Barbara said.

Sally typed a fresh copy that night with two carbon copies. She kept one and I thumbtacked the other to the bulletin board in the break room. I signed the letter and addressed the envelope to the CEO of Covington Shoe Factory. The boss wasn't a bad guy. He always came around at the holiday to wish everyone a Merry Christmas. If anyone could answer the employees, he could.

"PETERS, YOU STEPPED in a pile of dogshit when you wrote this. I got it from a VP who told me to talk to you since you're in my management line. Nobody upstairs is even going to talk to you about this. Just sit on it and don't rock the boat." The shift supervisor on my line was firm in what he passed on from up the management chain. "Truth is, you did a good job of spelling out things we've all been thinking. I wish I had better news," Bill Barton said. He'd only been promoted to supervisor a year ago and I couldn't blame him for not wanting to have trouble from his line.

Suddenly, my lasting machine didn't look so good and friendly anymore. I saw all the problems with the system, and instead, it became just a job I had to do. And it was a job I needed. Our family barely scraped by on my salary and Sally's piece-work job as a copy typist. My kids were going to the same shitty school I went to and probably wouldn't have an opportunity to become anything but a Dexter. I worried about what waited for them when they had to get a job. The shoe factory was the largest employer in the city with over six thousand employees. But jobs like that weren't always easy to come by.

"We can't just let this drop. They need to know that we'll strike if we don't get our demands heard. I'll bet the boss didn't even read the letter," Davy said at lunch. The news had spread fast and there were twice as many people in the lunchroom as usual.

"What do you want me to do about it? I typed and signed the letter. They could toss me out on my ear. I've had this job eighteen years and even if you've got eighteen years of shoemaking experience, that translates to exactly none in construction or road grading."

"Send another letter and tell them we're ready to strike if the company won't make a deal with us. They have to at least come to the table and discuss the problem. That's what it's all about," Jim Jeffries said. He was a good guy and seemed to always have my back lately.

"Yeah. I suppose I could do that. We'll need to circulate it to the other shifts and departments again. I'll have Sally help me put something together." I went home that night dejected and upset. I hadn't had an upset stomach in years but that night I could hardly eat a thing. If I did this, it was almost sure they'd fire me. I had to ask how much I trusted my co-workers to continue the battle now that it was started. And would Sally trust me to get something else?

Sally did. She typed up the letter and we made the duplicates like we had before.

> *We, the employees of Covington Shoe Factory, call upon the management to hear our grievances and meet our demands as stated in our previous correspondence. We have certain requisitions that can no longer be delayed. We remain ready to meet and negotiate a settlement in the next week.*
> *Sincerely,*
> *Randy Peters*
> *Representing the employees of Covington Shoe Factory.*

The letter was approved by the workers. I addressed the envelope and put it in the mailbox, followed by a dozen fellow employees who wanted to witness that it had actually been mailed. I sighed. This was going to turn out badly, I knew. But my co-workers were with me. And my wife. She kept saying I had management potential and might get reclassified as a Promoter.

That evening, we sat with the newspaper and began circling job possibilities in the want ads.

"PETERS! YOU'RE FIRED! Clean out your locker." It wasn't Bill, my line supervisor, who shut down the line. It was the department manager. Without a laster, the line couldn't make shoes. "The rest of you, make yourselves useful elsewhere. We're looking for a new laster if you know your place and can do the work. Apply at the front office." The manager turned on his heel and went back to the office he seldom emerged from. Bill laid a hand on my shoulder.

"I'm sorry about this, Randy. You're one of our best workers. But I warned you not to push it. Come on. Let's clear out your locker."

I shuffled dejectedly to the locker room where I had a clean pair of coveralls, my lunch, and a note from my wife that said she loved me and was proud of me. What would she think now?

Bill looked over my shoulder and I became aware that things on the factory floor were a lot quieter than usual. He rushed onto the floor and saw everyone in the department moving toward him.

"What in bloody hell is going on here? Get those lines up and running. You can't just leave here," he shouted. There was a note of fear in his voice and I started toward him to make sure nobody did anything stupid like trying to take things out on Bill.

"You fired Randy. None of this was his fault. We're all leaving with him. You replace him, you have to replace us all," Jim said.

"And you think the company won't do that? You're a few cards short of fifty-two."

"Only forty-eight cards in a pinochle deck. Stand aside, Bill. We're leaving."

They cleaned out their lockers, grabbed a few folding chairs and a deck of cards, and left the building. At first, it was just my department. As the day went on and word spread, most of the employees in the plant left their jobs.

"WE NEED SOME signs or people won't know why we're out here. Somebody needs to go to the office supply store and get some big sheets of poster board and some of those fat pens," Barbara said.

"I'd go, but I don't have money for all of that. Especially if we all just lost our jobs." I looked up at the speaker. I hadn't said anything since coming outside, but a dozen, then two dozen, and possibly a hundred workers were circling me. More were pouring out of the factory.

"What should we do, Randy?" I was shocked that they expected me to know what to do. It had all been their idea. Still, it struck me that starting this had been exciting. I felt like there was something meaningful I could do in my pathetic life. The time composing the letters with Sally were some of the best times we'd had lately.

"You could all just go home and go back to work tomorrow. They'd dock you a day's pay but you'd still have your jobs," I said. There were a lot of negative murmurs and head shaking. "You guys really want to strike?"

"Yes!"

"You know you could all be fired, just like I was."

"We'll get your job back!"

"Okay, then. Everybody dig into your pocket and give Big Al a quarter so he can go get sign-making supplies. We don't need poster board. Jim, go get some of those corrugated boxes from out by the loading dock. We can't have a strike without signs. Nobody would know what we're doing." Everyone started digging in their pockets and a team of workers headed for the loading docks.

THAT WAS HOW it started. Me, Randy Peters, shoe laster, suddenly became the union leader. Instead of going home, I walked the picket line demanding just wages and benefits. What a job for a Dexter.

Thomas Cyning

I'M A PRETTY GOOD NEGOTIATOR for a Promoter. I suppose it comes from watching my mother, Regina, put together deals over the years. But to me, there was no sense in the deal if it wasn't for profit. Profit means that someone wins and someone loses. I admire my mother's—and my son's—ethics, but they just don't get the point of being in business. Profit.

That's why I was so eager to make the deal as part of Fergie's team. He knows profit. I figured if I could strike a good enough deal for our family fortune, I could get Lydia to agree to selling off the Lincoln Arms and Munitions. That business still scared me. It was wasteful of me to order the melting and re-forging of all the barrels and magazines for that line of rifles, but they were not supposed to be there and I could only imagine what use they were intended for. I wanted profit, but not at the expense of people's lives. Nearly every night before I slept, I had a vision of Wilcox's crushed body after the warehouse incident. And with Wilcox gone, we still didn't know where they came from.

With a profitable clothing deal in Japan, we could step out from under the arms company and tell people we traded up. That was what I wanted.

"HERE'S TO OUR joint venture in Japan," Fergie said, raising his martini. We four partners raised our glasses.

"It's a sweet deal. You and Thomas must have negotiated the pants off them." Jason Harding, our attorney for this deal, took a long sip from his martini.

"We got them to loosen the ties a bit. I think we'll get them off soon," I said. "In the meantime, we have cheap labor, an existing factory, and a first order for our clothing before we've even opened the doors!" I was as happy as the rest of them—partly that Fergie had cut me in on the deal. Between the two of us, even with a translator, we had brought about an agreement that would profit the partners upward of ten million a year. In ten years, I could see that number soaring to a hundred million mark.

"Labor is so cheap there, I could see us moving the shoe factory over there, lock, stock, and barrel." Fergie grabbed one the oysters and gulped it down. "That would teach a lesson to those strikers."

"Would the quality be maintained if you moved the factory? There's a lot of difference between manufacturing cheap T-Shirts and fine shoes. I grant you, labor is being a pain in the neck right now, but everyone knows the standard of quality they get when they buy Covington Shoes," said Joseph Schwartz, the banker who had fronted much of the cash to be in on this deal.

"That's true. While I'd like to dump the whole lot of them, I realize 'Made in USA' trumps 'Made in Japan' hands down. But don't forget our discussions about the fad for canvas and rubber shoes. I've had enough time to consider their growth potential in the future. I foresee a time when young people wear nothing else." Fergie was a keen visionary when it came to his market. I'd followed his lead because I could see the reasoning Fergie had. If he said there would be a time when the youth of America abandoned leather shoes for canvas ones, then it was worth noting. It still made me shiver a bit to consider the degradation of society. *What is the world coming to?*

"Putting a canvas shoe factory in Japan sounds like a good idea. Count me in if you need a partner," I said. My capital was stretched to the limit with the new deal, but it would take Fergie a while to get his plan for this next venture ready to roll. By then, the clothing company we were opening now would have supplied enough return to replenish the coffers. And with luck we'd have the sale of the arms factory as well.

"Of course you are in, dear Thomas. You did a magnificent job in negotiating this deal. We make an excellent team."

A second round of martinis arrived and we gave our orders for salad, steaks, and desserts. By the time our food arrived with the third round of cocktails, the celebratory atmosphere began to shift.

"What are you going to do about this strike, Fergie? Not good news by any stretch." Jason was always looking for the problems. I suppose that's a good thing to have. It's what I have Jack Lenova for. But Jack was an Advisor. Jason was a Commander. Same occupation but vastly different outlook. Jason's loyalty depended on where he could find an advantage.

"Nothing." We looked at Fergie as if he were mad. "What I'd like to do is fire the lot of them and hire people who actually want jobs."

"Covington couldn't staff six thousand new hires. And the training time. You've got some skilled labor in there."

"Yes. No matter what I'd like to do, I'll temper my response. As it happens, this wildcat strike plays right into my hand. I was about to lay off everyone there for a month. We've begun to retool some of the outdated machines. While they are out on the street voluntarily, we're progressing quickly with the installation. Of course, when they return, there will be a few pink slips issued because the new machines require fewer operators. It won't be hard to figure out who the leaders were." We laughed and raised our glasses again. Me, a little nervously.

"So, you aren't going to the negotiating table at all?" For some reason I couldn't explain, this bothered me. Not enough to become upset, but more because an opportunity was being missed. Fergie was a Commander, like Jason. He was used to simply directing people to do what he wanted done and knowing it would be done. I had been taught everyone had something to say and I could learn from. My son was significant in teaching me that. I'd learned a lot in the Japan negotiations. *I need to get lessons in Japanese scheduled soon. I don't trust them when I can't understand what they're saying.* But not coming to the bargaining table spoke of a missed opportunity to learn about the employees. That bothered me. How could he exploit their weaknesses if he didn't know them?

"No. In two more weeks... a month without a paycheck... they'll be showing up for their jobs as scheduled. That's one thing you need to know about dealing with labor. They never plan ahead. This whole strike was decided in five minutes after a troublemaker was fired. It wasn't considered. It was an emotional response. Better by far not to let them think they have a place at the table at all."

"That's cold, Fergie. Cold, calculating, maybe even evil. But brilliant," Joseph, the banker, said.

I wasn't so sure. I wouldn't contradict Fergie but it gave me the same kind of gut feeling the arms factory did.

Meredith

I SET UP A MEETING with Regina as soon as I completed my research on the Kendrick family. It was mid-week and I didn't tell Liam I was going out to Buxton

House. I simply felt the matriarch needed to be aware another Leader was moving to town. Of course, it was not unheard of for a university to have more than one in attendance. It was, in fact, one of the best places for Leaders to meet and assess each other. I hurried to my meeting.

"From what I have discovered, Elizabeth Kendrick is the youngest daughter of the Kendrick family. She turned nineteen last month. It seems four of the Kendricks' seven offspring have been classed as Leaders. They sent one to Chicago and the youngest will be here."

"If they produce so many Leaders, her upbringing must have been extraordinary. Or she went to a school that automatically classified students according to their parents' wishes. I hope it is genetic."

"You're not upset?"

"No, dear. A gathering of Leaders' children is a known phenomenon. There are no restrictions on interclass marriages, though occasionally one's choice of a mate will affect their classification. But there is still an old prejudice from pre-classification days that one should marry within one's class. One Leader shows up and word gets out that he or she is looking for a spouse. An eligible match is discovered and sent to the same university. It seems Robert Livingston University has been chosen as the next gathering point."

"So, you expect Liam should be matched up with Miss Kendrick?"

"Not at all. One of the great benefits of Leaders amassing at a single university is the exchange of ideas and growth that occurs as they talk to others like themselves. Another male Leader is a year ahead of you at the university. Miss Kendrick may have been sent to assess him and might be completely unaware of Liam. Of course, she will know about Liam by the time she gets here since the real estate agent will certainly tell her. But she is but one of what will be at least a dozen young Leaders who will be sent here by next fall to prospect for a mate and to learn from their interactions. It is good to be aware of, but as long as Liam is aware that he should not fall head over heels for the first girl he meets, we shall be fine. I'm sure you and I are of one mind."

"Yes, Mrs. Cyning. I have already discussed with him the dangers of falling for the first pretty face he sees," I sighed.

"Exactly. Meredith, you are everything I hoped you would become."

16

Social Studies

Liam

MEREDITH PICKED ME UP Friday and we had a nice dinner while we caught up on what was happening at school and in our lives. It turns out she's been very busy.

"So, we have an appointment tomorrow morning to meet the architects at the condo to go over the plans."

"We do?"

"Well, I do. You don't need to come if you're not interested."

"No. I mean, yes. I'm very interested. I just didn't know. It's difficult not having you nearby. Thank you for including me," I stumbled. I'd been thinking entirely too much about the college party we were attending Saturday evening to even recognize that it is only part of the weekend.

"I thought you would like to take the opportunity for a little tour of the University campus. Perhaps we could pick out a couple of items at the campus store to expand your wardrobe and then go to the football game," she said.

"Football?"

"When the game ends, we'll have time to get a little dinner and then go to the party. Of course, if you have too much school work to do…"

"No. Not at all. Well, I have reading to do. Frau Dr. Meier assigned *Siddhartha* by Hermann Hesse. I'm to discover, by reading the book, why she assigned it to us. I think it's more than just because it is a classic treatise on Buddhism and enlightenment written in German. I can only read a few pages at a time before I need to put it aside and just think about it."

"I have read about the book, but I haven't read it."

"If I become enlightened, I'll share."

We retired for the night and I left her with a soft touch of my lips on her fingers.

"THIS IS GREAT!" I said. There was no other word I could think of. The furnishings in the apartment were rather old fashioned. The walls were papered in a floral print. It had a hominess about it that was very comfortable but I hoped I would be able to update it a bit.

"You are not stuck with the décor," Meredith laughed. "This is Mr. Singleton, the architect who has drawn up plans on renovating for you."

"Pleased to meet you, Mr. Singleton. I'm eager to learn what you have planned."

"Based on your assistant's description, we have a simple but elegant plan in mind. If you would imagine French doors here in the dining room, on the other side you would find a lovely study, done in a true gentleman's style with wainscoting and rich wooden bookshelves. Imagine your desk, your reading chair, and soft light. That part of the renovation and remodel is the most structurally significant. However, we plan to remove this small vestibule, leaving only a coat closet at the door. The remaining space will be used for the updated kitchen. I understand that not only are you a fine cook yourself, but that occasionally you will have a guest chef for special occasions. The kitchen will have more room for professional quality appliances. The other rooms will remain unchanged in layout but we are making several decorating thoughts available to you, depending on your personal taste."

"I can see it in my mind's eye," I answered. "Do you suppose we could make the look a little more modern? I don't mind a tasteful antique as a focal point but the amount and age of the furnishings in this room are overwhelming."

"I believe that would be an excellent choice and will have our artist draw up a couple of concepts for you," Mr. Singleton said.

"Some of the discarded antiques would work fine in the adjoining apartment," Meredith said. "I'll be happy to select the items and have them moved with your approval, Liam."

"I trust your guidance on that," I said. We walked out the door of the condominium and in a step were at the door of the second unit. The floorplan was a mirror of the first apartment but this unit would be vastly reduced in space with the loss of the dining room in order to accommodate my study. Meredith planned to leave the remaining space open other than the bedroom, removing the vestibule but not expanding her kitchen. "Will you be all right with the loss of so much space?" I asked.

"Oh, yes. It will be quite lovely. I plan to use the space as an open living/dining/office area. I'll simply use the furniture to define the areas. I am far less likely to be entertaining in my apartment than you are. I'll have a cozy conversation area with a low table for informal dining."

"If you are happy with it, I am happy," I said. "But don't spare an expense or make do with something that doesn't please you."

"OVER HERE IS the Student Union," Meredith said as she guided me across campus. Her dormitory had been a rather depressing building and the room she described sounded claustrophobic. I was glad she would soon be able to move to her apartment. "The Union has all the services we need. We eat in a common cafeteria, there is a coffee shop, a bookstore, and what we call the commissary. It's really just an extension of the bookstore that sells clothing, supplies, and even snack foods and refrigerated drinks. This is the building in which the bursar receives tuition and the housing authority assigns rooms. Essentially, it is the hub of college life. Let's get you a University sweatshirt. It might be a bit chilly in the stadium. It looks like it could rain."

Meredith led me into the commissary and we went down racks of clothes to find a sweatshirt in the school's brown and gold colors. I was surprised at how comfortable and warm it felt and wished Elenchus had adopted this mode of clothing instead of the navy blazer boys wore to class every day. She also chose brown wool knit hats we could pull over our ears.

"I'll like dressing like this every day," I said

"Oh, no. Not every day. While the atmosphere is more casual here, there's still a lot of pressure to meet a certain standard. Since there are always guests on campus who are looking for potential employment candidates, you'll find most students keep as high a standard of dress as they can reasonably afford so they won't be passed over at first glance."

"Is our society really so shallow that we judge people by their clothes?"

"You need only think about that for the answer to become clear."

We ate in the cafeteria and joined the throng going into the stadium for the one o'clock football game.

I'D BEEN COOL to the idea of going to a football game. I didn't think much of school sporting events and did not intend to compete, even though I loved running. The college game, however, carried its own excitement and I found myself cheering as loudly as the others in the stadium and sharing their disappointment at the close defeat of the home team. Meredith also carried a warming blanket, which she tossed across both our laps. It was a bit early in the season for a blanket on this October day, but she held my hand discreetly beneath the lap blanket.

MY PARENTS, OF course, wanted to inspect 'the new property,' as they called our apartments. We had picked up the keys from the management company when we met the architect and led them through the plans. Mother sniffed at the décor, but was pleased that we planned something more modern after the refit. I saw Father looking carefully at the plans, spread out on the dining table. That was one piece of furniture I thought I would keep. He made a mark on the plans and called us to look at it.

"You need a door. I'm sure you have discovered the door between your studies at Buxton House. You need the same access here," he said. I agreed but was not sure of his reasoning. "You and Meredith will have an increasing amount of collaborative work. You need to be able to interact freely without drawing the attention of your neighbors by going back and forth through the hall. I'm sure that is what led to the speculation about the former owners. You will be the youngest residents in this building. It wouldn't be wise to be on the gossipmongers' lips."

"I see," I said. "I hadn't thought of that."

"I actually marked the same thing on the architect's set of plans," Meredith said. "The way the doors are constructed at Buxton House, they ensure privacy when desired and access when needed."

"Well done, Meredith," Mother said. "I am happy that you were the first to join Liam's staff. It has been a long time coming. You'll need to consider hiring a valet for him when he moves to the college. This can be one of your early assignments."

"Certainly, ma'am."

We left the condos and my parents' driver took the four of us to a lovely restaurant for dinner. I was a little disconcerted at the idea of Meredith needing to ride in the front with David. I was sure there was plenty of room for four of us in the back seat. But that also reminded me of something Mother had said, so I brought the subject up as we were served.

"Mother, why would I need a new valet? What is wrong with Erich?"

"Oh, son. Do you have any idea how old Erich is?" Father asked. "He's seventy, if a day. He was your grandmother's tutor, my valet, and then your valet. While you were away at Elenchus this fall, he has semi-retired."

"He won't be terminated, will he?"

"Heavens no! Erich has a place with us at Buxton House for as long as he lives. I daresay your grandmother will keep him active when he isn't busy around the house. She always has." I was certain Mother winked at me.

"Now Meredith, I reviewed the work you did on the Lincoln Arms report," Father said. "A job that showed your worth immediately. You've been with us nearly four months now. What are your impressions?" Father liked to review things and usually had good questions.

"Liam is an easy person to assist and mentor. He takes suggestion well and learns rapidly. I enjoy being with him. I still find Buxton House a bit overwhelming, but have only recently had quarters there. We aren't there that frequently. I'm sure I will adjust. Please tell me more about the staff you expect him to need in the new residence."

"A valet, certainly. Someone nearby but not live-in. A young man needs privacy for his own affairs." My parents both laughed. "It would be good to have a housekeeper. Someone who could cook at least a few times a week and keep the apartments clean and tidy. Both positions could be part time at present with the possibility of full-time employment at a future date. I wouldn't rush to fill the roles. It is quite possible you might discover candidates at the University. You needn't limit yourself to established professionals in the area."

"I think that with a capable housekeeper, I could probably manage without a valet for a while. I have my driver's license now and Meredith has a car. Perhaps I'll want one of my own in the spring," I said.

"Young men and their cars," Mother laughed. "Remember that neither Dennis nor Erich are simply drivers. As you become better known you may need security. I'm sure nothing is required yet, but keep it in mind."

"Yes, ma'am."

All told, it wasn't an unpleasant evening with my parents. Dinner concluded with a nice apple crisp and coffee. My parents had Dennis drive Meredith and me to our dormitories to change while they enjoyed an after-dinner drink. I changed quickly and he dropped me at Meredith's dormitory so we could walk to the party together.

WE WERE GREETED at the Gamma Delta Epsilon sorority house by our hostess, Miss Carolyn Dubois. Indeed, everyone we met was very sociable. The women all wore party dresses and the men were in sport coats. I'd chosen my gray blazer for the evening. I figured this was not the time to make a statement with either my tweed or a brightly colored shirt. I might have been the most conservatively dressed man at the party.

"Miss Sauvage, I'm so glad you accepted our invitation. Mr. Cyning, on behalf of the Greek Council, let me welcome you both to Robert Livingston University."

"Thank you, Miss Dubois," I said as I took her offered hand. "I am looking forward to great things here."

"While I am already resident, Mr. Cyning will not begin classes until midterm," Meredith added. "We're so happy to have the opportunity to meet people and make friends before we're caught up in the pressures of academia."

I thought we were being a bit formal but we were taking our cues from our hosts and other people at the party were also introduced by their full names. There were far more women at the party than men, which I suppose was logical since the sorority had invited individual guests and not entire fraternities.

"What do you plan to study here, Mr. Cyning?" John Berringer asked me. He'd been introduced as president of the Greek Council.

"I'll have a varied course of study," I said. "I am advised that the University has an excellent program in history and in literature."

"An unusual course of study for a Leader," Miss Dubois rejoined.

"Not so unusual as you might assume. History and literature are the surest measures of human society. I agree that other disciplines are also important and my assistant, for example, is exploring social studies. I hope we will be able to cross-pollinate, as it were, so we can both benefit from the other's studies."

"You must have a very close relationship, Mr. Cyning."

"Miss Dubois, if we are to become friends, I hope you will consider calling me by my given name, Liam. I'm finding the constant Miss and Mr. appellations to be a bit stifling," I sighed, dodging the suggestion she made altogether. Meredith and I had agreed beforehand that for purposes of the party, we would be together as a date but she would maintain the role of my assistant.

"Wonderful. Please call me Carolyn. And this is John. Most of us here are quite comfortable on a first name basis but feel our way along as discreetly as possible in a new social circumstance."

"I do understand that, Carolyn. When Meredith joined my staff, it took us nearly three weeks before we used each other's given name. And we had known each other as children!" I laughed.

"If I might ask, Meredith, what does an assistant to Liam do?" John asked.

"It is a diverse responsibility," Meredith said. "Among the first things that I did was act as scribe and brainstorming partner on a consulting job Liam had this summer. I also organized a party and have spent a great deal of time organizing his files and library."

"I won't let her hide behind a secretarial role," I said. "Most recently, she has negotiated the purchase of an apartment for me and is managing the architect and renovation so it will be ready when I get here in December. And she is an excellent tennis partner."

"You won't be living on campus, then?" John asked. "I was told Miss Sauvage... Meredith... had visited several fraternities here inquiring about housing."

"We were encouraged by my parents and grandmother to find off-campus housing since there will be occasions that I need to entertain and I may also need to meet with clients," I said.

"Will you also be moving off-campus, Meredith?" Carolyn asked sweetly.

"I have acquired an apartment nearby so we can coordinate our endeavors." I thought Meredith handled that perfectly.

"Well, I do hope we will have more opportunities to socialize," Carolyn said, laying a hand on my arm. "Please, let me introduce you to some more of our guests."

Meredith

"THANK HEAVEN that's over!" Liam said as we walked back to my dormitory to pick up my car. We'd decided to drive out to Buxton House and simply relax on Sunday.

"Did you feel pressured?" I asked.

"Not at first, but perhaps I should not have suggested first names. Everyone got *far* more friendly from that point. Especially the women. And I couldn't help but notice you being chatted up by several of the men," he said.

"Yes. I thought we did a good job of establishing that we were together at the party, but it didn't seem to affect them when it came to asking me out," I said. Liam stiffened. "It's too bad there was no one there I could see myself spending more time with than at the party."

"Hmm. Too bad. The same can be said for the number of girls who pressed their phone numbers on me."

"Literally?"

"Oh, yes. I'm sure I have the slips of paper in my pocket here." He dug in a coat pocket and pulled out a dozen slips of paper. "I'll just throw these away when we get to Buxton House."

"Oh, don't do that. With such a huge initial splash, I'm sure you will be getting far more. We should do something with them that will commemorate the occasion. Perhaps pin them to the wall and see if they grow," I laughed. Poor Liam was quite flustered.

"I look at the names on these slips and cannot for the life of me remember which girl was which. I should have collected photographs."

"What a wonderful idea! I'll help organize them and see if I can remember which is which. Then you can decide if you want to take any of them out."

"Take them out? Look at this. Here are six names with the same phone number! They all live together!"

"That's a good thing to note, Liam. If you do take any of them out, the entire sorority will receive a report on it."

"That definitely puts them out of bounds, as far as I'm concerned."

"I don't think you would have any real problems," I said as we climbed the stairs to our rooms. "You are always a perfect gentleman. And I thank you for being my date tonight. You made the whole event tolerable."

"As your date," he said hesitantly when we reached my door, "may I kiss you goodnight?" I bit my lip. Well, we had spent the day together and held hands.

"Yes," I whispered. He touched my cheek with his fingers and it seemed I was magnetically drawn to him until our lips touched. And we stayed that way. Our lips spoke volumes to which we could give no voice. I surrendered.

It was Liam who pulled away and, while gazing into my eyes, lifted my fingers to his lips to lightly kiss.

"Goodnight, dear Meredith. Thank you for a most enjoyable day and evening." He let go of my hands and backed toward the door to his room as I placed my hand on the doorknob and pushed it open.

"Goodnight, sweet Liam," I whispered. And then we both bolted into our rooms. "Too soon. Too soon. Too soon," I whispered over and over to myself until at last I fell asleep.

IT WAS TOO cold for swimming or tennis on Sunday but it was a perfect crisp fall day for riding. We enjoyed a new level of camaraderie, at least in my way of thinking. Our conversation was free and easy. I was sure the horses and the ever-present Leonard were bored by our chatter.

"What do you think about John's challenge to me that history and literature, or general humanities, was not an appropriate study for a Leader?" he asked.

"I did have a degree of respect built for John," I answered. "I think he is legitimately looking for an answer—perhaps to his own studies. If I am not mistaken, he is an Inquirer. He wants to know the how and why of everything he encounters. His suggestion of a more scientific education shows more about his own character than that of a Leader."

"He was easy to talk to, I admit," Liam said. "I hope I get an opportunity to spend more time with him at some point. I think it would be good to know several Inquirers. I can't hope to understand everything the way they seem to."

"You probably need people of all classes around you. Think of the things you learned from Richard as a Cognoscente. And I know that you have benefited from Lonnie's approach to things as a Commander. I should probably not be your only Advisor," I said.

"Yes, I can see the benefits of having as wide a range of friends as possible. John reminded me of my friend Roald. I always learn something from him when we debate. I am less inclined to surround myself with Promoters."

"You mean like Carolyn?" I laughed.

"Yes. The social butterfly who introduced me to people of many classes but always tried to convince me she was superior to them or perhaps a better choice."

We rode on in silence for a while until I asked, "What have you learned about deciding why Dr. Meier assigned *Siddhartha* for you to read? Aside from being German literature, I've drawn a blank."

"Well, you haven't read it. I'll see if I can find an English translation," he said. "The story of Siddhartha is rooted in karmic Buddhism. We repeat life until we have learned the lessons it has to teach us and then we reach Nirvana, a stage of perfect oneness and enlightenment. I think Hesse's story tries to encapsulate that journey. Siddhartha is a Brahmin, which is the scholar class. But he doesn't find the answers he wants there. So, he leaves and joins the ascetics. They deny their bodies and seek spiritual enlightenment. Not finding it there, he wanders into town and meets Kamala. That's the same root as Kamasutra. Sensuality. But Kamala denies him that part unless he becomes a rich merchant, which he does. But not finding enlightenment as either a wealthy man or a sensualist, he wanders back to the river and simply sits and listens. And while listening to the river and helping the ferryman he discovers true peace in a simple life."

"I really would like to read that," I said. "But why did Dr. Meier assign it to you if not simply because it is good German literature?"

"I'm still working on that, but I think it has to do with the message that we go through different stages in life—different classes, if you will. I think she is getting at the idea that even our classes may not be permanent, but that we might progress through different stages of life as different people. I'm not stating it very well, but I think she means our lives are a discovery, not a given."

"I think you should develop that idea further."

OUR NEXT TWO weeks were filled with projects, assignments, and papers to be written. I discovered he could type, but the process was painstaking for him. I had no difficulty with his handwriting, so I gladly typed up his papers on the weekend.

"Meredith, it seems we've both been working too hard lately. Let's go out Saturday night and just have fun," he said.

"What do you have in mind?" I asked. We hadn't kissed since the night of the party and I was a little wary of what 'having fun' might entail. Still, we'd worked so well on our projects that the prospect was even more appealing than it had been before.

"At the party, I asked several people what was fun to do near campus. Several of them mentioned a place called the Rathskeller. It's apparently a bar that's very popular among the students. It has good food, three-two beer, and music. I'm not interested in drinking but the food and music sound like a great way to relax."

"I know the place. It's about a half-mile off campus on the other side of the shoe factory. I'm told lots of people walk over there. It's a little farther for you.

Why don't you have Erich take you and I'll walk to make sure I know the way? Then when we've had our evening, we can walk back to my dorm and I'll drive us back to Buxton House for the night."

"Agreed!"

EVERYTHING I'D HEARD about the Rathskeller was positive. It was a place easily accessible to students but far enough off campus that news of their behavior was unlikely to get back to the provost. I'd heard that even some of the factory workers stopped there after their shifts. Beer of the three-point-two-percent variety was served to anyone over eighteen. There were no hard spirits served at all and a staff of burly men enforced a cutoff if the bartender signaled it. It would be a perfect introduction for Liam to the college scene and possibly the first time he had ever worn his denim jeans off campus at Elenchus.

I walked along the sidewalk, occasionally being passed by other students who hurried by. About three hundred yards away from the bar, I saw Liam get out of Erich's car in front of the establishment. I hurried forward past the shoe factory where my progress was suddenly arrested.

"Just what we need."

"Alone and pretty. She'll do."

"What are you doing?" A man grabbed my arm and I opened my mouth to scream but one of the strikers clamped a hand over it. The last thing I saw as I was hurried through the picket line was Liam sprinting toward me.

17

Hostage

Liam

I OPENED MY CAR DOOR before Erich got a chance to get out and open it for me. It was bad enough having a driver, but I didn't want people to think I was a rich kid who got waited on all the time. I looked around and saw Meredith up the street, so I started walking to meet her.

Everything happened fast after that. Some guys in front of the shoe factory grabbed her and dragged her off the street. I took off running and was in front of the factory in less than a minute. I started through the picket line where she'd been taken. Hands grabbed me from every side.

"Whoa, boyo. Nobody crosses the picket line."

"I need to follow the woman you just snatched off the street," I said. "Right now."

"Who snatched a woman off the street?" the big guy said. "You must be kidding. Now go off and play with your college friends."

"And what do you think will happen if you shove me back toward the bar, say, and I go straight to a phone to call the police?" I growled. I wasn't backing down until I had Meredith back.

"They'd send a car around eventually and we'd tell them the same thing we just told you. What woman?"

"Look at me." The man stepped back and looked at me. I wasn't entirely happy with the way I looked. The staff had pressed my jeans with a neat crease down the front. I wore a white polo shirt and had a sweater over my shoulders, tied at my neck. "Now, look at yourself and your fellows here. Who do you think the police will believe? Do you really think I'm just another college kid?"

"Look now, you won't be telling the cops nothing." They grabbed me and a painful blow landed across my shoulders. My shirt was pulled out of my jeans and I lost the sweater.

"Listen! Do you really want to do this out here in public? Everyone will see you beating a college kid. Even if the police don't believe the story of the girl, they'll believe all those people watching you beat me." The strikers looked out toward the street. Two couples were standing next to Erich and half a dozen others were heading our direction from the bar. It could get very messy, very quickly. "Would you just take me to wherever you took her? Then we can have a nice civilized conversation. There's no reason to bully." I turned toward the people who were gathered and looked directly at Erich. "You won't try anything with these guys if I go willingly with them to where they took the young woman, will you?"

Erich clenched his fists but nodded his head. No doubt he'd called the others as he tried to catch me. The car was sitting beside him, still running. But the guy was seventy years old and I didn't want him trying to be a bodyguard. I'm a lot more solid than my size would make me appear.

"Take him to see Peters, then." The main speaker pointed to two guys who took me by the arms and marched me away as the rest of the strikers closed the gap behind us.

AN ARGUMENT WAS in progress and I could see Meredith being held in much the same way I was.

"Why the hell did you do this?"

"You said we need some leverage to bring them to the table. She's leverage. We have a hostage and they'll bargain or else."

"Or else what?" The leader turned and saw me. "Another? What are you guys thinking? Someone get out there and make sure there are no more!"

"Can I ask you something, mister?"

"Ha! Mister? I'm an unemployed shoe laster. Something you will never need to get your fingers dirty at." The fellow took a deep breath and let it out. "What's your question?"

"Was the purpose of kidnapping a woman off the street to have leverage to get the company to the bargaining table?"

"Yeah. It was a stupid move but we don't have any more options."

"Look at her. She won't work."

"What? Why?"

"She's way too pretty. Imagine yourself sitting at home watching the news and they put her picture up next to a picture of the picket line out there. Is she going to get you sympathy? I don't think so. People would be clamoring for the police to get in here and rescue her. None of us really want that. Someone would get hurt."

"I said this was a bad idea. Guys..."

"Not necessarily a bad idea, just poorly executed."

"What the... What are you talking about?"

"Well, think about those same people watching the news and they see a privileged boy who will never have to work a day in his life being held by desperate workers. Who do you think would have their sympathy then?"

"You mean you. Why would people know or care about you? Being pretty seems like a better strategy."

"I am William Thomas Cyning, heir to Regina Cyning of Buxton House."

"Oh shit!"

"I am volunteering to be your hostage and to keep the police from acting irresponsibly if you will let this young woman go."

"How would that help?"

"Miss, when you are released, please call Buxton House and ask for Erich Heinz. Tell him what you saw and ask to speak to Regina. Please deliver this message: I am asking the police not to be involved. We simply need the owners or managers of Covington Shoe Company to come to the bargaining table in earnest. I will remain with these people until they do. Will you do that?"

"Yes, L... Yes, sir. I will take that message." I caught her nearly calling me by name but she realized in time. It would be better if they didn't think we knew each other.

"There. You have my word. You have my body as your bond. Don't you think that's enough to bring the company to the table?"

"Christ. It just might. The bosses would all be ready to do whatever was necessary to help a Cyning. And you, girl? What are you?"

"I am just a secretary, sir."

"Will they listen to her?" the man asked me.

"Yes. If she carries out my instructions, Regina Cyning will see to it that the police do not interfere," I said. I hoped that was as clear as I could make it to Meredith that I wanted to be here.

The leader stood up straighter and looked at the closest circle of workers. "You two! Let go of the young woman's arms. Act like gentlemen and escort her out of the grounds so she can continue her evening. You will carry the message?"

"Yes, sir."

"Good." He waved at his men and they escorted Meredith from the circle as she kept looking back at me. "Now, you. Sit down here. Let him go. We have the word of a Cyning that he will be our hostage. You don't have to keep his arms pinned." We sat on rickety folding chairs facing each other. "Sorry about the dust-up out there. We've no intention of hurting you. I don't know whose bright idea this was but it all rose from needing leverage to bring them to the table. Our withheld labor doesn't seem to matter. They won't even discuss our demands."

"Please. May I know your name?" I asked.

"Randy Peters. I sent the letter to the management with our demands, so they fired me. When I was cleaning out my locker, all these people followed me. I never wanted to lead a strike."

"Yet it appears you are a respected leader. During our time together, call me Liam. May I call you Randy?"

"You're an okay guy, Liam. Not at all what we've always been told our betters are." He nodded.

"You've been told wrong. No class is better than another "

"Ha! That might be how you see it from the top, but any worker will tell you different."

"Then we need to figure out how to change that perception. May I see the letter that lists your demands?" I waited while Randy retrieved a copy of the letter from a card table.

"Here you go. I can explain anything if you don't understand it. We're not college-educated, you know." I scanned the brief letter. It was neatly typed. It used a few unusual terms but I could find nothing offensive.

"Okay. I see. This is serious stuff. You did a nice job of typing it up."

"My wife. We have a typewriter so she can do piece-work as a typist."

"She should be highly prized. Let's go through the list of... ah... your 'requisitions' as you put it, and make sure I understand them? This first one. Twenty-five cents an hour increase in pay across the board."

"We only got a nickel an hour increase at Christmas last year and they told us nothing was coming this year. A nickel an hour! What are we going to do with the extra two bucks a week?" One of the burly men who had held Meredith was standing close and was happy to offer his opinion.

"Mmm. I see. What'll you do with an extra ten bucks a week?"

"Ten dollars will put a meal on the table that we might have skipped to feed our children," Randy said. I looked sadly at the man as I began to understand their situation.

"I see. You ask for five days of paid medical absence each year?"

"Yes, sir. A lot of people can't afford to miss work, even if they're sick. So, they use their week of vacation if they're sick. We think we shouldn't go without pay another week if the illness is severe."

"You mean people come to work when they are sick?" I asked.

"Molly Amstel," the burly man next to us answered. Randy nodded.

"Molly was a fine worker. She got sick last year. Doctor told her she needed time to recover. After her vacation ran out, she was right back at her cutting machine. She died three weeks later and left three children behind with no one to care for them. She worked herself to death."

"What happened to her children?"

"All adopted but not all in the same family. Who can afford to add three mouths at once? But they're in the same school so they see each other every day."

I bit my lip. I couldn't believe people were pushed into these conditions. Oh, I knew it intellectually, but these men and women were the face of the Dexter class and were obviously being misused. I was on the verge of blurting out my anger. But that wouldn't help. I needed cold rational arguments. I continued down the list, discussing each point with Randy. A few points seemed frivolous at first. New chairs and tables for the breakroom? I discovered the rickety chair I sat on and which had twice threatened to collapse under my weight had come from the breakroom. New shoes? Randy explained that the workers couldn't afford to buy the product they made, so they bought a competitor's shoes for thirty percent less than Covington Shoes.

I WAS EXHAUSTED and glanced at my watch. We'd been talking for hours and it was past midnight.

"I'm afraid I can't deal with any more, my friend. Can we get some sleep and start on this again in the morning? I'd like to help you." I stretched and yawned, nearly toppling the chair again.

"Help us? More than by bringing them to the table?"

"Have you ever been in a bargaining room, Randy?"

"No. We've never bargained before."

"Then let me help. This is what I've been educated and trained for. Where do we sleep?" I looked around and saw a few people lying on the ground around fires in old oil drums.

"Uh... Sorry. There are six thousand of us on strike. The street frontage is only three hundred yards on this street and another four hundred around the corner plus the parking lot in back. That means we only have three to five hundred people on the picket line at once and work in shifts. There's no room for any more than that. So, most are home in their beds at least a couple of days between their shifts."

"This takes a lot of organizing. Who worked out the details?"

"My wife and me, mostly. She's behind us and a great encouragement to me. Some of the folks here don't have that kind of support at home. Husbands or wives are complaining to their mates to go back to work," Randy said.

"I'll stretch out over there if I may."

"If you're sleeping on the ground, so am I," Randy declared hotly.

"That's noble of you, Randy. Won't your wife want you at home?"

"Now that we have a hostage, I'm not letting you out of my sight. No offense. It's the only way I can make sure no one here messes things up."

"Sir? Here's your sweater. Sorry you... um... lost it earlier."

I looked up at the speaker, one of my original escorts.

"Let us forget the past, my friend. Thank you."

I WOKE UP stiff and cold. Someone had tossed a jacket over me during the night and I didn't know whom to thank for it. As late as Randy and I had talked the night before, I was still up before sunrise. I stretched and ran in place for nearly an hour. I obviously hadn't thought things through very well. I was smelly and damp and had no place to shower. Well, with luck everyone else would smell just as bad. Randy paused by the fire drum to warm himself as everyone else was waking up.

"Why do you do that?" he asked.

"I'm afraid my real life is spent sitting at a desk and studying. I need to exercise in order to keep from bloating like a whale." My stomach growled and I realized a second problem. I was hungry and had no cook to cater to me. It seemed Randy had the same idea. He went to the card table and pulled out his lunchbox.

"Sally, my wife, brought a lunch box for us this morning. Let's eat." He opened the box between us and pulled out a sandwich. He broke it in half and gave part to me. His wife had obviously not brought him enough to share but I took it gratefully.

"What is this?" One big bite of the coarse bread and meat spread was a new—and not entirely unpleasant—experience.

"Liverwurst. Doesn't take much to fuel a man for a day's work. And don't worry, she packed us another one for lunch."

"Randy, I've been thinking about your demands. They don't sound unrealistic to me but I need to find out what the company can afford and what it can't. For example, it would do no good to increase the company's expenses by ten percent if it meant ten percent of the workforce would be laid off."

"Do you think that's a possibility? The guys would never put up with that! To think a better life for us meant one out of ten of our coworkers were cut off? Impossible!"

"That's the point. I don't know if it's impossible or not. I need the details of the company's annual report. Can you get one?"

"I don't even know what it is. How would I know if I could get one?"

"It's a report the company sends to shareholders each year."

"I still don't know where I'd get one. None of us own stock." I filed that bit of information in the back of my mind.

"I think I know where I could get one but I would need to use a phone. Is there a payphone nearby?" I looked back at the factory as Randy shook his head.

"Closest, I suppose, is in the Rat Cellar over there. The owner of that bar… Well, he should have been a Promoter instead of a Cognoscente. He's been good to us, though. He brings the leftovers from the night before to us. He should be here soon. I'll ask if we can get you to a phone."

"I'll need to be closely escorted by workers. Maybe a dozen of them. It mustn't look like I'm wandering around on my own."

"Ah. Clever. I'll send out a call. We'll stretch the picket line all the way to his door."

Before too long, arrangements had been made through messages sent back and forth. Randy and I walked behind a picket line that stretched to the bar door. I was led to a pay phone and made my call.

"LIAM! WHAT'S YOUR status, son? I could get the police down there in an hour but your grandmother has forbidden it." My father was as anxious as I imagined he'd be.

"I'm well and am being treated as well as anyone on the picket line. I knew you would be concerned, Father, so I insisted they let me make a call to you to let you know I'm okay."

"It was a foolish thing to offer yourself in trade for Meredith. They might have kept you both and then where would we be?"

"I understand I took a risk, but I had little time to think of an alternate solution. They're pretty decent folk. The whole hostage thing was a spur of the moment act. They're getting desperate to get the company to the bargaining table. As foolish as it sounds, they thought having a hostage would hurry the company to negotiate. Of course, once they were committed, they couldn't really back down. I'm trying to de-escalate things." Father didn't need to know exactly how I was working on de-escalation. I was working on behalf of the employees.

"They should just all go back to work and accept what the company offered in the first place."

"Do you know what that is, Father? I've read the list of demands. I think a few things are unreasonable and I might be able to talk them down, except..."

"Except what, Liam. You have a plan. I can hear it in your voice."

"I really need to know where the company stands on this. That's the only way I'll be able to show them what's unreasonable. No one here is a stockholder, so no one has an annual report. You hold stock in Covington Shoes, don't you? Could you get me a copy of the annual report so I can show them exactly where their reasoning is wrong? Then when the company comes to the bargaining table, it will be much easier to negotiate." I was walking a thin line here. I didn't want to tip my father off too soon.

"What makes you think the company will come to the table? Fergie is convinced another week without a paycheck will put an end to the strike."

"Fergie?" I asked.

"Yes. You need to pay more attention to the business, Liam. Fergie is the CEO and majority shareholder in Covington Shoes."

"Well, holding me as a hostage certainly won't move him to the table. But..." I thought fast. What would concern Fergie more than having his employees on strike? "I haven't confirmed this but no one here looks like he or she has missed a meal. They've been on strike for three and a half weeks. I'd have thought they'd be more frayed by this time but they're in good spirits. You don't suppose someone— no one I know, but Covington does have some competitors who aren't entirely ethical—what if someone were subsidizing the strike in order to drive Covington into a loss position? I'd hate to see that, wouldn't you?"

"There are people like that. Do you think they're being subsidized?" Father asked. I could hear the worry in his voice. When dealing with a Promoter, nothing works like competition.

"Can't say for sure. I'll keep digging for information. Can you get me the report?"

"I'll send it with Erich. I need to talk to Fergie. It's good that you got on the inside so cleverly, son. You'll be wasted if you don't decide to come into our family business. You should take more interest in it."

"I'm only eighteen. Surely, nothing is set in stone yet."

"Right. Well, anything else you need?"

"I should speak to Meredith. I'm sure she's furious. Oh. And Grandmother."

"You're in luck. They're together. I'll patch you through to Mother's suite. Take care of yourself, Liam. I'm proud of you."

"Thank you, Father."

"LIAM! YOU IDIOT! They might have hurt you!" Meredith screamed.

"Calmly, dear." Grandmother was obviously right next to her.

"Please forgive me, madam. And you, too, Liam. I've been desperately anxious about you and your grandmother has been comforting me. I should be doing my job, not moaning. What is it you need next, Liam? What can I get for you?" She was struggling to remain calm. I needed to reassure her.

"When you are concerned for my health and well-being, there is nothing to be forgiven. I know you are distressed. How did it go last night?"

"Erich met me outside the picket lines and drove me straight here. In about five minutes, the house was on full alert. I don't think any of the strikers thought to notify anyone that you were being held hostage. Your father immediately called Mr. Ferguson to tell him you were being held. Ferguson wanted to send in the army or something to liberate you but by that time, your grandmother had contacted the police and other locals to inform them of the situation and that under no circumstances were they to attack or approach the pickets."

"Excellent! Grandmother, are you there as well?"

"I am."

"Do you think the police will continue non-interference? I don't want anything to set off violence."

"In this matter, my voice will prevail. The next time you do something like this, though, you will have to deal with them yourself."

"I hope never to do this again."

"We'll see. You're a Leader after all."

"I've asked Father to send an annual report with Erich. Could you see that he also brings my ski jacket and knit hat? My jeans and shirt are fine, but it gets cold here at night."

"Erich is with us and is nodding his head."

"Can you get us some appropriate news coverage? I'm certain Mr. Ferguson has kept this quiet as I've seen no reporters near the picket line. And I don't remember seeing more than a mention in the newspapers the past few weeks. I need some allies. I think I can resolve this if the company will come to the bargaining table."

"There is a reporter who wants a personal interview with me. I think she will treat it favorably. Don't abuse the favor."

"Yes, Grandmother."

"Is there anything else, Liam? Anything *I* can do?" Meredith pled with me.

"Mmm. I don't suppose you could get a hundred pizzas delivered to the picket line, could you? It would need to come from someone else, not us. We need someone who could be confused as a competitor."

"Ah! I think I know just the person."

"Who?"

"It happens there is another Leader attending the University."

"Really?"

"Don't be too surprised. That's an excellent idea, Meredith." I could just see Grandmother pacing up and down. "If you need additional credentials, I will provide them."

"Thank you, madam. Hang in there, Liam. We are all working for you."

"Grandmother. Meredith. The workers here have just cause. I need to find a way for Mr. Ferguson to win at the same time. It can't simply be that I'm not harmed."

"Exactly what you have been taught, Liam. This will determine if you are truly a Leader. Carry on."

"I love you, Liam."

"And I love you, Meredith. We have work to do."

I hung up and stood there for a moment in a daze until Randy suggested we get back to the factory. Meredith had just told me she loved me! *Me!* And I automatically responded with my love to her. It was insane. We were in love!

I realized Grandmother was in the room when we declared it. *Oh my!*

18

The Stakes

Meredith

THE WEEKEND was not what I had hoped for. I thought I would meet Liam at the Rathskeller and have a nice night out. We would walk back to campus and I would drive out to Buxton House. And perhaps I would allow another kiss. Just one. Or two. One taste and I was already addicted.

But strikers pulled me off the street and held me hostage. For a few minutes. Then Liam had burst in like a knight in shining armor and nobly offered himself in exchange for me. *The idiot!* Didn't he know a Leader was worth any number of Advisors? *No. Of course not.* To Liam, all people were worth the same. That was what made him a Leader. No other course of action would have been right.

I put him in this situation. I should have been more careful. Walked with a group instead of alone.

I made a call that was sitting on my list of things he needed. Food for hundreds of strikers.

"David Winzar's residence. This is Jonathan. How may I help you?" Ah, so the Winzar also had a personal assistant.

"Hello, Jonathan. This is Meredith Sauvage. I'm Liam Cyning's personal assistant and wonder if I might have a word with Mr. Winzar."

"Of course, Miss Sauvage. I'll get David." I waited only a moment for David Winzar to come on the line.

"What a delight to meet you again, Meredith. How may help you?"

"Do we know each other?"

"Meredith Sauvage, beautiful redhead assistant to Liam Cyning, efficiently cutting through the crowds of admirers and keeping him in tow."

"Where have we met?"

"The party at Gamma Delta house. I'm sorry it was a brief introduction and I only gave my name as David. Now you know my secret," he laughed. "I was trying to stay out of reach of the queen bee, so sadly I was unable to meet Liam."

"I remember. You were there and then gone. I believe you were the only gentleman present."

"I have other affections and try not to make an ass of myself in public. How can I help you today?"

"Liam has got himself into a bit of a bind and is calling on you as an independent Leader for assistance. Have you heard that he is being held hostage by the striking shoe workers?"

"No, I hadn't. Do I need to go negotiate a release?"

"Nothing like that. He is, I believe, doing the negotiating. But the workers on the picket line are suffering. We've sent over sacks of carrots and apples anonymously, but the workers really need food. I thought perhaps you might know of a pizza delivery service that you could convince to send a hundred pizzas to the workers," I said. I couldn't simply ask him to buy a hundred pizzas, though I knew he probably would.

"I see. Things are that bad? I'll have Jonathan go to work on it right away. They should be there by the evening meal. I hope we can all get together sometime in the near future. I'll be eager to hear of his adventure behind the picket line."

"I'm sure that can be arranged once this difficulty is behind us," I said. "Thank you so much, Mr. Winzar."

"Let's have none of that. We were introduced by first name. Please continue to use it."

"Thank you, David. Good day."

I disconnected, knowing that bit was done. I remembered David as a handsome and pleasant gentleman who might have been the only one in attendance I would have considered going out with. Well, Liam would have pizzas by Sunday dinner. Now what else could I do for him?

Liam

ERICH ARRIVED with the report and my ski jacket and stocking cap. In addition, he had several bags of apples and carrots. The pickets closed around the car
when he told them what he had and shielded a line of people carrying food into
the heart of their camp. Erich told them it had come from a friend of a friend. He
didn't speak to me but gave a nod in my direction.

I hurried back to where the fires were burning and sat to read the annual report.
What I read was staggering. It was impossible to conceive of a company which made
so much money and had workers so poorly cared for. I had very little experience with
these things but I was certain my father treated his employees better than this.

"Randy, there's a reporter at the front line who says she wants to interview
you. Also wants to verify that Mr. Cyning is being treated well." Randy looked up
from where we were studying the report. Davy from the slip-on loafer line was
pointing back toward the pickets. Randy glanced at me and I subtly nodded.

"Right. Well, you say she? Is she alone?"

"She has a guy with her she says is her photographer."

"Okay. Bring them both back here." Davy turned and left. "What are we going
to do?" Randy asked me.

"You, my friend, are going to greet her cordially and be as eloquent as you
can be as she asks you questions. The same as you have been with me. I've just
been getting you ready for this. Whatever happens, it's important that you not
take offense at anything she suggests and that you answer her questions fully. But
avoid the specific demands. This and a few photos of how we are subsisting out
here will be in the Monday newspaper. Probably front page. Up to this time, you
haven't received the coverage you should have. Tomorrow, everyone will know why
you are picketing the factory."

"I get nervous around people of upper classes." Randy wiped his hands on his
knees.

"There are no upper classes, Randy. We all have the fundamental rights to
life, liberty, and the pursuit of happiness. That some classes claim other privileges
based on their wealth does not make them better than you."

"Here she is, Randy." The crowd parted and a woman and her young male
photographer came into the circle. I winced as I recognized the photographer.

"What? Don't any of you have any manners? No introductions? Did you even
ask her name?" All the workers stepped back a step and Randy went directly to the

woman. "I beg your pardon, ma'am. We're not used to seeing people we don't know back here. I'm Randy Peters. I guess you could say I'm the union boss as that's the role my fellow employees have thrust upon me."

"A pleasure to meet you, Mr. Peters. I'm Angela Ritter. This novice with me is my new photographer, Lonnie ah... Ward." I breathed a sigh of relief that my friend had not been identified by the correct last name. Senator Porras had as high a profile in the city as the Cynings did. I wondered how Lonnie had been roped into this and by whom. Then the woman's name sank in. Ritter, as in Susan Ritter, Lonnie's girlfriend.

"We don't have much in the way of furniture, I'm afraid. Would you care to have a seat on one of our folding chairs? Careful. It's a little wobbly." Angela took the proffered seat, sitting on the edge, possibly not putting any weight on the chair at all. She glanced at me but kept her attention focused on Randy.

"Thank you for seeing me. I'm a reporter and have deadlines to meet. So, if you don't mind, can we get directly started?"

Randy nodded to her. "We know a bit about working under pressure. Please go ahead."

"We've not seen a strike in our city in many years. Can you tell me what inspired it?" Randy told about having sent a letter on behalf of the employees to the management and that he had been fired. When he cleared out his locker to leave, all the other employees had followed him. "You must have quite a leadership talent to convince them of that."

"Please, ma'am. I'm just a shoe-laster from the Dexter class. We've been told all our lives that we have no leadership ability."

"Really? What are the demands that you presented to the management which they found so heinous they would fire you?"

"It's a simple list, ma'am. We're falling behind the economy. We simply want to increase our wages to a living level. Second, we need time off when we are sick. We lost a beloved co-worker last year who literally worked herself to death because she couldn't afford not to work while she was sick. We believe machinery and equipment in the plant has suffered from lack of maintenance. This includes chairs for the breakroom, like the one you are carefully sitting on now, but also manufacturing equipment on which safety mechanisms have been broken or disabled. Wouldn't you think a company would want to take care of its own equipment? And finally, we make these shoes and we are proud of them. But none of us can afford to buy a pair. We end up purchasing inferior shoes made by our competitors. Don't you think it would be good for the company to have its employees wearing their product?"

"You are asking excellent questions. Let's delve a little deeper into each of these and into the company's response." Angela was an expert at interviewing and I was glad I'd briefed Randy so fully. But the union leader was handling himself naturally.

"Anything I can do for you?" Lonnie whispered after he'd worked himself nearer to me without appearing to pay attention to me. He raised the camera and clicked another picture of Randy.

"I'm glad to see you. As it happens, it looks like I'm going to need a lawyer."

"Have you committed a crime?" Lonnie couldn't keep amazement from his voice.

"No. Nothing like that. This needs to be a contract lawyer who'll work pro bono on behalf of the union to write and/or check any agreement proposed."

"You don't ask for much, do you? Geez!" Lonnie looked to make sure his reaction hadn't been noticed by anyone else. Angela was intent on Randy as he explained how much previous wage increases had been and what they were told about this year's lack. "If I pull this off, you're really going to owe me."

"I'll forgive you for all the terrible dating advice you've given me." We both choked back a laugh and Lonnie moved to a different photo angle.

"Now, I really need one last thing, Mr. Peters. May I see and speak to Mr. Cyning to assure our readers that he has not been harmed?"

"Of course, Mrs. Ritter. He's been sitting just behind you all this time. Mr. Cyning, would you be kind enough to answer a question from Mrs. Ritter?"

"Certainly." I stood and approached Mrs. Ritter.

"This seems to be a pretty mess you've gotten into. Have you been treated well here?"

"I believe my treatment is no worse and probably no better than the way everyone who walks the picket line is treated. Should I ask for better than that?"

"And where do you sleep at night?"

"Over there. The workers build fires in the drums you see at night. It's getting pretty cold out and they need to take breaks from walking the line to get warm and sometimes to sleep a bit."

"Where is your bed?"

"Would it be proper of me to ask for a bed when everyone around me sleeps on the ground? My jacket is probably warmer than theirs."

Just at that time there was a commotion and Davy came back.

"Randy, there's a pizza delivery truck here. He says he has a hundred pizzas for us."

"What? Who ordered that?"

"No one! It says it comes with compliments from David Winzar of Richmond, Virginia's House Winzar. I think that means he's a Leader."

"Mr. Cyning? Are Leaders banding together to pressure the company?" Angela demanded.

"I've never met this person," I said, not needing to feign surprise. Then a thought struck me. "Wait. I've been reading the company's annual report. Fascinating reading by the way." I picked up the report and began leafing through the pages. "Hmm. Here it is. According to the annual report, Covington Shoe Company faces vigorous competition from three companies. Look. One of them is Dominion Footwear of Richmond, Virginia." I tapped the report.

"Why would a Leader from the area of Dominion Footwear be sending support to the strikers of... Ah! I see," Angela quickly noted the names on her pad.

"It might only be a gesture of goodwill. I could make some calls to find out if a similar situation has occurred there and he's hoping we resolve this one in like manner. After this one is resolved, I mean." *Or my brilliant personal assistant might have contacted him and sold him on the idea of helping out another Leader.*

"Or he might be hoping to prolong the strike to give his local company an edge." Lonnie took pictures of the pizzas arriving and being distributed among the workers. One shoved a box at me.

"You eat, too."

Angela collected Lonnie and pushed him ahead of her as they left.

"**WHAT'S THE BOTTOM** line?" Randy and I had been talking well into the night again and I was even more impressed with Randy's sharp mind.

"Meaning?"

"What would it really take to walk away from the strike with everyone here feeling like they'd won?"

"I don't think that's possible. There are some who wouldn't be satisfied if they doubled all our salaries and gave us six months paid vacation." The men laughed and a few of those standing around tossed out names of people who fell into that category. Randy looked at one of them and motioned him over. "And there are those who would be perfectly happy if the company just said 'Come back to work and we'll forget this all happened.' Bob?" He looked up at the worker who had joined them.

"That would be me. I didn't want to strike in the first place, but I won't go against my friends on this. I'd never cross the picket lines. Things are getting pretty tight around my house. Them carrots and apples that showed up this morning? I've tossed a few in my bag to take home to the missus and kiddos. I don't want them to suffer any more than they have to."

"I wish it was in my power to provide for you all. No matter what you hear about the wealth of my family, neither I nor my counterpart who sent pizzas could make up what you are losing during the strike. It would take a Promoter to do that! And he'd want you to work in a factory." The guys all laughed. "So, those are the extremes. What would get most of the guys out here to go back to work next week and say, 'We won!' I need to know where the bargaining begins."

"I think our original list of requests is pretty close. I suppose if the wage increase came down a nickel, we'd accept that. If the safety standards were met on the machines, we'd manage to sit on the floor in the break room. We've lived for years not wearing our own shoes. I don't think we'd miss them in the future. The sick days, though, that's not an option. The wound of Molly's death is still raw and open. There was nearly a walkout that day."

"So, you'd sacrifice a little of the other demands in order to get that one. That's good. It shows you're already thinking of negotiating. What I'd like to do is set the starting bar a little higher. According to the annual report, the company is cash-rich and highly profitable. There is no reason I can think of that they wouldn't give a wage increase. It says here there are 6,000 employees. The company had $400 million in profitability last year. This request only comes to about three percent of their net profit. I think we can double that. Now, keep in mind this significant point of negotiating: Our initial offer has to be higher than the company will go but still sound reasonable. They will automatically come back with a lower offer. So, we don't want to start at the bottom line or we'll walk away losing. I think we should start with a dollar an hour wage increase. If we have to back off all the way to a quarter, we still win, right?"

"Clever. I get it. We have to give the company room to dicker."

"Right. Now as to the furnishings, how many people use the breakroom? It must be enormous."

"No. Most people go outside and eat on the bumpers of their cars—or in their cars if the weather is bad. And there are four breakrooms. The worse the furniture in them gets, the better a car looks. The real bottom line, though, is getting the safety equipment fixed."

"We've got that. But someone is going to get injured when one of these chairs collapses. An on-the-job injury is different than being sick and not having time off. If you have witnesses that say you were doing nothing wrong, the company could end up in a lot of financial trouble. We'll position this as saving the company from liability suits and ask that the breakroom be expanded to include a cafeteria where people can buy meals and have a nice place to eat their lunch. I don't think we'll get a cafeteria but we might get a larger breakroom or even some shelters outside with picnic tables."

"I'd never have thought of something like that. I'm not sure we should let the guys see this list before the bargaining starts. It'll raise their expectations and then they'll feel like they've lost when we get what we originally asked for."

"You're being smart, Randy. That's exactly what we don't want to happen. Sick time is a non-negotiable item, so let's build something around it we're willing to sacrifice. How about we ask for two weeks of sick time and two weeks of vacation time each year? Let me get these thoughts down. I think you're leaving more on the table than you intended to and we should make sure we've covered everything."

When I was finished, the list was longer than Randy's original list. Randy wondered at it but agreed to take it home for his wife to type up. I slept another uncomfortable night on the ground, but at least my ski jacket kept me warmer.

"MR. CYNING," DAVY said as he approached. "A Mr. Erich just showed up and told us to bring you the newspaper. Said it was important. He brought us sacks of oranges, too. Nice guy."

"Thank you, Davy. If Erich considered it important enough to get me the newspaper at this hour, I should look at it." Davy handed me the paper and began peeling an orange. I sat to read. The article was on the front page with a four-column photo that caught Randy, Mrs. Ritter, and me all in a good composition. I might need to compliment Lonnie on his photographic skills. I looked up at Davy. "Is Randy around?"

"He's out walking the line. That's one thing about Randy. He's our boss but whatever we need to do, he does, too."

"He should see this. Can you ask him to come here? He *needs* to see this. I don't think I should be seen out there, though."

"Right. Be right back."

I finished the article and nodded just as Davy returned with Randy.

"What's up?"

"The article from your interview is in this morning's newspaper. Mrs. Ritter was diligent in following up. She interviewed both Mr. Ferguson and Mr. Winzar." I handed the newspaper to Randy and turned to Davy. "Is Erich still waiting?"

"Yes, sir."

"I need to get a note to him. Randy, it looks like we are going to the negotiating table."

"This is stupid! He says he can't get in touch with us and if we don't turn up at the bargaining table in the board room tomorrow morning, he'll assume the strike is over and we should go back to work. He didn't try to get a message to us!"

"No, of course not. He's using the news to do his messaging. How many of you usually read the newspaper?"

"I do but I left the house before it got there this morning."

"He might have counted on no one seeing the message and then would have told the papers he tried but you didn't show up."

"What do we do?"

"I need to get this note to Erich." Randy looked over my shoulder.

"Gray suit, white shirt, red tie, and new Covington shoes? What…?"

"Do you have a suit, Randy?"

"Well, yes. We usually go to church on Sunday. Not always but pretty regular."

"You'll need to wear it tomorrow for the bargaining session. Did you get the new letter typed up?"

"Yes. Sally, my wife, was very impressed and I explained the reasoning that it wasn't really what we were going to get but was what we would start bargaining with. She was a little disappointed."

"That's why we aren't spreading it around. I need my suit as well."

"You wouldn't put a good suit on without showering, would you? We need to get you cleaned up. Davy, take the note to that Erich guy. Are we ready for this, Liam?"

"I don't know. We need to study the notes and think of every question Mr. Ferguson might ask."

"Why would he ask any questions? Doesn't he just tell us what he'll do?"

"Not the way he thinks. He'll start by asking questions and try to get you to admit that what you have written isn't what he should give you."

"I can't do this, Liam. I don't have any experience or know anything about negotiating." I looked at my friend. I thought I had instilled enough confidence in Randy to get him through this, but the man was out of his depth. "Can't you negotiate this for us?" It was what I wanted to do but I didn't want to suggest they couldn't do it for themselves. The idea of going head-to-head with Fergie excited me. Did I really have it in me to do a labor contract negotiation?

"Randy, I can be the spokesperson if you want, but you need to be right beside me. Every time he asks a question, I'll quietly consult with you. Then I'll answer his question. That way he'll know you are the one calling the shots."

"I trust you but I see why he needs to think it's me. I wish I could do this."

"You'll get more experience. Me? I've been in school all my life. I've been educated to do this but don't have any experience either. We'll get through it together."

I CAME UP with every question I could think of and Randy helped compose answers. I wasn't sure how we could prepare any better.

"Randy, Mr. Cyning. There's a gentleman and a lady to see you. Should we let him through?" Davy had become the official runner between Randy and anyone else who was needed.

"Did he say who he was and what he wanted?"

"Just said he's a lawyer."

I silently blessed Lonnie. "He's expected."

"And the lady?"

"Probably his stenographer."

A few moments later the two approached. The lawyer carried a briefcase and his companion carried a small case I identified as a portable typewriter.

"Mr. Peters. Mr. Cyning. I'm Alfred Smith, attorney at law. This is my secretary, Miss Loveland." I nudged Randy so he'd take the lead.

"I'm Randy Peters and this is Liam Cyning. I guess you know that. What can we do for you?"

"I'm here to help you, I hope. A mutual friend suggested you were going to need a contract lawyer. I'm here to offer my services."

"We don't have the money for a lawyer." Randy shuffled his feet.

"This is a pro bono offer. Uh... I shouldn't just use legal terms. Sorry. It means we're doing it for goodwill. I mean for free."

"Thank you for your consideration, but I understood the term. Liam? What's this about?" Randy asked.

"We'll need a signed agreement when we leave the bargaining table. It's the only guarantee we'll have that they'll honor what we agree to. Mr. Smith has kindly offered to provide the service of drafting it," I said.

"This is all overwhelming. Thank you, both. All three," Randy said.

"Right. I was told you have a typed document with the demands."

"Rick. Paul. Clear the card table so Miss Loveland can use her typewriter. We've got work to be done before morning. Do we have four chairs that are safe?" Randy called out.

People scurried around getting a couple more chairs and clearing the table. It was a little wobbly but Miss Loveland pronounced it good enough.

Randy and I sat opposite Smith as he read the typed page of new demands.

"This is good. It has the all basic words in it. Miss Loveland, please type another copy with two carbons. Now, who is going to negotiate?"

I raised my hand. "I'm afraid that privilege falls to me."

"You're young but Lonnie tells me you've been trained for this. Understand that you can turn to consult with me at any point. In fact, if you just need a minute to consider something, turn to me and take a minute. Don't feel forced to respond instantly and don't stammer around while organizing yourself. Silence is better than stuttering."

"Thank you for the advice. Good reminders." I'd heard all this in various courses but hearing a lawyer give the same advice reinforced the concepts and brought them to the fore. "How will we handle the contract terms?"

"Miss Loveland is an expert stenographer. She'll use shorthand to keep track of everything said in the meeting. We'll also keep notes. During our breaks, she'll type up the terms agreed upon and I'll start drafting the contract. It will take between half an hour and an hour to have copies of your contract prepared after the meeting concludes. I'm anticipating they won't have prepared for a formal agreement because they assume that meeting with you is all they need to do to satisfy the strike. I would guess Mr. Ferguson has prepared 'a stern talking-to' for his part of the meeting."

"My objective is a win-win. Can we keep the agreement phrased in non-inflammatory words?"

"Absolutely. Now let's look at the parts of the contract and how we want them worded."

It was a difficult afternoon and evening as we hammered out acceptable phrasing for each of the articles we wanted in the agreement. At the end of the evening, all we needed was to fill in the blanks with the final terms.

19

Winning

Liam

"LIAM, YOU NEED A SHOWER."

"Not much chance of that happening, Randy. Is there an outdoor faucet and a hose around?"

"I think I know a better way. The guys need to believe you're here as a proper hostage. I think I can get you out to my house, get you a shower, and get back before anyone is the wiser. Can you rise early?"

"I'm usually up by five."

"I was thinking four."

"Let's get some sleep then."

The plan worked flawlessly. I gave my ski jacket and University stocking cap to a guy about the same size as me who immediately lay down next to the fire barrel and went to sleep. Or appeared to. I left in Randy's car and, in the darkness, no one saw me. I hoped.

Sally Peters had a hearty breakfast for us when I came out of the shower. She was hospitable and not overly solicitous. She took her cues from Randy and greeted me as her husband's friend and nothing special. We'd been gone just an hour when I nudged my stand-in awake and took back my coat. At eight o'clock, Erich arrived with my suit and a newspaper. Soon after, Smith and Loveland arrived.

"Ah, good. You have a paper. Did you see the response?"

"It's like answering a challenge to a duel. 'The Shoemakers' Union will arrive at the appointed time and place. They will be accompanied by William Thomas Cyning as agreed upon in the terms of coming to the table. All items of concern will be presented at that time. We wish to thank the management and owners of Covington Shoe Company for agreeing to hear our grievances.' Are we ready for this?" I looked at my three companions.

"You look like a corporate executive yourself, Liam. No. You look better than most corporate executives. I'd peg you as a Leader at once," Smith said.

"Thank you, Mr. Smith. We need every advantage we can muster."

"Shall we head for the board room then?" Randy took a deep breath and nodded. He was obviously nervous, but we were on our way.

"LIAM! IT'S GOOD to see they kept their word." Ferguson said as we entered. "Well, conditions have been met. We have all come to the table. Come ahead, boy. We can leave now."

"Have they really been met, sir? Did you not promise to meet and hear their grievances?"

"Not exactly. We promised to come to the bargaining table. That's done."

"Do you generally conduct your business with deception and cheating?"

"You don't have a comprehension of business, Liam. You need to keep the other side off their stride."

"Why don't you show me how it's done, sir?" Fergie had to know I was goading him but he was far too proud to back down.

"Well, that would be a pleasure. Let's take our seats and have at this then." Ferguson sat at the center seat at the table and the two people with him looked surprised but sat as well. I walked around the table and sat opposite Ferguson. "Liam, that chair would be for the negotiator for the union. I can't be craning my neck to look around the table for him."

"Yes, sir." I calmly folded my hands on the table.

"Oh. You?"

"Is this not an appropriate venue for us to continue our discussion?"

"Very cleverly played. Please tell me who the people seated with you are. I assume one at least is from the esteemed Shoemakers' Union."

"Yes, sir. On my right is Randy Peters, shoe-laster, drafted by the employees as their union leader. On my left is Alfred Smith, our contract attorney. At the end of the table, our stenographer, Miss Loveland. And your lieutenants?"

"You surprise me at every turn. Very well. On my left is Leland Bennet, our Vice President of Operations. On my right is Arnold Rice, our Corporate Attorney. Now what are these demands the workers are making?"

"Have you not read the letter, sir?"

"No, no. When management brought up the issue, I simply told them to handle it and get rid of the problem."

"Let us present you with a fresh copy. We have prepared one for each of you." Smith handed the copies across the table.

"Very professionally done."

"Our stenographer was kind enough to type copies."

Ferguson read the paper, becoming more agitated as he read. Finally, he exploded.

"What? You can't expect me to take this seriously! This is not at all what I was told the asks were. This is way out of line!"

"Would you mind breaking that out a point at a time and telling me what is out of line?"

"A dollar an hour wage increase? That would be a substantial hit on our bottom line. We cannot afford that kind of labor increase."

"According to the annual report, the company had a net profit of $400 million last year. This represents a $12.5 million increase in expenses—just three percent. Is this what you consider a significant hit?"

"You have misinterpreted the numbers. Last year was an aberrant year. Various factors impacted our profitability that will not be in effect this year. Our net will be drastically reduced."

"Drastically? Can a company that drops drastically from $400 million in net profit to, say, $100 million even be considered as viable? Is Covington Shoe Company going out of business?"

"No! Nothing like that. We'll be a hundred million below last year. The shareholders are aware of this," he said. I needed to be wary. I knew Ferguson was an expert at this and even if he was willing to negotiate with me, he wouldn't be easily satisfied. It was likely that his 'drastic' reduction was no more than the union's demand.

"And we are asking for only four percent more. Am I correct in computing a $12.5 million impact on $300 million net at four percent?"

"That's simply too much of an impact on the bottom line. I'm a magnanimous man but I'm dealing with the money of my shareholders. I would have considered the twenty-five cents an hour I heard was originally proposed but this is ridiculous."

I felt Smith tap my leg and leaned over to the attorney so he could whisper in my ear. "He'll go higher. It's a gambit." I nodded and faced Ferguson.

"My attorney is very fast with math and has given me the numbers. Let me ask, Mr. Ferguson, what is the most valuable asset Covington Shoes has?"

"We have three primary assets. The real estate, including buildings, the machinery, and our raw materials," Ferguson said.

"And how big a liability do those items become if there are no workers to turn raw materials into shoes using the machinery in these buildings? No one here wants to cost the company its profitability, but assets have a value. Considering that, wouldn't you think seventy-five cents an hour would be a just compensation for what is really your most valuable asset?" I asked.

"I agree the workforce is valuable but there is a limit to what anyone will pay for an asset." He paused and scowled at me. I tried not to flinch. "Fifty cents and not a penny more." I turned to Randy and asked if that was adequate. Randy was struck silent and simply nodded.

"Miss Loveland, please record a fifty-cents per hour increase across the board as our agreement," I said. Ferguson looked at the secretary.

"Yes, Mr. Cyning."

The negotiations proceeded. Not everything went as smoothly as I had hoped. The equipment maintenance was approved with little discussion. Ferguson admitted that most of the faulty equipment had been replaced during the strike. He balked, however at improving the break area as simply being something the company did as a kind gesture. I argued that employees who left the building were the most often tardy returning to their stations. After Smith explained what he would sue for should a client become injured on the job and suggesting a dollar value for the gained productive time by keeping employees onsite, Ferguson finally agreed to replace the furniture but no more.

I barely got what the original document asked for in sick leave. "We can't be paying people to not work," Ferguson complained. He agreed to one week of vacation and one week of sick leave.

"Now this, you must agree, is simply frivolous. A free pair of shoes every year? That is the equivalent of increasing pay yet again. We have a compensation agreement in place on that."

"I can see your point," I agreed. I'd given this a lot of thought and even surveyed a number of strikers about the idea, asking them what shoes they wore to work. "What if this could be set up and have it not cost the company?"

"How can I give away a free pair of shoes and have it not cost anything?"

"When I was behind the picket line the past three days, I had the privilege of talking to many of the people—your employees—who were out there. They are fiercely proud of their work. Covington Shoes. They believe they are the best-made shoes in the world. But as I looked around, I saw that no one was wearing Covington Shoes. I'm wearing Covington Shoes, why aren't your employees?" I raised one foot above the table to display my new top-of-the-line pair of Covington Shoes. I'd only worn them once to the concert several weeks ago and Erich had seen to it that they were polished like a mirror.

"These are quality shoes. I would frankly expect a Cyning to wear nothing less," Fergie said. I knew my father wore Covington shoes and that Fergie would know it.

"Quality built by those employees. I asked a worker about why he was wearing Dominion Footwear. Can you imagine striking against Covington Shoes while wearing Dominion Footwear? I asked why and he told me Dominion Footwear was priced thirty percent below Covington shoes. If it weren't for that, he'd be wearing Covington shoes. Maybe not these top-of-the-line dress shoes, but certainly the casual or work shoes produced here."

"You can't possibly suggest we cut our prices by thirty percent. Let's go back to the scenario where you asked what would happen if a company went from $400 million to $100 million in profit in a year. An outright rebellion of the stockholders! There would be a sell-off of Covington Shoes stock and the price would plunge," Ferguson practically shouted.

"When a person walks into a shoe store to buy a pair of Covington shoes like I did just a few weeks ago, what was the markup of that pair of shoes? Certainly, Browning's wasn't selling them at cost, were they?"

"No, of course not. We sell wholesale. The typical retail margin is forty to forty-five percent."

"So why not offer a direct sale to employees at wholesale plus ten percent? That would put you at exactly the same price point as Dominion Footwear. For your employees only. You would still be earning more per pair from sales to your employees than from wholesale to retailers."

"And the next thing we would have is a worker selling shoes to his friends and relatives because he got them at a thirty percent discount." Ferguson sat back with his arms folded.

"Bravo! Yes! Let's let that happen!" I struck my hands lightly on the table.

"What?"

"Every pair sold to an employee represents a sale you do not currently have. Not just 6,000 per year, but perhaps a pair for each member of his or her family. Let's say 24,000 per year. But not only do you have a sale you did not previously have, you also have a ten percent markup over wholesale. It is more profitable to sell to your own employees than to your retailers. Isn't that worth some consideration? If an enterprising worker starts selling the shoes on the side, perhaps he should be moved into sales and be considered in the Promoter class rather than Dexter. Wouldn't those sales still be more than what you had before?"

"You're telling me that giving a discount to my employees for shoes bought direct will increase my bottom line?" Fergie grabbed a pad of paper from his attorney and started scrawling some numbers while we waited. "Damn it, Liam! That's brilliant. I agree. Miss Loveland, please record our agreement that employees will be able to buy direct from our Covington Shoes company store at ten percent over wholesale. I can't wait until I tell the board about this. Liam, you should become a Promoter."

I'd achieved all I was going to. Ferguson was happy with his win. The union would be happy with their win. I needed to walk away, but...

"There is one last thing," I said with a sigh.

"What? We have covered every point on the workers list of demands. I can't see what else would be necessary," Fergie said.

"This whole strike was caused by a simple letter with a request to bargain. It was suggested and reviewed by all the employees but it got the employee who signed the letter on their behalf fired. That employee is sitting beside me. When he walked out of the door, all the employees of Covington Shoes followed. Mr. Ferguson, I've suggested that your workers are an asset, but how much more of an asset is an employee who commands such loyalty and leadership? This is not on your letter but I am asking you personally. Will you please, reinstate Mr. Randy Peters as an employee with all benefits, back pay, and seniority restored? I ask this because I believe you are a just and honorable man who runs a great company and can afford to be magnanimous."

Ferguson looked at me for a long time. He turned to the company lawyer to consult with him. Finally, he turned to his vice president of operations before returning to me.

"I want you to know that hiring back a worker who was terminated for cause is never a good idea. But I see your point. As a personal favor to you, we will grant this request. Miss Loveland, please record that we have agreed Mr. Peters will be reinstated on his job with full benefits, backpay, and seniority. Can we call this meeting to an end?"

"If we may take a break, our agreement will be typed in half an hour and we can sign it as agreed pending union and board approval." Fergie looked at me and simply nodded his head.

Meredith

LIAM HAD SENT WORD to Erich that he needed his suit. Erich showed me the note. It wasn't worded the way Liam would have done even a week ago. Instead of asking for clothes suitable for a corporate meeting, he itemized exactly what he wanted. Suit, shirt, tie, and shoes. Liam was showing he had the situation under control and was making the decisions.

He was acting like a Leader.

My phone ringing startled me so much I froze in place wondering if this was Liam calling to say he was free. *Foolish.* It rang again and I rushed to answer it.

"Hello. This is Meredith Sauvage. How may I help you?"

"Meredith, it's Regina. I'm planning a party and would like your assistance."

"A party? Now?"

"Yes. We'll need to celebrate Liam's victory."

"You've heard? Has he won?"

"Dear Meredith, you don't understand how this works. *Everyone* wins."

"Yes, ma'am." No, I did not understand. This was a layer of Leaders I had not been shown before.

"Now, let's have the party on the Saturday after Thanksgiving. That will give things a chance to settle down. It will be a larger party than Liam's birthday, so we'll serve food from the buffet in the ballroom."

"I'll coordinate it with cook, Ma'am."

"I'd like you to help with the invitations since all the mportant guests are people you know."

"Really?"

"Yes. Your classmates, Miss Ransom and Miss Reese, with their parents, of course. Lonnie Porras and his sweetheart. Let's make sure both of their parents are invited. Miss Ritter's mother has been influential in this matter."

"His other school friends from Elenchus as well?" I asked.

"Yes. At least the two who came to the gathering you had in August. Liam expressed some desire that the next time we had a gathering in his honor, he would like it attended by his friends. I think he has made some new friends since then."

"Yes, of course. Should I assume you would also like Mr. Winzar to attend?" I said. I was beginning to see what she was after now. Everyone Liam had been in touch with the past three months would count as a new friend. I wondered about Carolyn Dubois and John Berringer.

"Oh! What a wonderful suggestion. I see you are understanding the process. Please indicate each is welcome to bring a guest and his or her parents if they happen to be in town. Now, who else?"

"Mr. and Mrs. Ferguson, of course."

"Yes. And don't forget *your* parents, dear." Regina's enthusiasm was contagious. I was scribbling down names as quickly as I could.

"Thank you, ma'am. And Richard and Donnie's parents. They'll need to get leave in order to travel home."

"I leave the rest to you, Meredith. I—and the University—will understand if you don't make it to classes this week. I don't think we'll send Liam back to Elenchus just now."

"I'll do my best, madam."

"I have always believed you would."

I collapsed in my desk chair. I'd been given a task by the matriarch. Perhaps it was nothing more than busywork to keep me active but it was work from Regina Cyning. I needed to get used to this. Regina's confidence that everyone would win was compelling. I'd been stewing with worry since Liam showed up behind the picket line. One day soon, Liam would give me tasks like this so I needed to get things in order and show I'm capable of handling them.

"MR. WINZAR, THIS is Meredith Sauvage calling."

"A delight. How may I help you? Another hundred pizzas?"

"No, the call is a simple thank you for the part you played in ending the strike. I'm sure Mr. Cyning will want to express his thanks personally," I said.

"Then you and he had better get used to calling me David. I could see his strategy from a mile away. When that reporter called, it was all I could do to keep from laughing. Do I take it that it's over?"

"They are still in negotiations, which I am told is a good sign. There will be a formal invitation, of course, but Liam is planning a holiday party in celebration and would like to entertain you and a guest on Saturday after Thanksgiving. He extends this invitation as well to your parents, should they be visiting for the holiday."

"As it happens my parents *will* be here. Would you mind terribly addressing the invitation to them at my address?" he asked.

"I will be delighted. Oh, and David, I assume you have good sources of information but we believe in sharing news we hear if we deem it important. As you know, Liam will join us at the university in January."

"Yes."

"I have recently been informed that Miss Elizabeth Kendrick will also begin at mid-term."

"Ah, yes. I recognize the name from something my parents said this summer. So, the gathering of the eligibles has begun. Well, perhaps I'll be lucky this time and discover she's a lesbian," he said.

"I beg your pardon, sir?" *Why on earth would he want the new student to be a lesbian?*

"As you will discover soon enough, Meredith, my predilection is toward my own gender. It would be convenient to find a wife who also had that bent. I'm sure we could still manage a conception, but we wouldn't need to depend on each other for recreation."

"I will keep my eyes open for someone who might fill the position. Please feel free to bring a guest of either gender to the party. No one will object."

"Thank you. Good day, Meredith."

"Good day, David." I busied myself composing the invitations. They would need to be handwritten, of course. It would be impolite to send typed invitations to a formal party.

"MISS SAUVAGE. MISS Sauvage." Lupe knocked insistently on my door. I needed to remind the poor woman that if the door was unlocked, she should just come in. I opened the door.

"What is it, Lupe?"

"Mr. Cyning called Erich to come and get him. The negotiations are finished. He said Mr. Ferguson is calling the press to meet at the picket line. You may want to watch the news."

"Watch? Indeed! I need to impress upon Mr. Cyning who his personal assistant is. I suppose Erich has left already." *Why on earth didn't he call me? I should have been the one to pick him up, or at least have ridden with Erich.*

"Yes, Miss. The family is gathering in the lounge to watch the conference and invite you to watch with them."

"I... I'll join them at once."

I was always comfortable with Liam. His grandmother was charming and always welcoming. We were getting on well. His parents, however, seemed remote or a bit standoffish. I didn't think they actively disliked me, but they still made me nervous. I hurried to the lounge. Regina was also just arriving.

"Mother! Just in time. They've just broken into regular programming. Meredith, please fix yourself a drink. Mother, the usual?" Thomas asked.

"I can get my own. Don't disturb anyone to wait on me," Regina answered.

"Brian is behind the bar already, Mother. He might as well mix your drink." Brian, in fact, rushed up to Regina with a martini and presented it to her.

"Thank you, Brian."

"Always my pleasure, Mrs. Cyning."

I had just reached the bar when Brian returned. He sent me to the front of the bar.

"No matter what the boss says, Miss Sauvage, when I am tending bar, I fix drinks for everyone. What can I make for you?"

"I'd almost join in the martinis but I think I'd better stick to non-alcoholic beverages for now. A tonic and lemon?"

"You're an easy one to mix for. Oh, look. The people are getting in front of the microphones." He finished pouring my drink and deftly twisted a lemon wedge into the glass. Then we moved closer to the television.

"THIS HAS BEEN a very long day. Of course, for some of you gathered here it has been much longer than a day. Your dedication and perseverance are noted." Ferguson had been the first to step up to the microphones and was trying to put everyone at ease. Most of the audience comprised striking employees. "I am happy to say, however, that after hours of bargaining, we have arrived at a solution I believe will please both the workers and the shareholders. Mr. Peters and I have signed an agreement that is ready for both union and board ratification. Yes. You have heard me right. We live in a world ruled by agreements, yet it strikes me as strange that in our closest relationship—that of employer and employee—we have never put pen to paper to formalize our relationship. This agreement spells out the settlement terms as well as steps forward that will enable us to keep pace with the economy and make sure our workers are fairly compensated as times change. When this agreement is ratified, we hope to never see a strike nor the necessity for one again." The workers seemed a little hesitant in their applause, but hopeful. "I would like your own spokesperson to address you at this time. Mr. Randy Peters."

I recognized the man from my brief time in captivity. He seemed like a fair enough man who was truly appalled that his fellow workers would kidnap someone off the street to hold as hostage. I felt he might have sent me home regardless of Liam showing up. I made a mental note to invite him to the party.

"Hi, guys. I guess you heard from Mr. Ferguson that we settled. We agreed not to talk about the specific terms in front of the cameras but I can tell you that Mr. Ferguson has agreed to terms as good or better than we originally asked. I believe this means good things for our working relationship in the future and we can once again take great pride in the shoes we produce and the company we work for. With a signed agreement, we can all return to work in the morning and you'll have an opportunity to review the agreement and vote to ratify." The workers let out a genuine cheer and applauded loudly. Ferguson stepped back to the microphones and placed a hand on Randy's shoulder.

"Please understand that at such short notice we cannot provide printed copies of the agreement immediately. Typewritten copies have been provided for the press and I am assured there will be printed copies available for all employees at the door tomorrow. Your representative and negotiator have done well for you. I'm happy to say we worked as a team. I will also say that Mr. Cyning, falsely reported as being a hostage, has been a welcome guest of both the workers and of Covington Shoes. He plans to return to his home now. Which is what we all should do. Let's be fresh when we clock in tomorrow morning."

There was more applause and cheering as the reporters tried in vain to ask questions. Ferguson, Randy, and Liam all turned their backs on the cameras and left with many workers slapping their backs and thanking them.

20

Homecoming

Meredith

"SO, LIAM SUCCEEDED in talking some sense into those strikers," Thomas said, raising his glass. Brian hurried forward with fresh martinis. "Fergie seems happy and the workers pleased with an agreement they don't even know the terms of yet." Thomas and Lydia laughed and toasted each other. Regina smiled and turned to me.

"We're having dinner in the dining room this evening. You and Erich will also attend. Please refresh your drink and keep me company until they get here."

"Yes, ma'am. Thank you. I was hoping I could greet Liam when he arrived," I said.

"Perhaps not in the fashion you would like," Regina laughed. "But you will be with the family."

Thomas took a call in the study and returned shortly to the lounge.

"Fergie says Liam acquitted himself well today. He sounded almost as proud of the boy as I am. Did anyone notice, by the way, that he was wearing a suit and tie? They looked new. You don't suppose he went out shopping while he was held hostage, do you?" Lydia laughed at her husband's lightheartedness. They turned to me. "Do you know anything about the suit?"

"If I am not mistaken, that is the suit Liam acquired just before school started as part of his fall wardrobe. Perhaps he has not had an opportunity to wear it before now," I said.

"Of course." Lydia toasted her husband again. "No doubt when the news of the meeting came out, his valet convinced the strikers to let him change. That would be just like Erich. Always thinking ahead." I just smiled and nodded my head. I didn't think it would make a difference if I told them Liam sent a note instructing Erich with exactly what clothes he wanted for the meeting.

"You must remember, dear," Regina whispered to me, "you are dealing with Promoters here." She took my elbow and led me back to the bar. "Have an appetizer, Meredith. You needn't be nervous. Promoters place a price tag on everything and have determined the exact value of Erich as their son's valet and you as his personal assistant. Apparently, Mr. Ferguson did not explain the extent of Liam's involvement. I think we can safely say, Thomas and Lydia will remain in blissful ignorance until he does."

The four of us continued to chat as we had hors d'oeuvres and either Thomas or Lydia was continually called out of the room to talk to an associate or friend calling to congratulate them on Liam's release. To a one, they considered the release to be the accomplishment of Thomas and Lydia. Lupe came into the room and whispered to Brian before rushing out again. Brian rang a small bell on the bar.

"Ladies and gentlemen, I am informed that Master Liam has just arrived."

Everyone moved to the hallway and we awaited Liam's entrance. I snickered to myself, thinking Liam might well come in from the garage with Erich. It seemed Regina understood exactly what I was thinking.

"No matter how much he would wish it, Liam will not disappoint his parents on his return home. Erich wouldn't let him. He will come in... just... about... now." The old woman proved psychic as Liam opened the door and family and staff applauded his entry.

"My son, the survivor, the conqueror, and the young Leader of our family—a Promoter's Promoter." Thomas made a rare display of embracing his son and turning him directly to his mother for like treatment. As soon as he was free, Liam embraced his grandmother and then turned to face me. I flowed into his open arms for a warm embrace that was all too brief.

He released me and we all went back to the lounge. Erich arrived from the kitchen at the same time and quietly blended in. I saw, however, that he was merely a step behind Regina just as I stationed myself behind Liam as he told of his adventure.

"It was a bit chilly at night. I mean, it *is* November. But Erich delivered my ski jacket and wool knit hat. It wasn't so bad then." Liam explained what the conditions were in the camp.

"On the ground? You slept on the ground?"

"It was like going camping, Mother. We had a nice campfire that was fed throughout the night and I shared the same conditions as the workers. It was that, in part, that allowed me to win their trust and let me guide them."

"Fergie was pleased. He said you did well and that is a good enough recommendation for me. He said, and I quote, 'I wish he were a Promoter or even a Commander. But, of course, he could no longer be a Leader then.' We had a good laugh at that." Thomas was on his third martini as far as I had observed. He may have started earlier.

Dinner was peaceable. Liam's father continued to laud praises on his son but it was obvious he didn't really know what Liam's role had been. And, he was becoming quite drunk. Finally, Regina saw fit to intervene.

"Lydia, we are obviously all exhausted. Poor Liam is nearly asleep in his chair. Why don't you and Thomas go to your suite for a nightcap and let the rest of us retire as well."

"Yes, Mother Cyning. I believe that is a good idea," Lydia said. She wasn't much more stable than her husband. Thomas stood shakily and Brian moved in to help Lydia support him as they moved to their suite.

"You've seen your father in a rare condition. He was truly very worried about you, Liam. Let us say he over-celebrated."

"Indeed, Grandmother. I hope he is fully recovered tomorrow. Oh, my. I suppose I need to get some sleep so I can get back to school tomorrow. It will be nice to sleep in a bed."

"Don't worry about that. I believe that after your adventure, you should stay here for the remainder of the week. And it is soon a holiday, so let's just say we are starting yours early. We have a lot of holiday planning to do."

"Thank you, Grandmother."

"You do look very handsome in that suit, by the by. Excellent taste. Goodnight, Liam. Goodnight, Meredith. Erich, would you escort me to my chamber?"

"Certainly, madam."

"Goodnight, Grandmother. Sleep well."

LIAM AND I strolled into the lounge. The dishes were being cleared from the dining room and staff bustled in and out but he led me by the hand to a loveseat as we talked softly. Brian brought a tray from the kitchen.

"Cook fixed your favorite baked brie, Master Liam. He said it seemed a shame everyone left the table before cheese and coffee. May I pour for you?"

"Thank you, Brian. Please tell Cook thank you from me as well. We do like his baked brie." Liam handed a cup of hot coffee to me and we each took a sip. "I know we should eat the brie, but all I want is to feast on your lips," he said. I nearly swooned and set the cup on the table before letting him lift my lips to his own. I was lost.

"Liam, I was so worried about you. Please, don't ever offer yourself in trade for me again. I couldn't have lived if anything bad happened to you."

"I understand your feeling, but I've suddenly come to understand what Leaders do."

"Really? Let us not disappoint Cook. Tell me about your epiphany while we have some cheese." Liam cut wedges from the pastry covered cheese and served me, then himself.

"When I was first told I was a Leader, I thought, 'What a waste.' Every other class, even Promoters, has a function. Yet Leaders don't produce anything. It seemed like an unneeded remnant of a bygone era. But I think I see what Grandmother was telling me about leading. We bring people together. I was able to lead the workers to a reasonable position. I was able to lead Ferguson to see how the workers' demands would benefit him in the long run. I negotiated a settlement between them that both were pleased with."

"You? Liam, do you mean...?"

"Yes. Fergie was a bit surprised when I sat opposite him at the table but he soon warmed to the idea, basically challenging me to a battle of wits and wills."

"That... and the workers let you represent them?"

"Yes. Isn't it amazing?"

"You are amazing!" I kissed him again and then rushed off to my room. It would not do to have the staff catch us making out in the lounge.

WHEN I ROSE in the morning, I went straight to work. Each invitation needed to be written in my best hand. I was sure other people simply typed invitations or didn't bother with them at all and used the telephone. That was not the case with the Cyning household. I clearly remembered the invitation I'd received to Liam's eighteenth birthday party. I had opened it with anticipation and thrilled to the contents. I was certain it was penned in Regina Cyning's own hand and it was her indication to me that I had been chosen as Liam's assistant. It was one of my most treasured possessions.

I called the kitchen and had breakfast delivered to my study. I didn't abuse that privilege, but Lupe was happy to bring it to me. As I ate and drank my coffee, I perused the guestlist and added the names of Randy and Sally Peters. Liam had spoken so highly of them that I couldn't help but think they were special and should be included on this list. Thinking I might spice things up a bit, I added the name of my former roommate, Hana Ito and guest.

At half past twelve, the phone rang.

"Meredith, will you have lunch with me? I'm afraid I've been so busy this morning I have neglected you. Please forgive me and join me for a bite to eat."

"Liam, you're so formal. Of course, I'll join you. Shall I meet you in the hall?"

"I need to wash and put on a clean shirt first. I'll knock at your door as soon as I'm ready. Until then."

"Yes, Liam."

I hung up the phone and went to my dressing room/bathroom. I looked at myself in the mirror and adjusted my makeup and hair slightly. Liam was putting on a clean shirt, so I quickly changed blouses. I studied myself critically, surprised at how anxious I was to please him. A few moments later, a light knock on my door brought me to attention and I opened it to find Liam, casually dressed in slacks and a polo shirt. He looked rather yummy and I took his arm as we went to the kitchen nook where Cook was setting out bowls of soup.

"Thank you for letting me get so much work done this morning. I had a lengthy phone conversation with the contractor working on our apartments. I'm certain he was capable of approving the marble tile, the kitchen layout, and on and on. I don't know why he needed my approval for every single thing," I said.

"You don't suppose the agent told him my name."

"That would explain a lot. I suggest we pay a visit to inspect the property. How about tomorrow afternoon?" I asked.

"As long as we don't give the poor man and his crew—what did your father call it?—apoplexy." We laughed and agreed to wear blue jeans and casual shirts. "I had a long hard run this morning. It felt good to be outside, even though I waited until the sun came up to get started. Then Grandmother met me and told me to call Mr. Peoples at school for my final assignment."

"What is your assignment? May I help?"

"I would appreciate your assistance when you're available. I'm to do an analysis of the labor dispute, tracking from the beginning to resolution. He stressed that it was not the same as a simple paper but I should consider it my graduation thesis," he said. "They don't expect me to return to school this term other than to present the paper."

"That's thrilling. You are graduating and heading to the University."

"I won't be finished with so much as the outline today. Would you like to go out this evening?"

"Since our date last weekend was so rudely interrupted, I think it could be arranged."

"I was thinking we might go north instead of into Covington. I've been told there is a cozy inn with a lovely dining room just a few miles from here. Should I have Erich drive us?"

"That has advantages. I am willing to drive if you prefer it to be just the two of us."

"Let's plan on that, then."

"I'll call to reserve a place. It might help keep things low profile to use my name instead of yours."

"Splendid."

I ATE BREAKFAST in my study once again, attended by Lupe. Liam and I had been out quite late the night before and I slept in a bit. Lupe busied herself straightening my bedroom while I ate and then she cleared my dishes.

"Lupe, thank you for cleaning up. Would you mind returning about eleven? I have things that need to be in the mail."

"Of course, Miss. Eleven o'clock."

I cross-checked the invitations and addresses I had. Over fifty people would be invited—and many would also bring a guest. Lupe returned promptly at eleven to help seal the envelopes and take them to the post. While we worked companionably together, there was a light rap at the door between the studies. I took a deep breath and went to the door.

"Mr. Cyning! I was not expecting you so early. Please forgive me. Lupe and I were just completing the invitations for the party. Is it urgent?" Liam straightened quickly.

"Not at all, Miss Sauvage. I wanted to clarify a couple of matters... about the architect's drawings... before we go to inspect the work. Please, just knock when you're free. I won't disturb you further." Liam retreated and closed the door to his study. I did likewise. I wondered what he really wanted. Lupe had scooted back toward the exit.

"Lupe, this is why there's an adjoining door. Mr. Liam and I will frequently need to meet. I *am* his personal assistant." Lupe nodded and relaxed. "Now about these invitations. Can you get them to the post so they are out today?"

"Yes, Miss. I'll go now. I'll make sure they are all in the mail immediately."

"Thank you, Lupe."

Lupe left and I went to the bath to look at myself in the mirror. I adjusted my hair and decided to keep the same blouse and slacks on so as not to create any surprises for Liam.

Finally satisfied, I opened the door between the rooms and knocked softly on Liam's side. It opened at once.

"I'm so sorry to have interrupted you."

"We were working on the party invitations. I believe I still have more than a dozen to write," I said.

"What is this party?" he asked.

"Let's say it's a graduation celebration for you," I said. "The truth is, I think your grandmother wants to show you off. But per your request, there are to be as many of your friends invited as possible."

"I was a bit of a snot to my parents after my birthday party," he said. "It would be nice to invite Fergie. I think we made real progress with each other."

"Consider it done." In fact, it was already mailed.

"We should have lunch and then go see how the contractor is coming with the apartments."

AS WE ATE, we talked about our date the previous evening. It had been simple and wonderful. We'd had dinner and simply sat at the table until the restaurant closed and we were the last ones there. And the kiss—we didn't mention it as we talked—I knew it was too late for me to resist falling in love.

Lunch was simple as well, just our usual sandwiches and salad. Liam wanted to know more about the party and who else was invited. He was very pleased his friends Roald and Remy were on the list. He would have little time to talk to them when he went to present his paper the first week of December.

"Who is Elizabeth Kendrick?" he asked.

"As it happens, she is another Leader—this one from Minnesota—who will begin attending the University at midterm. David Winzar expects there will be more Leaders gathering at the University and your grandmother suggested as many as a dozen. Apparently, this happens periodically, every six or seven years, so Leaders have an opportunity to get to know each other and build a network among themselves." I hesitated and then grinned at him. "I gather it is something of a mating fair as well. You might find the love of your life among them."

"Meredith, I..."

"Please, Liam. I revel in your company but we must stay open to the adventures of University life and not be committed at such a young age. I know you are fond of me as I am of you. Just try not to build boxes around us. Please?" If he had objected and committed himself at that moment, I would have been lost. He understood.

"Meri, I will not take back having said I love you. But I recognize the wisdom of your advice. I will stay as open to possibilities as I can, but I cannot help growing closer to you at the same time."

"Well, we should go off to see your new home. You'll be able to entertain there as long as you are discreet and only invite a few guests at a time. The building is mostly older people and they would object strenuously to loud parties."

"As you say. I can hardly wait to see the progress."

"MISS SAUVAGE, WHAT a pleasant surprise. Here to check up on our progress? I assure you it will be ready before Christmas." John Sturdivant, the general contractor, showed his nervousness about the surprise visit. I tried to calm him down.

"Not at all, Mr. Sturdivant. We were merely in the neighborhood and Mr. Cyning had not had the opportunity to see the excellent work you and your crew are doing. I just had to show him!"

"Mr. Cyning? Begging your pardon, sir. I should have recognized you from the photo in the newspaper." John snatched his hard hat from his head and clasped it in front of him.

"No apology is necessary, Mr. Sturdivant. There was no reason for you to recognize me nor to expect me. I'm just in such a good mood today that I wanted to see the progress. Think of it not as an inspection but as giving me a tour of my new home." Liam held out his hand and John had no option but to release his hard hat with that hand to shake. "Tell me, how are things going?"

"Oh, well, sir. Very well. Of course, there is little to do in the rooms on this side. The kitchen needed updating and expanding. I'm afraid the furnishings have all been stacked into the bedroom for now so the floors can be refinished. Lovely hardwood in this unit, sir. Lovely." John slammed his hardhat back on his head and led us into the new construction. "Here is where the big work is being done. We've cut a French door for access to your study. You'll find it easy to entertain guests should you have business as the hall cuts it off from the living spaces. The architect was very specific about the wiring and preparation for telephone lines. Both units will be ready for any office machines you need."

"This looks excellent, Mr. Sturdivant. I can picture the completion in my mind's eye. Meredith, do you think I should move my entire library here? Will there be enough shelving?"

"Yes, Mr. Cyning. There will be adequate library shelves in your study as I know your fondness for books. May I suggest, however, that you only move the most recent and frequently used books to the apartment. You will need room to add to your collection as we begin school in January. I'm taking a light load this semester and it still seems I've started a library of my own with the required texts," I laughed. Liam was like a child in his excitement to see everything.

"Good thinking."

"We've engaged a top craftsman to create the library shelves and cabinetry," John agreed. "If you'll step this way, you'll enter the smaller unit. It was very wise to put a door between them so you can consult with your assistant without running up and down the halls outside. As per the architect's drawings, the dining room, living room, and study are all shaped into a single open space to be divided by furnishings rather than walls. Per your instructions, Miss, the kitchen has also been renovated and updated."

"You are very proud of your work, aren't you, Mr. Sturdivant?"

"It is my trade. My reputation rests on fulfilling my contract with the utmost care. I employ both excellent tradesmen and top craftsmen. I hope you will find all of the work acceptable."

"I've no doubt I will. Meredith, do you suppose we might expand the guest list to include Mr. Sturdivant?"

"Yes, of course. Mr. Sturdivant, I will send you a formal invitation in the morning mail to a small gathering at Buxton House to celebrate Mr. Cyning's graduation from Elenchus on the Saturday after Thanksgiving. Would it be convenient for you and Mrs. Sturdivant to attend?"

"You would invite us to Buxton House for a party? Miss Sauvage, Mr. Cyning, the missus and I would be most honored." John was dancing from foot to foot and I could tell the first thing he would do when we left would be to call 'the missus.' I took Liam's arm and moved him toward the door.

"It is our pleasure and privilege to have a fine tradesmar as our guest. I have been thinking of some work I would like done at Buxton House, as well. It will give you a chance to get a feel for the old house. I'm afraid we've irterrupted your work long enough. I want to thank you for making this project go sc smoothly."

"Thank you, Mr. Cyning. We'll have it all finished and ready for you to move into by the winter holidays."

"THAT WAS WELL-HANDLED, Liam. You have become a real person to him," I said when we reached the car.

"What was I before? A mythical beast?" he laughed.

"In a way. There are few Leaders. It's the smallest class. So, most people never have a direct encounter with one. People tend to build up a mythos around Leaders. It takes direct contact to show the true human. Much as you did with Randy and the other Dexters."

"I see what you mean. Our society, our entire country, would not function without all the classes. You have said Leader is the smallest and Dexter is the largest. We don't dare let a barrier exist between the two. I think that is my life's work," he said. I looked at him with an overflowing admiration. To know that he, with my assistance, might deconstruct the barriers that have arisen between classes!

"I am so very proud of you!"

John Sturdivant

I TAKE MY WORK SERIOUSLY. I started as a carpenter but I was interested in all aspects of the building industry. I learned plumbing, electrical installation, and even worked on a crew pouring concrete foundations. My contracting license was secured years ago.

But ethical dealings are most important to me. I have never let down a customer. A handshake is a sacred contract to me. Liam Cyning struck me as the kind of man that would mean something to.

"What do you think, boss?" The crew was cleaning up at the end of the work-day and the boys often talked about the day's work.

"Good job."

"I meant about the high and mighty stopping by for a surprise inspection. I saw him look in every opening like he was checking for flaws in our work."

"Now, don't get upset about a surprise visit. Miss Meredith has stopped in nearly every week. Customers always want to check on the progress of their home. Mr. Cyning was no exception. If he was looking into every hole and crevice, I figure it was because he wanted to learn something, not to find fault. He's a good chap. Downright friendly," I said.

"Don't get too friendly with him." I turned to look at my electrician—an excellent tradesman himself. "From what I hear, Leaders can be all chummy in one instant and cut your balls off in the next. Who'd have thought a bunch of Dexters could get the best of a Commander like Ferguson? Did you read that agreement in the paper? He gave in to every demand those workers made. I tell you, that Cyning boy twisted the screws on a fellow who talks all the time about going to Buxton House."

"That's as may be. Ferguson sure sounded happy in the interview he did. He seemed to think he'd won some fantastic victory. We aren't on the inside of this. You're looking for evidence to support your belief. I'll base my beliefs on the evidence. I don't have much experience with Leaders, but I do have experience with customers. He was no different than any other customer who hired us to build or remodel. We do our jobs the way we always do and he pays his bills. No one's ever been cheated by a Leader."

"WE'LL NEED CLOTHES, John. Have you thought of what to wear? You'll need a new suit and I need a new dress. We can't go to Buxton House looking like we just came from a jobsite." My wife already had a catalogue open on the table with pages marked for suits and dresses.

"We should wait until we see the invitation before we run out to buy new clothes. Maybe they are having the party in the stable. I've heard they sometimes throw parties with a theme. We might need jodhpurs," I teased. My Rebecca was quite the excitable woman. A real Creator.

"Oh! You make me so flustered. We shan't order until we see the invitation but come and look at the pictures with me. Don't be such a spoilsport." I smiled at her and sat to look at the illustrations, agreeing that she would look lovely in a particular gown but that if the party was informal a certain dress would show off her good looks. Rebecca blushed. I kissed her on the cheek.

"Perhaps we should have dinner now and then continue our window shopping after." She hopped up from the table and soon brought steaming bowls of stew with freshly baked bread. I'd smelled it when I walked in the door and my stomach told me I needed to match smell with taste.

"I have never once regretted marrying you, John. You are good to me."

"And you are good to me. I'd say you are good *for* me, as well. You married a mere carpenter to become a wife and mother. I've always been thankful."

"My art would have made me another underemployed jeweler sitting at a desk typing letters. You made it possible for me to raise our family and take care of our home. I still have time to tinker with making jewelry a bit. Perhaps I'll go to one of those holiday craft shows and display a few pieces."

"Your jewelry belongs in a museum, not a craft show."

"Take me to bed, John. I'll show you art instead of craft."

21

Bracing for the Consequences

Liam

"I DON'T KNOW what I'm supposed to do at this party. Or even why we're having it. Grandmother dictated it. You sent invitations and made plans. What am I supposed to do?"

I suppose I was whining. I managed to coax Meredith into the library so we could sit comfortably to talk and sat next to her as she went over Cook's proposed menu for the buffet and the various seating groupings that would be available for people. We wouldn't try to seat fifty people in the dining room—or was it seventy now?—but the lounge opened to the ballroom and was large enough for several round tables at which eight or ten could comfortably sit and still have a small dance floor. I couldn't remember a larger gathering at Buxton House.

"You are, officially, the host. You have been seated at your grandmother's table often enough that you should know the duties and responsibilities of the host." She gave me a stern, lecturing tone, somewhat softened by her smile. I deserved the lecture.

"I should welcome each guest, see that they are introduced and refreshed, be genial, and welcome them to the table. Should I propose a toast?"

"No. In this instance it will be more appropriate to turn to your grandmother and let her also welcome the guests. She will propose the toast to you." Meredith scratched one of the items from the menu and suggested an alternative.

"To me? I'm the host!"

"You are also the guest of honor. Let your grandmother dote on you a bit," Meredith smiled and squeezed my hand. "Now, there'll be some guests you won't know. Most notably, the Winzars and the Kendricks. There'll be spouses and dates that you don't know either. I'll stay just behind your right shoulder to indicate who each guest is as he or she comes through the door. You'll greet them by name and welcome them to your home. Unless there's a line pressing to get in, it would be nice to say something personal to each one. Once you've appropriately greeted each guest, Erich or Ricardo will conduct them to the lounge and make sure they're provided with drinks as people gather."

"What about spouses and dates? You can't know each of them, can you?"

"No. I'll let you know by simply saying 'guest.' You'll then ask the one known for an introduction to his or her guest. There are several ways you can do this." Meredith stood and role-played several different introductions with me. We practiced until she felt I had it right. A formal party. *Why must I be subjected to this? Oh, woe is me.*

"This will be an exhausting evening."

"No doubt. But think of the reward you will have at the end of the evening when you find my door open. Of course, you will not open your door if you have seduced another guest to your bed."

"To my bed? I scarcely even know any of them!"

"Not so! You have seen several of the young women who will attend in their swimwear. Oh, don't forget Carolyn Dubois from the sorority And there is a single female Leader who will be seated near you," Meredith laughed.

"We certainly... We can't be expected to... It wouldn't be reasonable..."

"I'm teasing, Liam. With a party this large, it would be in exceedingly poor taste for you to seduce a young woman to your bed. Even if one should throw herself at you during the party. I wouldn't put *that* past any of them. And possibly some of the older women."

"Oh, dear! No!"

"Don't fret. Everyone will be aware all eyes are on them when they are with you." Meredith continued to laugh at my embarrassment and I relaxed. A little. "Now, about shaking hands with the guests. Gentlemen always offer their right hand and you should take it in a firm but non-threatening grip. If one is boorish enough to attempt to impress his superiority by squeezing too hard, ignore it. Do not enter into a contest. Women are a different matter. Few women grip in a handshake like a man, but if she does, treat it the same way. Most will offer their hand, you will take it lightly, and bow slightly over it. Do not succumb to the temptation of kissing her fingers. Not unless you plan to bed her."

We practiced the different handshakes. Most of this I'd been instructed in at Elenchus but it was fun to role-play it with Meredith. At last, I dipped my head enough to kiss her fingers. We took a quick look around to ensure we were alone in the library and came together for a genuine kiss. Meredith broke it off and pushed me away just as the door opened and Erich entered.

"You've been working very hard. I brought hot tea and cookies for you. You should take a break now and then, you know."

"Thank you, Erich. I don't know what I'll do without you when I move to the apartment." We each took a cup from the tray and sipped at the refreshing brew.

"Independence, sir. You will learn independence. Look at this as the first, and perhaps only, time no one will be minutely examining your life to see that you do everything correctly. No one will make up your bed each day or lay out your clothes. No one will wash your dishes or cook your meals. Will you rise to the occasion or will you awake one morning to find you live in a pigsty? This is the price of independence."

"I will try to follow your example, Erich. Thank you."

"You will do well and we will all be proud of you." Erich left us alone again and we sat with the cookies and tea.

"How did you know to break our kiss just before Erich entered?" I whispered.

"I would like to profess a fifth sense or secret code but I'm afraid it was merely coincidence. It's a good reminder to us, though, we are always subject to observation. It is also possible that Erich saw us and was waiting for the kiss to end before he interrupted."

"Oh. We really must be careful, mustn't we? I'm so sorry to have embarrassed you, Meredith."

"If there was a fault, it was as much mine as yours. As long as we are discreet, an accidental observation can be discounted as not having really happened."

"There will be another time, won't there, Meri?"

"I hope so."

"ARE YOU READY for Saturday?" Grandmother sat at the head of the table, as always, while Mother, Father, and I joined her for the Thanksgiving meal. Neither

Erich nor Meredith had been invited to this dinner. Meredith had gone home for a large gathering of her family.

"I have practiced, Grandmother. Meredith has been diligent in teaching me proper protocol and how I should comport myself. I find it overwhelming but will do my best."

"If I may ask, what is the purpose of this gathering?" Mother looked at her mother-in-law questioningly. "It seems to be putting a lot of emphasis on Liam's rather minor role in surviving being held hostage."

"Every young man should have a graduation party," Grandmother said. "Liam will be leaving Elenchus and enrolling at the University. Certainly, we can all be proud of that, *n'est-ce pas?* The guest list includes all the significant parties in Liam's childhood and emergence, does it not, Liam?"

"It does, Grandmother. I am very much looking forward to seeing Randy Peters and his wife again. And I understand David Winzar will also be attending. He's a student at the University and I'm sure he'll be able to give both Elizabeth Kendrick and me some useful hints."

"Don't forget Fergie," Thomas said.

"Of course not, Father. Mr. Ferguson and I have come to an understanding and there will be no shows of debate, I assure you."

"That is a relief. I admit, however, that it seems strange to have both sides of such a volatile issue attending the same party. Are you sure this is wise, Mother?" Grandmother nodded at Father's question and turned it back to me.

"Both sides of the issue developed a deep respect for each other. Much as I did. I spoke with Randy just after he received the invitation and found out he'd been in a meeting with Mr. Ferguson just the day before to sign the ratified agreement. I believe having them both at the party will show they have more binding them together than separating them. The way we've defined classes should not mean classes can't intermingle and learn from each other. I learned a lot from my time as Lonnie's roommate, from my time as Randy's hostage, from my time with Erich as my valet, and from my time with Meredith as my assistant and mentor."

"You've had excellent companions. There will be others attending whom you have not seen in a while. What do you think of Donnie and Richard?" Grandmother asked. She took another bite of turkey as she looked expectantly at me.

"We had a pleasant time when we saw each other in August. I remembered Donnie as rather rigid and ready to stand up to a fight at any time. Richard is a bit flighty, but he understands machines and especially weapons like no one I've met before or since."

"I've offered Richard a position with the arms company should he decide at any time not to pursue a career in the army," Father said. "His design work on the new magazine was excellent and I'll be paying him a royalty on production."

"That's great, Father. I'm sure Richard will look favorably on it."

"And do you understand why Lonnie Porras was chosen to be your companion at Elenchus rather than the others?" Grandmother asked.

"I believe so. Lonnie and I have had many opportunities to talk about it. On that day of my tenth birthday, Meredith stood up to my insolence and bloodied my nose. Richard stood in fear and Donnie in resolution where they were. Lonnie's concern was for me and seeing that I was cared for."

"Even I saw that," Mother said. "Lonnie always knew which side his bread was buttered on."

"He also displayed the intellectual character to challenge Liam," Father said.

"I've arrived at some conclusions regarding why Meredith was chosen as my assistant and mentor instead of Peggy Anne or Karen, as well. She showed the initiative to correct my behavior and the courage to do so when needed. As they grew up, the three girls chose different paths. I've no doubt Karen would make a great advisor, much as Mr. Lenova is to you, Father. But unlike Mr. Lenova, Karen is a Cognoscente. I believe she would always approach things from that perspective and not out of commitment to me. Peggy Anne would no doubt soothe me whenever I was upset, but her guidance would be based on a kind of gentleness I'm not sure I would respond well to. I may have misjudged all of these and ask you to correct me if I have, Grandmother."

"It is close enough. I believe we are ready for Saturday," Grandmother responded. "Or as ready as we will ever be."

"I WOULD MUCH rather negotiate another contract with Mr. Ferguson than host this party. Isn't a tuxedo too formal, Erich? Surely the Peters and Sturdivants won't have tuxedos, will they? I hate the thought of what it would cost them to come to this party."

"Mrs. Cyning has seen to it that costs were covered for all guests. You needn't worry about that. Now, let me look at your tie. Very good! I had no idea you had learned to tie such a perfect bow," Erich said.

"Would you believe we had a class in it? Not just tying a bow tie, but seven different knots and when each is appropriate. Four-in-hand, full Windsor, half Windsor, Eldredge, Prince Albert, Trinity, and Murrell. And we received a book with half a dozen others. When am I ever going to use an Eldredge knot? I'm not sure I have a tie of the right thickness to be able to tie it," I complained. It seemed complaining about the tie was safer than complaining about the party.

"You might be surprised. There are times and purposes for each. What did you use for your meeting with Mr. Ferguson?"

"Simply a full Windsor."

"Excellent choice. If you were going to a sportier event, however, and wearing your blazer, you might venture into some of the more avant-garde knots." Erich stood back after buffing a corner of my left shoe. "No, I'm sure you are ready."

"How soon do I need to be down there?"

"Twenty minutes. You can always arrive early and inspect the setup."

"No. I need a few minutes alone to collect myself. Do you mind, Erich?"

"Of course not, sir." Erich left and I locked the door behind him. I stepped into my study and made sure the hall door there was locked as well. Then I opened the door between the rooms. Meredith's door was closed. I was about to knock before I recollected myself. Lupe might be there and that would be embarrassing. I went to the phone. Meredith's phone rang three times and I was ready to give up before she answered.

"This is Meredith."

"Meri, can I see you? Just for a few minutes? I'm so nervous."

"Of course, Liam. Give me a moment to finish and I'll open the door."

I paced the room for at least three minutes before I heard the door click open. Meredith was heart-stoppingly beautiful. She wore a beige evening dress with puff sleeves and a vee neck with a wide sash belt cinched tightly just below her breasts. The full skirt touched the toes of her high heels.

"You are so beautiful!"

"You cut a dashing figure yourself. Now, I've not applied my lipstick yet, so you may kiss me but try not to muss my hair or dress."

"A kiss is all I desire." I pulled Meredith into my arms and kissed her, pouring my love into the all too brief kiss. It was becoming very easy to kiss Meredith. "Do you suppose we could ask Erich to fix us each a plate of food and have it delivered here so we don't have to go to this party?"

"Liam, you know better than that."

"I do, but it doesn't mean I don't think about it. I just needed to settle myself. You calm me, Meredith. When I don't know if I am ready for something, you give me confidence."

"Look within yourself, Liam. You did not have me by your side when you negotiated on behalf of the workers. You have all that is needed. Now you must put it to work. Go to your study and close the door. I need to apply my lipstick and then I will call you to meet me in the hall. One more kiss."

Meredith did not let me get too involved in the kiss and pushed me toward the door. I went through and she closed it behind me. I heaved a sigh and sat at my desk to wait for the call.

"MISS ITO, HOW lovely of you to attend our party. Welcome. And this?"

"Mr. Cyning, allow me to introduce Dr. Levi Abrams. He has been kind enough to escort me this evening." Hana Ito was as lovely and appealing as the first time I dated her. Lucky Dr. Abrams.

"Dr. Abrams, it's a pleasure to meet you. Do you work in the same hospital?"

"No, no. We met at a charity event some time ago. I was immediately smitten with Miss Ito. She will be an invaluable addition to our medical community."

"I welcome you both. Please allow Erich to show you to the bar for a cocktail."

"Thank you, Mr. Cyning." Hana winked saucily and I closed my eyes for a moment before turning to greet the next guests. My parents were standing not far from me, waiting for the arrival of some of their acquaintances. When Mr. and Mrs. Ferguson came in, they were quick to move next to me and conduct the CEO to the bar themselves.

"Senator and Mrs. Porras, welcome to our home. I am so glad you were able to shake free of your busy schedule," I said to the next arrival.

"I wouldn't have missed this opportunity, Liam. You and Lonnie have been inseparable for eight years and now I understand you will move on to the University. I do hope you'll stay in touch," the senator said.

"Definitely, sir. Lonnie and I are best friends and I value his advice on many things."

"Speaking of whom..."

"Lonnie. Susan. It's good to have you back at Buxton House."

"I didn't know I'd get a chance to get so dressed up this fall. Thank you for inviting me back, even after my boorish behavior the first time I was here." Susan dipped in a small curtsey and I took her hand to bow over it. I shook hands with Lonnie and met Susan's parents. I would have had a longer conversation but Meredith leaned up behind my ear.

"Liam, the next guest is David Winzar. His guest is Jonathan Summers. Behind him are his parents." I turned to greet the new arrivals.

"Mr. Winzar, I am so happy to finally meet you face to face. Welcome to Buxton House. Your assistance to the strikers was invaluable," I said.

"Mr. Cyning, now that we have met face to face and are to be school mates, I trust you will call me David and allow me the freedom of your first name. This is my friend and personal assistant, Jonathan Summers."

"Jonathan, my pleasure."

"Thank you, Liam."

"And these are my parents, all the way from Richmond, Virginia," David continued as he slipped past me to greet Meredith.

"It is a pleasure to meet you, Mr. and Mrs. Winzar." Grandmother was suddenly beside me. "Allow me to introduce you to my grandmother, Regina Cyning."

"How could one possibly mistake you for anyone else?" Mr. Winzar said. "Thank you both for including our family in this soirée. I fear David has not been getting out as much as we hoped when he came here."

"I think you will find that will change this year. Please, let me show you to the bar for a cocktail." Grandmother and the Winzars disappeared into the lounge and I continued to greet new arrivals. I was surprised that Richard and Donnie escorted Peggy Anne and Karen into the party. It was good to see my old school chums again. Their uniforms were immaculate and the ladies wore elegant gowns that accented their beauty. They were moved rapidly into the party so I could greet their four sets of parents.

"Oh, my God." I whispered. My exclamation caught Meredith's attention at once. She turned toward the door.

"That is Elizabeth Kendrick, followed by her parents, Mr. and Mrs. Kendrick. Please put your tongue back in your mouth and greet them properly."

Elizabeth Kendrick presented her hand and I bowed over it, nearly stooping to kiss it. Her blonde wavy hair hung in ringlets about her shoulders, which were bare in a strapless burgundy gown. Even in heels, she was a few inches shorter than me. Her smile was brilliant.

"Miss Kendrick, my home is brightened by your presence. Welcome."

"Mr. Cyning, your flattery will get you everywhere. Allow me to present my parents."

"Mr. and Mrs. Kendrick, I'm so pleased you happened to be in town this week-end. Have you succeeded in finding suitable lodging for Miss Kendrick?"

"A very nice and suitable apartment, I think. You would not believe the monstrosity of a house the agent tried to sell us. As if she was moving to town with an entourage and full staff rather than just a maid. I understand you also found suitable accommodation." Mrs. Kendrick seemed to take the lead in the conversation, but Grandmother was back and engaged both Elizabeth and her father.

"Yes. I was very fortunate. We had an architect do some drawings and the contractor who has managed the work is with us this evening."

"A very heterogenous group you've invited."

"I am pleased to agree. And every one of them a good friend. Please join my grandmother. I'm sure she would like to introduce you to the Winzars."

Only one other couple arrived after the Kendricks and I breathed a sigh of relief.

"Will you take my arm?" I asked Meredith softly.

"No, Liam. I'm not your date this evening. I'll not even be seated at your table. I need to check with the kitchen. Now is the time for you to circulate among your guests and be sure each is comfortable. And do not spend all your time ogling Elizabeth Kendrick. There will be time for that later. But not tonight. Go. I need to check on the buffet and make sure it's ready to serve."

I watched her disappear down the hall and took a deep breath. *Nothing to do but to do it.* I squared my shoulders and proceeded to the lounge where I was immediately caught up in talking to people who drew me into their conversations as I circulated. I was pleased to see my new friends, Randy and Sally Peters, engaged in a spirited conversation with Hana Ito and Dr. Abrams. The Sturdivants had no difficulty engaging all and were at one time with Cognoscenti and at another with Promoters. I noted that Mr. Kendrick pulled Sturdivant aside for a few minutes as well. This evening could be very good for the contractor's business. Then I spotted someone I'd not seen come in.

"Miss Loveland, there was such a press when you entered that I fear I did not adequately welcome you."

"Nonsense, Mr. Cyning. I fully understand the duties of a host and you did very well."

"And did I miss your escort in the press?"

"Ah, sadly, I have no escort. My brother was set to accompany me but he became ill on Thanksgiving Day and begged to be excused." I found the stenographer's information quite interesting. She was extremely competent in her role as a legal secretary but was a lovely woman, as well. Loveland was an appropriate name.

"Perhaps you would consider accompanying me to the buffet? I find I'm incredibly hungry and don't dare go to the buffet alone. It appears no one else will approach it until I do. Do you mind?"

"I would be honored, Mr. Cyning."

"Since we are to eat together, please call me Liam as my friends do."

"It's a pleasure, Liam. I'm Tiffany."

"What an unusual name."

"My parents are scholars. My father in Greek mythology. I'm afraid they went a bit overboard in naming me Theophania because I was born on Epiphany. It's all very complicated, but I prefer the shortened version of Tiffany."

"Beautiful. Ah, look! Cook has prepared some of my favorites. Try the baked brie. It will melt on your tongue."

As soon as I moved to the buffet, a line formed behind us. I was pleased to see that no one hesitated to follow. When I was seated with Tiffany, the table filled rapidly. The first to arrive were my one-time schoolmates. And Elizabeth. That was interesting.

"I just love men in uniform. Karen and Peggy Anne, I hope you don't object to my sandwiching myself between them. It makes me feel so important."

"Do you doubt your importance, Miss Kendrick?" I was surprised to find Donnie engaging her so readily. Karen looked at him and rolled her eyes.

"Oh, there are always moments. For example, when you insist on calling me Miss Kendrick instead of using my given name, Elizabeth. I thought we had agreed on this."

"Indeed. My pardon, Elizabeth." Before the conversation got further, I was surprised to be joined by Mr. and Mrs. Ferguson and by Randy and Sally Peters.

"My! I didn't expect you two to be together!" Tiffany exclaimed. Of those at the table, only she had been present at the negotiations with Peter, Mr. Ferguson, and me.

"We all had a lot to learn from each other," Fergie said. "Randy and I have been going over some of the finer points of labor relations. Liam, you opened a door for us to communicate. I hope you will join us again to make sure we stay on track. Right, Randy?"

"So true, Fergie. I've come to understand more about how the company is managed and the pressures you face. I believe our plan will alleviate a lot of the division between labor and management and ownership."

"What new plan have you evolved?" I was curious about what the meeting of the two extremes had come up with but I'd promised my father no debates tonight.

"Now, we aren't going to go into detail and get into a discussion of work here. Suffice it to say that Randy and I have devised a way to make workers shareholders. We believe that will make the realities of the business more tangible to those who provide the labor."

"It sounds brilliant. Congratulations."

"We owe it to you."

"What did Liam do?" Richard looked past Elizabeth to stare at me. "Don't tell me you were a bull in a china shop again." The veiled reference to the collapse of the pallets of rifles and death of Mr. Wilbur irritated me a little.

"No, no. Liam negotiated the settlement between management and labor at Covington Shoe Company. It was quite brilliant to watch. I doubted when I first met him that Liam could stand up to the pressure of a contract negotiation. I've seen a number of them that were near brawls. But he handled it beautifully. Wouldn't you agree, Mr. Ferguson and Mr. Peters?"

"That's true. Liam represented us at the table. I'm afraid if it had been left to me, it would have come down to fisticuffs as you suggest, Miss Loveland. But Liam showed us a different way of looking at things and also showed Fergie and me that we could deal with each other in a civil manner and not resort to contention."

"Randy, I believe you could have done as well yourself. But thank you for your confidence in me," I said.

"Liam—may I call you Liam?"

"We already agreed on that, Elizabeth."

"Liam, am I to understand that you took the part of the workers in this dispute and at your age of—if I am informed correctly—eighteen, you negotiated a labor contract with Mr. Ferguson here? You suddenly do not look so young to me."

"It was not only that, Miss Kendrick. Liam showed me a path to better productivity and increased profits. It was not only a victory for the labor union. It was a victory for Covington Shoe Company."

AFTER DINNER, I saw a small band setting up next to the dance floor.

"I don't remember this room being used before. Perhaps when I was very small," I said as I strolled around with Tiffany on my arm as I spoke to other guests.

"Come now, Liam. We are not such old fogies. While you were away at school, we had parties like this all the time."

"Grandmother?" I was surprised by her presence next to me. "I thought I was subtly conversing with Miss Loveland."

"Well, perhaps not all the time. Why don't you begin things by taking Miss Loveland to the dance floor? I don't think you will be allowed to leave it once you are out there. Just stay on the dance floor and partners will come to you."

I took Tiffany's hand and she followed me to the dance floor. As soon as we had completed a number, Elizabeth cut in. She may have been a bit surprised when Sally Peters took me for the next dance. Karen stepped in after that and whispered in my ear.

"You know I'm still available. Donnie is nice but it's not a permanent thing. Call me when things settle down and you are at the University." I thought it was strange that a woman in the company of one of my friends would make such a suggestion. I had danced with my mother and Grandmother's friend, Mrs. Grosvenor, when Hana captured me.

"I could get into an occasional date with such a handsome boy. If you think you could work around my schedule at the hospital," she said.

"But Dr. Abrams..."

"Is a dear friend and mentor. But medicine is just a job to him, not a calling. I'm afraid he really doesn't understand my passion."

"I see. I don't know how things will work out, Hana."

"Oh, don't worry. I'll still sleep with him. He's the only option I have at the moment. But I'm available."

I'd danced with nearly every woman at the party, inclucing Carolyn Dubois from the Gamma Delta sorority, who also made sure I was aware of her availability. I'd gone a couple of hours without a break, and I was ready to call it quits for the night. That was when Peggy Anne came into my arms as Richard danced nearby with Elizabeth.

"You seem quite comfortable with Richard."

"Yes. He's a doll. Do you know we talk by phone once or twice a month? I'm thinking perhaps I should move to be nearer to him when he knows where he'll be stationed."

"Do you think he'll take a commission? He doesn't seem very military, even in uniform."

"No, he's much better than that."

"Well, I wish you well. I was afraid... Well, a number of women have approached me this evening with suggestions that we get together again."

"Oh, Liam. That ship has sailed."

THE GUESTS FINALLY left. Many young women had reached up to kiss me on the cheek and I was sure I was smudged with lipstick. I was beyond exhaustion. It was past midnight and I was ready to head for bed. Meredith had disappeared into the kitchen to coordinate sending food to the homeless shelter. I saw her father follow her. The band had packed up but Kendall Sauvage was still playing on the piano in the ballroom. I turned toward the stairs when my father intercepted me.

"Walk with me, son." I accompanied him to the bar in the lounge where Brian poured both of us a glass of cognac. From there, we went to Father's study. He opened a box on his desk and removed two cigars, clipping them both and handing one to me. He held out a lighter. "Just suck it into your mouth and blow it out. You needn't inhale." I managed to get the cigar lit without choking as Father lit his own.

"Thank you, Father. To what do I owe this privilege?" Father had never before shared a drink and a smoke with me—not more than a glass of wine at dinner.

"I was honestly disappointed that you didn't turn out a Promoter," he mused. "You know I went to Elenchus, too. I know they teach what is necessary. I had my hopes. Mother attempted to coach me and show me the path, but I never could see the use for Leaders."

"I'm sorry to have disappointed you, Father."

"That's just it. It turns out that you haven't disappointed me at all, William. You have made me very proud to be the father of a Leader."

"I don't understand."

"I assumed you had coached the labor leader in the negotiations. I knew you could have walked free from the moment you were allowed to call me and ask for the annual report. But tonight, Fergie—and that fellow Peters—disabused me of my notions regarding what you had done. Your behavior that day—and your poise and behavior this evening—were ample evidence to me that you are everything a Leader should be. You brought together people of every class this evening. You set an example even your grandmother has never achieved. You are, in many ways, the hope for our future. Not as a family, but as a society. When I look at you tonight, I see a man I would follow. This drink and cigar are my toast to you, my son. I am proud of you."

"Thank you, Father." I was near tears at Father's declaration. He uncharacteristically put his arm around my shoulders and raised his glass.

"Here's to the future."

"To the future." I raised my glass to touch his. We drank down our cognac and took another puff from the cigars.

"Don't feel you need to finish that. Just leave it in the ashtray. You need some sleep, son. Keep your doors closed tonight."

I flushed a bit but looked my father in the eye and nodded. I laid the partially smoked cigar in the ashtray and went to my room.

22

Independence

Meredith

THOSE DAYS after the party were both hectic and relaxed. I made arrangements with my professors to complete the term from home. It wasn't difficult, as I had finished reading the texts and had only a term paper and exams to complete. But in the midst of that, Liam was completing his final paper for Elenchus. And I learned so much.

Liam's analysis of the labor issues at Covington Shoe Company was complex. Where he cited the issues brought forward by workers as the direct cause of the strike, his analysis delved into the tensions between classes and the perception that certain classes felt they were trapped and unable to advance. He mentioned Randy's observation that ninety percent of the students at his high school were classed as Dexter, a number that far exceeded the national average. While nearly half the population is classed as Dexter, having such a high percentage in one location spoke of a culture in which money and heritage played too large a role. He even suggested the teachers at that high school should be reevaluated to determine if they are truly capable of participating in class assignment.

I discussed his analysis as he wrote the paper and we brainstormed other aspects of the problem. Then I typed it in triplicate from his handwritten copy. I was privileged to attend his presentation and was happy to see his parents, grandmother, Mr. Ferguson, and Randy Peters in attendance as well. He even challenged

Elenchus, asking why there were no Dexters or Cognoscenti in the student body or on the faculty. He suggested the school was elitist, offering superior education to children of the wealthy and automatically classing them according to their parents' wishes. It was interesting to watch students and adults alike shifting uncomfortably in their chairs. However, his academic counselor, Mr. Peoples, was ecstatic over the presentation.

It would be an interesting year at the University if Liam continued to challenge the notions of class division that were so ingrained in our society.

IT WAS BECOMING very easy to kiss Liam goodnight. We frequently joined each other for events at the University, in the theater, or at the concert hall. I was comfortable holding his hand but concerned that we were progressing toward a relationship that would exclude others and inhibit his ability to grow as a Leader.

At the same time, I despaired that we were not progressing enough to suit my tastes. Each kiss made me desire the next. Sometimes, we spent ten minutes in the hall outside our rooms, kissing. It was all I could do to keep from inviting him into my chamber. I got in the habit of simply leaving the door between our studies open all the time, hoping he would open his.

And he did when we had work to do. But during those hours, he was a perfect gentleman and focused on the work at hand. Most of the time.

"What do you think of Tiffany Loveland?" he asked one day. I cringed. Tiffany Loveland was wonderful. She was bright and could challenge Liam on an intellectual level that was above mine. I didn't think she was smarter than I was, but my mode of working with Liam was more as support rather than as challenge.

"She's beautiful," I said simply.

"In a matter of beauty, I am more than satisfied with what I see before me now." His look was so intense—so hungry—that I felt the heat rise in my face. I shook it off.

"She is also very intelligent and has a way of responding to your questions with more depth of understanding than most people. Have you shared your paper with her?" I asked.

"No. We've talked about it on the phone. I've asked her out this weekend."

"I'm sure you'll have a lovely time."

"Meredith," he said, "you have pointed out to me that we are too young for a permanent entanglement. Do you not know I struggle every day not to fall to my knees and ask you to marry me? I feel the same about entanglements when I meet with any other woman, including Tiffany. I find her interesting, challenging, and beautiful. But I would cancel our date in an instant if you disapproved."

"I find resisting that entanglement to be very difficult," I sighed. "I fear I've already stepped too deeply into your life ever to extract myself."

"Well, that, at least, will never happen. You have become my best friend, my confidante, and my most trusted ally. I have little one-on-one experience with women. It is only since meeting you that I've become more comfortable in their presence. But I always look forward to coming home to you."

Our kiss that evening was more delicious than ever.

THE WEEK BEFORE Christmas, we moved from Buxton House to our apartments. From the moment we moved in, it seemed, the doors between our studies were seldom closed. There were family visits, of course. My parents wanted to see where I was living and my father wanted to cook for the combined families in Liam's kitchen. With Liam's parents in attendance as well as his grandmother, it was about the maximum number that would fit comfortably in his dining room.

He'd kept the antique dining set and a few other pieces in the living room, but most of the original furnishings had been donated to a second-hand store. We'd shopped carefully and I found out more about his taste for clean lines and open design with many decorative geometric patterns. He said the patterns led his eye in a kind of hypnotic way that allowed him to focus on only the problem before him.

Letters and phone calls had begun arriving at Buxton House before the holiday and I found it necessary to make a trip to the mansion two or three times a week to collect the correspondence and check the messages. Liam's role in the strike settlement and his photograph in the newspaper caused people to notice him for the first time. The party had been attended by enough people to begin spreading gossip about the newest Leader to emerge in our community. The Cyning name linked him to one of the oldest and wealthiest families in the state. Everyone wanted to become his 'friend.'

"I'm not sure how to filter these requests," I said. "Do you have any specific guidelines regarding what you would want to attend or with whom you would like to correspond?" He leaned back in his desk chair and clasped his hands behind his head.

"I suppose this is only an introduction to what will come," he said. "I think I'll invite us to dinner with Grandmother. She's dealt with it far longer than we have."

And so, we ended up in the rooms of the matriarch just two days after moving out of Buxton House. It was an informal and light dinner. I hoped the unique serving of French toast topped with savory shaved ham and cheese would be enough to satisfy Liam's appetite.

"I thought they would wait until after the holiday to start with the requests but people move so much faster these days than in my youth," Regina said. Erich also joined us but was content to quietly focus on his food rather than participate in the conversation.

"Some of them are worthy causes that I thought nothing about," Liam said. "Others seem frivolous at best. A few look like legitimate requests to work with someone on a specific problem."

"Party invitations, charitable events, and even date requests have come in," I said. "Some are still months away."

"You have only seen the beginning, I'm afraid," Regina said. "It is one of the key reasons I wanted to get you and Meredith established as a team early on. There are a few guidelines I can offer, but the real test will be what interests you. First, a Leader must be incorruptible. If your ethics weren't pristine, you would not have been classed as a Leader. So, the first filter is to determine which contacts are after nothing more than legitimizing their cause by association with you. No doubt, for example, there will be other labor-management disputes in which one side or the other wants to be allied with you. Now that the terms of the Covington Shoe Company agreement have been released, you will find people believing that you will either get a labor union more than it asks for or that you will lead the company into new areas of profitability."

"I certainly can't promise that! I was very lucky with Ferg e and Randy. It could as easily have been a failure," Liam said.

"Good. Don't assume success in one instance guarantees success in another," Regina said. "Now, charitable events are sent to you because you are from a wealthy family. You have funds of your own, but not the kind they are looking for. If you see a charity that particularly appeals to you, you need to bring it to the family to see if you can persuade us to join you in support. Otherwise, politely decline the invitation. I might say the same is true of party invitations. If it looks like fun and doesn't have an implied endorsement of a person or organization, go if you want to. I suggest that you not go unaccompanied. The hostage situation at Covington Shoes was a spontaneous event that turned out well. There is no guarantee the next one will be so benign."

"You think there is a real possibility that I would be kidnapped again?" Liam asked.

"Yes. Less now than when you were young and helpless. As an adult, you are more capable of defending yourself. But the temptation for criminals will still be high. Remember, any class might have a criminal element," Regina said, dabbing her lips with a napkin. "As to the dates you are being offered, the temptation is on your part. Do you really want to connect with random women? I would suggest you limit dating to women you already know. That field will expand rapidly once you enter the University setting."

We discussed the other kinds of correspondence and Regina impressed upon me the importance of my own ethics in dealing with them. Liam would depend on me to respond to people with the same standard of judgment he was using. It would be too easy to withhold information that I found unpleasant but would come back to bite me—or worse, Liam. I agreed.

THE WEEK BETWEEN Christmas and New Year's, Elizabeth Kendrick moved into her apartment, not far from where we lived. Liam immediately invited her out for a welcome to the University dinner date. He said it was fun and he believed Elizabeth would become a good friend in the future.

And then classes started and we were all too busy for any extraneous social activity. I'd had a few months to get used to the University experience. Liam came home in shock after his first day of attending lectures. It was not at all the learning environment he was used to.

Still, we found time to sit and relax together for a while in the evening or to study together if we had reading to do. I felt as at home in his apartment as in my own. He was very excited to share a dinner of fried chicken he made as a testament to his ability to feed himself. We were getting along well and I still cherished our few minutes of kissing before we went to our rooms.

Liam

I SAT AT MY DESK reading the assignment in the textbook, US History Since 1877. The rigid structure of the University, including showing up for lectures with a hundred other students, would take some getting used to. It was so different than the unstructured learning environment of Elenchus Scholé. I had attended three lecture classes, two labs, and a writing class and it was only Wednesday evening.

I glanced through the open door to where Meredith was working on correspondence. Seeing her in her space always set my mind at ease and let me set aside the stress of the University. She would separate out letters that had arrived for me into those she could reply to and those which required my personal attention.

I was thankful for the writing course I was taking. It was amazing how many letters I'd received since the party—and they were not all from guests. I received personal invitations to charitable events, requests to help with personal problems, and what I could only describe as love letters from women I'd never met. Meredith dealt with most things, simply asking me whether I would attend this or that event or if I was interested in a woman who had included her scantily-clad photo. *What would I do without her? I'm just so thankful for Meredith.*

We moved into our apartments two weeks after the party. Elenchus graduated me with honors after I presented my paper analyzing the Covington Shoe Company labor dispute and settlement. I found that I truly loved Elenchus and the learning environment I'd enjoyed for eight years. But it was disturbing to me that my education was elitist. I knew for a fact from my conversations with Randy and other laborers at the shoe factory that they were completely capable of engaging and learning in the same way I was. Mr. Sturdivant demonstrated some of the same techniques in relating to his contractors. There was no reason in my mind that Randy's high school should turn out ninety percent Dexters. It made me a little angry.

With school over, I immediately began setting up my new home. Those first weeks before the New Year's holiday were filled with enjoying independence and learning even better how Meredith and I would relate to each other. It was an exciting time. I could see a world of possibilities for us if we could maintain our good working relationship without entering a romantic relationship precipitously. I think we both had in mind that a romantic relationship was in the offing. I certainly enjoyed kissing her goodnight!

MY PHONE RANG and I picked it up automatically. If I let it ring, Meredith would pick it up and I didn't think that was necessary at the moment. "This is Liam Cyning. How may I help you?"

"Liam, it's Elizabeth. Can you believe the writing assignment Professor Harington gave us? It's like she's prying. I hate to write about something so personal. What are you doing?"

"Just now, I'm reading history. I figured I would get to the writing assignment later this evening. I agree, it is a very personal matter." The assignment given was: 'Describe the class you would want to be if you weren't of the class you are now. Why does this class appeal to you? How do you think it differs from others' perception of you? Expound.'

"I was hoping you could give me advice. Perhaps share a bit of what you are thinking."

"Hmm. Who else is prying?" I chuckled.

"Oh, come, Liam. Surely you want to know more about me. We Leaders should know each other well if we are to consider each other as possible mates. We can't say we have a lot of options." Elizabeth sounded a bit pouty. I'd taken her out to welcome her the first weekend she moved to town, between Christmas and New Year's. She was certainly beautiful and pleasant company, but I felt no spark between us. I felt none of the urgency she apparently felt.

"Elizabeth, you are so much more mature than I am. It's proven that girls mature more quickly than boys and I am simply trying to find my way in a new and unfamiliar environment. It is way too early for me to consider a future that is so far away. I'm not really ready to consider us as possible future mates. There's really no pressure to marry another Leader. At the University, we'll encounter few people of whom our parents would not approve."

"You don't care for me."

"That is not what I said. What would you do if we became involved this term and next term a perfect match showed up? My grandmother estimates there will be a dozen Leaders at the university next fall."

"If I found a better match, it would be necessary to extract myself from our relationship."

"Wouldn't it be better if the relationship we had was to become friends? Wouldn't we then be able to freely assess our possibilities without the urgency you are feeling now?"

"Liam, you ass. Do you know how much courage it took to call you and suggest something? And you respond in a perfectly reasonable way. It's very frustrating for a girl. Yes. Of course, it would be better to become friends and see what happened next. I just..."

"It sounds like you have something else bothering you. What is it, Elizabeth?"

"Oh, it's quite silly. I've just found that Carmen Ramirez will be arriving in the summer. We've met before and there is a bit of rivalry between us. Nothing serious, of course, just a feeling that anything one does, the other can do better. Perhaps you are under no pressure to find a Leader as a future mate, but my parents made no secret of the fact they expected me to find a Leader for my husband."

I laughed and shook my head. "All the more reason we should not become attached. How devastating it would be if I found Carmen a better match and needed to extract myself from our relationship?"

"That's awful!"

I supposed I would get a lot more of this kind of thing but I really had no plan to do more than casual dating for a long time. I was satisfied with my life right now and didn't really want to rock the boat. The whole concept of finding a Leader as a mate smacked of the very elitism I'd just spoken against in my diatribe at Elenchus. Of course, I wanted to maintain a friendship with other Leaders, but saw no reason to tie myself down to one.

"I tell you what. In the interest of improving our friendship, why don't we go out next weekend," I suggested. "Maybe Saturday night. We can see if David would like to join us. I'll see what is going on in town and make arrangements for a driver."

"Next weekend? Not *this* weekend?"

"I'm sorry. I have plans for this weekend."

"Redheaded plans?"

"Elizabeth. You're prying."

"I want you to know, Liam, that I only met her briefly, but I could tell I would become friends with Meredith."

"I believe friendship with Meredith would be a requisite for any kind of friendship between us. Now, we had better both get studying. Right?"

"Right. Don't put your essay off too long. It's harder to write than you might think."

"Goodnight, Elizabeth."

"Goodnight, Liam."

I sat, staring at the phone. In fact, I was not taking Meredith out this weekend. I would be busy with Tiffany Loveland. The more I'd gotten to know the stenographer, the more I liked her. She was a perfect example of profession being different than class. A stenographer might be assumed to be a Cognoscenti or even a Dexter. But Tiffany had a sharp and inquisitive mind. She took her job seriously but there was no question but what she was an Inquirer. In fact, the more I got to know her, the more I thought that if I were not a Leader, I would like to be an Inquirer myself. I set my history book aside and took out paper and pen.

"HAVE YOU COMPLETED your studies?" Meredith asked from the doorway between our apartments. "I thought I would make a cup of tea if you would care to join me."

"Thank you, Meri. I think I've gone as far as I can this evening. Why not come over and make tea in my kitchen while I wash my dinner dishes. Last night, I forgot and they were quite disgusting this morning."

"Yes. Learning to take care of things others have always done for you can be a challenge. You're adapting well. I guess I am as well. When I was at school, I took all my meals in the cafeteria. I didn't need to wash my own dishes. Of course, the story was very different at home. When I've managed to engage a housekeeper and part time cook, you'll have a much richer understanding of the people who help you. Do you suppose Elizabeth is learning that as well?" Meredith asked.

"It's hard to tell. I suppose you heard my side of that conversation. You know, she does have a maid living with her. I don't know if that means she can't take care of herself or if her maid is a personal assistant, like you. It seems her parents are already pressuring her to find a Leader as a mate."

"I'm sure that will come clear as you get to know her better. I'm interviewing housekeeper candidates to come by our units three times a week. I thought Monday, Wednesday, and Friday would be good times for her to be here."

We went to the kitchen and Meredith brought a fresh batch of cookies. She prepared a kettle on the stove and a teapot while I washed my dishes. I didn't dirty a lot of dishes when cooking. I felt I was progressing well and getting the hang of cleaning up after myself.

"I heard you ask Elizabeth out."

"Yes. I need to give David a call and see if he will join us. He might have some ideas about what to do or who should join us. Elizabeth unexpectedly commented she thought you might become friends."

"That's likely, as long as she doesn't become too class-conscious. I believe her type of leadership is very different from yours. I understand she's studying fashion design. She's struggling as much as you are with the new environment and the world she's been thrown into. She was at an all-girls school until just four weeks ago."

"That explains a lot, I suppose. I'm still struggling with the concept of dating. I'd rather just go out with friends."

"You don't seem to have much difficulty with Tiffany."

"Um... I... Uh... She's fun to be with. That's all."

"That is important. I think you are fun to be with. It is a basis for our friendship. If I found you boring, you would never find my door open." She poured water over the tea and took it and the cookies to the sitting room. I finished the last of the dishes and dried my hands before joining her. I sat on the loveseat next to her and put an arm around her shoulders as she leaned into me. It was so perfectly comfortable that I was tempted to just forget about ever dating anyone else.

"Am I always going to discuss my relationships with you? It seems so... callous."

"I hope you will. I want to be a part of all of you. I don't want you ever to think you need to hide your feelings or actions from me. But at this stage of our lives, it is important to develop a range of friendships with both men and women. If nothing else, it will keep us from becoming bored with each other."

"I have such a long way to go." I pulled her to me to kiss. She gave herself to the gesture and we both breathed deeply when we parted. Meredith poured the tea. "One thing I said to Elizabeth this evening is very important to me. And it comes from what you have told me. I don't want any difficult entanglements right now. I expect you to be with me all my life. While the idea of doing more than kissing gives me a frisson of excitement, I am in no rush to do more than casual dating. I'm only eighteen."

"And I will be twenty-one in the spring. Me, Peggy Anne, Karen, Hana, Elizabeth, Tiffany. You have only dated women who are older than you. You need to keep an eye out for one who is younger."

"I'm sure we will meet others in our classes. I promise not to look upon it as an unpleasant chore."

We laughed and sipped our tea and held hands as the loveseat rocked gently back and forth. I thought of all we'd discussed and looked hard at my feelings and desires.

"Meri, let us make a pact."

"What?" She looked at me skeptically with one eyebrow raised.

"Only this. I have told you that I love you. I stand behind those words. Therefore, I promise to always consider our relationship when making decisions about others. I know that this time of exploration might reveal unexpected paths for us—perhaps unexpected relationships. But I never want to disrespect you or to hurt you through my thoughtlessness. If you find me acting in such a way, please call me to account for my actions. I need you for that as much as for any of your duties as my personal assistant."

"Liam, I have grown to love you. I agree to considering our relationship when making decisions about others. If you find yourself in doubt because of my actions, please talk to me and let's resolve our differences. I'm sure there will be times when those differences rise between us. Beyond that, I will restrain my expectations and ask you to as well."

"Agreed," I said. They weren't wedding vows, but they were certainly kissing vows. I bent to her and she sealed her promise to my lips.

The End